WE COME IN PEACE

GERALD C. ANDERSON SR.

iUNIVERSE, INC.
NEW YORK   BLOOMINGTON

We Come in Peace

iUniverse books may be ordered through booksellers or by contacting:

iUniverse
1663 Liberty Drive
Bloomington, IN 47403
www.iuniverse.com
1-800-Authors (1-800-288-4677)

Because of the dynamic nature of the Internet, any Web addresses or links contained in this book may have changed since publication and may no longer be valid. The views expressed in this work are solely those of the author and do not necessarily reflect the views of the publisher, and the publisher hereby disclaims any responsibility for them.

ISBN: 978-1-4502-5858-6 (sc)
ISBN: 978-1-4502-5860-9 (dj)
ISBN: 978-1-4502-5859-3 (ebk)

Printed in the United States of America

iUniverse rev. date: 11/5/2010

PROLOGUE

Abraham watched as the men looked toward Sodom and Gomorrah. They headed toward the cities and Abraham wondered why they were headed that way. He remained in the presence of the Lord.

After the men were gone Abraham said to the Lord, "Will you sweep away the righteous with the wicked? What if there are 50 righteous people in the city? Will you really sweep it away and not spare the place for the sake of the 50 righteous people in it? Far be it from you to do such a thing to kill the righteous with the wicked, treating the righteous and wicked alike. Far be it from you! Will not the Judge of all the Earth do right?"

The Lord said, "If I find 50 righteous people in the city of Sodom, I will spare the whole place for their sake."

Again Abraham said, "Now that I have been so bold as to speak to the Lord, though I am nothing but dust and ashes, what if the number of the righteous is five less than 50? Will you destroy the whole city because of the 45 people?"

The Lord answered, "If I find 45 there, I will not destroy it."

Abraham asked again, "What if only 40 are found there?"

The Lord answered again, "For the sake of 40, I will not do it."

Then Abraham said, "May the Lord not be angry, but let me speak. What if only 30 can be found there?"

The Lord answered, "I will not do it if I find 30 there."

Abraham said, Now that I have been so bold as to speak to the Lord, what if only 20 can be found there?"

The Lord answered, "For the sake of 20, I will not destroy it."

Then Abraham said, "May the Lord not be angry, but let me speak just once more. What if only 10 can be found there?"

The Lord answered, "For the sake of ten, I will not destroy it."

Chapter I

Gomorrah, the City (around 3100 BC)

In Sodom the afternoon was getting started with preparations being made for another celebration in the city. The people of Sodom celebrated almost every day and gave no thought to the Lord. Their evil and wickedness was so great that the news of it spread all across the plains. Only the evil and wickedness of Gomorrah rivaled that of Sodom. Both cities were known for their evil and wicked deeds from across the Dead Sea and all points North and South.

The newly crowned king of Sodom, King Kfir, relished in his palace. He flung his cape back...flopped down in his chair and sighed out loud. He came to power by murdering the previous king and now was ordering the execution of all the servants that served the previous king.

King Kfir commanded, "Guards, bring out the servants of King Jarib and place the men to my left and women to my right."

The King's trusted servant answered, "Yes, sire."

The servants were brought before the King, the men on the left and the women on the right.

King Kfir looked them over, "Ah...nice...what a selection we have here. King Jarib had good taste. Today, some of you will live...and some of you will die."

He approached the men first.

King Kfir continued as he looked them up and down," You…you…certainly you…you and you… in the back over there…come forth. You will serve my pleasure for many years to come…or you will die. What say you?"

The first man selected boldly stated, "I…would rather die."

The King answered with a sheepish grin on his face, "Then…die you shall."

The King pulled his sword from its sheath and thrust it into the stomach of the man. The look on the man's face showed that he was in excruciating pain that riveted throughout his body.

He grabbed the King's shoulder and the King looked in his eyes and saw a plea for mercy. None was coming. It was too late. The king then turned the sword while in the stomach of the man…hoping to cause him even more pain.

King Kfir then said "Now burn in hell for eternity."

The servant's screams for his life was deafening. It continued until it began tapering off till his death.

The King looked at the rest of the servants and said "Anyone else desire to follow him?"

The King looked at every man as they nodded their head to do whatever the King desired.

The King envisioned being with each of them in his mind. He desired men equally as much as women. On occasion the King would entertain several women of his choosing in one evening. When he grew tired of them he would turn his attention to men. He loved the lewd and lascivious acts. He knew most of the men and women he had been with hated being with him. He remembered one night when a servant girl drank poison and died rather than spend another night with him.

The King then moved to the women that were placed on his right and looked them over smiling seductively and imagining what he will do with them later that evening.

The first woman he moved to was a very beautiful young woman. He gazed at her skin. He noticed that it was smooth and bronze in color. Her eyes were hazel colored and they captivated him when he looked into them. Her long black hair was shiny and when he touched it, it felt like silk. It ran down her back and ended just pass her hips. He knew she had been prepared to be the wife of a king from the day she was born.

The day for her to become King Jarib's wife was near but now King Jarib was dead. King Kfir chose her without giving any thought.

"You were bread to be King Jarib's wife but now you will be mine." The King said.

The next woman was an older woman and a concubine of King Jarib. She had served in the palace for seven years. King Kfir had secretly had an affair with her without King Jarib's knowledge.

King Kfir stated, "Rakefet…you are still a very desirable woman. Now I can openly love you as I have in secret. I will raise your status from that of concubine to my wife! You are of fine stock and I know you will give me strong and powerful sons."

King Kfir selected five more wives and three concubines.

He then returned to his throne and said "Take those I have selected…bath them in my finest oils… and prepare them for this evening's festivities."

His trusted servant asked, "What shall we do with the others?"

With a deep, dark cold heart the King said, "Kill them."

While the selected ones were removed, the King's guards pulled out their swords and began executed the remaining servants. He laughed as the cries of death filled his palace, and the streets of Sodom.

As the screams of death continued behind him King Kfir looked out the window. He saw tears rolling down the faces of the murdered servant's families, who stood outside the palace. He relished in watching them submerge in their pain. He saw it etched on their faces. He loved how the loss of life was so easily and senselessly erased. That was the way he knew life to be in Sodom and Gomorrah.

***

Dekel and Ilan were brothers and two of the few righteous people in all of Sodom and Gomorrah. Together they made up a total of 11 righteous souls in Sodom and Gomorrah. This total included Dekel and Ilan's wives and children and those members of Lot's family. Together these three families constituted enough righteous souls to spare Sodom and Gomorrah from destruction.

Dekel saw a woman who appeared to be desperately making her way somewhere. From a tavern about 100 yards away two men who were drinking heavily began shouting comments at her.

Dekel heard the first man who was short and stubby shout, "Hey missy come over here and sit with us for while. We need some company."

Dekel then noticed the second man who was older, taller but still looked out of shape add, "Yeah…where you off to in such a hurry?"

He then saw the woman hasten her pace as she appeared to try and get away from the men. They ran after her and cornered her in an alley.

Dekel was in ear shot of the alley and could hear what they were saying.

The second man said, "I got to her first so I get to have her first."

The first man responded, "No, you had the last one first, it's my turn."

The woman shouted "Leave me alone…please…I have children. I need to get to my children. Please let me go."

The second man swung and punched her in the face and she fell to the ground with blood spurting from her mouth.

The first man said, "Shut up wench. You're going to serve our needs and we don't care if you like it or not."

The woman cried out with a shrill that curled Dekel's skin. Dekel often came to the aid of others in need, never caring if his life was in danger or not. He believed that his life was always protected by the Lord.

His brother, Ilan was the more conservative one. He often thought things out rather than act impulsively. Dekel didn't have time to think the situation out. He had to act with or without the support of his brother.

Dekel shouted to his brother, "Ilan I am going to help her!"

Ilan responded, "No my brother. Remember we are in Sodom. If we interfere we can be executed."

Dekel couldn't take it and said, "I must help…no matter the cost."

The look in Ilan's eyes told Dekel that his brother would come to his aid even if he didn't support his impulsiveness. He had seen the look before. He knew it all to well.

Ilan said, "Then if we die…we die together."

The two brothers ran into the alley and fought the two drunken men. Dekel struck the first man with two quick punches, one in the stomach and the other to the face. The man went down quickly. He looked over at his brother and saw him winning the battle with the other man. He saw Ilan wrestled the other man to the ground…then punched him a couple times in the face. The fight didn't last long.

The brothers then turned to the woman and helped her to her feet. As she got to her feet, still dazed, Dekel saw the King's guard surrounding them.

The woman looked at Dekel and said softly, "I'm sorry."

Dekel looked at her.

He said to her, "Whatever happens is the Lord's will and I freely give my life in His name."

Dekel watched as the sergeant of the King's Guard walked around them with a cold look engraved on his face. He had a half smile on his face as though he was savoring the moment at hand…pondering his next move.

He then looked at the two brothers and said, "What do we have here? Did you assault these two men?"

Dekel responded "We did so helping this innocent woman. She was being attacked by them."

Dekel saw the woman look down as though she did not want to look the sergeant in his eyes. He thought she feared that she would be killed for resisting the drunken men.

The sergeant walked up to Dekel and said, "You are not from here… are you?

Dekel bravely said, "No we are from En Gedi…West of the Dead Sea."

Dekel thought that the hearing of this information was pleasing to the guard as his face was now poised with a sly grin on it.

His voice was noticeably joyful when he responded, "Well…do you know the punishment for a foreigner assaulting a citizen of Sodom?"

Dekel was about to answer but then he allowed Ilan to answer instead, "We were merely…"

The sergeant cut him off and continued, "Its death by execution."

Then he ordered his men, "Take them to the dungeon."

Ilan shouted to the guard "Wait…but…we were preventing a citizen of Sodom from being assaulted."

The sergeant spit on the ground and said, "You should have minded your own business."

Then he looked at the woman and said to the two drunken men, "Do with her as you please."

As Dekel was being taken away he saw the woman he had tried to rescue stumbling as thought she was still in a daze. She was not putting up much resistance.

She used what little strength she had to shout "Please…no…let me go…please!"

***

That evening King Kfir proclaimed a celebration in his own honor for the city of Sodom.

The King boastfully shouted, "Today, we shall celebrate my ascension to King and the uniting of me with my new brides. However, first we must attend to some matters of law. Bring out the criminals."

The Chief Priest came before the King and spoke, "Sire…I do not believe it to be wise to execute these two men today. Rumors are spreading that say the Hebrew Lord will destroy this place if ten righteous souls are not found amongst us. These two brothers are known for their righteousness and they are firm believers of the Hebrew God… Jehovah.

The King paused as if to consider what his Chief Priest had just said. He looked at the people then at the two brothers and finally back at his Chief Priest.

He thought to himself, "*If I chose to believe my Chief Priest then I would have to spare the lives of these men thereby causing the people to believe that I value the life of foreigners over my people. If I execute them and the rumor is true then my city will be destroyed. That's preposterous; a God would not destroy an entire city! We have done nothing to Him and who is to say that we do not have ten righteous souls in Sodom. I am a righteous man myself!*"

The King stood and spoke, "The Chief Priest has said I should spare the lives of these two foreigners because there is a rumor that the

Hebrew God...Jehovah will destroy our great city if ten righteous souls are not found here."

The crowd laughed and some shouted, "Kill them! There is no truth to this rumor!"

Another shouted, "Baal will protect us!"

Others shouted, "We cannot allow this crime to go unpunished. Kill them as you would any other foreigner!"

The King turned to his Chief Priest and said, "There...you hear the people have spoken. Besides who is to say that ten righteous souls are not amongst us."

He turned to the crowd and said, "How many righteous souls do we have here? Raise your hands if you are a righteous person!"

There were over 500 people in the square that day and all of them raised their hands.

The King said, "There...we have well over the required 10 people."

The crowd yelled, "Yeah!"

King Kfir looked again upon his Chief Priest. His face portrayed sadness and fear.

The Chief Priest said in a voice that confirmed the King's belief that he was sad, "You have doomed our great city to destruction. Even I know to concede that this Hebrew God is real and this rumor is true. The blood of all these people is squarely on your hands."

The King moved toward his Chief Priest and whispered in his ear, "Move from me or I will execute you as well."

He suppressed his desires to kill him but instead he watched coldly with evil in his eyes as the Chief Priest moved away and eventually out of his sight.

The King ordered the two brothers, Dekel and Ilan, to be beheaded.

The King began to speak as the men were brought in, "These men are from En Gedi and must be executed because they assaulted two citizens of our great city. Assault of a citizen of my land by a foreigner will not be tolerated!"

The two men were guided out by guards and led to a platform where the guillotine awaited them. The executioner stood poised to do his job. King Kfir had many meetings with his executioner. He knew he took pleasure in doing his job. The King knew that unlike his Chief Priest, he did not question whether it was right or wrong to behead these men; he just knew that he would enjoy doing it. The King liked that about his executioner. The first brother, Ilan was placed on the guillotine and the executioner wasted no time.

A man from the crowd shouted "Kill him! He assaulted our brothers. Kill him!"

The rest of the crowd joined in "Kill him, kill him, kill him!"

It happened...slowly the blade rose in the air...screeching a deafening sound as it rose...then... the axe fell...severing the head of Ilan from his body.

In minutes, his brother Dekel would also be dead. In the same manner as Ilan, Dekel's head was severed from his body. Both men were now dead.

The King sat back on his throne happy that he had just solidified his presence on the throne. He knew that if anyone doubted his ability to rule they no longer would after the executions.

As the crowd cheered the second execution, the King laughed out loud and heartily.

The King cried out to the people, "There...you see...no one has destroyed our great city! She still stands mighty as ever. Let's celebrate this day as my first day as King of Sodom."

***

While the celebration was getting started in Sodom the two men who were resting outside the city began to approach Sodom. The evening sun was losing the battle to the night sky over the city of Sodom.

The two men were met by Lot, who pleaded with them to come into his home and stay the night. Lot was a good man, from a good lineage. He was the nephew of Abraham, a man that God would bless to be the father of all nations. Lot accompanied Abraham on his journey to Canaan but when a conflict arose between the two, Lot traveled east to Sodom where he was currently living. Because of Abraham, Lot and his family had favor with the Lord and their lives would be spared.

Lot recognized that these men were Angels of the Lord and they intended to destroy Sodom and Gomorrah because the outcries against them have become so great.

Word traveled throughout the two cities of the arrival of the two men and later that evening the people of Sodom came to Lot's house to find them. Lot came out to meet the people of Sodom.

"Bring the two men out that you have hidden away in your home" said Elhanan who told everyone about the two men and appeared to be leading the mob.

He continued saying, "Let us have sex with them."

Lot said to the men, "No, do not do this wicked deed. I have two daughters who have never been taken, you may have them instead."

Lot's comments angered the mob even more. They demanded that Lot move aside as they continued to press their way to his door. The Angels of the Lord struck the people with blindness and they were not able to find Lot's door.

***

King Shemaiah, the King of Gomorrah, heard the news of these events and he feared for his life and the lives of his people. He had conversed with his friend, King Kfir, who dismissed the idea of the Hebrew God destroying their cities. King Shemaiah believed they were surly going to die when the sun rose the next morning.

King Shemaiah asked his royal priest, "Do we have ten righteous souls in the city?"

The priest responded "Surely we do not, sire. King Kfir of Sodom just executed two men who were known for their righteousness. After their execution the wives of these men took their children and fled the city. I believe Lot and his family are the only righteous people we have left in all of Sodom and Gomorrah."

At this news King Shemaiah fell to his knees and pleaded all night for the Lord to spare his life and the lives of his people.

He prayed to God, "Surely a God as great as you would not destroy a people begging to live?"

***

Lot rose early the next morning before the sun and ran into the city of Sodom to find his sons-in-law to encourage them to leave the city. He ran as fast as he could through the muggy morning air. When he reached the house of his sons-in-law he knocked on the door as loud as he could with his fist.

The eldest son-in-law, Galon, answered half asleep, "Father, why are you here so early in the morning hour?"

Lot came in hurriedly and said to them, "My sons please leave this city before dawn as it will surely be destroyed by the hand of God! Hurry!"

Galon responded "Father...don't make us laugh so early. We have celebrated all night and we are tired. Let us rest and discuss this later."

His other son, Dan, added "Surely you jest. God would not destroy us all. What have we done to Him? We did give a toast to Him last evening...did we not brother?"

Galon said through his laughter and while he was pushing his father to the door, "Go now father and let us rest. We are tired from last night's celebration."

They both laughed and went back to sleep. Lot, sadden by his sons not believing him returned home to get his wife and two daughters.

***

As Lot returned home, the sun was beginning to push away the night. The two men were standing in front of his house waiting.

The first Angel said, "We have taken an accounting of the righteous ones in Sodom and Gomorrah. There are but four righteous souls in all of Sodom and Gomorrah. They are you, your wife and two daughters."

The first Angel noticed Lot began to weep at the news that his family was the only righteous souls left in all of Sodom and Gomorrah.

The Angel of the Lord urged Lot, "Hurry! Take your wife and your two daughters who are here, or you will be swept away when the city is punished."

Lot hesitated so the Angel grabbed Lot, his wife and two daughters. He led them out of the city.

The Angel pleaded with Lot, "Flee for your lives! Don't look back, and don't stop anywhere in the plains! Flee to the mountains or you will be swept away!"

Lot turned. The Angel noticed his look of surprise.

Lot said, "No, my Lords, please! Your servant has found favor in your eyes, and you have shown great kindness to me in sparing my life. But I can't flee to the mountains; this disaster will overtake me, and I'll surly die. There is a town near enough to run to and it is small. Let me flee to it."

The first Angel responded "Very well, I will grant this request too; I will not overthrow the town of Zoar. Flee quickly."

The first Angel watched and when Lot began running to Zoar the angels turned toward Gomorrah to respond to the cries of King Shemaiah.

***

The King was slumped over his throne in distress. He felt the time was soon at hand. When he looked up he saw the two Angels standing before him. He was frightened but he didn't know if it was because of their sudden appearance or the impending news they were bringing.

The Angels spoke, "The Lord has listened to your cries all night. He has decided to grant you favor. Your people will be moved to another place. A place where life will not be easy but your people will live and have a chance to repent for their sins. For you, the evil you have done and led your people to do all of your days will be your own undoing. Your people will pass judgment on you. If they let you live, so be it. But if they want to take your life…Jehovah will not protect you."

The King responded, "I understand and I accept these terms."

***

King Kfir was standing in the window looking out over his kingdom. He looked to the skies and could see clouds forming in the skies above his city. The once bright sun that was beating down on Sodom was now covered completely as the anger of the Lord appeared evident.

Seeing this, the King looked down at his people and saw them running. He didn't know to what but they were running toward him. He looked in the sky and saw something hovering above him. He could hear his people shouting and yelling at being which he now believed was an Angel. Some wanted to be saved while others were cursing God.

King Kfir saw his sergeant of his guard burst through the crowd of people. He remembered the sergeant only because he had arrested Dekel and Ilan the previous day.

He was shouting, "You...you are trying to kill us all! We will have your heads for this!"

King Kfir looked to his right and heard his most trusted servant pleading for his life, "Please, do not kill me. I only did what the King asked. I had no choice! Please!"

King Kfir cursed him. He wished he had a sword to thrust through his heart and kill him where he stood.

Then he saw a woman who he knew was a prostitute shout, "I deserve to die. If there is room for me with Jehovah please take me. I know I have done wrong but I do not wish to die with this sin on me. Have mercy."

At the sound of the Angel's voice King Kfir's ears felt like they were going to rupture. The sound was so loud he could not clearly understand the Angel.

With his hands over his ears trying to suppress the excruciating pain, he saw the prostitute fall to her knees with joy. He could not understand why she was smiling and not in pain as he was.

He looked back into the sky wanting to curse the Angel. He saw the Angel raise his hands to the sky. He didn't understand what had just happened but down on the street a few people just disappeared into thin air. He believed this Angel was evil and trying to destroy him.

Then the Angel clapped his hands together creating a thunderous boom that rolled over the cities. The King was paralyzed. He could see his people were frozen in place as well.

He saw the Angel look to the Heavens above. In the distant sky, approaching at a rapid rate, he could see boulders coming toward him. The boulders were on fire. There appeared to be thousands of them.

He shouted to his people down below, "We're under attack! Sound the guard."

***

The Angel could hear and see everything that was being done and said in Sodom.

Lot's sons-in-law awoke when the boom occurred overhead.

He heard Dan say to Galon, "Father was right. We are going to die!"

Galon responded, "Fool, God would not kill us all. We have done nothing…"

Before he could finish his sentence, their house was destroyed by brimstone and fire.

The Angels rained down thunderous blow after blow igniting fires all over the cities of Sodom and Gomorrah. Screams of death and destruction as well as pleas for life, echoed throughout the cities. It was as if evil itself was being eradicated from Earth.

They heard the cries of a woman on the street as she was shouting, "No! Please don't let me die. Help me Lord please".

The Angel over Sodom saw a man running out of a brothel shouting, "Run, run…we can make it to Zoar. Run!"

Before he could make it ten feet from the brothel a wall from a nearby building fell on top of him. Similar scenes were played out all over of the city.

The Angels were saddened by all the death and destruction that was pouring down from the Heavens.

One said to the other, "If only ten souls were found, then we would not have to do this."

***

Alas King Kfir was the last one alive in all of Sodom. He stared out of his palace window at the destruction. He watched it as it was occurring. His palace had not yet been touched. Inside he knew the end was near.

He said to himself, *"What have I done?"*

He looked out the window one last time and approaching him was a large fireball. He noticed that it was the size of a small building. He looked down at his hands and he saw the blood of his people on them. He remembered that the Chief Priest told him that the blood of his people would be on his hands. Now he could see it with his own eyes but it was too late.

As the fireball got closer the King wept and cried out, "Jehovah, forgive my evil ways!"

He saw the Angel turn away from him.

The fireball struck the palace killing the king and destroying the last building in all of Sodom and Gomorrah.

***

As Lot, his wife and two daughters raced to the city of Zoar to escape the devastation, Lot's wife stopped. She knew Lot was behind her and as he caught up to her she felt his hand grab hers. Then she felt him try to pull her along.

She could hear all the wonder and power of the Lord occurring behind her. The temptation to look back was tugging mightily at her.

She heard Lot screamed at her, "Don't look back! You will be killed if you look back!"

She couldn't resist. She slowly began to turn. She saw all the wonder of the Lord as fire and brimstone rained down from Heaven destroying the cities of Sodom and Gomorrah. She saw the two men in their natural form as Angels of the Lord...wings spread out, hovering above the cities. She saw one Angel hovering over Sodom and one Angel hovering over Gomorrah. Simultaneously both turned and saw her looking at the destruction and in an instant she was turned into a pillar of salt.

Just then Lot felt her arm break away from his hand and he cried out, "Noooooooooo!"

***

Lot and his two daughters reached the city of Zoar and fell to their knees...thankful that they had been spared death. As the destruction was complete, the Angels of the Lord ascended to Heaven and quiet filled the morning air where once thunder and the pounding of the Earth consumed the airwaves.

Lot hearing that the destruction was done stood and looked over where Sodom and Gomorrah once proudly stood. Everything was destroyed. Nothing remained. All the people of Sodom, all the vegetation on the plains, all the buildings in both cities...everything was destroyed. Sodom and Gomorrah built just off the Dead Sea was once a beautiful land flowing with milk and honey. Now, it was desolate, burnt, smoldering, never to rise again...on Earth.

Lot fell to his knees and wept as he surveyed the place he once lived. He wept for his wife who could not resist the urge to look back. He wept the entire day and into the night.

***

The quickness of being moved to another planet in another galaxy made its new inhabitants believe they were still on Adamina. Adamina was the name the Gomorrites called Earth. King Shemaiah looked out and saw thousands of Gomorrites standing in a field crying out for death rather than being stranded. Everyone was complaining and wondering why they were sent to this desolate place.

King Shemaiah heard one of his guards speak out and tell the crowd that it was the King and his prayer to the God of their enemy that exiled them to this land. The crowd began to call for the King's head as payment for their isolation.

One of the King's servants shouted, "Sire, this place…it's barren and desolate. There's nothing here for us…we are going to die!"

King Shemaiah attempted to calm his people, "We must be thankful that we are still alive. The Hebrew God, Jehovah has granted us favor by sending us here instead of killing us. We were going to be destroyed in the destruction of Sodom and Gomorrah. Jehovah spared our lives by sending us here. We would be dead were it not for my pleading with Him for forgiveness."

One man in the rear of the crowd shouted "The King is a liar! The city of Sodom is laughing at us. They are probably in our city right now, enjoying my home, my cattle and taking my land! The King has led us to our death! He must die!"

The crowd began to yell, "Yeah, yeah!"

Another man shouted, "We saw no such destruction! He is lying to us! He has made a deal with the Devil to lead us to our death. We must kill him to save ourselves!"

King Shemaiah now fearing for his life pleaded, "No, my people, we are not here to die. We can build our homes again…here…in this land. Look…there is a mighty river flowing to the East…we can survive!"

The crowd began to move toward the King and his own personal guard did not help him.

Just when the crowd was close, General Birsha stepped up.

He stood up and spoke mightily "Stop! We must be civilized about our situation. We can't leave this place but we can make it our home. However, we cannot be led by this man any longer. We do not know if

17

our land was taken from us by his foolish prayers but we do know that we have been banished from our land."

The King thought General Birsha would support him but instead General Birsha pulled out his sword and turned to the King.

He said, "I have served you and Gomorrah for many years but this decision has led us to this perilous place and for that…you must answer."

The King responded, "You are my general and my best friend. How could you turn on me now? If you want to be king then fight me or be a coward in front of these people and kill a defenseless man."

The General took a sword from one of his soldiers and tossed it to the King.

He said, "If you want to die with a sword in your hands…then die you will."

General Birsha struck the first blow with a 360 degree spin aiming his sword toward the King's head. The King was a skill fighter. The King blocked it with his sword but defending the blow caused him to lose his balance for a moment. The General struck again with an overhead strike at the King. The King again successfully blocked this strike with his sword. The two swords remained locked together as the King forced his way to his feet.

The battle waged on for several minutes as each combatant tried to gain an advantage. Back and forth they struck blow after blow igniting sparks and sending them flying off into the air. The General was knocked to the ground with a mighty blow from the King and the King attempted to thrust his sword into the General's heart while he was down.

The General moved to the side and grabbed a rock. He flung it at the King but the King ducked. As the King ducked the rock, the General threw his sword at the King, stabbing him in the chest causing the King to drop his sword.

The King saw the sword coming but could not move quick enough to get out of its way. As he clutched the sword in his chest he saw General Birsha coming at him.

The General then quickly pounced on the King, grabbing his neck and placing his other hand on the sword in the King's chest. He slowly pushed the sword into the King as deep as it would go. The King saw him grinning at him with every inch knowing victory was in his hand.

General Birsha looked directly in the King's eyes and said, "Now you die and I take my rightful place as King of Gomorrah."

The King with his dying breath said, "You are a fool. You cannot lead these people. I know that I cannot win Jehovah's favor but you could and save our people."

The General spit in the King's face and said, "No...you are the fool! Baal is the one true god and he will save us. You die an idiot."

The new King of Gomorrah turned toward the mass of people and proclaimed his place on the throne.

He spoke, "Today we were removed from our great city on the plains of the Dead Sea. But now...I am King...I will lead you to be the greatest people on all of Adamina!"

His bold speech caused the mass of people to cheer zealously for the new King! They loved him and yelled, "Hail Gomorrah, Hail King Birsha!"

***

Later that evening as the sun over Gomorrah began to set; two moons began to appear overhead.

Ram, King Birsha number one soldier said, "Sire...look...in the sky."

King Birsha looked up toward the sky and was amazed at what he saw.

He said, "This is truly not Adamina. Never in my life have I witnessed two moons so evident in the night sky. Where are we? Get my scientist...now!"

The scientists were led to the King.

The Kings servant spoke as the King was pouring himself a drink, "Sire, the scientists are here for your questioning."

King Birsha said, "As you can see by the night sky, we are no longer on Adamina. Can any of you tell me how far we are from our home?"

Each of the scientist looked around but all of them were as confused as the other.

One scientist spoke up and said, "Sire, we do not know how far we are from Adamina or how we can get back there. But we will find the answers for you."

King Birsha sternly said, "You speak very carefully. I will grant you some leave. Find me the answers. You have one day to return to me."

The King ordered his men to make a camp in the area, "We must organize ourselves and form a government. We must build a city…a great city…even greater than that of Gomorrah. I proclaim the name of this world as Gomorrah after our city on Adamina. Ram will you be my new General."

General Ram spoke thankfully, "Thank you Sire."

King Birsha said, "General, gather the builders first thing in the morning. Your first mission is to design me a city. I am retiring for the evening. You…what is your name?"

Raanan was the former King's most trusted servant and he answered, "Sire, my name is Raanan and I was the King's most trusted servant."

King Birsha looked at him in the eye and spoke softly, "You are now my most trusted servant. If you ever betray that trust I will kill you with my bare hands…but not before I kill your entire family. Do you understand?"

Raanan's fear was evident in his eyes as he replied, "Yes…sire. I understand."

The King said to his new trusted servant with a pleasing tone, "Follow me."

***

The King went off toward the woods with Raanan. When they were alone the King received a visit from an Angel of the Lord.

Raanan fell to his knees and said "Lord, spare my family for we have done evil all our days!"

The Angel of the Lord replied to the servant, "You…and your family will have a place with Jehovah and He will bless your lineage forever."

The Angel looked at King Birsha and said, "King Birsha, you continue your wickedness even when Jehovah allowed you to live."

King Birsha interrupted and said, "Who are you and why do you come before me unannounced?"

Raanan answered, "Sire…he is an…"

King Birsha cut him off, "Shut up!"

The Angel continued, "Jehovah gave you favor by bringing you here. You continue to denounce Him and you killed the very man who had your lives spared. All of this you have done in minutes of your arrival. God will continue your isolation from Adamina for 5,000 years. Neither you nor your descendants will ever see Adamina again. Your lineage will cease to exist in one generation. Once your people attempt to return to Adamina you will be defeated but those who have given their lives over to Jehovah will live on.

The King defiantly stated, "You cannot dictate to me our future. I am King of this land and me and my people will find our way back to Adamina. We will conquer and rule over it forever!"

The Angel concluded by saying, "You openly defy the Lord thy God…Jehovah?"

The Angel of the Lord walked into the woods and disappeared as quickly as he had appeared.

Raanan stated "Sire we must repent and save our souls. Jehovah is real."

The King knew he could not allow any of this to come to the knowledge of the people. Therefore he turned to Raanan and said "This information cannot be allowed to be heard by anyone. I am sorry my friend."

The King turned and grabbed Raanan from behind. He placed his arms around his neck and slowly squeezed until there was no more life in him. Now the King believed he was the only one who knew of the visit by the Angel of the Lord.

***

In the bushes there was a man named Alon. Alon was a friend of Raanan. He watched as King Birsha killed his friend but he also saw and heard all that the Angel said. The Angel smiled at him as he walked away.

Alon returned to the camp and gathered his family and Raanan's family. He told them of the Angel and what the Angel had said to the King. He also told them that the King had killed Raanan. The King reported to everyone that a wild animal killed Raanan.

Alon's wife spoke, "This is madness. We will all be killed for having this discussion."

Alon calmly said to them all, "Jehovah will protect us. We will be the reason our people return to Adamina in the future."

Raanan's wife sadly said, "This Hebrew God did not protect my husband. Why should I follow Him?"

Alon placed his hand on her shoulder and said, "My friend gave his life over to Jehovah when he saw and heard the Angel of the Lord. You must believe that he would want you to do the same. He gave his life for it."

Then the Angel of the Lord appeared before them. They all immediately fell to their knees in reverence.

The Angel said to them, "Rise up for I am not the one who you should give reverence. I am but a servant as you are."

He helped Raanan's wife up by her arm and continued speaking, "Your husband is in Heaven with Jehovah. What Alon says is true. Your resistance will survive for 5,000 years and your descendants will return home to Adamina. You will also claim this world and turn it into a great and prosperous world that will rival Adamina. Jehovah has blessed your lineage and gives you favor. Keren, wife of Raanan, your son will be the first leader of the resistance. God has given this to him because his father showed reverence for Him and gave his life over to Him. From this day forward you all will be known in Gomorrah history forever."

Keren looking down and in a low voice said, "I will follow Jehovah."

The Angel of the Lord disappeared and all of them prayed and thanked God for showing them favor. That night the resistance was formed.

***

The builders of New Gomorrah approached the King with designs for the city.

The lead builder said, "Sire, we have spent the night drawing up plans for the new city. If you desire, we will show them to you."

King Birsha said, "Show me your work."

The lead builder spread the designs in front of the King and began speaking, "Sire, the land appears to be rich in materials necessary to build a new city, make weapons and provide food to survive. The city will be built off of the river. Your palace will have windows to oversee the view of the mountains and the river. It will be the very best view in all of Gomorrah. In the center of the city there will be a tower. This tower will be the tallest building in the city and overlook all of Gomorrah. The university's site will be on the North edge of the city. Its name will be the University of Birsha…after you my lord."

King Birsha in a pleasing voice stated, "This plan is pleasing to me. Make it so."

After the builders left the scientist came to visit the King.

The lead scientist stated, "Sire, we have put our collective minds together and at this time we cannot determine where we are. We need to see more of the night sky as it is not familiar to us. It will be difficult but in time I am sure we can find it."

The King knew that none of them would be capable of finding Adamina.

He said, "I know that you will not find it. I know that none of us will find it in our time. But, this day I command that Gomorrah's primary scientific agenda is to find Adamina and to find a way to return to her. Nothing in Gomorrah is more important than this agenda. Now go and begin your work."

The King knew that the Angel of the Lord spoke the truth and they would not return to Adamina in his lifetime. But he believed that Gomorrah would not fail at finding Adamina. He believed that the Gomorrites would return and take Adamina for their own.

The King continued, "Gomorrah will build its scientific community around its primary responsibility. That is to find and return to Adamina. We will build the mightiest army known to man and we will return to Adamina and take it back for it is our birthright to do so! In this I proclaim."

These words would become the motto which all Gomorrites lived by for the next 5,000 years. All those in hearing of the King shouted "Hail Gomorrah! Hail King Birsha!"

CHAPTER 2

GOMORRAH (5000 YEARS LATER)

King Abimelech was standing at the window admiring the view from his palace. He was thinking about how far his people had come in the 5,000 years of being exiled from their home on Adamina.

The royal palace sat beside the Dead Sea, the strongest river on Gomorrah. The palace sat high on a hill so it could be seen by everyone in New Gomorrah. The throne room overlooked the Dead Sea and the Zeeb Mountains. The view was breath taking. The backdrop of the mountains and the powerful river often gave Gomorrite kings a sense of strength and power over their subjects.

He was getting ready to make his annual kickoff speech at the New Gomorrah celebration. He was alone with his queen in his throne room.

"My queen", the King started, "This celebration shall be our last on this pitiful world. Before the year is up we will be on our way to Adamina. We will conquer her and rule over her forever!"

The Queen smiled and King Abimelech sensed a feeling of joy in his queen.

She replied, "My King, you are truly the greatest king to ever rule over Gomorrah. It is my honor to be the one chosen to be by your side. I cannot wait to crush the people of Adamina and take my place on the throne beside you."

The King let out a boastful laugh and the Queen joined him.

She then took him by the arm and asked, "My king please grant me one wish. Do not take a new bride this year. Let this celebration be ours alone."

King Abimelech looked at her and simply smiled.

In the 5,000 years that the Gomorrites lived in their new world they worked hard to improve the land and technology. King Abimelech smiled as he remembered the stories of how Gomorrah improved their farming and agriculture industries. Their handwork had led the way to moving a once barren land to a land filled with fruits and vegetation. Green grass now covered the grounds outside the main city and the mountains that stood nearby. This land was once desert land for miles. Trees with various different fruits grew in and around the new Pentapolis region. The few animals that were swept away with them had multiplied to become plentiful but not as plentiful as they once enjoyed on Adamina. The ration system that was instituted by King Birsha remained in effect throughout Gomorrite history.

The one industry King Abimelech was proud of the most was that of science and technology. He was proud that the kings before him had the foresight to see the need to be leader in this industry. He like his predecessors knew science and technology would enable them to return and destroy their emeny.

The builders built Gomorrah into a grand city. King Abimelech turned his view toward his grand city. The Twin Towers stood in the center of the main city and were called Esau and Jacob. They were the tallest buildings in New Gomorrah. New Gomorrah was the name of the main city on Gomorrah.

There were four other major cities on Gomorrah and each one was named after the cities on the plains of the Dead Sea on Adamina. Sodom stood on the other side of the Zeeb Mountains, West of New Gomorrah. These mountains were named Zeeb because it was where a creature similar to the wolf on Adamina was first seen.

Continuing his daydreaming, King Abimelech thought about the four other cities of the plains.

Admah stood to the North of New Gomorrah and provided the cattle and dairy products to the citizens of Gomorrah. The men of Admah were cattle herders from the day they were born. Each one passed on to his son the ways to herd cattle and produce meat for Gomorrah.

Zeboim was built to the South of New Gomorrah and provided most of Gomorrah's agricultural products. Zeboim grew predominantly all of Gomorrah's fruits and vegetables. The men of Zeboim worked tirelessly to cultivate the land to grow food.

To the East of New Gomorrah there stood the mighty and beautiful city of Zoar. The city of Zoar provided the place where the Gomorrite warriors were trained. The first training academy was built just off the Tigris River which ran through the center of Zoar.

Gomorrite warriors were placed in training almost from birth. Gomorrite kings desired to have a strong and mighty army at their disposal. Each king over the 5,000 years ensured the Governor of Zoar would have enough able men to train to become warriors.

All of the cities of the Pentapolis region were required to provide half of their male born population to the academy for training once the child turned six years old.

After each New Gomorrah celebration ended, half of the eligible male children were taken away from their parents and sent to Zoar. Here they would begin their training to become part of the Gomorrite army.

***

King Abimelech came out on the balcony of his palace to greet the people of Gomorrah on the morning of the first day of the New Gomorrah celebration.

The people of Gomorrah began to scream in reverence to the King, "Hail the King, Hail the great King of Gomorrah…Hail King Abimelech!"

The King stepped up to his pedestal, looked over his kingdom, raised his hands and began to speak to his people.

He boast, "My people…this is the last New Gomorrah celebration we will celebrate on this planet. My scientists have informed me that we will have the knowledge…and the means to find Adamina soon. We will return there just as the Basar foretold and defeat the enemy. Then we will be rulers of our home again!"

The crowd roared, "Hail King Abimelech…Hail Gomorrah!"

King Abimelech continued, "Today, as we have done in the past, we will start our annual week long New Gomorrah Celebration by passing on the young women who have come of age to their new husbands. As always I am relieving everyone of their normal duties to participate in the celebration. That is everyone except the scientist, who I require to continue their job of getting us all back to Adamina."

"Let the festivities begin!"

The people responded "Hail King Abimelech! Hail Gomorrah!"

The New Gomorrah celebration always began with the passing of all eligible brides to their husbands. After 5,000 years, the women of Gomorrah were still treated like property and bought and traded as such.

During the New Gomorrah celebration all laws were relaxed. Normally, it would be death by execution for a man to be with another man's mate. However, this rule did not apply during New Gomorrah week. It was always death by execution to be with any of the King's wives or any woman under 15 years of age.

King Abimelech shouted, "The women who have reached their 15th New Gomorrah celebration now stand before me."

King Abimelech looked at his Queen, smiled at her and reached out his hand for her to come forth.

As she was coming to him he spoke to the people, "As king it is my choice to take any of these beautiful women for my own. This year I will pass on all of them and spend my last New Gomorrah celebration on this planet with my beautiful Queen. Husbands you may take your new brides."

The men rushed toward their new prizes and proclaimed them as theirs. It was widely known that most of the women hated this moment and cried out in fear. However, they had no choice but to be with their husbands as it were customary and their law.

The King laughed as one Gomorrite man took his bride by the head, kissed her and threw her to the ground. She screamed as her new husband pounced on top of her, ripping her clothes, and continuing to kiss her...treating her like a piece of meat.

Passersby laughed at them and shouted comments to the man, "Eli, get a room!"

Another said, "Yeah...you must be starved!"

The man then rose, grabbed his new bride by the arm and took her home. Another young Gomorrite woman decided to fight back and her father intervened.

The father grabbed the young woman by the arm and said, "What are you doing? Stop disrespecting me and go with your husband. He has paid well for you!"

He then slapped her to the ground and motioned for her new husband to come take her away.

The King admired similar scenes as they played out in the square. The New Gomorrah celebration was in full swing. Those who were not getting new brides were taking up residence with anyone they could. Everyone in the square was drinking as much ale as they could hold as the celebration got off to a rousing start.

King Abimelech stood on is balcony and watch the festivities take shape. He and his Queen smiled looking back and forth at the events occurring on the streets of New Gomorrah. They laughed as the man struck his wife and pounced on her. The King cried out with joy as the father disciplined his daughter. He loved ruthless acts and encouraged them. He thoroughly enjoyed watching the entire carnage take place.

***

King Abimelech was bent on squashing the resistance that had lived as part of Gomorrite life since their arrival. No Gomorrite king had been truly successful at stopping the resistance. Instead many martyrs were made in the name of the resistance.

Many people had come to believe in the resistance but far more did not or they feared to believe in it. It angered the King that anyone would believe in the resistance. After 5,000 years the population of Gomorrah increased to well over 50 million people but only 1 percent belonged to the resistance. He was determined to change this.

After speaking to the people and before going to his private quarters with his Queen, King Abimelech retreated to his private office with General Idit, his top general and foremost military mind.

As they walked to the King's office, the General walked behind the King. Side by side the General towered over anyone, including the King. General Idit was a giant of a man. He stood six feet ten inches tall with muscles ripping through his entire body. No man dared challenge him and most feared him. His eyes always struck terror in the onlooker. When he walked he displayed his power and might. Secretly the King was intimidated by him also.

King Abimelech told General Idit, "General...please tell me that I will be the King that defeats this so called resistance and lead my people to Adamina as foretold in the Basar."

General Idit responded with assurance, "Sire, you have my word that this resistance will be crushed. I have spies all throughout the organization. They do not do anything without my knowledge. You do realize that Professor Hai is the leader in this resistance?"

King Abimelech demanded, "Professor Hai! Behead him at once!"

General Idit calmly responded to the King, "No, sire, we cannot."

King Abimelech was perplexed by the General's response, "You dare counter my command! I will have your head as well."

Again the General calmly stated, "Sire, let me explain. Professor Hai is the key to returning to Adamina and crushing the inhabitants. I believe he has the coordinates to Adamina and I know he has built a shuttle to survive the trip. He has not provided you this information for he believes he will be able to overthrow you as the ruler of Gomorrah."

"I have a secret group of scientist working on duplicating the shuttle he has built. With this shuttle I will send a spy to Adamina to spy on the inhabitants and await Professor Hai's arrival."

"Another group of my scientists are in the process of building two grand ships for the trip to Adamina. It will house your entire army, eight battle cruisers, and a fleet of fighters. Once we get to Adamina we will crush the inhabitants and kill Professor Hai as well."

King Abimelech was very happy to hear this news. It was his only desire to be the King who returns to Adamina and now it was all coming together.

While smiling King Abimelech said, "Your plan sounds good. I will not have him or you beheaded. Bring him before me. I will ask him if he has found Adamina. If he answers no, as I suspect he will, then I will kill his wife. That will satisfy my thirst."

General Idit said, "I will have them both brought before you."

***

Professor Hai was the Chief, Scientist at the University of Birsha. He was Chief of the Adamina Research Project. King Abimelech realized at a young age that Professor Hai was a talent and knew science better than many of his older scientist. When Professor Hai was but 22 years old he was given the responsibility for the Adamina Research Project. His predecessor was murdered for failing to provide results.

Professor Hai was a direct descendant of Adiel and as foretold by the Angel of the Lord, Professor Hai would lead the resistance in their return to Adamina.

He became the newly crowned leader of the resistance after his father was killed by General Idit. The General suspected Professor Hai's father of being a spy and when questioned about other members of the resistance, Professor Hai's father would not tell. General Idit made a public spectacle of him by beheading him at the start of a New Gomorrah celebration.

As the leader of the resistance Professor Hai planned an attempt to overthrow King Abimelech. The resistance was predicated on the belief that a government ruled by the people for the people could be formed. Professor Hai and his followers believed that a government could be formed that would promote peace and prosperity.

Being in the direct lineage of Adiel, Professor Hai knew the story of the Angel of the Lord visiting his ancestor. He knew the same Angel had visited King Birsha and told of Gomorrah's attempt to return to Adamina and their eventual defeat. Anyone caught telling that story was immediately brought before the King and executed. It was one of the greatest crimes that could be committed by a Gomorrite.

In his laboratory Professor Hai was working with his lead assistant, Tamir, whom he trusted immensely. Tamir was also a member of the resistance.

As a young man of 18 years, Tamir was banished from his home in Zeboim for asking about Jehovah. His parents did not want to see him executed but instead he was treated like an outcast. Professor Hai found him two years ago on the streets of New Gomorrah stealing food. He took Tamir into his home and trained him to be his assistant.

Professor Hai said to Tamir, "With these new breakthroughs we can travel to Adamina in this small shuttle and arrive in six to eight months."

Tamir replied, "The King will be pleased that we have made this discovery. He may even promote me in status. Then I will be respected by all Gomorrites."

"The King cannot know of this Tamir." Professor Hai quickly replied.

Professor Hai continued to say, "We must attempt to overthrow the government and make our home here on Gomorrah. If we fail and only if we fail will we launch this shuttle and go to Adamina.

There are only three seats available on this ship. They will be for you, me and my daughter, Malka. The King cannot know because he will use it to make war with Adamina so he can rule it. Do you understand what I have said Tamir?"

Tamir sadly responded, "Yes, professor, I do understand and I will not divulge this information to anyone. What about your wife?"

Professor Hai spoke in a sad voice but knowing it was the right solution, "She agreed to stay behind, in the shadows. Her work in the resistance will be needed here on Gomorrah."

Tamir asked, "Professor, have you found Adamina?"

Professor Hai answered with happiness, "Yes, I have located Adamina. It was very difficult to find because Zilah lies between Adamina and Gomorrah. Zilah blocks the view of Adamina nine out of ten months of the year. It was only by the blessing of God that I found it."

Tamir ask, "How long will the trip to Adamina take?"

Professor Hai answered, "The shuttle is capable of reaching warp five. It should take us approximately six months to arrive there."

Tamir asked, "Professor shouldn't we go to Adamina and take it for ourselves? Gomorrah is our home but it is not Adamina. I have heard stories that Adamina is rich with food and water. We would not have to worry about rations. We could eat for days. We could make it a peaceful place and rule over it ourselves."

Professor Hai could not believe his young assistant made such a statement.

He grabbed Tamir by the shoulders and said to him with some anger, "Gomorrah is our home even if the planet is not flowing with milk and honey as that of Adamina. We cannot just go to another planet and take what is theirs for our own. If we did such a thing we would be no better than the evil that resides here. This same evil caused us to be swept away in the morning light and brought to this baron and forsaken planet. Gomorrah is ours and we must do what we can to turn our society into a peaceful God fearing society."

Just then the King's guards burse open the door to Professor Hai's lab and shouted "The King requests your presence…now!"

Professor Hai snapped at the guards, "How dare you barge into my lab and talk to me that way. Do you know who I am?"

Professor Hai rarely threw around his status as chief scientist but he was startled by the entrance of the guards and was afraid something was happening. Something he was always afraid would happen.

The guard stood stern and confident as he responded "Come with us peacefully or we will drag you there through the streets."

Professor Hai looked at Tamir and stated "Tamir put away these materials while I go see what the King needs."

Tamir responded with concern, "Yes, Professor…I will take care of the lab."

***

As Professor Hai was being led out of his lab, at his home, his wife was being taken from their home by guards and led to the palace.

The Kings' guards kicked open the door to the Professor's home and pointed their weapons at Professor Hai's wife and daughter.

The senior guard yelled, "Come with us…now…or we will kill your daughter!"

Professor Hai's daughter Malka could see the fear in her mother's eyes.

Her mother spoke calmly, "Malka, do not be afraid."

She then held her tightly and whispered into Malka's ear, "I am a child of Jehovah and he will care for me in this life and the next. I love you."

Malka through her tears returned the love in spoken words, "I love you mother."

Two of the guards walked over and snatched Professor Hai's wife by the arm and led her out of the quarters, through the streets and to the palace. Malka could hear the citizens of Gomorrah as they yelled obscenities at her mother as she passed through the streets, and she could see that some of them even spat on her.

One woman yelled, "Traitor, kill her!"

A man standing next to the woman followed suit "Let me have her first. She will make a good prize for me!"

Malka looked with disgust as she saw the man motioning to unzip his pants as he yelled.

The guard shouted back, "I will have her before you!"

Then he laughed and continued to drag her through the streets. Professor Hai's wife prayed every step of the way. She knew her life was probably over but she kept her faith in the Lord.

Another man shouted, "Look! She's praying. Baal will not save you now!"

The group laughed and continued to shout at Malka's mother as the guards led her to the palace. Malka continued to watch from the window until her mother was out of sight.

Malka slumped down to the floor and cried. She suspected that she would never see her mother again. On many occasions she and her mother talked about what to do if this would happen. She prayed that she would never have to live through this day but now it was becoming apparent that she would.

***

The resistance received word that Professor Hai and his wife were taken to the palace. Lieutenant Oded was a trusted member of the King's army and a resistance member. One of his men found him in a local bar.

The man rushed over to the Lieutenant and said, "Sir, Professor Hai and his wife have both been taken to the palace by guards. You never know who is working for that stinking resistance."

Lieutenant Oded quickly looked up from his drink and said, "How do you know they are resistance members?"

Lieutenant Oded realized his mistake as soon as he saw the expression on the man's face. He looked shock at the question. It was clear that was not the reply he expected.

He replied, "Professor Hai is a respected scientist...why would he be taken to the palace under guard unless he was a resistance member."

Lieutenant Oded knew the man was right. Why would the King have the professor and his wife brought to his palace under guard unless he suspected them of treason? Since he was a high ranking official in the King's army, Lieutenant Oded decided to go over to the palace and find out what was going on. Because of his status he would be allowed in the throne room without question.

***

The guards brought Professor Hai's wife into a room just off the throne room. They threw her down on the floor and drew lots to see who would have her first. She watched them with tears in her eyes. She silently prayed to Jevohah to stop them from raping her. If she had to die for the plan to succeed then she was ready to die. She did not want to be raped. She did not want her daughter, Malka to remember her that way.

She continued to watch and pray as the men laughed and laughed. Each man drew his lot until one was chosen. The guard who won went over to Professor Hai's wife and knelt down.

Professor Hai's wife kicked him in the face and tried to get away. There were too many of them in the room to escape. They threw her on the ground and two of them held her down.

The guard who won the lot had pulled his pants down when an officer walked in the door. At the presence of the office all of the guards jumped to attention.

The officer asked, "What is going on here?"

The highest ranking guard answered, "We were just going to have some fun before she is killed."

The officer replied, "What if the King wanted to have some fun...as you put it? Do you think the King would want to follow you?"

The guard answered, "No sir."

The officer ordered, "If any man lays a hand on her, I will kill them myself. Is that clear?"

They all answered, "Yes, sir."

Professor Hai's wife looked at the officer. She thanked God for sparing her the embarrassment of being raped. Then did a double take as she could have sworn the man mouthed the words "I'm sorry" to her. She suspected the man was a resistance member. She did know that whoever he was God had sent him to stop her from being raped.

***

The Professor was brought before King Abimelech who was waiting in the throne room. Professor Hai had often been brought into this room. He always marveled at the design of the throne room. It was filled with gold ornaments as Gomorrah had plenty of gold as a resource. The throne sat against the South wall of the room so the King and Queen could easily see the view of the Zeeb Mountains, the Dead Sea and anyone who entered the room.

The entrance to the throne room was on the North wall. Anyone who entered the room would process directly to the throne and kneel before the King. The guards brought Professor Hai in front of the King. The guards and the Professor kneeled down to show reverence to the King. The guards then released Professor Hai and proceeded back to the entrance of the room.

Professor Hai saw Queen Metuka seated at the right of the King in the place of honor. Professor Hai feared her more than the King. He believed she was more ruthless, wicked, and evil than her husband. She was the first wife of the King and commanded as much. She was the only Gomorrite woman who could command the men of Gomorrah to do her will.

General Idit was standing to the King's left. He asked the Professor to have a seat.

There was a small chair in front of and just to right of the King. Professor Hai knew this chair as he had sat in many times before. If the King liked you, you would be offered a seat in this chair. The chair was made of solid gold and had three rubies set across the top back of it.

The Professor responded, "No thank you, General Idit. I prefer to stand."

General Idit responded in anger, "That wasn't a request. Have a seat!"

Professor Hai knew the command structure on Gomorrah. He was not a fool to openly challenge the General. He also knew General Idit was a giant compared to him. He would not have a chance against him in a fight.

Professor Hai nervously and quietly responded, "Yes sir."

General Idit began, "Professor…the King and I were talking about Adamina and we were wondering what is the status of your research. I mean…after all…it's been 10 years now that you have been researching the whereabouts of Adamina. The King has proclaimed that this will be the last New Gomorrah celebration on this planet. Are you going to make him out to be a liar?"

Professor Hai thought carefully of a response to the question. The King requests a status of The Adamina Research Project a few times a year. Professor Hai had been able to stall him in the past but he believed his tactics were not working any longer but he had to continue to try.

As he pondered his response he glanced at Queen Metuka, then the King and back at the General. Queen Metuka had a sinister smile on her face as if she could not wait to see what would happen next.

Professor Hai then looked at the King whose face was frowned with utter disgust.

Professor Hai knew that he was going to die this day but he answered anyway, "Sire, I am closer than I have ever been to finding Adamina. I just need a little more time. I am sure I will find it soon. I'm sure I will find it before the next New Gomorrah celebration. You will not be a liar."

As the professor finished speaking, he saw Lieutenant Oded entered the throne room from the side entrance. This entrance was only used by high ranking officials of the military. He stood to the side of the door where he could see everything that was going on in the throne room. Professor Hai knew he was there to protect the secrets of the resistance.

The King threw his head back in apparent anger, stood up from his throne, and walked as though he were throughly disgusted down the solid gold steps.

As he headed over to the General, King Abimelech spoke.

His voice was stern and angry, "Professor…I believe that motivation is a factor in determining how fast a person can complete a task for me."

Professor Hai watched as a man was dragged into the throne room.

King Abimelech continued, "This man has been imprisoned for two years in my jail. For the last thirty days he has not been fed. He will not tell me who he was working with when he was caught stealing food from the storage bins."

King Abimelech reached for a plate of the meat.

He continued, "As you know a normal man will not eat Zeeb meat because of the possibility of the poisons killing you. However, if a man has been sufficiently starved will he be motivated to eat the meat without regard to the poisons? What do you think?"

Professor Hai was to frighten to answer.

The King placed the meat on the ground. The meat of a Zeeb can be poisonous if not properly clean. Care must be taken to ensure all the hair from the animal is removed. If the slightest bit was ingested death would occur in seconds.

It was also found by Gomorrite scientist that some people had a natural immunity to the poisons. The number of people with a natural immunity was under 1 percent.

The man, who had been brought in, had obviously not eaten in a long time. He was very frail. You could see his rib bones and his skin was sunken in from the lack of food. The King placed the meat in front of him. He looked at the plate of meat on the floor for a few seconds then he began to visibly salivate.

Before Professor Hai could answer the King looked at the prisoner and said, "You my friend appear to be very hungry. This plate of Zeeb meat is all yours but remember the risk of eating such meat."

The King then ordered the guards to release the man and without hesitation the man began to eat the meat. He was eating fast, using both hands. The King, the Queen and the General all broke out in laughter watching the prisoner eat the plate of meat.

Before he could completely finish the plate of meat the prisoner paused. The Professor suspected the poisons were beginning to take effect. He continued to eat the meat.

The man began to shake feverishly clutching his frail body and foaming from the mouth. The effect of starvation was so great that despite the poison beginning to work he continued to try and eat the meat. Within minutes he was dead.

The King turned to look the Professor in the eye and said, "You see Professor...when sufficiently motivated a man will eat a plate of meat that he knows is poisoned."

He continued, "You...you have had no motivation to this point. So I must give it to you. Here...here are two beautiful young virgins for you to have for yourself. They were promised to two fine understanding

Gomorrite men. They are a prize that you can enjoy for many years to come. All you have to do is give me the coordinates to Adamina. How about it, Professor, what do you say…is this a fair trade?"

The Professor's belief in Jehovah would not allow him to partake in such things. He did not believe in the Gomorrite ways and taking this offer from the King would violate his beliefs. Furthermore he knew something was wrong because the King did not make such offers. He normally killed first and thought later.

Professor Hai lowered his head to the ground and answered praying for the best, "Sire, I do not have the coordinates to Adamina. I am sure I will discover them soon. I would not keep this information from you."

King Abimelech stated, "What a shame because I believe you do have the coordinates. I believe you…for some reason, are deceiving me…or you are incompetent."

The Professor pleadingly, with tears forming in his eyes begged, "Sire, I am not deceiving you…"

Before he could finish his sentence General Idit cut him off, "Silence! How dare you blatantly lie to the King?"

Professor Hai could see the anger growing in the King with each passing moment.

He raised his hand at the General to halt him from speaking and in a cold and calculating voice he spoke, "We will soon see if you are or not."

He then shouted, "Bring her in."

A sensation rolled up and down the Professor's spine as the words filled his ears. He hoped the King was not referring to his wife or daughter when he commanded the guards to "bring her in". Pain filled his heart as he saw that the King was having his wife brought into the throne room.

The Professor now feared the worst would come to his wife and not to him. What could he do? If he admitted now that he had the coordinates it would mean that he had been lying to the King all this time. For this he would surly die and the resistance would be no more. Professor Hai was caught in a circumstance that he knew no way out.

He began to do the only thing he could, pray, to himself, *"Jehovah, I turn this situation over to you. I know that all things happen for a reason and this sacrifice will lead to the fall of the evil of Gomorrah and to the believers returning home to Adamina. I know my wife trust her life with you as I trust my life with you. My Heavenly Father, I turn it all over to you."*

Professor Hai's wife looked at him. Her eyes told him not to tell the King what he wanted. Professor Hai knew she could not speak those words because the King would know they were members of the resistance. They had many discussions in the past in preparation for a moment like this one. A moment they both prayed would never happen. He knew this would be the last time he would see his wife again.

The King looked at the Professor and said "How is your motivation now Professor? Will you tell me what I want to know?"

The Professor had tears rolling down his face.

He continued to plead with the King, "Sire, I do not know the coordinates to Adamina. I cannot tell you want I do not know. Please do not harm my wife. Take my life for my incompetence instead. Please!"

The tears continued rolling down his face as it was evident that he was hurting at the thought of losing his wife forever.

The King was slowly pacing the floor and made his way to the Professor's wife.

He then looked over his shoulder to the Professor and said, "No, Professor…even though you are a pitiful man, you remain far too valuable. I let your daughter avoid her birthright to be given as promised to her husband during the New Gomorrah celebration solely because you asked. Yet, you still have no information for me. I should kill you just for being a weak man. Gomorrite men never cry! Now you must be properly motivated."

At these words the General moved over to the King and handed the King his sword. This sword was handed down from king to king. It was forged form the best metals Gomorrah had to offer and was perfectly balanced to the touch.

Gomorrite kings only used this sword for special occasions. Professor Hai attempted to jump up and come to the rescue of his wife but the King's guard held him in place.

King Abimelech turned toward the Professor and said "Now, you will be properly motivated."

Professor Hai shouted, "No!...Don't..."

The moments it took the King to rare the sword back and thrust it forward seemed like hours for Professor Hai and his wife. The Professor's mind raced to when he and his wife first met.

She was promised to him by his father's best friend. Both Professor Hai and his wife were born in the same year. At age 15 as promised she was given to him to marry. They grew up together so Professor Hai was happy to marry her and he knew she was happy to marry him.

Professor Hai's mind then flashed to the day their daughter was born. It was the happiest day in their lives. To see the smile of the child they brought into the world was truly a blessing from the Lord. He remembered how much pain his wife was in that day but how much joy they both had seeing their daughter born into the world.

Professor Hai's mind flashed to the night when both him and his wife vowed to never provide the King with any information that could help him get to Adamina. They both agreed that no matter the situation they would rather die than to allow that information to get to the King. Now the Professor was watching his wife fulfill that vow. She was about to die believing that her death would someday allow the resistance to have victory over the King.

She looked at her husband one last time and mouthed the words, "I love you."

The King turned, and looked at Professor Hai. In one swift, unfettering motion he thrust his sword into Professor Hai's wife. He let out an excruciating sound that made the room feel as though he thoroughly enjoyed his work. Once the sword was through her body and she fell over, the King removed the sword, stepping to the side to ensure no blood would spill on his royal clothing.

Professor Hai's wife grabbed her wound and as she fell to one knee, she looked at her husband and uttered her last words aloud this time, "I love you."

The blood gusted out of her and flowed over the throne room floor. She did not scream.

After she uttered her words of love she fell completely over and died.

The Professor could not contain himself. His emotions could not be concealed.

He screamed "No…"

Then he fell to the floor as she did and in a soft, whimpering tone he returned her words, "I love you."

The King reached back as if to hand his sword to someone. A servant ran to the spot and took the sword from him. It was his duty to ensure the sword was thoroughly cleaned and placed back in its royal place on the wall behind the throne….waiting for the next time the King wanted to relieve some stress. As the servant took the sword, the King made his way back to his throne, wiping his hands.

He then stated to Professor Hai with his back turned to him courting his robe about himself, appearing proud of his newest deed, "Now Professor, if I do not receive the coordinates to Adamina in one day…your daughter will be next. But she will die only after I have publicly had my way with her."

The Professor looked at his wife lying motionless on the floor and to himself vowed he would see both the King and the General die. He asked God to help him end this ruthlessness and defeat this enemy.

The Professor never wavered on his faith in Jehovah. Many of the resistance would have quit after witnessing such evil. However, this only made the Professor stronger. He longed for his wife but he knew that she would have rather died than to have her husband give the coordinates to the King.

***

Lieutenant Oded was sick to his stomach at the events that had transpired in the palace. He wanted to leave but he knew he could not. He had to stay and watch to be sure the Professor did not give any information to the King. If necessary he would have killed the Professor himself to prevent the information from being released.

Lieutenant Oded left the palace and went around the side of the building where no one was standing. He vomited everything he had in his system. The sight of watching an innocent woman die sickened him but he vowed that he would do his best to overthrow these ruthless leaders.

Lieutenant Oded then went to resistance headquarters where several others had gathered. No one knew what had happened until the Lieutenant arrived.

When he came through the door a young woman asked him, "Lieutenant, were you at the palace? Professor Hai and his wife were taken there."

The Lieutenant was visibly saddened by what he saw. He had to hide his emotions in public for the sake of remaining a spy among the General's ranks.

He looked the young woman in the eye and said, "I was there...I witnessed one of the worst things I have ever witnessed. He could not tell them what they wanted to know and he kept his faith. He is the strongest man of faith I know."

She said to him as she began to cry and hold her hand to her mouth, "What are you saying?"

The Lieutenant continued, "The King asked the Professor for the coordinates to Adamina. The Professor told him he didn't have the coordinates. I don't know if the Professor has them or not but the King murdered Professor Hai's wife right in front of him! He has no heart at all!"

A young man jumped up and said, "Where is the Professor?"

The Lieutenant responded, "They let him go. He probably won't come straight here for fear of giving them our location. He's probably going to tell Malka. She should find out from him and not from anyone else. The sad thing is people are laughing about it in the streets. Gomorrites are evil!"

The woman who had answered the door took the Lieutenants arm and said in a comforting tone, "Lieutenant, you know not all Gomorrites feel that way. We all share Professor Hai's pain. We have all experienced it as well. One day, with God's help we will overthrow the King. We just have to be patient and wait on the Lord."

The Lieutenant's head was down as he began to say in a sad helpless tone, "Sometimes I wonder if it is all worth it. Sometimes I wonder if we have been deceived all this time."

An old woman in the back of the room had been rocking in her favorite chair and listening to the events being described by Lieutenant Oded. Lieutenant Oded always looked up to her because she was a very wise woman who had survived the life of Gomorrah for over 100 years.

She responded to Lieutenant Oded's comments, "I have been on Gomorrah for over a 100 years son and I can tell you I have seen my share of ruthlessness. I have seen innocent people like my own parents murdered in front of me for no reason. I have seen women beaten and attacked over and over again. I have seen so many children turned over to old men for their sexual desires that it would make a sane person sick."

"What we are doing here is bringing about change and change isn't easy. It's hard. You have to be strong. You have to trust in the Lord because there is no other way out of this life but through Him. Now that Angel promised that we would defeat the King of Gomorrah and live in harmony on Adamina. The "Bible" says so and nothing or no one can make me believe otherwise."

The Lieutenant looked at the old woman and said only one word "Amen."

***

Professor Hai was stunned as he stumbled into the Beth-Peor Square where his quarters were located. He knew he had to get to his daughter before anyone else could tell her what happened.

People in the square saw the Professor and yelled at him.

One man shouted, "What a fool, he should never have gone against the King!"

A man at a bar shouted to the Professor, "Professor...do you want one of my wives...well you can't have any!"

They all broke out in laughter at the Professor's expense.

Professor Hai could hear everyone in the bar near him as they broke out in laughter. One man came over and helped him to his feet and then poured ale in his face while two women spat on him. They all laughed and mocked the Professor but for him his only goal was to get to his daughter.

Once he arrived at his quarters he found his daughter sitting in the corner of her room with tears in her eyes. She ran to him.

Professor Hai just celebrated his daughters 15th birthday a few days ago. He had convinced the King to spare her being given to anyone. Now she was in danger of being killed because he could not turn over the information he had to the King. He had to step up the plan to overthrow the King.

Malka, as she was crying along with her father she said to him, "Father, what happened? Where is mother? What did they do to you?"

Professor Hai attempted to get enough strength to tell her what happened. He feared he would not be able to say it her. He looked at her and attempted to wipe the tears, ale and spit from his face with a cloth that she handed him.

Through his tears he said, "Malka…your mother…she is…the King murdered her! He murdered her right in front of me because I would not tell him the coordinates to Adamina. Please forgive me. Please forgive your weak father."

The Professor could not hold back the full force of his tears any longer. He broke out into tears of pain and anger as he could not get the image of the King thrusting his royal sword into his wife…the only woman he had ever loved.

He couldn't look Malka in face because he felt she hated him. He did not want to hear her next words for he feared it would confirm his thoughts.

Malka said to her father, "Father, please take us away from this place. I cannot take it here any longer."

Professor Hai was glad to hear that she didn't hate him. He tried to comfort her as much as he could.

Professor Hai responded, "We will be leaving soon or the King will be dead. I can promise you that much, my child. No matter what happens in the coming days, know that I will always love you!"

Malka said, "I will always love you father. Nothing will ever change that."

Professor Hai said, "Malka…your mother was strong. I felt her eyes telling me not to tell the King what I knew. She knew she would certainly be killed but I could tell that she would rather die than for me to tell the King."

Malka looking down as she said, "Father she told me that I should not hold anything against you. She told me that she might have to sacrifice her life to prevent the King from finding out any information. She made me promise to understand that you were not to blame."

Professor Hai deep in thought comforted his daughter some more and told her, "Your mother was a great woman. She understood more about this than any woman I know. I will always love her."

Malka looked her father in his eyes and softly spoke, "She told me many times that I had to be strong like her. The resistance needs us to be strong even if it meant that we might die for it. I will always remember how strong my mother and father are. I will never lose my faith in Jehovah. Never."

At that moment Professor Hai knew he had to move up the timetable for the resistance to strike. He began making contacts to all the members that evening to set up a meeting to finalize plans for the overthrow of the King. Professor Hai was not thinking with his mind... instead was thinking with his heart and his heart was hurting...he wanted revenge.

***

After Professor Hai left the palace King Abimelech and General Idit were in the throne room.

King Abimelech reveling in his act of violence said, "How long before we know the coordinates to Adamina?"

The General quickly and with confidence replied, "My spy is on his way over now. We should know in a few minutes."

The King looked at his queen, caressed her chin, and softly said to her, "My dear, as I promised you a decade ago we will be the first royal couple to rule over Adamina in 5,000 years. The plan is starting to come together."

Queen Metuka looked at her husband with a smile and in a soft tone spoke to her king, "I knew you would be successful my King. You are the greatest King in the history of Gomorrah."

General Idit interrupted, "Sire, we must go and meet my spy. We must keep his identity a secret."

King Abimelech responded without taking his eyes from his queen, "Even from my queen?"

The General was careful with his words, "Sire, I desire that no one know his identity but you and I."

King Abimelech still looking deep into the eyes of his queen sternly spoke, "You are the best general I have ever had. Therefore, I will continue to give you some leeway in these matters. Let us go. I will return soon my love and we will begin our New Gomorrah festivities together."

***

King Abimelech went to his private office while the General went to get his spy. A few minutes later they both joined the King in the King's private office. The King cracked open a bottle of his finest wine for the occasion.

General Idit spoke first, "Sire, I present to you my spy. He has been successful in infiltrating the resistance and he has stolen the coordinates to Adamina."

King Abimelech quickly turned and looked at the man with disgust. He despised the resistance so much that he wanted to kill anyone associated with them. His hatred was so deep he wanted to kill this man who was working undercover for him. He resisted his temptation and welcomed him into his private office.

King Abimelech placed a phony smile on his face and stated, "Welcome. You have the honor of being one of very few to enter my private office. Here, have a sip of my best wine. Not many have had that pleasure either. Do you agree General?"

General Idit said, "This is a great honor to be in the presence of the King...especially in his private office. Many come to the palace and conduct business with the King but very few see this room. In fact, most of his governors have not had this honor. You should be proud."

The man voice cracked as he responded, "Sire...thank you for inviting me here. It is an honor to serve you and Gomorrah."

King Abimelech asks the spy, "Who is your father?"

The spy answered still with fear in his voice, "My father was Saar of Sodom. He was a soldier in your army. He was killed by a resistance member who was fleeing the city. For that I want to play my part in destroying their existence forever! I despise the stinking resistance. I feel dirty every time I am near them."

King Abimelech was excited to hear these words. He looked at the man as a father would look at his son. When the spy entered the room that day he was on death's door but now he was loved.

The King boastfully spoke to his new found friend, "Then you shall have your revenge. Do you know the man who killed your father?"

The man responded with anguish, "His name is Lieutenant Oded."

He then turned to the General…there is no mistaking the hate that is firmly in his eyes.

He says, "He is a high ranking Lieutenant in your army."

General Idit responded intensely, "I am rarely surprised by anything but this information surprises me. Are you sure about this?"

The spy spoke with renewed confidence in his voice, "General… sir…I have never been sure of anything in my life. He had to kill my father or he would have been exposed. My great king…my real name is Samuel. General Idit instructed me to change it because the resistance would have known who I was and not trusted me. So many times I wanted to kill Lieutenant Oded with my bare hands but I waited. When you give me the word, I will kill him…slowly…and painfully."

King Abimelech spoke with joy at the words that he heard, "I like this one General. He is highly motivated to perform the task at hand. Tell us what the resistance is up to Samuel."

Samuel was smiling as he said, "I stole the coordinates to Adamina for you. The resistance is going to go there if they fail to overthrow you. I do not know when the attempt will come but I'm sure to find out that information soon."

He handed the General a small piece of paper containing the coordinates to Adamina.

Samuel continued, "Professor Hai has a small shuttle craft designed for three people to travel to Adamina. He will use this craft if the resistance fails to overthrow you. He plans to go to Adamina and send back help to defeat you."

The General while looking at the coordinates stated, "Good work Samuel. We will send someone to Adamina today. When our battle cruisers get to Adamina Professor Hai will be killed."

King Abimelech said, "Excellent plan. Samuel you will be rewarded greatly for your work. When we take over Adamina I will make you a governor over your own land."

Samuel responded, "Thank you Sire but I would rather have a chance to kill Lieutenant Oded with my bare hands instead."

King Abimelech smiled, put his hand on Samuel's shoulder and said slowly, "You can have both…can't he General Idit?"

General Idit said with a grin, "Yes Sir."

They all laughed boldly and drank wine to celebrate what they believed to be an impending victory over the resistance and over Adamina.

CHAPTER 3

THE RESISTANCE

Professor Hai now realized that he must make preparations for the resistance to overthrow the King. The King gave him one day to provide the coordinates to Adamina. Professor Hai knew he could not provide this information to him, so his only choice was to launch the attack earlier than planned. He scrambled to begin making contact with the resistance leaders to schedule a meeting for the evening hours.

The resistance was headed by Professor Hai with 12 leaders in honor of the 12 tribes of Israel. Each leader was kept in the dark about the other leaders for fear of too many people having too much knowledge about the organization. Only Professor Hai knew all the leaders of the resistance and he kept the information to himself.

The 12 leaders were Aaron head of the Zebulun tribe, Dave head of the Simeon tribe, Daniel head of the Reuben tribe, Eben head of the Naplatali tribe, Gideon head of the Levi tribe, Israel head of the Judah tribe, Lemel head of the Joseph tribe, Reuben head of the Issachar tribe, John head of the Gad tribe, Sivan head of the Dan tribe, Rafeal head of the Benjamin tribe, and Yanisin head of the Asher tribe.

The Professor's mind focused on Gideon. All of Gomorrah considered Gideon a mighty warrior. He was looked upon as the equal of the General as they both grew up training to be warriors.

Then the Professor's mind jumped to one of his closest friends, Israel. Israel was a born leader of people. He grew up a farmer in the

Zeboim region of Gomorrah where he farmed vegetables. Israel once told Professor Hai that he received a vision that he would be a great leader on Gomorrah and because of him many lives would be saved. He joined the resistance and it was immediately recognized that he was a skilled leader of people. Professor Hai realized he needed to promote Israel to leader of a tribe. In doing so Israel became leader of a tribe faster than anyone in resistance history.

Professor Hai turned over the responsibility for planning the attack to Israel and Gideon. He knew that if a successful plan could be made, it would come from these two men working together.

He instructed Gideon and Israel to meet before the meeting that evening to go over the plan. He wanted to be sure there would be no problems with the plan since it is now going to take place during the New Gomorrah celebration. The plan was originally scheduled for execution two months after the celebration.

***

Israel went to Gideon's hiding place. Once Gideon saw him riding up on his beautiful stallion he came out to greet him.

Gideon greeted his friend with a smile and a hug, "It is good to see you old friend. I wish it was under better circumstances but it is good to see you."

He saw a similar smile of happiness on the face of Israel as he returned the gesture, "My friend it is good to see you as well. I miss our conversations and fellowships. The time is getting near and we must play our roles in ending this tyranny of ruthlessness on Gomorrah."

As Israel hugged Gideon he continued saying, "Our leader has paid a high price for his faith on this day. We must not let him down. We must not let the Lord our God down."

Gideon had only heard the news of the lost of Professor Hai's wife from the Professor himself when he contacted him regarding the meeting. Because Gideon had to live in the caves outside of Admah he was not privy to much of the news inside the city of New Gomorrah. At the mention of it by his long time friend Israel...it sadden his heart some more.

"The news did not reach me until Professor Hai informed me himself," Gideon was able to get out before gasping. "The Professor is a strong and faithful man. I only hope that I can be as strong as he if I am placed in that position."

Israel told his friend, "You are one of the strongest, bravest men I know Gideon. I believe if you were in a similar situation, you would have the intestinal fortitude to maintain your faith. Let us both pray that you will not have to endure such a situation and that we will end this reign of evil before the rise of the sun tomorrow. Come let us review the plan that will go down in history as the greatest plan every created."

The two of them went into the cave where Gideon was hiding from General Idit's men.

Gideon spoke as he led his friend to his office in the rear of the cave, "This plan must be coordinated...a simultaneous attack of the two greatest powers on Gomorrah...New Gomorrah and Zoar. If we bring down the two strongest areas of Gomorrah then our success will be imminent. My army will attack New Gomorrah from the North. We will send small squadrons of men into the city undercover. They will position themselves strategically around the city. Once we attack, they will unveil themselves and attack from within. Our primary objective will be to secure the palace and capture the King and General Idit. Taking out the leadership will greatly hinder their army."

Gideon continued, "At the same time, you and your men will attack Zoar. Taking the barracks by surprise should enable you to defeat the Gomorrite army and stop any reinforcements from coming to the aid of New Gomorrah. The other regions will not be as much of a threat after we have captured New Gomorrah and Zoar."

Gideon noticed Israel's head was shaking as he was talking.

Israel placed his hand on the shoulder of his friend and revealed his feelings, "My friend, I respect you as a leader and a skilled fighter. Your plan is brilliant as always but I do not feel I should be the one to lead an army against Zoar. My skills are that of a leader...a motivator. A warrior...I am not. Yanisin...now there is a warrior. He should be the one to lead the army against Zoar."

Gideon did not trust Yanisin. His hate for Yanisin was as strong as his hate for General Idit. He knew Yanisin from their days in Zoar. Gideon was older than Yanisin but he followed his career.

When Gideon found the Lord and fled to the hills from the Gomorrite army. It was Yanisin that led the troops to find him.

A couple of years later Gideon heard that Yanisin was forced to follow his path. It was told that the King was going to execute Yanisin so he fled in disgrace.

Yanisin was introduced to the resistance by other members who had come to trust him. Gideon believed he was a plant and never trusted him.

While pouring a cup of water, Gideon spoke calmly to his friend, "My friend, I have confidence and trust in you but I do not have the same for Yanisin. Despite my pleadings the members of the resistance still feel this man can be trusted. I do not feel we should place the greatest plan in our history in the hands of a man who cannot be trusted."

Israel replied, "Yanisin has earned trust from all of us my friend. Please consider my request and allow him to lead the army against Zoar."

Gideon with great reservations agreed to allow Yanisin to lead the army against Zoar. The two men sat down at a table with a map of Gomorrah and plotted out their plan.

Gideon spoke, "Once we have captured the King and General Idit, you will assume temporary leadership of Gomorrah. After the governor of each region has conceded victory to us, we will announce to the people that a new government is in place and they will have the right to vote for their leaders. It is my prayer that you become the permanent leader of this world my friend. I do not believe there is anyone better for this position than you."

Israel smiled and said, "Thank you for your kind words my friend. We should send for Yanisin and bring him in on this plan."

Gideon still believing this would not be a good move but not wanting to offend his friend turned to his guards and said, "Go and retrieve Yanisin, leader of the Asher tribe. Bring him back here. Do not allow him to leave your presence and blindfold him before bringing him here. Do you understand?"

The guard quickly snapped, "Yes sir."

The guard rode off on his horse en route to retrieve Yanisin. Israel and Gideon continued to talk while they were waiting. They both knew it would take awhile for the guard to return with Yanisin so they reminisced about their youths and the events that lead them to this day.

***

The Professor had returned to the university. He had work to do before the meeting that evening. He had to ensure the ship was ready in case they needed it. He left instructions with Malka to be ready to leave if he could not get to her. The adrenalin was flowing through the Professor like the blood flowing through his veins. He was hoping that the day was fast approaching that they would be free of the ruthless reign of kings of Gomorrah.

The Professor quickly came into the lab where he found Tamir working and said, "Tamir, we must ready ourselves. Tonight will be a great night in the history of Gomorrah. Tonight we attack the King and his army in the name of the Lord."

Tamir's face went from sympathy to shock.

"Professor, we are going to go ahead with the plan tonight," asked Tamir?

The Professor clutched Tamir's shoulders and with the excitement of a child he told Tamir, "Yes my friend. The plan has been put into place and tonight we will attack the King and his army. If we are successful we will not be ruled by ruthless kings any longer. However, if we are not, then we will be on our way to Adamina in hopes of getting help for our plight. Let us hope that we defeat the King and when we make our trip to Adamina it will be to make new friends and not to ask for help."

Tamir replied, "Professor, we will win this battle and the King will be dethroned. Then we will have a government by the people, for the people…as it should be!"

The Professor and Tamir readied themselves for the evening's events. They prepared the ship in case it became necessary to leave Gomorrah and they finalized plans on the meeting. They agreed to meet at the shuttle when the battle started in case they had to leave.

***

General Idit sat in his office reared back in his big black leather chair pondering the events that would take place over the next few days.

He knew the Professor would not provide the coordinates to Adamina and he suspected that something was about to happen. He relished his chance to wipe out the resistance. Just as the King desired so mightily to be the King to return to Adamina, the General desired mightily to wipe out the resistance especially Gideon. In the midst of his thoughts his private communicator that he used to get information from his spies rang.

The General answered the phone, "This is General Idit authentication code Jordan449."

The voice responded, "This is Rafeal authentication code Zeeb711. I have received a message from the Professor. We are meeting this evening to discuss a plan to overthrow the King. I do not have any details as of yet but I will contact you when I do."

The General was pleased to receive this information and responded, "Rafeal, you have pleased me on this day. Find out the details of the plan and contact me immediately. I want to wipe out this resistance and when I do, you will be greatly rewarded."

Rafael told General Idit, "Sir, I will contact you after the meeting with all the details. You will crush this resistance before sunrise... forever!"

The General and Rafeal hung up their respective communicators and again the General reared back in his chair. He only hoped that he would have a chance to kill his nemesis, Gideon. He remembered the last battle he and Gideon had. In this battle, Gideon humiliated him to the rest of the men. They were only 18 years old at the time but General Idit has never forgotten that day. It was a sunny day like any other day in the region of Zoar and the heat was immense. The war games for the day had just ended and the general remembers how he was relishing in his victory over Gideon's team.

The General saw Gideon walking back into the square where the men normally gathered after the war games to laugh and exchange stories of the day's events.

The General pointed at Gideon, laughed and said, "Men, here comes the loser now!"

The rest of the men standing around all broke out in laughter but Gideon and his men did not. Gideon walked right down the middle of them toward General Idit.

Gideon sternly said to the General, "You have no honor, no tactical skills, and you are a worthless warrior and a coward."

This angered the General and he challenged Gideon, "You had better be ready to back those words up. Back up men so I can show this loser how to be a warrior!"

The General then stepped toward Gideon and threw a punch at him. Gideon sidestepped the punch and countered with a combination to the General's stomach and jaw. This sent the General backwards, falling to the ground.

Gideon shouted, "Get up and take your beating like a man!"

The General got up and ran toward Gideon with his head down hitting Gideon in the midsection. Gideon grabbed the General by the waist, picked him up and threw him over his shoulder.

The General landed on his back. The General's first instinct was to grab his back with his left hand. He then got up again, grabbing some dirt on the way up and flung it at Gideon.

Gideon grabbed his eyes and the General stepped to him hitting him in the face three consecutive times causing Gideon to go down.

Gideon quickly got up and performed a round house kick hitting the General on the side of his head, and then he pounded on him with several punches causing the General to fall backwards. General never forgot that dizzy feeling. He wanted Gideon to feel that and more. But what was worst were the words Gideon said next.

Gideon put his finger on the General's head and said laughingly, "Men, here is your leader. He is a sorry excuse for a warrior. He has to cheat to win a battle but one on one he is no match for a true warrior."

Gideon then pushed the General's head with his finger and the General fell helplessly to the ground where he stayed. The men broke out in laughter at the General's expense. Even his own team members laughed at him.

Humiliated and stunned he vowed to someday have his revenge. Shortly after that fight, Gideon announced he had found the Lord and fled for his life.

The General waited for his revenge. The Gomorrite soldiers never captured Gideon but General Idit knew one day Gideon would be captured and he savored the moment when he would take the pleasure of killing Gideon for himself.

***

Gomorrah's long 30 hour days provided ample time for the resistance to gather its forces and ready them for attack. The guard that was sent to retrieve Yanisin had arrived at Yanisin's quarters and was met by one of Yanisin guards. The guard put his hand up making a motion to stop.

Yanisin's guard asked, "What is your business here?"

The guard responded, "I am here to bring Yanisin back to an important meeting. He must come with me now."

Yanisin's guard instructed him to, "Wait here and I will see if Yanisin is available."

The guard replied, "He must be available. There is no other option."

Once inside Yanisin's guard went to Yanisin's private office to inform him that the guard was present and asking for him. Yanisin stood up and walked behind his guard making his way outside to see what the guard wanted.

Once outside Yanisin asked, "What is it my friend? Why have to come here at mid day to see me? It is dangerous not to be taking part in the festivities but you make this trip. Is it that important?"

The guard did not flinch at Yanisin's questions.

Instead he simply replied, "I have been instructed to escort you to a very important meeting. We must go now without hesitation."

Yanisin stared at the guard but did not reveal what he was thinking. If he were not working as an undercover spy for the General he would have killed the man without blinking an eye. But, as a resistance member he was to show patience and respond to the request.

Yanisin smiled and spoke calmly to the guard, "Where is the meeting and why the rush? No matter. I will hurry myself. Give me one hour and I will be ready."

The guard replied, "Sir, I cannot…we must go now."

Yanisin thought better of this and decided to give in.

He said, "Then now it will be."

***

As they approached the cave Gideon's guard led Yanisin through the entrance and then to Gideon's office where Gideon and Israel were waiting. The guard removed the blindfold from Yanisin and motioned for him to join the group.

When Yanisin saw it was Gideon he had to contain himself over the joy of this opportunity. Yanisin was a young lieutenant when he was sent out to find Gideon and bring him back to the King. Yanisin's failure in this mission nearly cost him his life.

When he returned without Gideon, the King ordered Yanisin to be beheaded for his failure. Instead, the head of the King's army at the time offered Yanisin a chance to redeem himself by going undercover with the resistance. His sentenced to death by the King gave him a chance to provide the resistance with evidence that he was not loyal to the King any longer.

The first five years undercover was the worst for Yanisin. No one trusted him. No one believed he had turned against the King. He had to work 18 hours or more a day just to eat. The resistance watched him carefully. It was not until Yanisin saved the life of a prominent leader within the resistance that he started to convince members to trust him.

Once he won their trust he climbed the ladder of success but always informed the General of his every move. He never forgot how Gideon was the cause of him losing his family and friends.

He blamed Gideon for having to work so long and so hard to become a valued member of the resistance but now he would have his revenge. He would see Gideon die at the hands of the General.

Yanisin managed a smile and some words, "Gideon my friend. It is good to see you after all these years. I pray that you are alright."

Gideon snapped back at him, "You are not my friend and I am not glad to see you."

Israel interrupted, "Now gentlemen. We must put our differences aside and handle the business at hand. Tonight we will begin a campaign that will go down in Gomorrite history as the campaign that changed everything on Gomorrah for all of its people. What happened in the past must stay buried in the past. Today we move forward."

Yanisin agreed, "I agree my friend. I do not believe we have had the pleasure. As you probably know I am Yanisin, leader of the Asher tribe. And you?"

Israel smiled and shook Yanisin's hand.

With pleasure he responded, "Yes, I do know who you are and it is a pleasure to meet you. As you know the secrecy of the leaders of the resistance is necessary so that no one person knows all the names of the leaders. It is good to know you my friend. My name is Israel, leader of the Judah tribe."

Gideon did not extend a welcome to Yanisin instead he turned his back to him and sat in his chair.

Yanisin said in a sarcastic tone, "Regrettably, not all feel as you do Israel."

Israel continued, "Yanisin, we have decided to bring you in on the plan to overthrow the King and his army. In the early morning hours we will launch and we need you and your regiment to take up a position around Zoar. Your attack will be coordinated with the attack on New Gomorrah. This plan is predicated on secrecy therefore it is paramount that you not discuss this plan with anyone...even your own men. Is that clear?"

Yanisin was excited at this opportunity. Now he could lead the regiment he commanded right into the hands of the General's army and lead Gideon right into the hands of the General. He would be a hero on Gomorrah and obtain his rightful place in the kingdom. He may even be promoted for his sacrifice.

Yanisin, while remaining calm, looked Israel in the eye, leaned toward him and spoke softly, "I will die before I divulge this plan to anyone. It is an honor to be chosen for such a prominent role in the downfall of the kingdom. I thank you both for this opportunity."

Gideon quickly added, "It was not my idea to bring you in but Israel believes you can be trusted. If you are working for the General, I will kill you myself."

Yanisin stood up and Israel stood with him placing his hand on Yanisin's shoulder, "Now gentlemen we must contain ourselves. We cannot allow bitterness to come between us."

Yanisin pushed Israel's hand away and said, "It is okay, I will continue to pray for Gideon. Remember my friend, when you found

God and asked others to believe in you? I only ask and am given the same opportunity. I have done nothing over the years but prove my allegiance to the resistance. When will you give me a chance?"

Gideon looked sternly in Yanisin's eyes and said with a bitter coldness, "I will never give you that chance."

Israel seeking to dissolve this situation said, "Gentlemen do we at least have an agreement on the plan. Each one of you will command a prominent army in the plan. You both need the support of each other to complete this attack. Tomorrow...if you like you can be enemies, but today, you need to work together to accomplished our goal. What say each of you? Can we do this or must the resistance wait another 5,000 years?"

Gideon begrudgingly said, "Yes."

Yanisin with a smile yelled, "Yes!"

Israel happy to see that both sides are willing to make this plan work spoke boastfully, "Today we plan for victory and tomorrow we shall have it. If two mighty men such as the two of you can come together for a common goal than I am sure that we can come together as an army and take control of our land. To the resistance!"

Yanisin shouted, "To the resistance!"

Gideon raised his cup, drank some wine and walked out of the room. Yanisin knew he was still not convinced that he was loyal but it didn't matter. Yanisin would have his revenge.

***

After the meeting with Gideon and Israel, Yanisin returned to his quarters. He instructed his men not to bother him with anything for at least an hour. He retreated to his private office where he retrieved his private communicator. He was about to pass on the most vital information that he had ever had the chance to tell the General.

As he was searching for his communicator he imagined how he would be given the best house available in the main city. How the King himself would decorate him with honors and he would be able to marry again.

He would not have to deal with resistance women. He was disgusted by their very behavior. He was disgusted with their dedication to abstinence from sex until marriage.

He remembered several of them and what he would do to them if they survived the General's onslaught. The General had promised him his pick of them all if he delivered the resistance over to him. Now he would get his chance.

After finding his communicator he quickly dialed it to contact the General.

The General answered, "This is General Idit, authentication code Jordan449."

Yanisin could hardly deter his excitement he responded, "This is Yanisin, authentication code Moses373. General Idit, sir, I have the battle plans of the resistance of you. The fools have granted me the privilege to leading one of the attacking forces in the plan. The resistance will attack at zero three hundred hours in the morning. They are hoping that all of the troops will be celebrating New Gomorrah and not realize what hit them. Sir, what are your instructions?"

Yanisin could hear the excitement in General Idit's voice. He knew that soon his reward would be given to him because he delivered the enemy into General Idit's hand.

General Idit asked Yanisin, "What of Gideon?"

Yanisin smiled and answered, "Sir, he will be leading the attack on New Gomorrah. He will be approaching the city from the North. Some of his men will slip into the city to appraise the situation and take out any guards. At zero three hundred hours they will attack and Gideon will come right into your hands. Sir, when you kill him please make it slow and painful…and please allow me to watch."

General Idit replied, "You have done well Yanisin. I am pleased with you. I will honor both of your requests. If the resistance is crushed you will be promoted in rank and given back all your assets and more."

Yanisin happily responded, "Thank you sir."

After hanging up with General Idit, Yanisin sent his personal guard to get Rafael. No one knew that Yanisin and Rafael were brothers. When Yanisin infiltrated the resistance, his brother was recruited by the General to infiltrate the resistance as well. Yanisin had Rafael change his name and falsified documents to cover his background.

Yanisin was responsible for ensuring that Rafael successfully got into the resistance and moved up the latter. With Yanisin's help Rafael was able to become the leader of the Benjamin tribe.

Rafael arrived at Yanisin's quarters and was brought into his private office.

The guard brought Rafael into the office and announced him, "Sir, Rafael, is here as you requested."

Yanisin happily replied, "Welcome my friend. Guard, you may be excused."

The guard replied, "Yes, sir."

After the guard left, Yanisin continued, "My brother it is good to see you again. Soon we will be able to announce our bloodline publically again and live as brothers would. I have learned the plan of the resistance as they have anointed me leader of the forces to attack Zoar. What fools these resistance leaders are. Now we will have victory and be able to resume our lives as they should be...as true Gomorrites!"

Rafael was delighted at this news and hugged his brother with joy and asked, "My brother this is truly good news. Have you informed the General of this plan?"

Yanisin answered, "Yes, I have just informed the General and he offered me a high position in the army if we succeed in crushing the resistance. My brother, I will bring you with me and together we will have great power in Gomorrah."

Rafael remarked, "Thank you my brother. Allow me to assist you in crushing the forces that plan to attack Zoar."

Yanisin responded, "You will have the honor to fight alongside of me. Together we will crush the vermin and eradicate our world of them forever!"

Rafael said, "I must go now. It would not be good of us to go to the meeting together."

Yanisin agreed, "Yes, go now and I will see you later at the meeting."

After riding for many hours to get back to the caves Yanisin finally arrived. He was excited to know that the end of his masquerade was almost over. He had clutched in his hands his communication device to contact the General after he learned the identies of all the leaders.

As he approached the entrance to the cave he was pulled aside by a stranger.

Yanisin asked, "What is this, my friend?"

The man replied, "I am a friend. They are searching everyone who enters the cave. They will find your communication device. Give it to me. I will take it in for you and return it once inside."

Yanisin ask, "How do I know I can trust you?"

The man answered, "The code word is ga'al."

Yanisin smiled and handed the device to the stranger. Ga'al was their code word when the General's spies met in the field and didn't know each other. Yanisin now knew he had another friend at the meeting.

***

The bright sun of Gomorrah was finding its way to its nightly hiding place and the celebration in New Gomorrah began to hit a fever pitch. Every night the celebration intensified in New Gomorrah and the surrounding regions. The resistance members found it harder to evade these activities at night so they stayed in their homes to avoid detection. However, on this evening a meeting of the leaders of the resistance was necessary to prepare for the forthcoming battle. All the leaders were instructed to meet Professor Hai at the caves where Gideon was hiding.

None of the leaders knew all of the other leaders and this was the first time that they all were meeting together. Now all 12 leaders would meet each other just before the biggest battle in their 5,000 year history.

As the last members were entering the cave, Professor Hai stood up to begin the meeting. As he stood his thoughts jumped to his wife and how she had sacrificed her life to keep the secrecy of the resistance and in her honor this battle would be waged. He reminded himself of the merciless act that the King had done in front of him…killing his one and only love…his one and only wife.

Professor Hai finally managed to speak, "The love of my life…left us today."

He felt a deep sigh roll across the room.

He continued, "For many years she fought for change. She helped to keep the resistance organized. She taught the young women of our clan how to live as a saved woman. She took care of me and our daughter but she was more than just a wife and mother. She was a wife, mother, leader, teacher, preacher, friend, and fighter to us all. In her name I proclaim this battle…this battle will change the ruthless ways of our people…this battle to take Gomorrah from under King Abimelech and General Idit's rule."

The leaders all stood and clapped their hands mightily. Professor Hai could sense the heighten emotions in the room.

Professor Hai continued, "Today we present to you the plan to overthrow the King. In the early morning hours of tomorrow morning, we will enact this plan. I present to you, Gideon, leader of the Levi tribe and our foremost military strategist, to brief you on the plan."

***

Gideon stood and walked to the front of the room. The caves he lived in for many years had been carved out into a mighty fortress. The room they all were meeting in was a conference room where Gideon had many meetings with his troops. Now he was about to brief the leaders of the 12 tribes on the most historic plan in the history of Gomorrah. He knew everyone in the room had at least heard of him and respected him. He respected many of them as well.

Gideon calmly began, "My friends, this plan has been prepared to ensure victory of the resistance over our enemy. The main threats to our success are the city of New Gomorrah and the region of Zoar. We must defeat both at the same time to ensure victory. If we are not successful we will not win.

Timing will be everything. We must time the attacks to commence at the same time. In the confusion, the King's army will not be able to defend both places. By taking out Zoar along with New Gomorrah there will be little to no reinforcements available to assist New Gomorrah."

"Everyone in this room will stay here until the first hour of the day. At that point you will be released to take command of your forces and take your positions. Thirty minutes prior to the third hour of the day small squadrons of men will enter Zoar and New Gomorrah; take up positions, and subdue any guards not participating in the celebration. There will not be many of them since security is often lax during the celebrations."

"At precisely the third hour of the day, the forces led by me and Yanisin will attack New Gomorrah and Zoar respectively. I will approach New Gomorrah from the North. The primary objectives in

New Gomorrah will be the palace, King Abimelech and General Idit. Once we have secured our objectives the rest of New Gomorrah should fall without much of a fight.

Yanisin will attack Zoar at the training barracks. If Yanisin and his men can subdue the barracks the region of Zoar will fall easily and New Gomorrah will have no reinforcements."

"Once we have control over Zoar and New Gomorrah we will move out to the other regions and take control of them as well."

"I cannot empathize enough the importance of surprise in this plan. I also cannot empathize enough the importance of taking the palace and the barracks at Zoar first. These places are the strongest held places on Gomorrah. If they fall the rest of Gomorrah will fall and we will be able to institute our own government. Are there any questions?"

Saul, the leader of the Gad tribe, spoke up, "Giving us two hours to gather and ready our forces is not enough. We will need more time to make this happen."

Gideon answered, "We cannot allow more time. Concern for secrecy makes this necessary. For the first time in our existence all 12 leaders are present in this room. Now we all know each other. We cannot allow anyone to leave this room without being sure our plan has a chance of success."

Aaron abruptly responded, "This means that we are not to be trusted. Is that right?"

Gideon continued in a calm voice, "I am staying here myself. I ask nothing of each of you that I am not placing on myself. Any of you can be captured after you leave here and tortured for information. This part of the plan is for your protection as well."

Israel stood and remarked, "Gentlemen, we should not take personal any part of this plan. We have thought out each phase of the plan for many years. This is the best plan in order to take control of Gomorrah. The hour has now reached the 26th hour of the day. We have five hours before you will be allowed to return to your forces and ready them for this battle. Let us eat and drink in celebration of our impeding victory!"

Everyone in the room stood and clapped their hands. Some hugged others, happily anticipating the end of the ruthless leadership of Gomorrah. All of them adjourned to the dining room where a feast

We Come in Peace

had been prepared for them. The leaders of the 12 tribes, Professor Hai and each leader's second in command attended the feast.

***

It was early in the 28th hour of the day. The celebration was in high gear on Beth-Peor square. Malka was in her quarters wondering what was going on with her father. She knew of the big meeting with all the leaders of the resistance. She knew a battle was soon to be fought and that in the case of defeat she would have to get to the shuttle and leave for Adamina.

One part of her wanted to go to another world but the other wanted her people to see freedom. She prayed to Jehovah to let her see both. She listened as the celebration continued in the square beneath her. The drinking, eating, cursing, sex and violence all made her sick to her stomach. She hated life on Gomorrah.

In these times she remembered her mother taking her in her arms and telling her stories from the Bible. Her mother had memorized many stories and told them to Malka. Malka wanted to remember them just as her mother remembered them. Now without her mother she sat on the floor of a dark room remembering those stories and how they provided comfort to her. She thought in one way or another, this would be the end of this wretched life.

***

General Idit calmly and confidently made his way to the private office of the King.

As he approached he yelled, "I am here to see the King. Announce me!"

The guard at the door of the King's private quarters adhered to the General's request and went in to announce him. In seconds he returned and motioned to the General to enter. The General eyed the guard as he walked through the door.

He wanted to strike fear in the hearts of everyone he came into contact with. He didn't care if they were his men or not. Striking fear was his goal.

He saw the King behind his solid oak, burgundy in color desk. Anyone else would acknowledge it's beautiful design. That is anyone else except General Idit. General Idit noted the Kings family crest etched into the front of it. The thought of his families crest adorning the front of the desk flowed across his mind.

The General began to inform the King, "Sire, I have discovered an attempt to overthrow New Gomorrah and Zoar in order to takeover Gomorrah. The resistance is planning this attack to start at the third hour in the morning. My men will be ready for them and we will crush this attack within minutes. Also as you promised I will be able to exact my revenge on Gideon."

The King stood up from behind his desk and snarled, "Assure me that this is the day the resistance will end and be no more."

The General assuredly responded, "It will be so. I guarantee it."

After a slight pause the General continued, "My plan is…"

The King cut off the General, "I don't need to know mere details. Just defeat them and bring the leaders before me. You can have Gideon for yourself but the others are mine! They will die swiftly and publicly."

The General proclaimed, "So it will be Sire…so it will be."

He walked off with a confidence that only he could. General Idit was cold and calculating. He wanted his revenge and he could not wait to have it.

***

During the last hour of the day, Yanisin slipped off from the rest of the tribe leaders claiming to need to use the shirutim. He had reacquired his communication device front the stranger. Now he was prepared to use it.

While away, Yanisin pulled out his communicator and relayed the details of the meeting to the General including the names of the leaders. He then returned to the dining room with the others.

***

The General gathered his colonels together. General Idit knew he could count on his number one colonel, Colonel Harel. Colonel Harel was General Idit's top assistant. General Idit planned to give him the highest responsibility…to capture Gideon.

General Idit welcomed his friend Colonel Harel, "Welcome my old friend. It is good to see you again. We have pressing business to attend to this evening."

After a brief pause, General Idit continued, "I realized the previous king sent you on an expedition to find new land to cultivate and add to the land already occupied by us. I need to pull you off of that assignment now. Tonight you will be responsible for capturing Gideon."

Colonel Harel asked, "Sir what about the Shehar?"

The Shehar were a pest to General Idit but not as much as the resistance. To General Idit the Shehar were just a primitive tribe of people who did not deserve the attention of the Gomorrites.

General Idit answered, "Leave them be. We have no time for them."

Colonel Harel sighed and smiled, "Then I will capture Gideon for you. What would you like me to do?"

General Idit explained, "You will go to the Northern edge of New Gomorrah. You will take cover and hide in the Vardar building complex leaving all lights off so Gideon will think the complex is unoccupied. When he leads his men through the gates your men will begin shooting them down from an elevated position. It will be like shooting fish in the water."

Colonel Harel laughingly replied, "I love this plan. I assume we are to leave Gideon alive."

General Idit answered, "Yes. He is mine. Do not start shooting at them until they are more than halfway through the gate. This will ensure that Gideon, who should be leading them, is out of range and you can hit all of his men. You should post several men past the Vardar complex to capture Gideon. This is where you should be positioned as well. Place your best lieutenant in charge inside the building complex."

Colonel Harel declared, "This victory will go down in history and Gomorrah will be free of this resistance forever."

General Idit agreed, "Yes my friend it will be over and you will be relieved of your duty with the Shehar as well."

Colonel Harel had a perplexed look on his face as he replied, "Why? I want to stamp them out."

General Idit said, "You will be needed here to command the Gomorrite army."

Colonel Harel responded, "Sir, I am puzzled, what about you?"

General Idit responded, "I will be on my way to Adamina…leading the invasion force. We are allowing the leader of the resistance to take a shuttle to Adamina. Then we will know for sure that such a trip is possible. We will then take an armada of troops and ships to Adamina and take it over. We have been building these ships for years and tonight all of that work will show its fruits."

Colonel Harel excitedly responded, "This is truly great news. I did not know all of this was going on. You have done an outstanding job keeping it secret."

General Idit sat down and proclaimed, "Our forces are the greatest ever. I have kept scientist in a secret location where no one knows of them except me. They have been working for us for the past ten years. Advancements that Professor Hai made were being expanded to war capability. We are ready to crush the resistance and Adamina all at the same time. Wait until we unveil the battle cruisers."

Colonel Harel replied, "I will attend to the responsibilities in your absence. Tonight I will ensure me and my men are ready to crush the resistance."

General Idit replied, "Go my friend and gather your troops."

The two men made a toast to Gomorrah. Colonel Harel then departed to gather his men.

***

After the first hour had come Professor Hai returned to his quarters where he found Malka asleep on the floor. He woke her and they gathered their things together in preparation for the long journey that he hoped would not be necessary.

Professor Hai panted, "Malka, wake up my daughter. We must get to the shuttle and be ready in case our plan fails."

Malka half asleep answered, "Father…you are back. I am ready Father, I have been preparing all evening."

Professor Hai rushed to the door saying, "Then let us leave now. Tamir should be waiting for us at the craft."

***

Israel was sitting in his office. He looked up at the clock on the wall and saw that the time was just after the second hour. He knew the plan of attack was nearing. His thoughts were skipping around on different parts of his life. He reminisced of the times he and his father worked in the field together.

His father told him on many occasions that he would be a great leader of people someday. His mother often spoke of the greatness that hung over him. How he would someday lead his people. She spoke of a vision that she had of Israel meeting with a group of strangers who would provide help to his people, freeing them from the ruthless reign of kings.

He wondered how his mother had gotten the vision so wrong. The victory would come with his friends not strangers.

Now just minutes away from a history changing event, he thought of the many things that would have to be done once victory was achieved. He took out a pen and paper to begin writing them down when suddenly the door flung open and his thoughts were interrupted.

"Sir, I have to speak to you. It is urgent!" His personal assistant, Isaac was shouting as he ran into the room.

"We have traced a communication that was sent from Gideon's cave during the dinner. We traced it to General Idit's office! Someone in the group is a spy!"

Israel's heart dropped to the floor.

He said with sadness evident in his voice, "Who? We searched everyone as they entered the cave. No one had a communication device on them."

Isaac grimaced, "Somehow one came in and it was used. Sir, we have a recording device in the General's office. Should we try and retrieve it?"

"Who can we trust," asked Israel?

"I will go myself," Isaac insisted. "I will contact you as soon as I return!"

***

The distance to New Gomorrah was short. Isaac would not have far to travel to get to the General's office. He also had one of the fastest horses on Gomorrah.

He arrived at the General's office shortly after leaving Israel's office. He pretended to be cleaning the General's office as was often his detail. When he was sure no one was around he retrieved the recorder from the General's office. Knowing he would be searched when he left, Isaac placed the recorder in the crouch of his pants. He knew the guard would not search him there.

Just after Isaac finished hiding the device General Idit walked through the door.

"What are you doing here," the General commanded?

"Sir, I am Isaac, and I am on detail to clean your office. I was just finishing up…"

"Get out…now," the General huffed!

Isaac quickly gathered his cart and left the General's office. The guards did not search him because the General wanted him out of there in a hurry. Isaac quickly returned to Israel's quarters to listen to the recording.

As Isaac was running through the streets of New Gomorrah the people were too busy celebrating to pay him any attention. He hoped on his horse and set out to Israel's quarters.

He arrived at Israel's quarters 30 minutes before the third hour of the day. He rushed into Israel's office and hurriedly pulled out the recorder and pressed play.

***

Israel was shocked to learn who the traitor was and it made him sick to his stomach.

He moaned, "What have I done? I have killed my best friend."

Isaac did not recognize the voice and asked, "Sir, who is the traitor?"

Israel answered, "It is Yanisin. I asked that he be the one to lead the forces into Zoar. Gideon warned me that he could not be trusted but I believed Gideon was just being paranoid. Now I see he was right."

Isaac sighed, "We must warn him."

Israel through his tears responded, "They do not have communicators. We did not want them used for fear of tipping our hand to the General's army. Now we have sealed their faith."

Isaac yelled, "Sir, I will ride my horse and then run as fast as I can to get to Gideon's men!"

Israel slumped down in his seat and cried. If he had not asked that Yanisin be given the responsibility for leading the forces against Zoar his best friend's plan to overthrow the King might have succeeded. As it stood now he would be lucky to die quickly. Israel got himself together for he knew he had to warn the Professor that the plan was going to fail.

***

Professor Hai and Malka reached the shuttle where Tamir was waiting for them.

Tamir shouted, "Sir, I thought something happened to you. Where have you been?"

"I was at the meeting and I had to get my daughter. The streets are not safe tonight. The celebration is in full force," exclaimed Professor Hai.

Tamir informed the professor, "Sir, I have completed all of the preflight checks like you told me to do. I believe we are ready."

Professor Hai sneered, "We have to wait…"

Just then his resistance communicator rang and he answered it.

"Professor…Professor I must speak with you," yelled Israel!

Professor Hai asked, "What is your authentication code?"

Israel replied, "I forgot… my code is Adamina699."

Professor Hai responded, "My code is Adamina731. What is it Israel?"

Israel was desponded when he spoke, "I have made a grave mistake my friend. Yanisin is a spy and it was I who requested he be allowed to lead the forces against Zoar. I believe he has told General Idit our attack plan."

The Professor could not believe his ears. All of this careful planning… everything was now about to end right before them. They had no chance now with General Idit knowing they were coming. The Professor had to leave and hope that he could find help on Adamina.

Professor Hai spoke, "My friend, I must leave for Adamina and hope that we can bring back help to defend against the King and his army.

71

Our long awaited plan will not work but we still have God on our side and in the end we will prevail."

"You must take control of the resistance in the aftermath. It will be difficult as many will begin to question God. You must keep their faith that I will return with help. Remember the Bible says that both Gomorrah and Adamina will be free of ruthless Kings. Keep the faith my friend."

Israel sadly responded, "I cannot be the leader of the resistance. I am not worthy of such a position after my decision today ended any hope of us winning this battle."

Professor Hai shouted, "Israel you must get it together. We all believed in Yanisin. The fact that he was selected to be a leader of one of our tribes was our downfall...not his selection in this plan. He would have informed General Idit had he not been selected to lead the forces against Zoar. He had us all fooled. You are the best man to lead the resistance. We need you to keep it together."

"He will be ready to lead the resistance, Professor. Go now and be assured the resistance will survive in spite of this setback," declared Raya, wife of Israel.

The Professor did not realize Raya was in the room and that she heard most of the conversation. The Professor recognized her voice as she spoke. She was friends with Professor Hai's wife and the Professor trusted her judgment and loyalty as he did his friend Israel.

Professor Hai was more confident as he spoke, "Thank you Raya. I leave my friend in your capable hands. Ready him to take my place and most of all do not let the resistance die! Shalom, my friends."

Both Israel and Raya said in unison, "Shalom."

The Professor, Tamir and Malka buckled themselves into the shuttle craft and the Professor initiated liftoff procedures. The craft rose slowly at first. As it picked up speed it began rising high in the sky and towards space itself. Professor Hai recalled similar attempts made by Gomorrite scientist to send a ship into space but failed on numerous occasions. However, the Professor made all the corrections and was sure this one would not fail.

The Professor proclaimed with his communicator still on so Israel and Raya could hear his last words as he was going into space, "This is the first spacecraft to fly away from this ruthless planet. I pray that what we find on the other end of this journey will be friends and alleys capable of helping us free our people."

***

The third hour fell upon Gomorrah and celebration activities were commencing throughout the land. At Zoar, Yanisin stood on top of a hill and ordered his men through the gate to attack the barracks where they believed soldiers would be unprepared for them.

As the resistance soldiers were halfway through the gate, Yanisin watched as the governor ordered his men to begin shooting at them. He had arranged for the Governor's men to hide out of sight until enough of the resistance fighters and entered the city. One by one resistance fighters were shot down from an elevated position with laser blasts.

Yanisin listened to the screams of their defeat and celebrated with his brother. The lasers lit up the night sky like fireworks. The cries of defeat were deafening to the ear.

***

About 20 yards behind Yanisin was another man. This man was called Tomar. Tomar was sent by Israel to avenge the eventual defeat of the resistance. As Tomar crept up behind Yanisin, another man appeared on the hill. Tomar recognized him as one of the men from the meeting. He knew him as Rafael.

Tomar saw the two of celebrating the events unfolding before them.

Tomar heard him say to his brother, "This is a great day my brother. The resistance is dead!"

Tomar spit his anger to the ground. He would kill them both.

Yanisin agreeing with his brother proclaimed, "On this day---"

Before he could finish a laser blast from Tomar cut them both in half killing them instantly. Tomar stayed and watched his brothers get slaughtered. He fell to his knees and started praying for their souls. After he could not take anymore he returned to Admah to find Israel.

***

Gideon stood proud of what he was about to embark on. His initial squadrons had already entered the city and he believed they had taken up their positions subduing any of the Kings guards. Gideon instructed his men to ready themselves as it was two minutes prior to the third hour of the day.

Running as fast as he could was Isaac. Stumbling several times on the way but never stopping as he could not give up even if it seemed impossible. He had to try and get word to Gideon. Nothing else was more important to him. In the distance he could see some figures moving about in the darkness. He hoped it was Gideon and his men.

As he was running he remembered how Gideon saved the lives of over one hundred resistance members one day.

General Idit's army had cornered them near the Jordan River and was poised to kill them all. Gideon arrived and he and his men fought off the soldiers. Gideon was like no other soldier Issac had ever seen. He defeated over 20 men by himself that day. Issac believed he was truly anointed by God Himself.

The third hour hit and Gideon and his men ran toward the city with Gideon leading the way. The guards at the gate were instructed to pretend to be caught by surprise and to not fire a shot.

Isaac was running shouting, "Gideon…Gideon…no…Gideon…do not attack!"

From the shadows leaped a soldier from the King's army. He stood over six feet, ten inches tall and weighted over 300 pounds of solid muscle. Isaac saw the giant but could not stop. The guard struck him in the face with a massive blow. Isaac felt his jaw shatter.

Issac watched as the guard knelt down to him. He could not utter a sound as his jaw was broken. He recognized the special clothing worn by the guard. This man was one of General Idit's Elite Warriors. Isaac knew he was about to die.

The guard did not say a word he just carefully placed his hands around the neck of Isaac, smirked, and began to squeeze. Isaac grabbed his hands by instinct but he did not have near the strength to remove the soldier's powerful hands. The warrior slowly and slowly squeezed until all the life in Isaac was gone.

***

Gideon led his men throw the North gate of New Gomorrah… down the street and passed the Vadar building complex. All the men were yelling confidently as they ran toward the city. Once Gideon himself was well pass the complex, laser blast starting raining down on the men.

Gideon turned and his heart dropped as the screams of death filled the air. He knew Yanisin had to be the reason for this defeat. Gideon started to run toward his men but someone grabbed him.

The Colonel grabbed Gideon by the throat and commanded, "Put your weapons down or Gideon dies!"

Gideon shouted, "Shoot them, they will not kill me! Shoot them."

Gideon's men had tears in their eyes. The shock of their easy defeat caused them to give up easily. They laid down their weapons and raised their hands.

Gideon continued to shout, "No…he's going to kill you! No!"

Dan, Gideon's right hand man stepped forward and looked Gideon in the eyes. He spoke calmly and soft, "Then we die in the name of Jehovah."

Colonel Harel was visibly upset.

He ordered his men, "Kill them all!"

Colonel Harel held Gideon and made him watch everything.

Gideon shouted, "I will avenge all of you! I will avenge you!"

Colonel Harel whispered in Gideon's ear, "Not on this day or any other. Today you die as well…and General Idit will be your executioner."

Colonel Harel laughed loudly…threw Gideon to the ground and spat on him.

As he threw Gideon to the ground he shouted, "Chain him up and prepare to take him to the General."

***

Israel knew now that the General had the names of all the leaders of the resistance. He fled to the hills in hiding with some of his trusted men. There they would have to live out their lives as Gideon had done. His heart was deeply saddened by the news that all the other leaders had been captured.

***

Colonel Phinehas, one of General Idit's high ranking colonels brought the leaders to the throne room in chains. Just as Colonel Phinehas was bringing in the leaders, Colonel Harel was bringing in Gideon. Now General Idit had nine of the 12 tribal leaders of the resistance. He knew their leader was on his way to Adamina. He also knew Yanisin and Rafael were leaders and spies for him. That left only one leader remaining...Israel.

General Idit looked over the leaders.

He called over Colonels Harel and Phinehas and asked, "Where is Israel?"

Colonel Phinehas replied, "He got word that we were rounding up all the leaders and fled. I have men searching the mountains for him. We will find him and bring the coward to you."

General Idit sneered, "See to it yourself."

Colonel Phinehas quickly replied, "Yes sir."

General Idit paced the floor in front of Gideon. Gideon kept his eyes to the floor. He was chained with a 5 inch steel rod across his back and his arms were around the rod. His feet were chained together with a chain that allows him to walk at half steps. He was on his knees on the floor. It was obvious that he had been beaten by the guards as they brought him to the palace. The General was admiring his opportunity to get his revenge for the humiliation that Gideon caused him.

General Idit had the other leaders of the tribes lined up behind Gideon. They were all chained up in the same manner as Gideon. None of them would look up at the General.

***

King Abimelech came into the throne room. As he entered the door he stopped and paused looking at the leaders of the resistance with disgust. He wanted to crush each one of them with his bare hands.

King Abimelech growled as he processed in, "These are the leaders of the so called resistance! You disgust me...all of you. Did you really believe that you could overthrow me? Did you really believe that you could defeat the mightiest king in the history of Gomorrah? I will ensure that your blood runs through the street of New Gomorrah so that all will see that I cannot be challenged!"

The King then turned to his guards and commanded, "Take them to the gallows in the center of the city. We will make an example of them to the people."

The guards responded together, "Yes sir."

King Abimelech looked at General Idit and asked, "What do you desire of this one?"

General Idit answered, "First, I want him to be taken to the post in the center of the city. After I have had my fill of whipping him like a dog, he will hang until he is dead."

King Abimelech smiled, "This will be fun to watch but first let us take care of the other so called leaders. Resistance members have weak hearts. It will pain him to watch them die."

General Idit responded, "Yes sire."

***

The King stood on the palace balcony overlooking the center of the city. He could see the gallows very well from his seat. King Abimelech, General Idit and Queen Metuka were all present on the palace balcony waiting to see the death of the leaders of the resistance.

King Abimelech boasted, "Today we have captured the leaders of the so called resistance. They dared to challenge me and they have lost! Now their measly, pitiful lives will end on this day."

"One of the cowards eluded capture for now. His name is Israel. If anyone provides information that leads to his capture...or death...I will give 100,000 talents."

"Bring out the leaders and place them on the platform."

The guards brought out the leaders of the resistance and placed each one under a noose. It was obvious that King Abimelech planned to hang them all.

King Abimelech commanded, "Bring out Gideon to watch his friends die."

***

The guards brought out Gideon and forced him to kneel down in front of the gallows. He prayed for the souls of his friends. He noticed that Israel was not among them. He prayed that Israel would be protected from harm and that he would be able to reorganize the resistance. He knew his life and the lives of his fellow leaders could not be saved.

***

General Idit was standing in the booth as one of his men approach him from behind.

The guard whispered in his ear, "General, I am sorry to report that Yanisin and Rafael are dead."

General Idit was now very angry. He planned to avenge the death of his most honored spies. He was going to take out his anger on Gideon after the leaders were hanged.

Realizing the General was not going to respond the guard decided to retreat to the shadows.

***

King Abimelech noticed the leader of the Joseph tribe, Lemuel, as he started whispering something.

King Abimelech shouted, "What is he saying?"

A guard near the platform replied, "Sire, I believe he is praying."

King Abimelech ordered, "Stop him! Stop them all!"

The guards began shouting at them to stop. The Gomorrites began mocking them…making fun of them and laughing at them.

One citizen hopped around and fell on his knees in front of his friends.

He said, "Jehovah save me…please save me!"

His friend responded, "Die you fool! Die!"

Everyone laughed at the skit and continued mocking the resistance leaders and their God.

King Abimelech ordered, "Place the noose around the traitor's neck."

The guards began placing the nooses around the necks of the leaders. The leaders continued to pray without ceasing. The nooses were tightened around their necks.

Some guards took shots at the leaders as they were putting the nooses on their necks. One guard struck Lemuel in the stomach.

He shouted, "You started this!"

King Abimelech shouted, "Now these traitors are an example to all who desire to challenge me. Death will come to those who come against me. Remember this day...for today is the day...that I...King Abimelech...have become the greatest king to rule over Gomorrah!"

A roar came up from the crowd that was so loud the ground seemingly shook.

King Abimelech ordered, "Release the gallows and let them hang!"

With what seemed like a thunderous snap, all of their necks were broken and each one lay helplessly dead...the life ripped from their bodies.

***

Gideon dropped his head and cried for his friends. General Idit laughed at Gideon's tears. General Idit slowly made his way down the steps and to the square. He was ready to exact his revenge.

For years, Over and over, General Idit had to hear how great a warrior Gideon was from everyone. He could even tell his own men believed that Gideon was greater than he was. Now he would put an end to all that talk.

Each step he took down to the square inspired his revenge more and more. It fueled his anger to the point that when he arrived he was highly motivated, as King Abimelech would put it, to whip Gideon to within an inch of his life.

King Abimelech sat back in his seat, looked at his Queen and said, "This will be good. Finally General Idit will get his revenge."

The General walked out to the grounds. As he walked he reached out his hand and on cue a soldier placed a whip in it. It had five leather straps at the end of a wooden rod. Each strap was a foot in length and had a fisherman's hook at the end of strap.

He wanted to extract some flesh from Gideon with each strike. The General wanted to whip Gideon until he was tired and then hang him until the life was out of him.

General Idit ordered the guards, "Remove his shirt. I want him to feel each and every whip across his back."

The guards removed Gideon's shirt and General Idit began striking him over and over with the whip. The leather straps cut into the skin of

Gideon. The hooks dug into his skin and made gouges in his body. Flesh was flying into the air every time General Idit pulled the whip back.

Each blow created bright red marks on Gideon's back. The more strikes across his back the redder it became until it was covered in blood. General Idit grunted loudly as if with each blow he was trying to cut Gideon in half and King Abimelech bellowed out laughter with each strike.

The crowd cheered louder and louder with each anticipated strike. Roaring for more and more…screaming for death…the crowd seemed to care little about life…especially the life of a traitor.

No one man could have sustained the punishment being handed out to Gideon. He was truly the strongest warrior anyone had ever seen.

As Gideon fell over from the pain, one of the Gomorrite soldiers ran over and placed him upright again. Each time he fell a guard picked him up for more abuse.

From their view in a small building just off the square some of the women and children of the resistance watch and cried for Gideon and their fallen comrades. With each blow more and more tears flowed out from all of them.

One woman pleaded to the Heavens, "Please, God make him stop… Please!"

Another shouted, "I cannot watch any longer."

After nearly a hundred blows General Idit stopped. He gathered his breath and ordered the guards to pour alcohol on Gideon knowing it would cause him severe pain.

Gideon bellowed out a scream as the alcohol hit the numerous open wounds across his back.

General Idit looked at Gideon as he lay pitifully on the ground, moaning in pain, his back now covered with blood, alcohol, and dirt. He walked over to him, lifted Gideon up by this hair and spit in his face. He then dropped Gideon back down to the ground. Gideon rolled over in pain. He could not reach his wounds because of his chains. All he could do was cry out in agony.

General Idit looked up in the balcony at King Abimelech as he laughed and enjoyed the punishment he was putting on Gideon.

General Idit noted the look on Queen Metuka face. It was filled with excitement. He thought, *"She was truly an evil woman."*

General Idit then turned back to Gideon and snarled, "Look at you...pitiful Gideon...the great so called warrior. Look at you. All of these years I have waited to get my revenge and now I am enjoying each second of it. You disgust me. My friends Yanisin and Rafael were killed by your people. I exact revenge on their behalf as well."

Gideon looked up from the ground and managed to utter the words, "You are still a coward. No matter what you do to me, I am still a believer in the one true God...Jehovah!"

This angered General Idit even more. He turned and slapped Gideon across the face with a powerful blow. Then he grabbed Gideon and dragged him up the steps of the gallows himself. Once there he threw Gideon down on the platform beneath one of the hanging ropes.

He yelled at the guards, "String him up...now!"

The guards hurried to Gideon. Gideon cried out again as the guards securely placed the noose around his neck and tighten it enough so his neck would not snap right away. They wanted Gideon to hang for a while before he died.

Gideon looked at King Abimelech and then to General Idit and announced, "Jehovah will avenge me...both of you will burn in the fires of Hell for all eternity. This...I do in the name of my God... Jehovah!"

Then in a cold emotionless voice, General Idit commanded the guard, "Pull the level!"

With one swift pull Gideon legs went out from underneath him and his body began to kick for several minutes as the noose tighten around his neck. He kicked and kicked as he struggled in vain to free himself. His arms remained chained behind his back and around the steel rod. He could not get free. After what seemed like a lifetime the noose slowly choked all the life out of him.

With his last breath Gideon proclaimed, "Father...I give my life to you!"

Gideon's body went lifeless on the platform before all. The crowd became silent and the clouds above Gomorrah began to get dark. It was a darkness never seen by Gomorrites before. Many of them ran in fear.

A thunderous explosion rolled across the sky unlike any other ever heard before. The rain began to pour down from the sky and the wind raged with anger. The greatest warrior of the resistance had died.

One man standing in the rain and part of the now silent crowd asked, "What have we done?"

General Idit stood there proud of what he had done. The rain was soaking his body from head to toe but he wanted to take in every moment of this revenge.

***

In the small room the women and children of the resistance were crying feverishly as the life of Gideon was lost forever. Many hoped that he would lead them to victory but now he hung dead in the center of New Gomorrah as the thunder rolled across the sky and rain poured down washing his body free of the blood and dust that once covered it.

One small child who stood looking out the window looked up and asked her mother, "Mommy...is God crying too?"

CHAPTER 4

GOMORRAH, THE DAY AFTER

While Professor Hai and his party were traveling to Adamina, General Idit and King Abimelech were making plans to follow them.

General Idit was in his private office relishing in his victory over Gideon. He was renowned for his tactical skills and his rise to general was faster than anyone in King Abimelech's army had ever done. He saw his opportunity 10 years ago when there was an uprising against King Abimelech and it appeared that the King would be overthrown. General Idit's plan impressed the King so much that he executed the previous general and replaced him with General Idit.

It was early the morning after the execution of the resistance leaders. King Abimelech was in his private office with General Idit. They were discussing the plans for the destruction of Adamina.

King Abimelech spoke first, "General, where do we stand with the completion of my armada?"

General Idit replied, "We are nearing completion of the ships. Each ship is as big as a region. They both will hold eight battle cruisers and each cruiser will have a full complement of fighters."

"After we launch our electromagnetic pulse, we will deploy the battle cruisers over the major areas of Adamina and launch the fighters at that point. Once the fighters have secured the major cities, the cruisers will land and the ground troops will clean up each city. "

King Abimelech responded, "This sounds like a great plan. When will we be able to leave?"

General Idit answered, "We should be able to leave in a few days. However, the journey will take us longer due to the size of our ships and payload. My scientist predicted that it will take approximately one year for the journey. In this time we will run multiple simulations and tactical drills to ensure the troops are sharp."

King Abimelech asked, "How long will it take Professor Hai to get there?"

General Idit answered, "My scientists tell me it will take him six months to get to Adamina. We will arrive six months after that."

King Abimelech asked, "Good, what if the Adaminians have the ability to fight us in space?"

General Idit replied, "My scientist inform me that there is a gaseous planet in close proximity to Adamina. This planet has a storm that has been raging for years. We can hide our ships in this storm while you take a shuttle to Adamina.

You will tell them that you are on a peaceful mission from the planet Shalom. Your mission is to make contact with new people and share technology with new people. You will tell them that you have a peace envoy waiting to share our knowledge with them."

"Once they grant you permission to bring your people you will return to us and then we will bring the ships to Adamina. Instead of landing and taking refuge on the planet our fighters will launch our pulse and then begin our assault on the planet. By then, it will be too late for them to respond. We will destroy them easily."

While pouring a glass of his finest wine for himself and the General, he happily responded, "This may be the greatest plan you have ever devised my friend. I want to see these ships today."

General Idit replied, "I will take you myself."

***

One of Israel's men came running up the mountain with news for him. He found Israel in a private room readying himself for a meeting with two of his close friends. He was trying to come up with the right words to say to them...to convince them to join him in reorganizing the resistance. He wanted to ensure the resistance remained alive just as Professor Hai wanted. He could not let Professor Hai or Gideon down.

Israel's man came into the room and said, "Israel...I have learned that the General has two great war ships almost completed and ready to journey to Adamina! We must stop him."

Israel looked surprised by this news. He knew that Professor Hai believed that his ship was the only ship that was capable of such a journey. He thought, "How did the General build these ships?"

Then he asked, "Are you sure about this information? How did the General manage to build these ships without the Professor knowing about it?"

The man replied, "He built and maintained a secret laboratory that Professor Hai did not know about. He stole all of the technology that Professor Hai created and had his scientists use them for military purposes. He also had his scientist working on technological advancements as well. The General got the coordinates to Adamina from a resistance spy."

Israel said, "This is truly more sad news for an already depressed people. How can I gather our forces to continue the battle when it looks so bleak for us? How can I ask them to maintain faith if I too question my faith? No...I must not question my God, Jehovah. He is all powerful and in the end I know it will be true...we win!"

The man asked, "Do you think we can stop the ships?"

Israel answered, "We can try in the name of our Lord, Jehovah."

***

In the caves of Mt. Sarai, Israel wept over the loss of his friends. Instead of a celebration and forming a new government, the resistance was mourning the loss of over 1000 soldiers and hearing rumors that King Abimelech was ready to set out for Adamina. This troubled Israel's heart and he wanted to do something to prevent it from happening.

Israel called a meeting with Moses and Abram, two men that he knew without a doubt he could trust. These men worked for Gideon and were part of the smaller squadrons that infiltrated New Gomorrah before the slaughter. Both made it out without being captured but their faces were recognized and reported to General Idit and King Abimelech.

The King issued a bounty on the heads of Israel, Moses and Abram. King Abimelech promised a gracious reward to the one who captures or provides information that leads to the capture of these men.

Israel spoke, "Gentlemen…we must reorganize the resistance. We cannot stop because of the events of today. Instead we must forge ahead in the name of the Lord and our fallen comrades. Today we lost over 1000 members but we must show a passion for survival never before seen on this planet. We must rally the members and keep them focused on Jehovah. They must believe. They must believe!"

Moses placed his hand on the shoulder of Israel and responded, "We will do whatever is necessary to continue the resistance. You have my full support."

Abram disagreed, "My friends…this is not a wise idea. We must remain in hiding and temper our response. We are all wanted men. This puts our lives and the lives of those we love in jeopardy. If we go forth with this, nothing will happen but more loss of innocent lives."

Moses angrily replied, "You cannot be a coward! We must continue the fight or be slaves to the king. I will never give up!"

Israel interrupted, "Moses my friend…do not let us be moved to anger. Abram brings good points to the table and we must be sure of what it is we must do. Surely if we act in haste we will make more mistakes."

Abram added, "My friend Israel, you are wise. However, it was you that suggested Yanisin command the troops at Zoar and this lead to loss of my best friend…Gideon. How can we follow you now?"

The words of Israel's friend Abram struck deeply into his spirit. He sat down in his chair and quietly prayed for strength.

Moses clearly angered even more, "You are an idiot! We all thought Yanisin was true to the cause. Now you place all the blame on Israel. Gideon would not like your words."

Abram spoke, "I will not follow you. Instead I will retreat to a place where no one can find me or my family. There, we will live in peace."

Moses angrily said, "Then leave us. Never come to us again."

Israel stood again and sadly added, "My friend this is not a wise decision. We must stand together in this time. Surely no one is more saddened by the events of today than me. I can only continue to keep the resistance together in the aftermath. This I must do not for me but for those who lost their lives today…especially, my good friend, Gideon. He would have wanted nothing else. Can you not see that?"

As he was leaving the cave Abram turned and said, "I cannot follow you."

Moses yelled, "Good riddance."

***

General Idit took King Abimelech to a secluded area outside the region of New Sodom. To the naked eye there was nothing there but wasteland. The ground was not fertile for crops and grass could never grow there.

After they arrived at a spot where there was a stone with E=MC2 on it, General Idit stopped and kneeled down. He moved the stone upward like a lever. From the ground a keypad rose up and General Idit typed in the code 38103.

Once he typed in the code the ground in front of them began to move. Something was rising up out of the ground. It was larger than the keypad. General Idit saw the the look of apprehension on King Abimelech's face. He decided to inform him that an evaluator was coming. After it arrived, General Idit instructed his men to wait above ground for him and King Abimelech to return.

When the evaluator reached it's destination the two men stepped out.

King Abimelech spoke, "Oh my. Thank Baal for he has blessed us. General you have done an amazing job."

General Idit responded, "Yes sire, thank you. These are the two ships I spoke to you about earlier. Each of them will carry eight battle cruisers and our entire army. With these ships we will destroy Adamina and you will be ruler over her just as the Basar foretold."

King Abimelech replied, "You have outdone yourself General. I knew when I first met you that you were the right man for the job. Your accomplishments will be remembered forever. You will always be known as the best general in the history of both Gomorrah and Adamina. Take me inside one of the ships. I wish to see it."

General Idit motioned for the King to go to the ship on the right and they began walking toward it. The stairs to the ship were already down as there were many technicians and scientist working on her.

General Idit and King Abimelech climbed the stairs and entered the ship. General Idit gave the King the grand tour of the ship. General Idit had this particular ship designed specifically for King Abimelech. He showed King Abimelech his private quarters and his private office. His quarters were big enough for him to carry four of his wives and his queen.

All seemed to be in order and the Gomorrite army was ready to leave Gomorrah and journey back to its home world…Adamina. General Idit and King Abimelech disembarked the ship and left the underground warehouse for the surface. Once back on the surface they found the men just as they left them. They all returned to New Sodom and then back to New Gomorrah.

***

One of the guards that were with General Idit and King Abimelech was loyal to Lieutenant Oded. Lieutenant Oded was waiting in New Gomorrah for General Idit and the men to return from their secret visit with the King.

Lieutenant Oded was never allowed to go with the General on these trips. The General told Lieutenant Oded that he only took men he personally trained. He felt he could trust them more. It was hard for Lieutenant Oded to find someone who would be sympathetic to the resistance but in Lieutenant Yaniv he did.

Lieutenant Oded knew Lieutenant Yaniv was a devout Gomorrite when he was a teenager. However, seven years ago lieutenant Oded attended Lieutenant Yaniv's 25th birthday party at his home when guards burst through the door. They arrested Lieutenant Yaniv's father because they believed he was in the resistance. They dragged Lieutenant Yaniv's father out of the house and to the square. Lieutenant Oded watched as General Idit immediately executed him for treason.

Three days later Lieutenant Oded and Yaniv discovered that the General never suspected Lieutenant Yaniv's father of being a resistance member. Instead he was punishing Lieutenant Yaniv for taking Renana as his bride.

Lieutenant Oded knew General Idit loved Renana. He heard him say on many occasions that she was the most beautiful woman General Idit had ever seen.

Lieutenant Oded like many believed she was very beautiful. Her hair was black as the night sky and her skin was just the right texture to match it. When she smiled she appeared to light up the room with her beautiful white teeth. She was warm, loving and full of spirit.

***

Lieutenant Oded was just finishing his shift in the late evening of the third day of the New Gomorrah celebration. His troops spent many hours drilling as they were getting ready for battle. Lieutenant Oded believed that this was a futile effort because Professor Hai ensured him that travel to Adamina would be decades away for the Gomorrites. Lieutenant Oded ensured all of Professor Hai's research had been destroyed. He had to continue to play the role in order to continue to fool General Idit and King Abimelech.

***

The royal party arrived back in New Gomorrah at the same time as Lieutenant Oded shift ended. Once the party arrived at the palace General Idit walked over to Lieutenant Yaniv and the men. When the General arrived where they were standing, they immediately snapped to attention.

General Idit ordered, "Lieutenant go and find Lieutenant Oded. When you find him place him under arrest for treason. Bring him back here and lock him away in the prison."

Lieutenant Yaniv replied, "Yes sir."

He then turned to his men and said, "You heard the General move out."

The men did an about face and headed out of the palace to find Lieutenant Oded. Lieutenant Yaniv knew it was odd that General Idit ordered that he be placed in prison. They usually executed men for treason on the spot. He was worried for his friend because there was something different about this one.

Lieutenant Yaniv ordered, "Sergeant Abner, take Private Gad and Private Gera with you and search the North and East parts of the city. Sergeant Yachin, take Private Nathan and Private Paz with you and search the South and West parts of the city. I will search all the officer's quarters and private bars. Go now and report back to me in two hours."

The men split up and went off to search their designated areas. Lieutenant Yaniv gave them those places because he suspected Lieutenant Oded would not be there. He knew the most likely place would be their meeting place. He pondered what he was going to do? His contact with the resistance was going to prison. How would he get word about the secret underground warehouse and the code to the resistance? He had to figure a way. He had to be the one to find Lieutenant Oded.

***

Lieutenant Oded knew the royal party would be returning so he headed to the meeting point where he would meet Lieutenant Yaniv to exchange information. He arrived near sundown and waited to see if Lieutenant Yaniv would arrive. He normally waited a couple of hours and if the Lieutenant did not show then he knew there was no information to pass on. They would meet after any trip Lieutenant Yaniv made or weekly.

Lieutenant Oded had been waiting an hour when Lieutenant Yaniv arrived. The look on his friend's face worried him. Lieutenant Oded had not seen this look of distress and dismay on Lieutenant Yaniv's face before.

Lieutenant Oded asked, "What is it my friend? Is there trouble?"

Lieutenant Yaniv responded, "Yes my friend. I have to arrest you and take you to prison."

Lieutenant Oded surprisingly questioned, "Why? By who's order?"

Lieutenant Yaniv answered, "General Idit walked up to me and my men. He instructed me to find you and arrest you. He said treason and he surprisingly ordered me to place you in prison which you know is unusual. What will we do? I have information that needs to get to the resistance. If you are in prison who will I give it to?"

Lieutenant Oded said in a low; sadden voice, "He must have discovered that I am a spy. He must not be on to you. Take me to prison but before you do let me go to headquarters in the square. I will pass on the information. After that I cannot help you any longer. I cannot be sure of who to trust any longer. You will be on your own."

Then Lieutenant Oded looked at his friend with glassy eyes.

Lieutenant Yaniv said calmly to his friend, "Tell me your contact. I must have faith that this person can be trusted. If we are ever to succeed then faith…not fear…has to be our guide."

Lieutenant Oded took his friend by the arm and whispered, "Come with me."

They both left the meeting spot and made their way carefully to resistance headquarters. It would be the first time Lieutenant Yaniv had seen the headquarters and they him. Lieutenant Oded was the only person who knew that Lieutenant Yaniv was a resistance member. Lieutenant Oded was the only contact Lieutenant Yaniv with the resistance.

When they arrived at the headquarters they both burst through the door, closing it quickly behind them. They were out of breath because they ran secretly all the way. They prayed no one saw them.

Maayan turned as the men burst into the room and she shouted, "What is this?"

Lieutenant Oded placed his finger over his lips and whispered, "Shhhhhhh."

Maayan whispered back, "Lieutenant, what is going on and why have you brought this man here?"

Lieutenant Oded explained, "This is my good friend Lieutenant Yaniv. He has been working for us for seven years now. I have told no one of him because he is in very deep. Most of my information has been provided by him. He is to be trusted. However, now we have a problem.

Maayan asked, "What is the problem?"

Lieutenant Oded continued, "Lieutenant Yaniv has been ordered to arrest me and place me in prison. We do not know why I am being placed in prison but that was the order given by General Idit. Lieutenant Yaniv must comply with this order so that he is not discovered. Pray for my safety. Pray for all of our safety."

Varda, another woman in the room asked through her tears, "Why should he turn you in. You can go to where Israel is and hide there. We cannot watch another of our members be put to death. I cannot take it any longer. I just cannot!"

Lieutenant Oded placed his arm around her and comforted her with some words, "Varda, I will be safe. Jehovah will protect me and someday we will be together. I promise you."

Varda asked, "How can you make such a promise?"

Lieutenant Oded answered, "The events of the past few days have left many of us questioning our faith. Mine is not to question what Jehovah has set forth. Instead mine is to continue down the path for which I have started. Jehovah is the answer. He is the truth and He is the way. Never should we question that belief. My faith will remain solid and if I die...I do so in His name...Jehovah."

Lieutenant Oded and Varda were deeply in love. Varda fell in the arms of Lieutenant Oded and cried. He held her as tightly as he could and whispered in her ear.

He said, "I love you."

He then released her and said calmly with love and care, "I must go now. We cannot allow Lieutenant Yaniv to be discovered. I love you."

She whispered to him, "I will always love you."

Lieutenant Oded turned to his friend Lieutenant Yaniv and instructed him to tell Maayan the new information he had discovered. Lieutenant Yaniv told her all he knew including the code and the two of them planned to meet each week to exchange any information.

Varda ran up to Lieutenant Yaniv and shouted, "You take care of him!"

Lieutenant Yaniv said sternly, "I will die before I let them kill him."

Lieutenant Oded interrupted, "You cannot my friend. The resistance needs you to remain a secret. You cannot risk your life to save mine."

Lieutenant Yaniv looked at Varda and said, "I know what it is to love and be loved. I will not allow him to die even if it means I must die."

Maayan spoke, "Enough of everyone volunteering to die first. We will all live. Let us pray that Jehovah protects us all from death and no one has to die."

Lieutenant Yaniv agreed, "True words of wisdom."

The two lieutenants left for the palace. Lieutenant Oded sensed Lieutenant Yaniv did not enjoy taking his friend to the palace to be imprisoned. However, he knew it had to be done in order to keep him from being discovered.

They were 200 meters from the palace entrance for the military when Sergeant Abner and his men ran up to him.

Sergeant Abner spoke, "Sir, you found the traitor. Shall I take him to his cell?"

Lieutenant Oded did not make eye contact with any of them. Lieutenant Yaniv motioned for Sergeant Abner to take control of the prisoner.

Sergeant Abner shoved Lieutenant Oded and yelled, "Move it along you traitor!"

He then took the butt of his laser and hit Lieutenant Oded across the back.

Lieutenant Yaniv yelled, "Don't injury him. You don't know what plans General Idit has for him."

"Yes sir," yelled Sergeant Abner as he continued to take Lieutenant Oded to his cell.

***

Maayan successfully passed the information received from Lieutenant Yaniv to Israel. No one knew what was being kept in the underground fortress but they all agreed that it had to be penetrated to see what was down there. As far as any of them knew no one was down there that was sympathetic to the resistance. Israel and Mosses were devising a plan.

Israel asked, "What do you think General Idit could be hiding under the ground?"

Moses replied, "It is my greatest fear…but it can only be a ship to travel to Adamina. He would not hide anything else except a new food supply. The General does not strike me as the kind of man that would care about food to hide it"

"I fear you are right. This mission will require a scientist. If it is a spaceship then we must find a way to sabotage it," added Israel.

"Do you know of someone we can truly trust" asked Moses?

Israel pondered the question for a minute then he spoke, "We must go visit Aaron, Jacob and Ananias. We must see if one of them can be trusted. I am not sure of any of them. Before we make a selection we should do a thorough background check. We cannot afford any more mistakes."

Moses was shaking his head agreeing with his friend, "Then, we should leave now."

"Agreed," added Israel.

***

Aaron was a scientist who was the only equal to Professor Hai. He gained his intelligence through hard work and long hours of study. Professor Hai was a natural but Aaron had to work at it. For that Aaron was always envious of Professor Hai. In fact, he hated Professor Hai. He dedicated his life to proving he was the better scientist.

When General Idit came to him and offered him the position of building the two war ships he jumped at the opportunity. He had been working the project for over five years. The last year he and all the others involved in the project were living in the underground warehouse.

Aaron had expanded Professor's Hai discoveries in the areas of warp engine technology and laser weapons. It was through Aaron's advancements that all Gorromite soldiers were armed with laser rifles now. The King still used his swords for traditional executions but the new weapon of choice was the laser rifle.

Aaron was sitting in his office when one of his junior scientists came in.

The scientist asked, "Sir, we're ready to test the engines."

Aaron responded, "Excellent, I'll be out in a minute."

The scientist said, "Sir if I may, how does it feel to be the scientist that leads us back home? I mean your discoveries in warp drive technology have advanced us light years ahead of what Professor Hai did."

Aaron replied, "It feels great. Now that we are able to sustain our electromagnetic pulse for 30 minutes, we should easily defeat the inhabitants of Adamina."

The scientist said, "And it's all because of you."

"Thank you. Now let's go test those engines."

***

Israel and Moses arrived at Aaron's home and were met by his wife. She informed them that Aaron had been killed by resistance fighters. She swore that she would have her vengeance on them. Israel and Moses left knowing that the house of Aaron would not help them.

94

Moses asked, "Why did we kill Aaron?"

Israel answered, "To my knowledge…we did not."

***

When Israel and Moses arrived at the home of Jacob they found him in his laboratory looking down a microscope. Jacob heard them walk in and suddenly turned around.

He shouted, "Who are you and what are you doing in my home?"

"I let them in," his wife said to him. "Jacob, listen to them. You both have the same ideas."

Jacob said, "What are you talking about woman?"

His wife responded, "It is time you leave this lab and put your research to work. Just listen to what they have to say."

Jacob was a proud and boastful man. His scientific career had been destroyed by General Idit when the failed to create a ship that could fly in space. Jacob knew that he could accomplish the project if he had been given more time. Now he was relegated to working in his home lab trying to find answers to science questions.

After the embarrassment by General Idit, Jacob decided he would find a way to space but give the information to the resistance. He swore he would make General Idit pay for stripping him of his scientific status in front of all of his peers and the people of New Gomorrah. To Gomorrite scientists this was a worst punishment than death.

"You gentlemen are resistance members," asked Jacob.

Israel answered, "Yes. We are here because we need scientific help. We believe we know where the General is building his ship to go to Adamina. We must stop him."

Jacob said, "I already know where he is building them. The ships are as big as the region of Zoar. They will contain battle cruisers. Each battle cruiser will contain numerous fighters. They will massacre Adamina unless I find a way to help them and get the information to them. Professor Hai left to soon."

Moses asked, "There is more than one ship?"

Jacob answered, "Yes, there are two ships, each with battle cruisers and each battle cruiser has fighters. The war ships can hold a compliment of 50,000 soldiers each. Their drawback is that it will take them longer to travel to Adamina than it took Professor Hai."

Moses inquired, "Is there a way to disable them?"

Jacob responded, "The ships are heavily guarded and you will not be able to get inside. All of the members of the project were moved to the warehouse and housed there. The lead scientist, Aaron, is out to prove he is a better scientist than Professor Hai. This has been his project for the last five years." Israel interrupted, "Aaron? We were told he was dead."

Jacob continued, "He is not dead. General Idit did not want everyone to know about the project. To explain why a high profile scientist disappeared he told everyone the resistance killed him. In other words he lied. Are you surprised?"

Moses asked, "How can we disable them?"

Jacob looked at Moses, shook his head and replied, "It's nearly impossible. You will have to connect directly to the computer system and upload this virus. All of the ships respond to a signal from the royal ship. If you input this virus directly into the system, it will tell all the ships to shut down. Basically they will go to sleep. Their shields will be down, communications will not work…everything will be down. They will be vulnerable to defeat. "

Jacob continued, "The two biggest problems will be to find a way to connect directly to the computer core and to strike soon thereafter. If not they will have time to eradicate the virus. Aaron is very good. He probably will find a way around the virus in 10 or 15 minutes. You cannot use the computers on board the war ship because it will be detected. You will have to use one of the fighters.

If the Adamians are capable of capturing one of the fighters then they will have an advantage. But they have to be able to hack the system and upload the virus. Professor Hai is very capable of doing this."

Moses added, "Well we hope to have people on the ships. Maybe one of them will be able to get the virus and the information to Professor Hai in time. Thank you for helping us."

Jacob conveyed, "I must get on that ship. Is there a way for me to get onboard?"

Moses countered, "That will be impossible. They will recognize you and General Idit will never allow you onboard."

Jacob grabbed Moses by the shoulders and sternly said, "I must."

Israel added, "We will try my friend. For your help we will try. May I ask why you need to be onboard?"

Jacob answered, "I want to see the end of General Idit."

Israel summated, "We all do."

∗∗∗

Israel and Moses went to find Ananias but was told the same story that they were told about Aaron. They could only assume that Ananias was a member of the project as well. They returned back to the cave to discuss their options.

Moses stated, "Our best option is to rely on Lieutenant Yaniv to provide the information to Professor Hai when the ships arrive at Adamina."

Israel said, "I agree. We must inform Maayan. She will inform him of our plan."

Moses stood up and as he was leaving he closed by saying, "I will take it to her personally. We cannot trust anyone. Take care, my friend."

Israel said loudly, "Take care."

∗∗∗

"Ananias," shouted Moses as he entered resistance headquarters!

Ananias responded, "Moses, it is good to see you!"

Moses asked, "I was told you were killed."

Ananias replied, "I was taken away by force. General Idit is building war ships to go to Adamina. I found a way to get out and get this word to you. I need some explosives in order to sabotage the ships."

Moses acknowledged, "Yes. We can get you some. David, get Ananias a small amount of explosives."

Ananias said, "I will need a larger amount. You see the plan is to launch the ships using smaller rockets around each ship. At take off these rockets will ignite and lift the war ship off the ground. Just before the warship is in orbit the rockets will separate and the warships will go to warp. If we blow the rockets at the precise time we can destroy the ships."

Moses replied, "But we planned to have resistance members on board. They will die trying to get the information to the professor."

Ananias responded, "It is the best plan."

Moses asked, "What if it fails?"

Ananias answered, "Then the people on board will be our last hope."

Moses then motioned for David to retrieve the explosives.

David acknowledged Moses' order and went to retrieve the explosives.

Moses was happy to finally have some good news to share when he returned to Israel. The war ships will be sabotaged by Ananias which will kill General Idit and King Abimelech but several resistance members will die as well. He thought, *"They will have to be told of the danger."*

***

It was now day five of the New Gomorrah celebration and the citizens of Gomorrah were thoroughly enjoying themselves. The news of them returning to Adamina had now made its way around all of the regions. Everyone was happy to know that they were going home after 5,000 years.

The evening of the fifth day saw Ananias sneak back into the warehouse compound. He had the explosives hidden in his quarters and tonight it was time for him to act. In two days General Idit and King Abimelech were going to launch the war ships to Adamina. He went to his quarters and retrieved the explosives.

He concealed them in a bag marked spare engine parts. He also gathered his computer so he could present the look that he was going to the war ship to do some last minute work. When he opened the door to his quarters he was shocked at what he saw.

General Idit was sneering at him.

He said in his usual cold voice, "Welcome back, my friend. We did a roll call the other evening and no one could find you. We decided to keep an eye on you to see where you were going. I was hoping that you were sneaking out to get something from a pretty little lady."

"However, what do we find? We find you sneaking into a place that we are suspicious of being run by resistance members. Search him!"

General Idit's guards grabbed Ananias and began searching him. It wasn't long before they found the explosives in his bag. The guards showed the General what they have found. Ananias stood tall and strong. He wanted to give nothing to the General. He vowed not to cry for his life.

General Idit continued, "Well. I would never have suspected that you were a sympathizer. We will watch you hang, unless you tell me who you are working with. If you tell me than I will let you live."

Ananias looked directly into his eyes and said, "Jevohah."

General Idit replied, "I would have had more respect for you had you said Baal. The only thing your God has gotten you is dead. Now scream for your life."

Ananias said, "Never."

General Idit replied, "Take him to prison and lock him up. Tomorrow's New Gomorrah day will begin with the ending of your life."

General Idit began to laugh loudly. Ananias' eyes watched him as they were taking him away. He silently prayed, *"My Father in Heaven, protect my friends. Bless their mission to end this reign of evil against our people. Bless them in your name."*

Ananias could see as everyone turned to see what was making General Idit laugh so much. Some sneered at Ananias while others spat at him. They all showed disdain for him.

***

Aaron ran over to General Idit.

"What is going on? Where are they taking Ananias, "Aaron shouted as he got closer?

General Idit looked at him sternly and he felt a chill go up his spine. He wished he had not asked the question.

General Idit answered, "He is a resistance member and he will die tomorrow."

Aaron replied, "But sir, I need his help to make the final calculations."

General Idit did not even look at him.

He simply said, "Find another way."

***

The next morning Ananias was hanged in the square and left there for all to see. It was another resistance member killed by the General.

99

The mood back at the caves was a quiet and depressed one at best. Abram had come to mourn with Israel and Moses over the loss of Ananias. When Moses saw Abram he did not even argue with him. They both were too sad to fight with one another.

Maayan walked into the room and broke the silence, "Why do we continue to do this? Each time we attempt to turn the tide of the battle in our favor all we do is lose another good man. You preached of faith the other day. How can anyone have faith now?"

Israel answered, "If we give up now or anytime we disrespect the names of those who have fallen before us. We have to keep trying. Faith is all we have. We cannot allow General Idit or King Abimelech to take that away from us."

Abram then spoke up, "Are we not to lose the battle here in order to win the battle over the skies of Adamina?"

Moses shouted, "What are you talking about now? Are we in for more quitter talk?"

Abram continue, "No my friend. In the time I have had since the failed overthrow I have studied the word."

Israel interrupted, "How did you get a copy?"

Abram continued, "Professor Hai left it behind. In it the word says that the resistance would fail here on Gomorrah but and with the aid of an unknown friend, we would prevail."

"Evidence of this victory will be witnessed by two giant fireballs over the skies of Adamina. We keep trying to win here when the real victory has been foretold to happen over Adamina."

Everyone in the room was quiet. They were all asking themselves if this was true. Their sacrifices were not in vein but it was only to secure a victory over Adamina.

Israel stood and spoke first, "Abram, if your interpretation of the word is correct then by getting Jacob's information to Lieutenant Yaniv we have done what we can to secure victory. It's all up to them now. We must begin to focus on a plan of action after the war ships leave."

Moses walked over to his friend Abram and extended his hands, "My friend I am truly sorry for not listening to you the other day. You were correct. Had I listened Ananias would still be alive."

Israel added, "You cannot blame yourself. Everything happens in God's world for a reason. Now we understand our role. Let us plan for what to do after the ships leave."

Moses stated, "After the ships leave there will not be many guards. We can easily subdue them and begin to put in place our government."

Just then Jacob walked in the room and he expressed, "Science must be at the head of that government. If any of the ships escape and return here we must be able to defend ourselves."

Happily Israel responded, "Jacob! You have decided to join with us!"

Jacob replied, "Yes my friend. I will help rid this planet of the likes of General Idit forever."

***

It was the final day of the New Gomorrah celebration and the morning festivities were under way. King Abimelech wanted this to be a closing ceremony that the people of Gomorrah would never forget. On this day he planned to announce to the world that they were on their way to Adamina. He would display his two new ships for all to see.

In his bedroom King Abimelech was up and pacing the floor. Queen Metuka was lying in the bed and attempting to comfort him.

Queen Metuka said, "My King, my love. You are pacing the floor like you have much to worry about. You are the King of this entire world. No one can challenge you. Why are pacing the floor?"

King Abimelech continued pacing and looking down at the floor. He then looked at Queen Metuka with concern in his eyes.

He asked her, "What do you think of General Idit?"

She responded, "General Idit is a loyal and dedicated man. You should not be concerned about him?"

He replied, "I am concerned that he may be trying to overthrow me. He built these ships without my knowledge. He built an entire underground warehouse without my knowledge. I have a right to be concerned."

She offered, "I can send one of my maidens to him to gather some information. I know he is sweet on Vered."

King Abimelech replied, "Do it."

***

Vered entered the private chambers of General Idit while he was in the showers. She climbed in the bed and waited for him to come out. She loved General Idit because he was a strong man. When he came out of the shower Vered was lying in his bed. She had the covers draped over her to show just enough skin to get him excited.

General Idit said, "Are you trying to get a seat on the war ship to Adamina? If so, this is a good start."

Vered smiled and moved around under the covers in a seductive manner. General Idit looked at her and smiled. She got excited as he allowed the robe to fall to the ground and climbed in the bed with her.

Through the kisses Vered said, "King Abimelech thinks you are trying to overthrow him. What should I report back to him?"

General Idit, "Tell him I am loyal and dedicated to serving him."

Vered replied, "Hmmmm…now serve me."

***

Thousands of Gomorrites lined the desert fields waiting for King Abimelech to arrive. King Abimelech heard the cheers ring out over the desert and along with shouts of "Gomorrah" echoed. The fanfare had reached a fever pitch when the ground began to move. From what seemed like out of nowhere King Abimelech, General Idit, Queen Metuka rose up from the ground. The cheering got louder and louder as the elevator rose higher and higher. King Abimelech raised his hands to silence the crowd.

He then began to make his speech, "Today my citizens…today we will unveil to you the tools in which we will return to Adamina and defeat the Adaminians!"

Cheers quickly filled the air. The excited crowd of Gomorrites jumped up and down and shouted for joy. King Abimelech raised his hands again to silence them.

He continued to speak, "This closing ceremony is the last on Gomorrah. We have crushed the resistance…found the way to Adamina and now…now we have the means in which to get there. The journey will take us approximately one year to travel. Once we reach Adamina we will destroy the inhabitants of our land and take it back. The Basar has foretold it all to us and today we embark on the fulfillment of that prediction.

Again cheers filled the air.

King Abimelech silenced them again and continued, "Now feast your eyes behind us…and watch the single greatest scientific accomplishments of all time come before you. Citizens of Gomorrah, here are your…warships!"

The ground began to shake for miles. Dust and sand filled the air. The crowd began to move backwards for fear of the unexpected. What was coming up from the ground? It felt like the ground was quaking. Some people could not keep their balance and fell to the ground. There was so much sand and dust now in the air it was blocking the sun.

Slowly you could now see something emerging from the ground. It was bigger than anything that any of the people had ever seen. Their eyes were amazed as the two extremely large ships slowly rose from underneath the ground. The sheer look of them inspired fear in the onlookers. They were mighty and powerful.

After a few minutes both ships were now at ground level. They were tall as a building and wide as city blocks. The ships were ready. They were ready to take off and head to Adamina for their mission.

The crowd began to shout louder than ever. They were excited about returning to Adamina. They were excited about the opportunity to defeat the Adaminians and to live their again. King Abimelech's ego was raised to it's highest height.

*****

Lieutenant Yaniv was meeting with Maayan during the final New Gomorrah celebration.

Lieutenant Yaniv began, "It does not do my heart good to know that King Abimelech will be heading to Adamina to attack an unsuspecting people. I know the Bible says that this is the way it is supposed to be but I am still saddened by it."

Maayan replied, "I feel your pain. However, we must believe that in the end we will win."

Lieutenant Yaniv continued, "Here are your papers to get on the ship. You will be my wife's handmaiden. There is one for Varda as well. While both of you are onboard the ship we will come up with a plan to free Lieutenant Oded and get the information to Professor Hai. We may not succeed at this mission. We may all die trying but we have to try. Are you in?

Maayan responded, "I am in and I know Varda will be in as well."

Lieutenant Yaniv concluded, "Good. Both of you are to come to my home and we will go to the ship from there."

Maayan replied, "We will be there."

***

Jacob, Israel and Moses were meeting at the caves during the closing New Gomorrah celebration.

Moses said, "Lieutenant Yaniv could not get you credentials to board the ship. It is very well because we will need you here. I have given the Lieutenant the virus and the instructions for loading it on the computers. Now, it will be up to him to succeed. We have done all we can do."

Jacob added, "Then we will wait until the ships leave."

Israel announced, "Let us pray for their success."

***

The next morning the final boarding was taking place and systems were readied for takeoff. The two Gomorrah war ships were ready to begin their year long journey to Adamina. In Lieutenant Yaniv's quarters Renana, Varda and Maayan were getting use to their quarters.

Renana said, "We must ensure that no one discovers our identity. We must be very careful how we conduct ourselves. This is not like being on Gomorrah. It is a much smaller environment and we can easily be discovered if we are not careful."

Varda asked, "What is that?"

Renana was placing something in a case and hiding it in a compartment in their quarters. Lieutenant Yaniv had this compartment built in his quarters to store information where no one could find it.

Renana answered, "This is information we will use only if my husband cannot get the virus to Professor Hai."

Maayan said, "Thank you for allowing us to stay here with you. We will not divulge any information. We must do this to stop these ruthless leaders."

***

Both war ships were loaded, sealed up and ready for takeoff. The countdown had begun. In the tower overlooking the launch pad was Colonel Harel.

Colonel Harel ordered, "Contact King Abimelech."

The communications officer replied, "Gomorrah tower to Royal One over."

The Royal One officer replied, "Royal One here."

The communications officer asked, "Colonel Harel would like to speak with King Abimelech."

King Abimelech came on the line, "This is King Abimelech."

Colonel Harel asked, "Sire, are you ready to begin countdown?"

King Abimelech answered, "Yes. Begin countdown now."

Colonel Harel replied, "Begin countdown. Have a safe journey Sire."

It was now two minutes before the war ships would takeoff headed for Adamina.

***

Israel stood outside the cave looking out to the desert land. He could see the massive ships sitting on the launch pad from his viewpoint. His heart did not know where to stand. The Bible assured him that victory would come over the skies of Adamina. His friend Abram taught him that this was to be.

However, he felt like he was doing nothing by letting these war ships leave. He felt he should be disabling them somehow. But many have tried and many more had died. In the end he knew he had to leave the ships alone and pray that his friend Lieutenant Yaniv would succeed.

The rockets ignited on both war ships. Smoke rose from underneath them and bellowed outward. The sound of the engines of the war ships filled the air and could be heard for miles around. Israel watched as slowly each ship rose higher and higher in the morning sky. Now they had rose so high that they could be seen from every point on Gomorrah. Each ship turned and pointed toward space. The rockets on the side of the ships were separating and falling back to the ground.

***

Colonel Harel stood stern looking up at the ships rising off into space. His face held a smile as he knew Adamina would soon be under Gomorrite rule. Even more he was proud of the opportunity to run things on Gomorrah.

He never noticed the men coming up behind him. One man in particular held a blade in his hand. He thrust the blade in the back of Colonel Harel.

Colonel Harel screamed with agony. He never even saw the face of the man who took his life.

***

Israel looked down...fell to his knees and began to pray. Two men one on each side knelt down beside him. They all prayed. When Israel looked up he realized that he did not know either of the two men praying with him. They wore clothes that he had not seen before. Israel was afraid.

The man to Israel's right spoke first, "Do not be afraid. My name is Isaiah. This is my friend Joseph. We have been familiar with the word of God for many years. Together we will stop those ships from being successful in their mission."

Israel was shocked at what he was hearing. He thought to himself, *"Who is 'we'?"*

CHAPTER 5

FLEE TO EARTH

Professor Hai calculated that it would take 144 Gomorrite days to reach Adamina at maximum speed. They settled in for the long journey with plenty of food and water to make the trip. The Professor and Tamir stocked the ship for months prior to their departure so no one would suspect anything out of the ordinary. The small spacecraft had only two levels so there was little privacy available. The long journey would be a test for all of them to stay sane.

As Malka looked out the window at her home planet she could see a tremendous cloud formation forming. It was bigger than anything she had ever seen in her life. From the clouds she could see what appeared to be lightening strikes. The clouds were dark…almost darker than space itself. They continued to form until they covered the entire planet. After a few moments she could not see her home world any longer.

She yelled, "Father…look!"

Professor Hai and Tamir looked out the window and to their amazement they saw the same thing Malka was seeing. They did not realize what the cloud cover meant but it was bigger than anything they could remember.

***

The evening settled in on Gomorrah. Under the cover of darkness resistance members moved in and recovered the bodies of Gideon and the other leaders. They wanted to bury them with honor on the hills behind the region of New Sodom. This area was reserved for those who served honorably in the resistance. The celebration continued in high gear so no one noticed as the bodies were being removed. Resistance members worked quickly and quietly.

***

The 144 days were coming to an end as the small spacecraft had reached viewing distance of the planet the occupants called Adamina. As Tamir and Malka slept Professor Hai who was awake, marveled at the sight of Adamina.

He said aloud, "My God, there she is…we have returned home. Tamir…Malka…wake up…we are in viewing range!"

As they both woke, they could see a beautiful ball that appeared to be sitting on air in the distance in front of them. Professor Hai loved the blue and white with accents of brown and green mixed in it. He compared it to Gomorrah where brown was the dominant color. Gomorrah's water supply did not compare to that of Adamina.

Malka joyously said, "It looks so peaceful…full of happiness. Father it is a wonderful sight for a people who have seen nothing but pain all their years."

Tamir looked at her with a stern look and spoke defensively, "Gomorrah is beautiful as well."

Malka asked, "What do you mean. I hated Gomorrah."

Tamir continued his defense, "Gomorrah is our world. We do not know if this…Adamina…is any better."

Professor Hai interrupted, "It has been a long journey. We are almost at the end. Let us not fight any longer."

Tamir asked, "Professor how will we accumulate ourselves into their world? We cannot just land and tell them we are from Gomorrah."

Professor Hai answered, "As we get closer we will tap into their communication grid to find out any information we can. We will use this translator to learn their language. I was able to perfect it by using the Shehar's language."

"We cannot go directly to their leadership. Just as Tamar noted we do not know if they are any better than the King. What we will do is watch their behavior. After we have enough information then we will decide what to do."

***

Waldorf, Maryland is a small city located approximately 20 miles South of Washington DC. It was a beautiful summer evening and the stars could be seen miles away like lights in the distance. Pastor Larry Bell was winding up another revival service at his church, Redeemer Life Ministries. It was the third day of a five day service.

"This is a beautiful evening that the Lord has created," Pastor Bell announced. "Our first week in our new building and it is truly been a blessing from God. They said 'it couldn't be possible'. Oh...but God... God said 'it is...possible'. We are all living witnesses to the power of the almighty God and Jehovah is His name."

As the members of the service were leaving the church many of them gathered outside talking and fellowshipping together. In the night sky a small object appeared to be falling to the Earth. Pastor Bell could see it from his car.

He decided to drive over to where the strange object appeared to fall. He wasn't the only one to arrive on the scene. Two members of his service, Solomon and Gabriel also saw the object and arrived shortly after the Pastor.

***

Professor Hai said "Wait...they should leave in a few minutes. We don't want anyone to see us arriving here. We don't know what their intentions or fears might be of us."

"Father, I'm scared," Malka said with a meek voice. "Are you sure they can't see us?"

Professor Hai reassured his daughter, "Malka, our stealth technology bends the light of the visual spectrum and prevents the eye from seeing us. We can remain in this position for up to 6 hours before our energy consumption will be drained. They cannot see us."

Tamar said, "Your translator will be tested here Professor."

Professor Hai replied, "Yes, it most certainly will."

Malka asked, "Father does the King possess this stealth ability?"

Professor Hai answered, "No my child, I hid this technology from everyone."

Tamir angrily intervened, "Professor you did not trust to tell me of this technology?"

Professor Hai calmly spoke, "This technology can only be used with smaller objects but I did not want to put anyone in position of having to secure this information. With it King Abimelech would have been able to attack Adamina without being seen. It is far too dangerous to provide to anyone."

***

Pastor Bell stood overlooking the area where he believed the object fell from the sky. A few minutes later Solomon and Gabriel joined him.

Solomon remarked, "Pastor, did you see something fall from the sky?"

Pastor Bell answered, "Yes. I thought it fell in this field but I don't see anything."

Gabriel added, "I don't either and I am sure it fell here... somewhere."

Solomon commented, "I guess it wasn't a figment of all of our imaginations. Where could it be?"

Pastor Bell examined the ground as both Solomon and Gabriel watched. Pastor Bell was a very determined and detailed oriented man. From his days on the streets of South Carolina he was admired as a leader of people. No one could have seen him leading his own flock of believers when he was a young but now that he has grown up he could not be seen doing anything else.

He looked closely at the grass on the ground. Solomon and Gabriel both looked at each other.

Pastor Bell turned to them and said, "If you guys want to leave you can. You don't have to stay here for my benefit. I'm a tedious man and I like to explore. I'll see you guys tomorrow night."

Without hesitation Solomon said, "Okay Pastor, we'll see you later. God bless."

Gabriel added, "Pastor we can't just leave you out here by yourself."

Pastor Bell responded without looking back at them, "I will be okay. There is nothing out here that can harm me. You two go on. I'll be fine."

Gabriel replied, "Okay sir. We'll see you tomorrow night."

Pastor Bell answered both of them, "Good night my brothers. God bless you both."

As the two men walked back to their car, Pastor Bell continued to study the ground. He believed something was not right out there. He didn't want to bother Solomon and Gabriel with it but in his heart he knew something was out there.

Before Pastor Bell became a pastor in the church he spent 20 years as a member of the United States Air Force. That and his current position of pastor, allowed him to come into contact with many people of various backgrounds.

Pastor Bell's contacts were from many nations. He knew people who could not openly worship Christ. He formed a network that would help these people come to the United States and form a new life so they could worship freely and openly.

Pastor Bell noticed that the grass was straight everywhere except in one rectangle sized area. Since the grass was not very long most people would have easily missed it. However, Pastor Bell and his keen eye saw that there was something on the ground but he could not see it. It was invisible.

Professor Hai whispered, "He knows we are here."

Tamir offered, "I will kill him?"

Malka shouted, "Father...No!"

Professor Hai bellowed, "Tamir...I cannot believe you would suggest such a thing."

Pastor Bell stood up and looked in their direction. He heard the voices.

Pastor Bell yelled, "Is somewhere there?"

***

Professor Hai was puzzled. He then realized that the sound spectrum still could be heard. Even though the hull of the ship was between him and the stranger, if a sound was loud enough it could be heard.

Malka surprisingly looked at her father and whispered, "Father... can he hear us?"

Professor Hai answered, "Yes my dear, he probably heard us. I must go out and talk to him."

Tamir intervened, "No. Allow me to talk to him. If something were to happen to you..."

Professor Hai cut him off, "No Tamir. I must do the talking."

Professor Hai was becoming increasingly concerned about Tamir. Some of the things he said sounded like a true Gomorrite, not a true member of the resistance. Professor Hai knew he had to make first contact. It was the only way to be sure things went well.

Professor Hai scanned the grounds to ensure no one else was around. He then opened the door to the ship and walked out to meet Pastor Bell.

As the spacecrafts door lowered, Professor Hai stepped out.

Professor Hai stepped from the ship and spoke calmly, "My name is Hai. Professor Hai and I am from the planet Gomorrah. I have come here in the name of Jehovah to ask for help for my planet. We are ruled by a ruthless king and his general. Please do not harm me or my party."

Professor Hai saw the profound look on Pastor Bell's face. He waited for a response to his statement.

After a few moments Pastor Bell finally responded, "My friend. This is too much to take in all at once. If it were not for your invisible ship I would question your story. You mentioned Jehovah. How do you know of God? How can I even understand you...and you me?"

Professor Hai continued, "What is your name?"

Pastor Bell replied, "I'm sorry...my name is Pastor Larry Bell. Everyone calls me Pastor Bell."

Professor Hai asked, "What is a pastor?"

Pastor Bell answered, "A pastor is a person who has spiritual care of a number of persons. I serve Jesus Christ, the Son of the one true God...Jehovah."

Professor Hai asked, "I know Jehovah because he saved my people from death when He destroyed the cities of Sodom and Gomorrah. This story has been passed down for years. I have come in the hope that I can secure support for our plight."

"Regarding our ability to understand each other, I created this translator. Its matrix has only a few languages that I was able to store in it but it has the ability to translate what I say to and what you say to me. Also we tapped into your communication system and learned your language."

Pastor Bell replied, "The Bible doesn't mention this information."

Professor Hai spoke, "About 5,000 years ago my people lived here on Adamina. They were and still are a wicked and depraved people. God heard the outcries of the people and decided to destroy our city and the people in it."

"The King of Gomorrah plcd for the lives of his people and begged Jehovah not to destroy them all. God, in his infinite mercy, swept away the people of Gomorrah to a far away nearly baron planet. Jehovah knew that not all of the people wanted to continue their wicked ways. Some wanted to change their ways and resist the kings and their rule."

Professor Hai continued, "For 5,000 years we have stayed in the shadows waiting for an opportunity to overthrow the government and put in place a government that would be ruled by the people. Six months ago we tried and failed. I then boarded this craft with my daughter and assistant to come here to ask for help. We are the descendants of those who were swept away in the early morning light from a city on the plains of the Dead Sea. A place called Gomorrah."

Pastor Bell reiterated, "You are descendants of those who lived in Sodom and Gomorrah?"

Professor Hai answered, "We are descendants of the people of Gomorrah. The people of Sodom were destroyed with their city."

Professor Hai watched as Pastor Bell began walking in a small circle. He then noticed him opening a book. He then showed it to Professor Hai.

Pastor Bell said, "See here my friend, my Bible says Gomorrah was destroyed along with Sodom. It says and I quote, 'He looked down toward Sodom and Gomorrah, toward all the land of the plain, and he saw dense smoke rising from the land, like smoke from a furnace'."

Professor Hai pointed out, "My friend it speaks of the land where the city once sat but not of the people that lived there. We can debate the specifics of our Bibles all night but we must hide this ship and talk with your leaders about sending help to my planet."

Pastor Bell explained, "My friend, I will gladly assist you but as far as telling my world about your situation…well I do not believe it would be wise. Not everyone on Earth believes as I believe. In fact most do not. This world has many beliefs about God."

"Now you are living proof that the Bible is true. I do not believe it will be received well."

"Also we do not have the technology to travel to other planets. How could we help?"

Professor Hai responded, "I do not know but we must find a way."

Pastor Bell said, "I have contacts that can help you find a position within the scientific world. In this position you could design the technology to help us travel to your planet…which you will conveniently discover. Will others be coming here from your planet?"

Professor Hai answered, "No…we had the only working spacecraft and I destroyed the plans for it. It would take them many years to find a way to get here. They do not even know where this planet is so we do not have anything to worry about."

Pastor Bell placed his arm around Professor Hai and said, "This is a new beginning for both of us and we must make the right decisions and stay the course. First, we must hide your ship. I have about 20 acres of land south of here…outside a town called La Plata. I keep several items there that can help. Can it still fly?"

Professor Hai was happy that his first contact with someone on Adamina was one that was forged by God. He believed Pastor Bell to be a Godly man and he placed his trust in him.

Professor Hai answered, "The ship can still fly but what about your ground vessel?"

Pastor Bell replied, "'Ground vessel?' Oh…you mean my car. We can come back for it later. Let's go."

***

The next morning Pastor Bell started out bright and early. His wife woke Professor Hai, Malka and Tamir with the aroma of an exquisite breakfast and then informed Professor Hai and Tamir of his plan. Malka had not come to breakfast yet.

Pastor Bell spoke quietly as if someone were listening, "We have a network setup in which we bring in people from other countries that are not able to freely and openly worship Christ as we can here. We give them new identities and establish employment for them. The network has many members and I believe we can help you get into the science community. The first thing you'll need to learn is that we call this planet Earth. Why do you call it Adamina?"

Professor Hai looked up from his breakfast, swallowed and answered, "That is the name our fore fathers gave our home world. It is named after the first man...Adam. What does Earth mean?"

Pastor Bell thought for a moment and then replied, "That's a good question. The word Earth comes from German and Old English but as to how we started calling her 'Earth'...well that I don't know."

Professor Hai signed, "Interesting. This food...it is truly outstanding."

Pastor Bell's wife responded, "Thank you so much."

Pastor Bell added, "But we do know of Adam and Eve. The story is one of the first in the Bible...the book of Genesis."

Malka came running into the kitchen yelling, "Father...they have a device that shows moving pictures on it!"

Pastor Bell laughingly stated, "It's called a television Malka. We watch news, sports, weather...basically it's a tool to stay informed and entertained."

Malka excitedly said, "Father...come see. It is like nothing I have seen before!"

Professor Hai, Tamir and Pastor Bell went into the living room and they looked at the television. Pastor Bell demonstrated the television and they were marveled by it.

Pastor Bell concluded by saying, "Now we have to go and see a man about your new identities and where you will live. Remember even he can't know that you from Gomorrah. That information must stay with only me. Trust me...our society is not ready for visitors from outer space."

***

Pastor Bell called his sister Lorraine Williams, who was a professor at the University of Maryland, College Park.

Lorraine was a tenured professor at UMD and she had a PhD in Biotechnology. She was known in her field as a very knowledgeable professor and respected by her peers.

Lorraine saw her brother's number on the caller ID and answered, "My brother. Hi'ya doing this fine morning?"

Pastor Bell replied, "I am fine my good sister. I pray you are blessed."

Lorraine responded, "Yes…I…am. What can I do for my baby bro today?"

Pastor Bell began to ask, "I have a serious situation that I am going to need your help with. It's imperative that we meet at some point today. I have a meeting this morning at nine, but after that I will need to meet with you. Are you available?"

Lorraine answered, "I have classes until noon. After that I can make some time for you at about one o'clock in my office. Can you come to the university?"

Pastor Bell said, "I'll be there. Bye sis."

Lorraine replied, "Bye little bro."

As she was hanging up the phone she knew that something was different about this conversation. Her little brother would always laugh and joke with her no matter what the situation. This time he was all business. She prayed that he was safe and began getting ready for class.

***

Malka was amazed by all the sites and people she was seeing in Washington DC. To her this was a dream that she could only hope that she would never wake up from. She saw men and women walk side by side in the streets. She remembered how that was unheard of on Gomorrah.

She asked herself, *"Could this be the same place her ancestors had been swept away from in the morning light?"* It was so different than the place she grew up and called home all of her life.

While sitting at a light Malka watched a man who was sitting at a bus stop. She then saw a woman walk up to the bus stop. The man stood up and offered his seat to the woman and the woman sat down.

Malka shouted, "Father! Did you see that? That man got up and gave his seat to that woman! Father I love it here. Can we please stay forever?"

Pastor Bell smiled as he said, "That is common..."

Tamir interrupted, "Why do you persist to want this place over our home world? Gomorrah was not that bad."

Malka sternly replied, "For a man."

Tamir said, "Professor I miss Gomorrah. I miss my friends. This place is so strange to me."

Professor Hai said, "Tamir, you will meet new people here. They will be your friends and you will love it here. Someday we will return to our home world and hopefully put in place a peaceful government."

Tamir said, "Thank you Professor. I needed that."

***

Pastor Bell sat silent in the car as he thought about the two gentlemen he was about to meet. He trusted them emphatically. Charles Jackson works for the Department of Immigration and Naturalization who Pastor Bell met through church.

Pastor Bell like everyone else calls him Charlie. Pastor Bell like being surrounded by educated men who could hold in-depth conversation with him and help him with his mission of providing places for people to worship.

Albert "Big Al" Watson was the other man Pastor Bell was meeting. Big Al is a government employee who has experience in witness protection. He was the perfect man for Pastor Bell to have formed a relationship with.

Pastor Bell's BMW sedan made its way down Maryland Ave SW and pulled in one of the available parking slots. Pastor Bell instructed his new friends to remain in the vehicle until he returned. He then got out of the vehicle and headed to the usual meeting place...in front of the Ulysses S. Grant Memorial.

As he was walking toward the memorial he could see that his two friends, Charlie and Big Al had already arrived. He did not know what he was going to tell them about the Professor and his party but he would think of something.

Pastor Bell spoke first as he arrived, "Gentlemen."

Both men nodded their heads as an acknowledgement to Pastor Bell. They didn't want to do much talking because they could never know who might be listening to them.

Pastor Bell continued, "I have two males and a teenage girl that we need to get into the program. She is around the age of 16. Both men are scientist and have solid knowledge in science, specifically computers and engineering. What can we do for them?"

Big Al spoke up first, "Pastor you know things are kind of hot right now. We just placed a couple last week. We might need to lay low on this one like we agreed."

Pastor Bell replied, "I know we agreed to lay low for a while but this one dropped in from nowhere. We must place them and then we can lay low."

Charlie added, "I'm good on my end. I don't think I will have a problem because the last couple really didn't need my help. However, if you need me to do something else Pastor just speak the word and I'll help you out anyway I can."

Big Al said, "You know I'm always down too but it's hot around my way. If we do this I will have to bring someone else in. They can be trusted. But after this one we have to lay low for a while. I mean it."

Pastor Bell reached his hand out to Big Al and said, "Thanks. I will not bother you for a while but just to let you know this one is bigger than any before it. When do you think the identities will be ready?"

Big Al answered, "Give me a couple of days. I will have to confer with my friend. Do you have pictures of them?"

Pastor Bell reached in his pocket and pulled out the pictures that he had taken of the Professor, Malka and Tamir, the night before.

He said, "Here they are. It's important that they are able to get jobs in the scientific community."

Big Al replied, "I got it boss. I'll contact you in a couple of days."

Charlie said, "Anything you need from me?"

Pastor Bell answered, "Yes, we will need papers showing them to be American citizens. It must appear that they were born and raised in the United States. Also can you contact our friend to setup an educational background. We'll make both of them graduates of UMUC. My sister will vouch for their credentials. We also need a work history for them."

Charlie replied, "Got it. I'll let you know when its set."

Pastor Bell gratefully said, "Thanks. I owe you guys more than you can know."

The three of them parted ways. Pastor Bell headed back to the sedan where Professor Hai and his party were waiting. He was thankful that Charlie and Big Al never asked where Professor Hai and his party came from. As he approached his vehicle he could see someone talking to them through the car window.

His heart began to race as he feared that they may be talking too much. He had to stop them. He set out running as fast as he could. The vehicle was about a quarter of a football field away from him. As he got closer to the vehicle he overheard the end of the conversation.

Malka was saying, "I am sorry we are new here and do not know where anything is. Here comes our friend maybe he can help you."

The stranger replied, "Thank you."

Then he turned and said to Pastor Bell, "Sir, do you know how to get to the National Air and Space Museum?"

Pastor Bell was elated that the stranger was only asking for directions. He thought for sure Malka in her haste to live on this planet that she had given out vital information. He was much more relaxed as he came to a stop.

Pastor Bell was breathing heavily after running as fast as he could but he answered, "Yes…if you go down Maryland Ave to Independence, you will find it on the right side of the road."

The Stranger said, "Thank you sir. Have a nice day."

Pastor Bell stood there relieved and said, "You're welcome…and God bless you!"

***

Lorraine Williams sat at her desk in her office after a morning of instruction. She told her assistant that she was not to be interrupted until her brother arrived. She had a ton of papers to read and wanted to get started. She was quietly in thought reading when the buzzer sounded and startled her.

"What is it Jackson," she shouted?

Andy Jackson was Lorraine's assistant for the past several months and had a habit of getting under Lorraine's skin. She liked him and knew he had great potential but he was very weird to her.

"Your brother is here, ma'am," he replied.

"Thank you. Please send him in and stop saying ma'am," she answered!

Pastor Bell and his crew came in Lorraine's office. She was surprised to see her brother bring others with him. Now she knew something was amiss.

Lorraine asked, "Who do we have here, little bro?"

Pastor Bell hugged his sister and answered, "These people are some new friends of mine. I need your help with them. Please meet Professor Hai, his daughter Malka, and his assistant Tamir."

Each nodded their head as they were being introduced to Lorraine and she gave a similar response while looking over the rim of her glasses. She was perplexed as to what the nature of their visit to her office was.

Lorraine said, "It's nice to meet each of you. What can I do for you?"

Pastor Bell said, "You might want to sit down for this sis."

Lorraine still perplexed said, "Okay."

Pastor Bell began, "What I'm about to tell you must stay between us. No one outside of this room can know what we are about to discuss. I trust you as my sister to keep this between us. Can I count on you?"

Lorraine answered, "If that's the case than I suggest we take a ride. I'll drive since you have that little car."

Pastor Bell replied, "Little!"

They left Lorraine's office and exited the building.

The five of them got in Lorraine's Navigator and drove off down Route 1 headed toward the 495 beltway.

"Ah, now this is room even for five," Lorraine signed.

Pastor Bell laughed, "You're funny big sis. Can we get down to business?"

Lorraine asked, "Why all the business talk now? You use to be more fun."

Pastor Bell replied, "I'm sorry. It's just this situation is more serious than you can imagine. You see my friends here are not from here. By here, I mean Earth."

Lorraine looked and said, "Are you out of your ever loving mind? Do you think for one minute I'm going to fall for that one? I have a PHD and it's not in stupidity."

Pastor Bell calmly said, "I am not trying to run any game on you my sister. I am speaking the truth. Their spacecraft landed in a field near the church. I found my new friends in a cloaked ship."

"I have arranged for them to get new identities which will take about two days to accomplish. In the meantime I need you to teach them the nuisances of our world. They don't know of such things as cars. We have to teach them these things so that they can integrate themselves into our world. Will you help?"

Lorraine paused as she gave it some thought. Could this really be true? Her little brother was always truthful but he did play the occasional gag on his friends and family members. However, he had never done anything of this magnitude. If it is true then why would people from another planet come here?

Lorraine responded, "Okay, say I believe you. I need to know more."

Pastor Bell replied, "You will. I will tell you everything tonight at my house. They are good people from a bad planet. We must help them."

Lorraine said, "I will be there at seven. Why don't we just take them to the President? We can land the ship on the White House lawn. We're sure to get help then.

Pastor Bell replied, "Do you really trust our government like that? Remember Roswell?"

Lorraine answered, "You're right."

She then turned the vehicle around and headed back to the university. Still in shock she attempted to teach them little things on the journey back. Malka asked what seemed like a thousand questions and Lorraine struggled to keep up with them.

***

That evening Lorraine came to her brothers house and sat down to talk with Professor Hai and his group. She specifically pointed out to Malka that women were not second class citizens on Earth and that they are treated as equals to their male counterparts. She told them that women of Earth were allowed to pursue any occupation they desired. They chose their own mates and most countries if not all were not subject to prearranged marriages.

She told them that many of the nations of the world allow their citizens to worship whatever God they chose. She pulled up the Internet and showed them the many churches in the DC Metro area where people worship Jehovah openly and freely. Malka was so happy and impressed with all this information that she could not contain her joy. Lorraine could not understand why Tamir stormed out of the room.

Lorraine asked, "Was it something I said?"

Professor Hai answered, "Please forgive my assistant. He says he is having trouble adapting to this world. He misses his friends back on Gomorrah and to hear how great it is to live here while they are suffering is bothersome to him. I will reassure him that our mission has not changed and we will find a way to get back to Gomorrah and free our people."

Lorraine said, "Whew, I thought I upset him."

Professor Hai added, "He also is not used to following the instructions of a woman. Back on Gomorrah women are treated as property. My daughter had the advantage of my teaching. Therefore she is more advanced than the typical Gomorrite woman. Give him time. He will come around."

Lorraine said, "Forgive me Professor but I think there's something else going on with him. I hate to say this but I get a bad feeling about him."

Pastor Bell jumped in, "You have to forgive my sister."

Professor Hai responded, "No, no, it is okay. I am beginning to have my own doubts."

They finished discussing different topics that evening and the Gomorrites learned many things about Earth. The evening ended well into the morning hours.

***

Tamir stood on the deck for a minute then he turned to come back in the room. He heard Lorraine saying she had a bad feeling about him.

He said to himself, *"if we were on Gomorrah I would slit your throat for speaking such words."*

He gathered himself together and returned to the room. He wants to act apologetically so no one would suspect he was a spy. Staying undercover was growing difficult for him.

***

After obtaining all the necessary documents and employment, Pastor Bell found apartments for the Gomorrites. Professor Hai and Malka got a place in Sheffield Greens apartments while Tamir got a one bedroom apartment at Holly Station apartments.

Lorraine was able to use her influence to get Professor Hai an assistant job as a scientist with a major university while Tamir was hired as a graduate assistant at a different university.

Malka enrolled in high school in Waldorf, Maryland as a junior. This was a totally new experience for her as Gomorrite women were not educated. The first person Malka met was Shannon Tyler, a girl in her homeroom class.

Shannon saw Malka walk in and knew she was new so she approached her and said, "Hi, my name is Shannon. What's your name?"

Malka hesitated as she almost said her Gomorrite name. Her father and Pastor Bell reminded her countless times to forget that name and use her Earth name, Liz Mitchell.

Liz responded, "My name is Liz…Uh Liz Mitchell."

Shannon laughingly said, "Well, Uh Liz, you must be new here. I haven't seen you before."

Liz replied, "I am…me, my father and cousin moved here from overseas."

Liz was happy to have gotten that part of the story right without hesitation. She had spent hours practicing it in the mirror.

***

"Professor Simmons, is it true that you are experimenting with new weapons technology for the military?" The reporter who had interviewed Professor Simmons on several occasions stuck his recorder in her face again and caught the world renowned scientist off guard.

Professor Simmons answered sternly, "No comment and get that out of my face please."

Professor Cassandra Simmons was a renowned scientist and a leader in her field. She hired Professor Hai based on her good friend Lorraine's recommendation and on a hunch that he knew much more than he was admitting.

During the interview he seemed to be trying hard not to show his intelligence. Professor Simmons could tell he was very knowledgeable… too knowledgeable for a low level assistant position. She decided to trust her friend but keep an eye on Tony.

As she made her way to her office she passed Professor Hai now known as Tony Mitchell in the hallway.

Professor Simmons said, "Tony, you're here early. What are you working on?"

Tony answered, "I'm just double checking some numbers I entered yesterday."

Professor didn't believe him but she chose to let it slide. She suspected Tony was working on a side project of his own and didn't want to tell her.

CHAPTER 6

EARTH, A YEAR LATER

Shannon and Liz had bonded in their friendship. They did everything together. Liz was careful not to divulge her past but she truly enjoyed the peace and freedom of being on Earth. She hoped this time in her life would never end. She had forgotten everyone on Gomorrah. She didn't want to tell her father but she didn't care anymore. Sometimes she felt guilty about her feelings but when she thought about the things that she went through the guilt went away.

Liz did spend hours thinking of her mother. She began to realize that her father had a crush on another woman. At first she was angry that he even noticed another woman but then she realized that he deserved to go on with his life also. It was making him happy and she saw him smile more than she ever had in her life.

The school year was off and roaring for Liz. It was all so knew to her. She was enjoying all of it. She found that the little knowledge passed on to her was enough to propel her to the top of her class.

Her friendship with Shannon was a blessing to her. It was as if destiny had found them and placed them together. Liz felt they would be friends forever. The fall was coming to a close and old man winter was right around the corner.

***

Tony had become fond of Professor Simmons but tried to hide his emotions. He was also ashamed of them as well. It had only been a year since his wife was murdered on the throne room floor of the palace mouthing the words "I love you". He had not forgotten that pain and he had not forgotten his first love. Now on Earth he was beginning to enjoy his freedom. He was falling in love with another woman.

He was use to relationships being prearranged and since the execution of his wife he had not been attracted to anyone else. Professor Hai possessed more science knowledge than everyone on Earth but he did not know how to ask a woman to go out on a date with him.

This was something they did not do on Gomorrah. He was not even sure he should ask her because of his secrets. He decided to ask Lloyd, a co-worker, how relationships were handled. Then if he could get the courage…he would ask Professor Simmons out on a date.

"Tony!" Professor Simmons yelled from across the parking lot of their building.

It was early on a Monday morning. Both Tony and Professor Simmons were reporting for work. Tony always reported to work early. He liked the smell of morning and fresh reminder of freedom. He had not seen Professor Simmons at work this early before.

When Tony looked back to see her, he saw a beautiful spectacle of a woman. She was getting out of her car and it appeared to him that she was moving so eloquently that it had to be in slow motion. Every part of her body was pleasing to his sight and he found himself lusting for her. He chastised himself for his feelings as the haunting image of his dying wife flowed across his mind.

He answered, "Good morning Professor Simmons."

Strutting toward Tony as if she were in a rush she asked, "How was your weekend?"

Tony answered, "My weekend was pleasant and very peaceful. How about you? How was your weekend?"

She cocked her head to the side and with a sleek smile she replied, "You seem to be a man who loves peace and quiet. Did you come from a large family or something?"

Tony shyly responded, "No… I just enjoy the peace of this world…I mean…of my life. I feel for those people who don't live in a peace."

Professor Simmons happily remarked, "You're strange Tony. Okay... well, it's been a year now since you started with us and to be frank with you...I believe that you have more talent than you are letting on. I have an opening and I would like to promote you to one of my primary scientist positions. What do you think?"

Tony's first response was one of excitement but he quickly tempered his enthusiasm and realized that accepting this position it would mean that he would have to have his background thoroughly investigated. It would not be long before questions would rise and the possibility of his exposure could not be allowed to happen.

Tony responded, "I am happy with my position now Professor Simmons. Thank you for considering me."

Professor Simmons stopped in her tracks and looked at Tony.

"I just offered you a position that is almost double your current salary and you're not interested? Okay, I know something is wrong with this picture. You are far to wise a man for this. We need to talk. Tonight after work, we will go to Sonya's on 9th and I Street for dinner and some conversation. Don't say no because it's not an option," demanded Professor Simmons.

Tony responded, "Yes, ma'am."

He now had his date and he didn't have to ask for it. He was going to dinner with Professor Simmons and he was so excited about it that he couldn't concentrate on his work. What was he going to do? What was going to say? He couldn't take the job. That was out of the question unless Pastor Bell could come up with something to help him. He had to contact him to see what could be done. This was an opportunity he could not miss out on.

***

Ashlee Davis was an employee with the Department of Energy. She had become friends with Simon Bell, who was a security guard in the same building. Ashlee and Simon would often trade comments as she was going in and out of the building. She was attracted to him but she didn't think he noticed her in the same way.

Ashlee was a 26 year old nurse and she enjoyed her work at the Department of Energy. She had just graduated from Central State University and was on her own. She was raised in the church and continued to go as an adult. She was always smiling and her friends liked having her around.

On this particular Monday morning Ashlee was walking into the building with her friend Marion.

"Girl, there's your man," whispered Marion.

Ashlee responded, "He doesn't even see me like that. We're just friends."

"Why? What's his problem," asked Marion?

Ashlee replied, "You have to ask him that question."

Simon welcomed them to work, "Good morning ladies. You both look beautiful today."

In unison they both responded, "Thank you."

Ashlee asked, "Can you come see me at break time?"

Simon replied, "Yes ma'am."

She then turned and continued walking with Marion.

Marion looked at her and said, "I know why you said that."

Ashlee asked, "Why?"

Marion replied, "You trying to let him know you're interested. Tell the truth."

Ashlee responded, "I am interested but the boy won't react. I don't know what else to do except for me to ask him out. You know I can't do that you know. The word says 'A man that finds a wife......'"

Marion continued, "I heard that. He'd better move or he's going to lose out."

***

Charlie Baxter was enjoying his new surrounding but he hated the people. He particularly felt the women were out of place. He couldn't wait for the armada to arrive and destroy the inhabitants of this world. Then he would put their women in their place.

He was also tired of playing the role of Tamir, the young assistant to Professor Hai. He thought, *"How stupid the great Professor Hai is to allow a spy to work right next to him on his biggest projects."*

He couldn't wait to see Professor Hai's expression when he realized that he was a spy for General Idit.

Charlie was making his way home through the DC Metro traffic. He had stopped and made some electronic purchases while on his way home. He needed these items to make a communication device so he could send word to General Idit regarding Professor Hai and his activities. He also wanted to provide him with the weapons capability of the Adaminians.

He was thinking about the parts he had just acquired and what else he needed to make the device when the red and blue lights illuminated behind him. He thought hopefully the police officer was not stopping him but he soon realized that he was wrong. He pulled his vehicle into an alleyway off of New York Avenue and the officer pulled in behind him.

Charlie waited for the officer to get out of his vehicle. When the officer approached his vehicle, Charlie swung open his car door and stepped out. The police officer stopped and put his hand out in front of him.

He instructed Charlie, "Sir, stay in your vehicle."

Charlie made a move to get back in the vehicle then swung around in one motion and fired two quick shots with his .38 revolver and silencer. The officer was dead before he hit the ground. Charlie looked around to ensure no one saw what just happened. He then got in his vehicle and left the scene as though nothing happened.

   ***

Pastor Bell was working in his office when the phone rang. He recognized the number on the caller ID and answered it.

"How's it going my friend," asked Pastor Bell?

"Pastor...I have news but I don't know if we can do anything about it," Tony responded.

Pastor Bell asked, "What is your news?"

Tony hesitated and then said, "I have been offered a promotion to a primary scientist position. I know this will take some doing because of my background but this will put me in a position to finish my work on the warp engine. Is there any way I can get this promotion?

Pastor Bell thought for a minute. He had some contacts in an investigation agency but he would have to find out what agency Tony's department used.

Pastor Bell replied, "Let me make some calls and I will get back with you. Try and stall them in the mean time."

Tony said, "Thank you Pastor. Also I have a date with Professor Simmons tonight."

"Wow! When did this happen," asked Pastor Bell?

"Today…but it is only to discuss the promotion offer. I wish it were more," replied Tony.

"Take it one step at a time my friend," consoled Pastor Bell.

"I will my friend. Sometimes I feel guilty that I haven't returned to Gomorrah to free my people. I think about their suffering and I feel bad that I am living so freely. Last night the guilt overwhelmed me and I cried myself to sleep." Tony replied.

Pastor Bell said, "You should expect days like that. Your people would understand that these things can't happen overnight. Our technology is not near yours and our government does not take kindly to aliens. No offense."

"None taken," replied Tony.

Pastor Bell continued, "You see there have been rumors that aliens came here in the past and the government concealed it from everyone. We believe they even experimented on them. I can't let that happen to you my friend."

Tony responded, "I truly understand. That is why I need this position to build a warp engine for your world. With it they will be able to go to Gomorrah and help us overthrow the King and his General."

"I'll get back to you as soon as I know something," said Pastor Bell.

"Thanks Pastor. Have a blessed day," replied Tony.

"Bless your bones my friend," responded Pastor Bell.

***

This Monday was just another Monday for Solomon. He arrived at work at his usual time and sat at his desk to have some oatmeal. His co-worker Michele Fishburne popped up at his cube to chat.

"What's up Sol," asked Michele?

"Come on you know that's not my name. Solomon…why do you persist," replied Solomon?

Michele was smiling as she like teasing him, "Because you make it easy."

Solomon replied, "Okay…okay. How was your weekend?"

"Cool. I didn't do much. I got my car washed. Went to a cook out around 6 and Sunday I just chilled at home with my sister and her kids," said Michele.

"I didn't do much either. Me and the wife went to a friend's house and watched movies. We went to church on Sunday and did some work around the house the rest of the day," Solomon commented.

Solomon saw his best friend, Gabriel, pop up at his cube. He worked on the same floor as Solomon and Michele.

"What's up playa? Oh…hi Michele," asked Gabriel.

Solomon replied, "What's up?"

Michele replied, "Hey Gabriel."

"Hey man, are you going to do the war games this weekend," asked Gabriel?

"You know it," said Solomon.

Michele sighed, "You boys and your toys. Why do you guys do that mess?"

"It's fun. We get to pretend we're in charge of a military regiment and attack another regiment. It's all about strategy, baby," Solomon exuberantly replied.

***

Pastor Bell had been busy all morning making phone calls to friends in an attempted to get Tony's background tighten. He wanted to help Tony get the position that Professor Simmons was offering him because it would help Earth discover warp drive and travel to Gomorrah.

Pastor Bell realized that Tony was probably the single most important key to the direction of mankind. He represented proof to the world that the stories in the Bible were in fact true. He knew people all over the world would not want to accept this fact but an entire race of people from the land that Earth knew as Gomorrah returning home to Earth would be irrefutable proof. He had to get his background solid so he could get this position.

***

Tony's heart raced as the day was beginning to wine down. Tony and his co-worker Lloyd was talking about Tony's impending date.

"So man…you excited," asked Lloyd?

Tony replied, "Yes, I am excited and I am a little nervous at the same time."

"Look, just take it easy and relax. Take things as they come. There's no need to rush anything here. She obviously thinks highly of you so just be yourself," said Lloyd.

Tony said, "You are right. I will relax. After all, this is just a meeting about a possible promotion…not a romantic affair."

Tony noticed a figure walk in the room out of the corner of his eye. He stopped himself from saying anything else because he didn't want everyone to know how he felt about Professor Simmons.

"What are you boys talking about," asked Professor Simmons?

"Nothing ma'am, I was just getting ready to leave," said Lloyd.

Tony didn't say anything as he watched Lloyd leave the room. After Lloyd left Tony stood quietly, not knowing what to say. Then he saw Professor Simmons look at him and stroll over to him with smile on her face that looked flirtatious to him.

"Is there something you want to talk about," asked Professor Simmons?

"Um…no…well yes…are we ready to go to dinner," asked Tony?

"In about 10 minutes. I'll meet you in the parking lot," Professor Simmons answered.

She walked out of the room on her way back to her office. Tony breathed a breath of fresh air as she walked out of the room. He caught himself looking at her figure as she was walking out. Then his heart dropped as she looked back and caught him looking.

***

It was late afternoon and Pastor Bell was in his study sipping on some Earl Grey tea and reading Romans 8:6 in preparation for his next sermon. His wife, Lynette came into the room carrying his cell phone.

"Your phone was ringing so I answered it for you. Here you go," said Lynette.

Pastor Bell reached out his hand, smiled to his lovely wife and thanked her. After 25 years of marriage, he still loved her. To him there was no other woman and there could be no other woman. She supported him in everything he did. She was his helpmate.

Pastor Bell answered the phone, "Hello."

"Pastor," the voice on the other end said. "All is set up. This background will pass CIA level scrutiny and we have secured the investigators cooperation. It cost us a lot so I hope it's worth it."

Pastor Bell replied, "Thank you. Trust me, it is. I am in your debt."

The voice responded, "No sir. You are doing great things for these people by giving them a chance to worship in public. Without you they would still be living in tyranny. Thank you and take care."

Pastor Bell said, "God bless you."

He hung up the phone and prayed that he was doing the right thing by helping Tony. He then reached for the phone to call Tony knowing he would be on his date with Professor Simmons. He didn't want to interrupt but he was sure that Tony would want this information.

***

Tony and Professor Simmons arrived at Sonya's on 9th and I Street in Washington DC around 6:00 pm. Tony was outwardly excited about the opportunity to have dinner with a woman that over the past year he had come to admire.

Tony thought she was smart and attractive. He thought back to the first day he met her. Lorraine introduced them in her office. When Tony shook Professor Simmons' hand he felt something ignite inside of him.

Her smile, her soft skin, her brilliance were all amazing to him. He never knew a woman could be all those things in one package.

The women on Gomorrah never had the opportunity to excel the way Professor Simmons excelled. He wondered if his wife would have flourished in the same manner.

Professor Simmons' voice broke the silence.

"Hello there. Are you dreaming," she asked?

"Oh I'm sorry. I let my mind stray off a bit. This is a nice restaurant," replied Tony.

Professor Simmons took a deep breath and said, "Yes it is. Tony I need you to be honest with me. Why would you turn down this promotion? I believe there is more than meets the eye with you."

After sipping on some water she continued, "You came to me through my friend Lorraine and she wouldn't lead me down a bad path. But who are you...really? I mean, the advancements that you have made in the area of warp drive technology just don't add up to an inexperience scientist. I know you have a considerable amount of knowledge that you are keeping to yourself. Tell me what the real deal is Tony."

Tony looked down at the table and he knew he couldn't share his origins with her. He wanted to tell her everything but he knew he couldn't betray his trust with Pastor Bell. Professor Simmons would be a great asset to helping his people back on Gomorrah but she also was head of a research lab ran by the government. If he was wrong about her, where would that put him...his daughter...and his friend...Tamir? He couldn't chance it.

Tony mustarded up a reply he even half believed.

He explained, "There is nothing special to tell. I am the man you see before you. I do a lot of reading and studying because I love science. This promotion...I am just not sure I am the right man for the job. I don't have the political skills you possess."

Professor Simmons signed, then she said, "Okay the offer is on the..."

Tony's cell phone rang to cut Professor Simmons off. He looked at the ID and saw it was Pastor Bell. Maybe he had good news? Maybe he could accept this position.

He answered, "Hello."

Pastor Bell responded, "I know you are at dinner so I'll make this real brief my friend. Accept the job."

Tony contained his happiness and replied, "Thank you. God bless you."

Pastor Bell said, "God bless you my brother."

Tony then looked at Professor Simmons as she was telling the waiter what she wanted to drink. The waiter then motioned to Tony for his order. Tony told him he wanted water and the waiter left.

He then looked at Professor Simmons smiling and said, "Professor Simmons..."

She cut him off and said, "Call me Cassy please."

Tony resumed, "Okay...Cassy...I will accept the position."

He saw the look of shock on her face.

"Well...I must admit...I am surprised at the sudden turnaround. Why?" she asked.

Tony said, "I have given it some thought and you appear to want this more than me. I will give it a try and I hope not to let you down."

Cassy said, "Okay, I know you still hiding something but I'm going to go with the flow right now. I do have my eye on you. I will put your name in tomorrow. In the meantime you will be working down in the basement on a special project for me. The bad news is that there are no windows, TVs, cell phones, land phones, or Internet. There is no way to communicate with the outside world where you will be working. For eight hours you will be totally isolated."

She then asked, "Can you handle all of that?"

Tony thought about it for a minute and answered, "Yes...I believe I can handle that. What is the project?"

Cassy answered, "We can't discuss that until tomorrow morning. Let's just enjoy our dinner for now."

CHAPTER 7

WE COME IN PEACE

It was a long arduous journey but Lieutenant Oded managed to keep his sanity even in the ship's prison. He did not know how the resistance was going to get the information they had in their possession to Professor Hai but he knew that God would provide a way.

General Idit didn't allow any visitors to Lieutenant Oded's cell so he spent most of the time alone. The General did allow him to have exercise time. He wanted him fit and strong to stand execution at the hands of Samuel.

Varda slipped in for visits when she could. Lieutenant Oded was pleased that she had gotten on the detail that brought him food. Just seeing her was enough to keep him encouraged throughout the long trip.

On occasion his friend, Lieutenant Yaniv, would help Varda get in to see Lieutenant Oded. Lieutenant Oded discussed, when he could, with Lieutenant Yaniv different ways they could get off the ship safely and destroy it at the same time. They had not come up with a plan.

Lieutenant Oded instructed Lieutenant Yaniv to hold on to the transmitter because he could not risk having it on him when the guards searched his cell.

***

The Gomorrite battle cruisers were crossing the Norma Arm of the Milky Way galaxy and the final plans were being reviewed by General Idit and his staff. The war ships were preparing to stay out of sight while the peace envoy proceeded to Adamina.

"Gentlemen we have reliable spies already in place on Adamina and when we get in range, all of their military strength will be given to us. This information along with the pretense of peace will give us a decided advantage against our enemy," shouted General Idit.

He went on to say, "Our scientists have told us that Adamina is heavily populated but that will not be a problem for our army. Our men are trained and ready to take back what is rightfully ours. Most of the planet's inhabitants are out of shape and weak. We are a race of warriors! We were born and bred to win this battle! They may have more people than we have but we are the better trained army…and we are more determined."

General Idit had no information on the shape of the citizens of Adamina. He often lied to enhance or motivate his men.

The General had every soldier's attention in the room as he spoke. He demanded attention and was quick to punish the slightest mistake.

General Idit slowly walked around the room while talking and when he reached the sleeping young soldier he pulled out a piece of rope and wrapped it around the soldier's neck. He pulled on it tighter and tighter until the soldier could not breathe anymore.

He could not stand insubordination. He strived for perfection in his life and expected nothing less from his troops.

***

At the Drake Observatory Professor Roland McKay and his assistant, Malcolm Richardson was working early in the morning when they observed a small object in the night sky.

"Professor, there's something in the sky," said Malcolm.

"Young man there is always something in the sky. Can you be more specific," replied Professor McKay?

"Sir, it looks like…it looks like…well… a space craft," Malcolm shouted!

Malcolm saw King Abimelech's shuttle on approach to Earth.

He continued, "Professor shouldn't we call someone?"

Professor McKay responded, "Malcolm, I'm already on the phone."

***

Lieutenant Colonel Wade Simpson was a man with just over 20 years of military experience. He had fought in both Gulf Wars and now was in charge of monitoring the North American Space Administration's deep space radar. Lieutenant Colonel Simpson received a call from Professor McKay.

He answered the phone, "Professor…we're kind of busy right now… what can I do for you today?"

Professor McKay replied, "Colonel…we have spotted what appears to be a spacecraft headed to Earth."

Colonel Simpson said, "We spotted it as well and we have begun attempts to communicate with it."

Professor McKay said with deep concern, "Colonel you need to know this may be the single biggest day in Earth's history. Be careful how you proceed."

Colonel Simpson replied, "No pressure…thanks Professor."

***

NASA continued to contact King Abimelech's shuttle. On board the shuttle attempts to communicate were coming in from several different places on Earth.

The royal communications officer asked, "Sire, which one should we respond to?"

King Abimelech responded, "Answer the first one that attempted… this NASA place. Give them the honor of speaking with me first."

NASA communications continued to try, "This is NASA Deep Space Radar to unidentified object, please respond."

Several attempts with the incoming spacecraft were met with no response. Lieutenant Colonel Simpson received a call from Marshall Tucker the Director of the Kennedy Space Center.

Marshall asked, "Colonel…have you received any response from the space craft?"

Colonel Simpson answered, "No sir. We're still trying to contact them but we have not received a response. I recommend we go to DEFCON 2."

Before the Director could respond to the Colonel's recommendation a response came over the NASA communication system.

The royal communication officer announced, "NASA Deep Space Radar...we are a peace envoy from the planet Shalom. We are here to make peace with you. Please do not attack us."

Everyone in the room looked at each other. Colonel Simpson was mystified at the realization that they were the first to receive contact from aliens from another planet.

The royal communication officer continued, "We request permission to land on your planet. Will you please grant it?"

Marshall excitedly shouted, "Colonel, tell them we must contact the President prior to granting them permission. Ask them not to enter Earth's atmosphere until we can contact the President and respond to them."

Colonel Simpson answered, "Yes sir."

***

The Director shouted to his secretary, "Get me the President... NOW!"

She responded, "Yes, sir."

She punched the automatic button to dial the number to the White House and get the newly elected President on the line.

"President Davis' line," the voice came over the phone and said.

The Director's secretary stated, "The Director of the NASA's Deep Space Radar needs to speak with the President Priority One."

The president's secretary responded, "He's in a meeting right now can I take a message."

"No," she retorted. "We must speak to the President now...it's a national emergency."

Just then the Director got on the line and stated, "If you don't get me the President now, you will be packing groceries next week."

The president's secretary responded, "Just a minute sir."

President Davis answered the phone, "Tuck, this had better good."

Marshall stated, "Mr. President, we have established contact with an alien space craft approaching Earth. They are a peace envoy...on a peace mission. They have requested permission to land. How should we proceed?"

Marshall rushed to get all his words out to the President that when he finished he realized he had to take a deep breath.

The president could not believe what he was hearing from his Director. He had personally vouched for Marshall Tucker to receive his current position. Now he was beginning to question if Tuck was sane.

President Davis seriously responded, "Tuck, I'm not in the joking mood. You called me out of a very important budget meeting. Tuck, I vouched for you personally. Are you making me regret that? Now what is it truly?"

Marshall answered, "Sir, I am being straight with you. Please...you must give us direction in this issue. I can patch the communication through to your office so you can speak directly to the space craft."

President Davis asked, "Does any other country know about the space craft?"

"Sir, we believe that China might have spotted the space craft as well. If we want to be first we had better move fast," said Tuck.

President Davis said, "Patch me through."

The President then punched the intercom on his phone and instructed his secretary to get the Vice President, the Secretary of Defense, the Chairman of the Joint Chiefs of Staff, and the National Security Advisor in his office now.

***

King Abimelech's crew consisted of Pesach, a loyal member to the King and his personal aide, the royal communication officer, and two of the King's personal guard. The King was reviewing the plan on a secure line with General Idit.

General Idit stated, "Sire, we must convince the Adamians that we are on a peaceful mission from Shalom. Pesach should attempt to contact our spies currently on Adamina and get whatever information they have from them now. We cannot wait until you land because the transmission might be detected."

The King ordered Pesach to send the transmission.

The voice of the President came over the communication system to the Gomorrite ship.

President Davis announced, "This is President Charles E. Davis of the United States of America. I welcome you to Earth."

The King looked at his aide and said, "What is this Earth they keep talking about?"

Pesach replied, "It is probably the name they go by now instead of Adamina. We should call them by that name since that is what they are using."

King Abimelech responded, "This is King Abimelech of the planet Shalom. I represent a peace envoy that request permission to land on your planet...Earth."

The President said, "It is an honor to speak with you Sir. We know that you come in peace but what is it that you wish to achieve with your visit?"

King Abimelech answered, "We are here to establish a friendship with your world. Our planet is dying and we are searching for a new place to live. We have met many new friends in our journey and we wish to count you among them. Maybe some of our people will be allowed to dwell on your world. In return we can provide our technology to you. Most importantly I hope that we can become friends."

President Davis replied, "This is truly an honor to welcome friends from another world but we must be cautious in our behavior. I hope you understand."

King Abimelech responded, "I expect no less. If I were in your place I would do the same."

President Davis asked, "How many are in your party?"

King Abimelech answered, "There are five of us. My assistant, my communications officer and two personal guards accompany me. We are peaceful people. We do not have any weapons on board my ship."

The President replied, "King Abimelech...you have permission to land and my people will forward the proper coordinates to you. It is an honor to welcome you to our planet. However, please be aware that we do not have one leader of our planet. Instead our planet has several leaders under a United Nations accord. Once you have arrived I will take you in front of the United Nations to formally welcome you to Earth."

King Abimelech said, "It is an honor to visit your planet and I hope both of our worlds can become friends."

The King sat back in his seat and smiled as he began to see his plan coming together and the takeover of Earth in a few days would be complete. He would then be ruler of Adamina, what he feels his rightful place in the universe.

***

In the White House Situation room the President, Vice President and his staff were discussing the arrival of King Abimelech.

President Davis began, "Today we are about to embark on history. Today we are about to be remembered as the people who greeted the first visitors from another planet. Our names will be forever remembered in history. Think of the possibilities. If we can convince them to help us build ships that can reach the stars as they have, then we will see Star Trek come to life right in our back yard. Today is history and let us be ready for it."

The Chairman of the Joint Chiefs of Staff, General Starks cautioned, "Sir, we need to ensure that this is the right plan of action. Our troops need to be ready in case this is a rouse or something."

President Davis responded, "I don't think so Ted. They obviously have the ability to come here on ships. If they wanted a fight then they would have picked it already."

General Starks said, "Sir, they may be trying to ascertain our defensive capabilities. We may be giving them the time they need to assess us. I recommend we put our troops at DEFCON 1."

Vice President Woods joined the conversation, "I agree with the President. We should extend an olive branch and not nuclear missile. If they wanted to attack us they would have."

"I'm afraid I second the words of General Starks. There's nothing wrong with a little precaution," said Secretary of Defense Robert Parker.

"Okay…a little precaution maybe. But certainly not DEFCON 1. Set the DEFCON level to 4 but we are not to engage these people in any kind of threatening way. Security is to back way off and take no gesture as a means of attack. Remember they requested to land here and they did so in the name of peace. Let's not be the one to escalate matters. Now we must attend to our guest," stated President Davis.

"Sir, what do we do about the public? If they land that ship on the White House lawn then everyone will see it. I advise that we create a cover story," recommended General Starks.

President Davis turned to his staff and sternly said, "We will not deceive the public on this issue. We will not have another Roswell on our hands. No one is to create a cover story that we may or may not have to continue lying about. We will tell the public the truth this time and trust that they can handle it. David...can you handle the press release?"

Vice President Woods answered, "Yes sir. I will put together a speech and make an announcement to the public."

As the Vice President was speaking one of General Starks' aides came in and whispered something into his ear.

General Starks looked at the President and Vice President and said, "We have another problem. Other countries are beginning to call and questioned our right to allow the aliens to land on Earth. What should we tell them?"

Vice President Woods answered, "Tell them they are landing on United States soil through United States air space. We have the right to allow whomever we want to land on our soil. However, we will agree to bring this matter to the United Nations for further discussions. Do you agree Sir?"

President Davis pondered for a moment and then agreed. He adjourned the meeting and went to meet the visitors.

***

Linda Hayes was a roaming reporter for WWAS channel 6 news and she was racing to the scene of a usual report. She rushed to get herself together as the truck raced through the city. Her lipstick fell to the floor as the driver turned a corner.

Outside the hectic atmosphere of the van was Washington DC. Linda noticed that tourist and citizens were walking along the streets as normal. She though, *This day isn't any different than any other normal day in the city for them.*

It was a warm day in the city and the sounds of it were as natural as always. Linda heard all the sounds that she usually heard on the streets. She finally took a minute to look out the window. She saw tourists racing from site to site trying to see all that Washington DC had to offer. Many visitors gathered on Pennsylvania Avenue gazing at the White House. For many of them it was the first time in their lives that they had the opportunity to see the White House in person.

From their view the White House stood approximately the length of a football field away but even to get that close marveled many tourists. There they stood snapping pictures of family members using the White House as a backdrop. Everything was as it should be until…

As Linda got close she could see people pointing to the sky. The news truck came to a screeching halt just outside the barriers blocking vehicles from entering Pennsylvania Avenue in front of the White House. The truck nearly struck the barriers but before it could even come to a complete stop Linda and a camera crew were already leaping out of the vehicle. They went running down to where all the people were standing.

Linda heard someone shout, "Look…its some kind of ship!"

Everyone looked up in the sky and she was amazed to see that it was a ship like they had never seen before. It was descending downward and appeared to be landing on the White House lawn. She thought, *"Was this some kind of new technology?"*

One man said, "No planes can fly over the White House!"

Another man pulled out his cell phone and dialed 9-1-1. He had it on speaker so Linda could hear it.

The voice answered the call, "This is 9-1-1…how can I help you?"

The man said, "There's something landing on the White House lawn!"

The voice said, "Sir, do not make prank calls here…it is a felony offense."

The man continued, "It's not a prank!"

The voice continued, "Sir I will have to re…"

She was cut off by her supervisor.

Linda instructed her camera crew to start filming. With the zoom lens they could see the ship close up. She marveled in its design. Nothing like it had ever been seen before. It was white with a gold horizontal stripe going down the side until it met an emblem that looked like a family crest.

Linda was ready to begin her report.

The Cameraman started, "Five, four, three, two, one and go."

Linda began to announce, "I'm here…live in front of the White House with hundreds of people who have witnessed what can only be called a spacecraft landing on the White House lawn.

We do not know if this is some kind of new technology being demonstrated by the government or if in fact we have visitors from another world. All attempts to reach the White House have not produced any results."

Linda reported, "We are witnessing what has to be the arrival of visitors from another planet. As we zoom in on the greeting that is taking place on the White House lawn between President Davis and what appears to be at least five people who were on board the craft."

"Wait…we are now receiving word…that…yes…President Davis has announced that there will be a news conference concerning the ship and the visitors in 30 minutes. We are on our way to the White House briefing room! This is Linda Hayes reporting from Pennsylvania Avenue."

Once off camera Linda screamed, "Let's roll I want to be in the front of the room! This is the biggest story of our lives. Let's move people!"

***

President Davis led the royal party to the oval office.

President Davis excused himself, "King Abimelech…forgive me…I must attend to some business. Please…have a seat. My assistant will get you a drink."

King Abimelech replied, "Thank you President Davis. We await your return."

Once outside, President Davis was cornered by his aides.

"Sir, you really should have more security with you. Our top leaders are all in that room. At least let me put one security officer in the room" ask the head of the Presidents security team?

President Davis responded, "Okay…two outside the door and one inside the room with us. He is to remain in obscurity, do you hear me?"

The security team chief responded, "Yes and thank you sir."

President Davis looked himself over and returned to the oval office where King Abimelech was waiting.

***

President Davis came back in the room followed by a member of his security team. The secret service agent remained at the door and the President took a seat next to King Abimelech.

President Davis began speaking, "Well King Abimelech...I trust you find the brandy to your liking?"

King Abimelech replied, "It is very good sir...I thank you. You should try some of my wine on Shalom. It is also very good. One day before our planet dies I will have you over to my palace in return for your hospitality."

President Davis said, "That would be great King Abimelech. "

King Abimelech began saying, "It has been a long journey for my people. When will they be allowed to join us on your wonderful planet?"

President Davis answered, "We have to take you before our United Nations assembly. We asked for and was granted an emergency special meeting later today in New York City. At this meeting the President of the United Nations will formally welcome you to Earth. Before the day is out I am sure you will be given permission to bring the rest of your envoy to Earth."

King Abimelech asked, "So how is it that you don't have one leader for your world?"

President Davis answered, "In our history no one group of people has ever ruled the world. We believe in each nation governing themselves. Therefore there are many nations and leaders over all of them."

"Don't get me wrong there have been attempts to unify the world under one leadership. Some attempts were hostile and a few peaceful but to date none have worked. "

King Abimelech replied, "However, you must admit things would be smoother under one leader...would it not?"

President Davis responded, "Given this situation...yes it would. However, we have never had a visitor from another planet before. This is a first for our world. Maybe now we will pursue a world with one leader."

King Abimelech announced, "Well…let us toast to brotherhood and peace. May we become good friends now and forever?"

President Davis raised his glass in a toast to celebrate the occasion. He wondered just how great his legacy as president will become now that he was the man who allowed the visitors to land on Earth.

***

"Carolyn, I need a speech and I need it yesterday. It must strike an accord of peace and not of fear and concern. The people must believe that these people are here in the name of peace. They must know that King Abimelech is here on a peaceful mission," shouted Vice President Woods as he hurried back to his office.

Carolyn Jeffers, the Vice President's speech writer replied, "Yes sir. I'll get right on it."

Vice President Woods commanded, "Yesterday Carolyn…. yesterday!"

***

Charlie was at his job and some of his co-workers ran to the television to see the news report. Charlie ran with them to see what was happening.

Charlie asked, "What is going on? Why is everyone running to the television?"

One of his co-workers responded, "There's a strange spaceship landing right on the White House lawn. This is history man!"

Charlie pushed his way to the front of the group. When he got in view of the television he saw the camera zoom in on the passengers exiting the spaceship. He saw King Abimelech and his royal court exit the shuttle.

Charlie smiled. Now he knew he would no longer have to pretend to be one of these miserable Adaminians. He was ready to kill Professor Hai and his daughter. He even wanted to kill Shannon because she annoyed him so much. But most of all he wanted his revenge on Lieutenant Oded.

The co-worker asked Charlie, "What are you smiling so hard about? I think I have never seen you smile before."

Charlie responded, "You are right my friend. It is history and a great day in it as well!"

***

As the meeting was taking place in the oval office the news conference was beginning in the White Housing briefing room. The room was packed to capacity with reports and cameramen. Before the Vice President could come out and deliver the speech he received a phone call from the head of WWAS Jack McClusky. Vice President Woods suspected that Jack wanted the first question to go to his reporter at the White House.

Vice President Woods answered the phone, "Jack…I was expecting your call. I'm surprised it took this long."

Jack answered, "I couldn't get to you. It's almost impossible to get through to the White House."

Vice President Woods replied, "That's understandable considering what's going on. You want the first question to go to Linda, right?"

Jack responded, "What good is having a friend in the White House if you can't leverage them."

Vice President Woods said, "Jack I'll take care of you. You knew I would even if I hadn't spoken to you. Gotta go my friend."

Jack replied, "Thanks my friend. I owe you."

Vice President Woods said before he hung up, "You always will Jack."

***

The White House Press Secretary said, "Good morning. Today is a momentous day not only for the United States but for entire world. Today Vice President Woods will brief you on the landing of a spacecraft on the White House lawn about an hour ago.

Please no questions during the briefing. Once he is done then he will select three questions. If he calls on you…you get one question and no more. Ladies and gentlemen…I present to you…the Vice President of the United States."

Everyone in the room began clapping as the Vice President came into the room. He was accompanied by two secret service agents, his assistant and his speech writer. Vice President Woods took his place on the podium and settle himself in to speak.

Vice President Woods began his speech, "Good morning ladies and gentlemen here in the White House and around the world. Today at 9:32 am Eastern Standard time we received a communication from a space craft containing five men from the planet Shalom."

"This planet is approximately 20 light years away from Earth. The peace envoy made this long journey from their planet in the hope that they could establish peace between our worlds. They lost some lives in the process but they hoped that it would be worth it in the end."

"The members of the shuttle asked for permission to land on our planet in the name of peace. President Davis granted permission for them to land and we provided them with coordinates that would put them down on the White House lawn for this historic event.

"President Davis and I want to iterate to everyone that this is a peaceful meeting of two worlds and nothing more. There is nothing to fear. President Davis is having conversations with the leader of the envoy as we speak and he has been assured that peace is at the center of this visit."

"The leader of the envoy has requested permission to bring a peace envoy consisting of approximately 1,000 people. These people will land in several countries to exchange ideas and ways of doing business.

The Shaloman people are willing to give us technology to build our own warp driven spaceships, translator devices, as well as medicines that can cure aliments that we have not been able to cure on Earth.

In exchange they want us to provide some land for some of their people. Their world is dying and they estimate that in 10 years the planet will become uninhabitable. They are willing to provide us information to help prevent the same thing from happening here."

"Later today the peace envoy will go in front of an emergency assembly of the United Nations to be formally welcomed to Earth and to request permission to bring the rest of their peace envoy to Earth. All the world's leaders will be able to state their opinion and vote on this historical event."

Vice president Woods looked directly at Linda Hayes.

Then he concluded by saying, "Now, I will take questions. Ms. Hayes from WWAS channel 6."

Linda asked, "Sir, Do we know if these people are descendants from Earth?"

Vice President Woods answered, "We do not know that as of yet. Until the United Nations grants permission for the envoy to land we will not be conducting any experiments. The Shaloman scientists are eager as I'm sure our scientists are to get to work on things of that nature.

"Now I'll take one from Diane of WKOR News 7."

Diane Allen, a news anchor for WKOR asked, "Sir, I noticed that we are at DEFCON 4. Are we sure this is not a ploy to trick us to have our defenses down so that they can attack us?"

Vice President Woods replied, "Diane…I assure you and the rest of the world that we have taken precautions to prevent any surprise attacks. These people are humble people and if they wanted to attack us they could have without asking permission. The last one will be from Allen of WWNS radio."

Allen asked, "Sir, if you say this is a peace envoy and it has taken them a year to get here how is it that they know how to speak our language and why are they hiding the rest of their people in the stars somewhere?"

Vice President Woods responded, "Well Allen that's actually two questions."

The room chuckled a little.

Vice President Woods continued, "They are 'hiding' their ships and people in the stars because of any preconceptions by us. If they had shown up at our doorstep with two very large ships, would we have believed they were here in peace?

As for our language I am told they have a translator that is actually translating our language to them and allowing us to hear them in our own language. They have marvelous technology that we have only seen on Star Trek. They are also willing to share this technology with us."

"Imagine the possibilities that are at our fingertips right now. We will be able to speak and understand everyone in the world. No more language barriers. Unfortunately, linguist will be out of work."

Again the room chuckled as the Vice President attempted to keep a light and humorous atmosphere.

Vice President Woods continued, "That's only the beginning of what we can learn about them. I am told that there are a multitude of planets out there that are Earth like. With our new ships we will have the means to explore them. Our population problems will be solved. No more real estate problems. We will be able to move those who want to move to another planet. We will have interplanetary travel back and forth between planets."

"My friends this is a historical event and we have the pleasure to live this day and see it come to life. Do not allow prejudice and fear to rule you. Instead let's roar into the unknown and learn from our new friends. Thank you and have a great day."

The White House Press Secretary retook the podium and announced, "Thank you for attending this news conference."

Vice President Woods walked off the stage as the reporters began dialing their respective numbers. He suspected they were trying to be the first to report the story from the White House.

***

It was the end of the work day and Tony made his way up from the basement and his isolation. Tony had to be in the basement at 6:00 that morning and was not released until 2:00 that afternoon. He was tired and ready to go home and rest. He had to go to the main office and check out for the day.

When he arrived he saw a group of scientists gathered around the television watching the speech by Vice President Woods. He saw Professor Simmons and she appeared to be excited. As he got closer he saw her turn and run to him.

"Tony," she shouted, "You've got to come and see this. It's about our visitors from the stars."

Tony was taken back by her words and looked at her confusingly. He asked, "Visitors...what visitors?"

She answered, "Oh...I forgot you haven't been in touch with the outside world. Come see this."

Tony joined the others watching TV. He looked at the television which was showing footage of the royal court exiting the shuttle. The sight sent a sudden chill up and down his spinal cord. His legs went limp and he had to catch himself to avoid falling to the floor. His worst nightmare had come to life. He saw King Abimelech as he arrived on Earth.

These were the faces of people he thought he would never see again. He shutter at the sight of King Abimelech shaking hands with the President of the United States. His stomach churn inside as the two leaders posed for a photograph.

Professor Simmons broke his thoughts by asking, "Tony...are you okay?"

Tony did not say a word. He continued staring at the screen as if he was seeing ghosts.

The footage switched to Vice President Woods telling of the King's long journey from Shalom. Tony realized that he was the only person in the room who knew that was a lie. Tony could not image how they got to Earth. He had destroyed all of his documents and research. He never gave him the coordinates. He wondered, *"How did he do it?"*

Tony turned and ran to his car.

Professor Simmons shouted, "Tony...where are you going?"

He still didn't answer. His only thought was to get to his daughter and he drove home as fast as he could to get there.

***

Shannon and Liz were running home as well after they saw what was taking place on the news. Liz, like her father was terrified. Her greatest fear had come to life. The man who killed her mother and so many others was now on the same planet as she was.

Shannon shouted as they were running, "Liz, what in world are you so worried about? This is the greatest day in our history. We get to see visitors from another planet! I'm so excited!"

Liz looked coldly at her but she realized that Shannon did not know what she knew. If she did she would shutter at the thought of these people being on Earth.

Liz yelled, "Shut up! I have to get home in a hurry. I can't stop and be excited about this with you."

***

As Tony drove up to the apartment he saw Shannon and Liz running down the sidewalk. Tony hated that Liz had brought Shannon with her. This was not the time to involve outsiders.

Tony almost yelled but caught himself, "Why did you bring Shannon? This is not the time."

Tony turned and rushed to the front door. Liz and Shannon followed. Once at the door, Tony hurriedly opened it. He allowed the girls to go first but then got angry when they stopped at the door almost blocking his way in. As he got in he saw Charlie standing there with a gun pointed at them.

Charlie ordered, "Close the door and raise your hands in the air."

Tony said, "Charlie...what are you doing with that thing? Put it away."

Charlie responded, "I can't do that Professor. I have lived among you and the rest of these idiot people long enough. Now my King is here and we will take this place as our own! You...my friend...have outlived your usefulness."

Tony was shocked for the second time today. He began to doubt that the Lord had granted him any favor by bringing him to Earth. Now he thought he would be the tool to destroy the planet he had come to love so much and the planet were he was born still would not be free. How could God do this to him?

"Tamir, how could you? You have been my assistant for years. You know of peace. It was you who gave my research to the King? You caused the lost of so many lives of our friends and family back on Gomorrah," asked Tony?

Charlie, proud of deeds responded, "My name is not Charlie and it is not Tamir. I am Samuel. I will have my revenge on you and the resistance for killing my father...especially Lieutenant Oded!"

"It was difficult to smile and pretend to help you but now I can take my rightful place as governor in the Kings new government here on Adamina. We will make slaves of these pitiful people and I personally will see to it that they do nothing but work for our leisure."

Tony asked, "Your father? Lieutenant Oded did not kill your father. If you are Samuel then your father was one of us. General Idit found this out and had his men kill him. Lieutenant Oded found his body lying in a ditch behind the palace. His last words were for Lieutenant Oded to save you...his son!"

Charlie yelled, "You lie! I do not hear your words!"

Tony continued, "It is not a lie. In all the years you have known me...have I ever once lied...about anything?"

Tony appeared to have Charlie attention. He appeared to be hesitating. Tony was hoping that Tamir had come to see him as an honest and forthright man.

Charlie said, "General Idit came to me after the death of my father and told me Lieutenant Oded was the man who killed him. I wondered how he could know that so fast."

Tony noticed that he had Charlie thinking about it.

Tony took this opportunity and said, "Samuel, your father was a very good friend of mine and Lieutenant Oded. One thing is for sure... Lieutenant Oded would not have killed him."

"I remember clearly the night Lieutenant Oded found the body. He came to headquarters and mourned the death of your father. He wanted to go to the palace and kill General Idit that night. I stopped him because we needed him to stay undercover for us. He wanted to go and find you...take care of you like your father...his friend asked but General Idit had already gotten to your quarters. After that no one could find you for years. We all thought you and your brothers were dead. My friend I assure you...Lieutenant Oded did not kill your father."

Tony saw tears beginning to stream down Charlie's face. Tony now knew he had gotten through to him. He actually felt sorry for Charlie. He had spent all these years betraying the resistance...the organization that his father supported. Tony couldn't hate him even though he had betrayed and helped caused the death of his wife.

Charlie turned the gun to his head and said, "I do not deserve to live any longer!"

Tony yelled, "Samuel no! Your father would not want this! You can still help us."

Charlie through his tears asked, "How?"

Tony said, "Look...General Idit thinks you are still on his side. All you have to do is feed him some misinformation. Hopefully we can get to Lieutenant Oded and any other resistance members on board the ship. Maybe they have a way to destroy the ships. Help us Charlie. Don't kill yourself!"

Tony watched closely for any sign that was reaching Charlie. He thought of him as a son. He could not stand to see him kill himself. Tony began to notice that the arm that Charlie held the gun in was slowly dropping down.

Tony was caught off guard as Shannon jumped over and grabbed the gun from Charlie. Tony grabbed Charlie and began to console him. Tony motioned for Liz to join them.

After a minute Liz screamed, "What are you doing?"

Tony shouted, "Liz…what is it?"

Liz pointed at Shannon and Tony turned only to receive his third shock of the day. Shannon was now pointing the gun at them.

Tony said, "Shannon…you don't understand what is happening here. Let me…"

Before he could finish Shannon fired a shot and Tony thought the swish sounded loud as a cannon as the bullet passed through the barrel, silencer, and finally through the heart of Charlie.

Tony could not believe that Charlie who just a minute prior was going to take his own life was now dead on the floor in a pool of his own blood.

Shannon said, "Weak…he was a weak man. All he had to do was finish both of you off. Well…I guess it's up to me now!"

She aimed the gun at Liz but Tony stepped in front. They both shouted for their lives. As Shannon began to squeeze the trigger the front door flung open knocking the gun out of Shannon's hand and knocked her to the floor. When her hand was hit she squeezed the trigger and the shot went through the front corner of the roof. Tony hoped that no one was at home in the apartment above it. Tony grabbed the gun and pointed it at Shannon.

Pastor Bell asked as he surveyed the room, "What's going on here? I heard all the shouting as I was getting out of my car. Charlie…is he… dead?"

Tony answered, "I am afraid so…at the hands of this one."

Pastor Bell said, "This child? Why on Earth would she kill Charlie?"

Shannon answered, "You all will die at the hands of my husband… General Idit! He will come for me and kill you all."

Pastor Bell looked at Tony and said, "I guess our visitors are from your planet."

Tony responded, "Yes they are. I must get in touch with Professor Simmons. I have to tell her the truth about them. Earth cannot trust these wicked men."

***

They bounded and gagged Shannon until they could figure out what to do with her. Tony and Pastor Bell left to get to the church and then to take care of Charlie's body. Liz was frustrated and mad with Shannon. She had truly betrayed her. She used her to stay close to her father. For what reason…Liz had to know for what reason.

Liz screamed, "How…how could you do this. We were 'girls'! That's what you always said!"

"You do not know the pleasures of being with a man like General Idit. I pity you. You make me sick," replied Shannon in a low tone filled with hatred!

"You betrayed me over a man like General Idit! How could you be so stupid," asked Liz?

"It was easy. I just pictured your death each day," replied Shannon.

Liz said, "I cannot believe the General would allow you…a woman to make this journey alone. Who was with you?"

Shannon replied, "There were three of us in the beginning. My sister and a scientist in the General's army came with me. Daniel was his name. Pathetic man…he fell in love with some Adamain woman. The fool…he wanted to marry her. He was going to turn on my husband when he arrived. He was going to tell the Adamians who we were. I slipped in his apartment and killed them both. I made it appear like a robbery. Stupid Adamians…they believed it was.

Diana…my sister began to enjoy the life of Adamain women. She wanted it for herself. She was my sister but I puked at the sight of her. How could she turn on her people? I poisoned her meal and watched her as she gagged, kicked, and screamed for her little life."

She said, "I don't know you at all."

***

The following morning, the emergency assembly of the United Nations met in New York City to discuss the arrival of King Abimelech and his peace envoy. King Abimelech and his peace envoy were introduced and formally welcomed to Earth.

The President of the General Assembly made the welcome, "We the people of Earth welcome King Abimelech of the planet Shalom to our humble planet."

The members applauded and the President continued, "Our planet is not like your planet Sir, in which one person rules. Our planet is ruled by many and each has a voice here in this assembly. Therefore we cannot grant you leave to bring your entire envoy to Earth as of yet."

"However, if you can be patient, I am sure we will all agree that in the interest of peace your entire envoy waiting amongst the stars will be welcomed to join us here on Earth."

The King stood and acknowledged the United Nations President and said, "It is an honor to be here on Earth. We first saw your planet in the stars what you would term a decade ago."

"Then one of your years ago we started this long journey to meet you. The journey has been rough and some did not survive it. We gathered much information and in the interest of peace we will gladly share it with you."

"As a gesture of good faith we offer you the schematics to our translators. With these you will be able to understand everyone you come into contact with in your own language. There will be no need for someone to translate for you."

"In our journeys to other worlds we saw this as a valuable asset to have in our possession. I strive for peace and brotherhood for our two worlds!"

Everyone in the room applauded the comments made by King Abimelech. He noted how gullible they were as each of them displayed a sense of brotherhood and peace on their face. King Abimelech knew he was succeeding in his quest to convince them that this is a peaceful mission.

He waved his hands at the leaders of the Earth and in his mind he thought of hanging them all in front of the people. He thought this would get the attention of everyone and place him as the feared ruler of this world. The throne of Adamina was within his reach. He would contact General Idit and let him know all was going according to plan.

***

All the countries of the world were excited and worried at the same time. Ashlee sat on the train and listened to people as they talked around her. Marion was with her and they both laughed at some of the comments.

Some people warned that the visitors were going to attack, some said they are beautiful people and want to live harmoniously with us. Some knew that attack was for sure to come in the days to follow. Everywhere Ashlee went she heard nothing but the news of the visitors.

While on a blue line subway train Ashlee heard a homeless person warn everyone, "They will destroy us…they will destroy us! You will see…you will all see!"

Others laughed and said, "We have friends from another world. There is nothing to be afraid of."

Marion inquired, "So what do you think?"

Ashlee replied, "I don't know what to think. I guess it's understandable that there could be other people in our universe. We shouldn't be thinking that we are the only planet with life on it. But as far as them wanting to attack us or not…I don't know. I don't think anyone really does."

Marion responded, "You're right. All we can do is keep on living and praying."

A young man was listening to them.

He leaned over and said, "This is all a Hollywood movie trick!"

They all laughed and continued throwing out ideas and jokes to anyone who would listen.

***

Solomon and Gabriel were having lunch at Union Station in Washington DC. Everyone in the restaurant was discussing the visitors.

Solomon said, "Man, I can't believe the times we are living in. Visitors from out of space...I would have never dreamed of seeing something like this in my life."

Gabriel responded, "You and me both. Do you think it's real? I mean, do you really think they are here in peace?"

Solomon replied, "All I can say is this is an exciting time and we should sit back and enjoy it."

***

In Waldorf, Maryland, Pastor Bell was having a meeting with his leaders and the subject was the visitors. He had to attend this meeting but his mind was certainly on Tony and Liz. Tony had agreed to wait for him to return before calling Professor Simmons. Pastor Bell had to get out of this meeting so he could get back to them.

Pastor Bell spoke, "My friends we are facing something that we have never faced in our lives before. We must pray for our brothers and sisters from the stars as well as the people here on Earth. Our leaders must be guided by the Word of God and not by their own ambitions. Many people are trying to make money from this but we must be of good conscience and treat these visitors as our brothers and sisters."

One of the leaders asked, "Pastor the Bible doesn't speak on visitors from outer space. How should we proceed in this issue?"

Pastor Bell responded by saying, "We have no way of knowing if Earth was the only planet that God inhabited with his people. There is a massive universe we live in and these people are God's people just as we are. We don't know if Eden was actually on Earth or there is another planet out there called Eden. These people are human just like we are and therefore we must believe they are God's people as well. There is no difference and the Word of God is never wrong."

In his mind Pastor Bell was thinking what on Earth can we do against these people. I know that they are our worst enemy but I can't tell anyone this information. If Tony tells Professor Simmons then she will have to tell more government officials. Then I'm afraid my friend will be imprisoned or worst. Who knows what the government will do with him once they know that he's from Gomorrah. Will they even believe him?

He asked himself, *"Should I have taken them to the authorities in the beginning? I guess it's to late for that kind of talk. We just need to convience Professor Simmons for the threat and go from there. God please be with us."*

***

"Sire, they are truly falling for our plan. How much longer will we have to keep up this despicable kindness," Pesach asked the King.

King Abimelech responded, "Don't worry my loyal subject. The attack force will be given authorization to land any day now and Adamina's defenses will be caught on the ground. We will crush them like grapes!"

Pesach asked, "Sire, I have not heard from our spies."

King Abimelech replied, "Not to worry Pesach. The Adamians do not have weapons that can contend with us. Even if Professor Hai is able to warn them, we will still destroy them!"

***

Aboard one of the cruisers, Lieutenant Oded was taken from his prison.

One of the guards said, "The General would like to speak to you."

Lieutenant Oded responded, "What choice do I have?"

The guard said, "None."

The guard then grabbed Lieutenant Oded while the other one supervised. Lieutenant Oded watched as a Gomorrite woman walked by him and caught the attention of the guard who was doing the supervising.

At that moment the guard who grabbed Lieutenant Oded slipped something into the Lieutenant's pocket. Lieutenant Oded looked at him and the guard nodded his head to show allegiance.

As the other guard turned his attention back to them, Lieutenant Oded straighten up and started to walk with them to see General Idit.

Lieutenant Oded was brought into the conference room where General Idit was waiting. Lieutenant Oded saw it had a view of the stars that was no less than astounding. He had not seen the stars during any of the trip.

General Idit said, "Lieutenant...gaze upon the galaxy and all her stars...her wonders. There, Adamina lies ready for the taking. Is it not more beautiful than anything you have ever gazed upon?"

Lieutenant Oded responded, "It is truly amazing but I'm sure you did not call me here to look upon the stars of Adamina."

General Idit turned to him and said, "Right to business...I can respect that. In fact, I liked that about you Lieutenant. I was truly saddened to confirm that you were a traitor."

Lieutenant Oded said, "I doubt that."

General Idit responded, "Correct. I was happy...very happy."

Lieutenant Oded asked, "Why have you kept me alive all this time? Is it to be the first hanged on Adamina?"

General Idit answered, "Your death will come soon. I promised a young man, you might know as Tamir, that he could have the honor of killing you. He thirsts for it so much. After all he thinks you killed his father."

Lieutenant Oded was confused, "Tamir...I do not even know his father."

General Idit smiled and chuckled, "But you do. Except Tamir's real name is Samuel. Now do you remember his father?"

Lieutenant Oded looked coldly at General Idit and said, "You are a coward, a liar, and a murder! You killed Samuel's father!"

General Idit laughed and boastfully said, "Yes I did...and it was very enjoyable watching him beg for his miserable life! Then I got to turn his son into a spy for me by blaming his father's murder on you. Now I will get to see Samuel kill his father's friend. What a world we live in."

Lieutenant Oded responded, "Your day will come."

General Idit replied, "Yes...but not this day. Take him back to his cell."

Lieutenant Oded felt the guard grab his arm and guide him out of the room. There was only one guard taking Lieutenant Oded back to his cell. It was the same guard that had slipped the object into this pocket earlier.

Lieutenant Oded asked, "Why are you..."

The guard quickly quieted him, "Shhh."

He then motioned for Lieutenant Oded to continue moving.

Once they were close to the cell the guard began to say, "There are cameras all over the ship except in this area. General Idit does not expect that they are needed back here.

The object in your pocket is a communicator. Professor Hai has a receiver. Send him the information on the file and he will be able to defeat our ships. However, if we cannot get off the ships we will die along with the Gomorrite forces."

Lieutenant Oded asked, "Why are you helping me?"

The guard answered, "Samuel was not the only son Saar had. My name is Zur, the youngest son. I learned of the General's assassination of my father years ago. I tried to find Samuel but I could not.

Then I found out he was working with Professor Hai under a different name. I did not know what to think so I remained quiet until I could figure out what to do.

Several of us obtained these communicators in the hope that one of us would succeed in transmitting the information to the Professor. I know that I would not have a chance because I am always with other guards. "

Lieutenant Oded said, "I don't know if I can trust you...anyone for that matter."

Zur asked, "What have you to lose?"

Lieutenant Oded thought about it and agreed that he did not have any other options at the moment. He would keep the communicator.

Lieutenant Oded asked, "Why don't you send it now?"

Zur said, "We are not in range. We have to be in orbit around Adamina for it to work. We could not use a stronger communicator for fear that it would be picked up by the ship. You are in the safest position on the ship because there are no cameras back here. Please trust me."

Lieutenant Oded said, "You will have to let me know when we are in orbit."

Zur said, "Someone will if not me. Thank you my brother and may God be with us all.

***

Pastor Bell and Tony attempted to hide Charlie's body. At some point the smell would alert a neighbor that something was wrong.

They had managed to avoid detection with all the screaming because everyone was so involved in the news of the visitors.

They drove the body to the field where they hid Professor Hai's shuttle a year ago. By the time they dug the grave and buried the body is was very early the next morning.

Somehow Tony had to get word to the resistance that he was still alive. Then he had to explain to Professor Simmons who he really is and that their new found friends were bent on destroying them.

CHAPTER 8

THE WARNING

The next day the sun was high in the morning sky. Pastor Bell returned to the apartment where Tony and Liz were waiting. Shannon was still bound and gagged. Pastor Bell didn't know what he should do but together they would decide. He thought, *My God, in a few hours this country…this world…might be in a war and the outcome could depend on what they decide now.*

"Pastor Bell…it is good to see you again. I was beginning to worry," said Tony.

Pastor Bell responded, "How are you sir?"

Tony replied, "It's not been easy but we're hanging on. Liz had to keep Shannon gagged because she continued to scream and shout out obscenities throughout the night."

Pastor Bell took a seat on the couch. He looked over at Shannon who was sitting in the corner of the room. He thought, *Her stare is so cold."* Pastor Bell could feel the air of hatred in the room.

To Pastor Bell the room felt chilling and it held a hatred he had never felt in his life. He silently prayed for Shannon's soul.

He knew his friends, Tony and Liz, felt this cold, bitter hatred before. He wondered how they dealt with it every day of their lives.

Pastor Bell said, "What are we going to do? If we do nothing Earth may be destroyed. On the other hand if we do tell them about you then we open us ourselves up to criminal charges. I'm willing to do this if necessary. Only you know just how bad these people can be."

"Imagine your worst nightmare coming to life and multiply that by 100. Still you would not know the terror these people can employ. They thirst on their desire to inflict pain on anyone. They take joy in spilling the blood of the innocent. They won't care about you or anything you stand for. They will trample over anyone who stands in their way of taking this world back," Tony proclaimed.

He continued, "I will contact Professor Simmons and determine the best way to turn myself in to the authorities. Hopefully she will help me get word to your leaders that King Abimelech can't be trusted. I will keep you and Liz out of it. Take Liz with you so I will know that she is safe," asked Tony.

Pastor Bell insisted, "Tony...I can't let you take all of this on your shoulders. I have to be there for you during this time."

Tony responded, "Sir...you have been there for me and my family since the day we arrived. I am thankful to God for placing you near that open field a year ago. Were it not for you I do not know what we would have done. Please take my daughter so that no one can find her. If something were to happen to me, at least I would know that she is still alive. The war...if it comes...will need people like you."

Liz said, "I can't let you do this father."

Tony replied, "My child. You are all that I have left. I must protect you. Your mother gave her life so that we could come here. Now I must make a sacrifice. You will be safe with Pastor Bell. He is a good man."

"Pastor, please take Malka to a safe place. I must do this to have a chance to save your world and mine."

"I will take her my friend and she will be safe. Be blessed my brother...be blessed," replied Pastor Bell.

Liz moaned, "Father...no..."

Tony begged, "Liz...my child...please go. Please. I cannot do this without knowing that you are safe."

***

Pastor Bell and Malka walked out of the apartment and Tony sat down on the couch and pondered his next move. He really liked

Professor Simmons and this was going to be hard for him to do. Also there was Shannon and what to do with her?

Tony tuned Shannon out as she continued to grunt at him. He kept watch over her because he knew she wanted to get free of her bindings and kill him.

Tony continued to ponder whether he should call Professor Simmons or not. He wished there was another way. No matter what he thought about he kept coming back to the same answer. The only way Earth was going to have a chance against the Gomorrite army was for him to turn himself in to the authorities. He would make the sacrifice and call.

He picked up his cell phone and search through his recently dialed list. It didn't take him long to find her number and hit the green button to dial it.

She answered.

"Professor Simmons, I must talk you," Tony's voice sounded anxious.

"Tony, you were supposed to report to work today. I haven't seen or heard from you since you ran out of here yesterday. Where are you and please call me Cassy," asked Professor Simmons?

"I'm sorry but there are things that you do not know about me. However, the time has come that you should know. Please come to my apartment so we can talk," replied Tony.

"Tony, I don't think I should come to your home. People might talk...more," Professor Simmons responded.

Tony could sense her smiling over the phone.

"Cassy this is very, urgent. Please come over now," Tony said sternly.

"O...kay...I will be there in an hour," said Professor Simmons.

After hanging up the phone he sat there and thought about all the horrific things he had witnessed in his life.

He remembered his wife and how brave she was. He thought of his family...his mother and father. They were brave people as well. He thought about the times when his mother would tell him how special he was and that he was destined to do great things.

He remembered what she often said to him, "Destiny has its way of working things out for us". She was right. Destiny was God and he would work things out for them. He dropped to his knees and began to pray.

***

Shortly after Tony finished praying, Professor Simmons arrived. When she entered the room she saw a young girl bound and tied up in the corner of the room with a look of hate impressed on her face. Professor Simmons did not understand what was going on and the questions were mounting in her mind but first she had to hear Tony out.

"Professor...I mean...Cassy, please understand I could not divulge any of this to anyone in the past and you will now understand why I hesitated on taking the job opportunity you offered me in the past," stated Tony.

Professor Simmons sat down and replied, "Okay, go on. Why is she tied up? Who is she?"

"Cassy...please be patient. The visitors are not who they are pretending to be. They are an invasion force from a planet named Gomorrah," stated Tony.

"Gomorrah," questioned Professor Simmons. "That was the city people believed God destroyed in the Bible. We all know it was only a meteorite. You see..."

Tony cut her off and continued, "God did destroy our city."

Professor Simmons interrupted, "Our city?"

Tony continued, "Cassy please. My people use to live there. But they were and still are an evil people and God destroyed our city along with the city of Sodom. However, my ancestors plead for their lives and asked God not to destroy them with the city. The Sodomites laughed and didn't believe they would die or that their city would be destroyed."

After a deep breath he continued, "God knew that most of us were still an evil people and would always be that way. Because of that we were whisked away to another planet to live. We call it Gomorrah after our original city. Even though God blessed the land with enough food and water for us to live on, my people hated living on Gomorrah. They believe that their birthright is to rule here on Earth which we call Adamina."

"The scientists of my world were asked to find Earth and create the technology to get us there. That was our primary mission for 5,000 years and I discovered Earth many years ago but withheld the information from the King. I continued to lead him along making him believe that I was not able to find it. My wife paid a high price for that deception. The King killed my wife because he knew I had the coordinates and didn't provide them to him."

"My assistant was a spy for the King and that is how he came by the coordinates to your world. For that I am truly sorry. "

"The resistance, which I am the leader, planned an uprising to overthrow the King and end his reign over our people. Unfortunately we didn't realize the King had spies amongst us and he discovered our plan. Me, and my daughter fled to come here to Earth. We were to make our home here and live out our lives in the hope that we could get some help to return to Gomorrah and overthrow the King. They are not here in peace...they are here to take over Adamina...Earth"

The Professor was astounded by this information and she replied "Wait, didn't they say they were from a planet called Shalom? Why would they conceal the name of their home world?"

"They know that history has taught you the evilness of the name Gomorrah. If they told you they came from Gomorrah then you might not believe that they are a peaceful people. The welcoming envoy is really an attack fleet designed to take your world by surprise, defeat you, live in your cities and make slaves of all of us."

"How can they tell the difference between me and you" asked Professor Simmons?

"Our blood contains a high concentrate of titanium oxide. Many believe that it is a curse of the devil." If you test my blood you will find it too contains titanium oxide. This is necessary to prevent our sun from burning our skin. In the early years we had to inject titanium oxide into our bodies to help against the sun. These injections lead to a natural buildup of titanium oxide in our bodies as we evolved.

Our evolution also included the development of a second eyelid. The extreme brightness on Gomorrah caused many to become blind in the early years. However, with this second eyelid which allows more of the sun to be blocked out, blindness is no longer a major issue on

Gomorrah. We have evolved differently than you because we were removed from this planet," answered Tony.

Professor Simmons looked in Tony's eyes. She could see something that looked like a second eyelid. She began to ask herself, *"Could it be possible that she was wrong and the Bible was right. Could Sodom and Gomorrah's destruction be the work of God and not a meteorite as she argued on several occasions? Could she now be in the presence of a man from another planet in the universe?"*

She had so many questions and not enough time to answer them all. She now realized that if all of this is true then Earth could be in trouble and something must be done. However, what if it wasn't true?

Professor Simmons said, "Tony, I want to believe you but you're asking me to take this all in and believe it so fast. I don't know if I can do that."

Tony responded, "The longer you wait the less time Earth will have to defend itself."

The Professor replied, "O…kay…that's no pressure…none at all. Give me some solid evidence. Something I can take back other than your word."

"Your evidence is sitting right in this chair," said Tony as he pointed at Shannon.

Professor Simmons looked at Shannon. She thought she saw a look that desired to kill but now her face held a pitiful look. Shannon motioned to have her gag removed so she could speak. Tony removed the gag.

"Miss…he's been holding me against my will now for days. He's delirious and he concocted this story. He's made me some sort of villain in all of it. Please let me go. I've been tied up for hours. Please," Shannon pled.

"This is not true. She is a wife of General Idit. The most evil military mind in the history of Gomorrah. You cannot believe her," said Tony.

Professor Simmons was perplexed and did not know who to believe. She questioned herself, *"Was Tony having some sort of mental breakdown? Was this girl that she had met for the first time telling the truth? What should she do?"*

Shannon added, "Miss I think he hit his head on the floor while the news was replaying the visitors landing. He probably has a concussion and got it all confused in his head… he doesn't know what's real and what's made up. For God's sake…me and Liz are best friends! Please help me. Ma'am…I haven't even been to the bathroom."

Professor Simmons yelled, "Tony…what's wrong with you? The poor girl hasn't even been to the bathroom. We have to get you some help."

Professor Simmons started walking over to Shannon to free her so she could go to the bathroom. She chastised herself for believing Tony's story. Professor Simmons began untying Shannon.

Professor Simmons continued, "Tony, we have to get you to…"

Bang! As soon as her hands were loose Shannon struck Professor Simmons in the face with her fist knocking her to the floor. Professor Simmons was stunned and rolled over trying to get her bearings.

She saw Tony attempt to grab Shannon. Shannon swung at him with the dinette chair that she was tied too. Tony blocked the blow but it knocked him off balance.

As the battle raged Shannon was shouting, "I will kill you both where you stand! My husband will not go easy on you. He will have his way with you…you pitiful Earth girl! Then he will give me the honor of killing you with my bare hands."

Shannon then turned and ran for the door; she unlocked it and ran out of the apartment. Professor Simmons felt terrible for what she had done. She should have believed Tony.

Tony ran after her and Professor Simmons ran after him. They got in the street and Professor Simmons saw Shannon running down Smallwood drive. She started to run after her but Tony grabbed her by the arm.

She said, "Tony, I have to go after her. This is my fault."

Tony replied, "If you do it will attract attention. Let her go. What could she do?"

A neighbor up on the balcony asked, "Is everything okay down there Tony?"

Tony responded, "Yeah Ted everything's okay. Just have some issues with my daughter and her friends. You know how teenagers can be."

Ted responded, "Yeah tell me about it. Have a good one."

Tony replied, "Thanks Ted…you too."

Professor Simmons looked at Tony and whispered, "I'm sorry. I should have listened to you."

Tony responded, "It's okay. Destiny has a way of working things out. I still have evidence if you need it. I can take you to my ship."

"Tony...I have to call the FBI. I have no choice," said Professor Simmons.

Tony replied, "I understand. I just hope we can stop this invasion."

***

Professor Simmons was completely rattled by the events surrounding Shannon. She pulled out her cell phone and looked up the number to her good friend in the FBI, Paul Wakefield. She thought that she could not risk telling him much over the phone so she would get him over to the apartment alone. The two of them could decide what to do after that.

She dialed the number and waited for it to ring.

The phone rang two times on the other end before FBI Agent Wakefield answered, "Hello Cassy...how are you today?"

Cassy got right to the point, "Paul...I need you to come to 111 River Cross Road, Apartment 121 in Waldorf. Its urgent but I need you to come alone."

Paul attempted to calm her down, "Can't a brother get a hello?"

Cassy responded, "Sorry...hello Paul. Can you get here...quick?"

Paul had never heard Cassy like this before so whatever was going on it must be urgent.

He replied, "Give me about 2 hours."

Cassy asked, "Can you get here sooner than that please?"

Paul responded, "I'm on my way out the door now."

Cassy turned and told Tony, "Agent Wakefield is on his way. Tony... I'm not sure how this is going to play out but just know that I have your back."

Tony half smiled and replied, "'Have my back?' What does that mean?"

Professor Simmons smiled back now knowing why Tony didn't know all the slang.

She responded, "It means that whatever happens I will be there for you."

Tony replied, "Thank you Cassy."

They made small talk while they waited for Agent Wakefield to arrive.

***

FBI agent Paul Wakefield arrived at the Mitchell apartment 30 minutes after speaking to Professor Simmons on the phone. The two had known each other for the last ten years and were close friends.

Professor Simmons greeted him at the door, "Paul...glad you're here. Come on in."

Paul replied, "Hi Cassy...you said this is urgent."

Professor Simmons put her hand on Paul and said, "Paul it's a long story but the short version goes like this. In the Bible the story of Sodom and Gomorrah is true. I know...we had this discussion a couple of years ago and I don't need you to remind me that I argued you down that it was just a meteorite."

"The Bible doesn't tell us the expanded verision, the version where the people of Gomorrah are moved to another place in the universe. For 5,000 years they have tried to find a way back here to Earth. King Abimelech succeeded. He is from Gomorrah...the planet...not Shalom as he says. They are here to conquer Earth. He is here with the intent to take over Earth. He's not here in peace."

"Tony here is also from Gomorrah. He is part of a resistance that wants to overthrow King Abimelech and his ruthless rule. He has been living here for a year. I know that was a mouthful but that's the short version of the story."

Paul looked at her with disbelief written all over his face.

He said, "Is this some kind of joke? Come on, Cassy today is a very busy day. We are providing support to the Secret Service to protect King Abimelech and the President. You dragged me over here to play a joke on me?"

Professor Simmons replied, "Paul you have known me for 10 years so you should know I would not joke about something like this. We have to get word of this to the President."

Agent Wakefield quickly responded, "You have to be kidding me. I would have to be asinine to take this to my Director...much less the President."

Tony replied, "Agent Wakefield…if I take you to my spacecraft will you then believe? The more time we waste, the more time they have to attack. We must get word to the President."

Professor Simmons snapped her fingers and shouted, "I got it! We took blood samples from the King and his court. If I take one from you and it matches then that will be proof. How's that Paul?"

Agent Wakefield responded, "Okay…but I will have to take him into custody. If he is an alien, who has been living among us for a year, then there will be questions to answer."

Tony replied, "I am ready for whatever procedures you wish to use. Your custody could not match that of Gomorrah."

Agent Wakefield searched Tony and placed him in handcuffs.

Professor Simmons asked, "Is handcuffs really necessary?"

Agent Wakefield replied, "I don't know If there's a book on taking aliens from another planet into custody but I'm sure it would include handcuffing them."

Tony said, "Cassy its okay."

Agent Wakefield said, "Okay…lets head down to headquarters."

The three of them left the apartment. Tony's neighbors were outside looking at him and whispering things. Ted who lived upstairs was shaking his head as Tony was being led out by Agent Wakefield.

Agent Wakefield heard them talking.

Ted said, "I was getting ready to call 9-1-1 a little bit ago because I heard a ruckus down there. I don't know what's going on but something ain't right."

The other neighbor responded, "It's always the quiet ones."

***

Shannon was out of breath from running as fast as she could to get away from Tony and Professor Simmons. She ran into a wooded area off of Smallwood drive not far from the apartment complex. She searched for a specific tree as if she had been to this wooded area before. She found a tree marked "M and I 4ever". She fell to her knees and began digging up the ground looking feverishly for something. After a few moments of digging she found it.

Shannon said to herself, *"Yes. Here it is. Now I can contact my husband."*

Shannon turned on the device and began saying, "Mazal to General Idit, Mazal to General Idit."

Instead she got Pesach.

He responded, "This is Pesach. General Idit is out of range and cannot be reached. What do you have to report?"

Shannon responded, "I was captured by Professor Hai and his friends but I escaped. They are trying to get word to the President that we are going to attack them. What are my instructions?"

Pesach asked, "Where is Samuel? He was supposed to kill Professor Hai."

Shannon responded, "He got soft. Professor Hai convinced him that General Idit killed his father and not Lieutenant Oded. He was going to side with Professor Hai. I killed him and tried to kill Professor Hai but they overtook me before I could succeed."

Pesach replied, "Find Professor Hai and kill him before he can tell anyone our plan. If he has told anyone else…kill them as well. No one can know of our plan."

Shannon responded, "Yes. I will do as instructed."

Pesach said, "I will inform General Idit that you have done well."

Shannon replied, "Thank you."

Shannon knelt down to the ground again and retrieved the gun she had planted there as well. Once she ensured the gun was loaded and she was ready, she headed back to the apartment complex.

***

Agent Wakefield pulled the FBI sedan out of the apartment complex and onto Smallwood drive. As soon as the vehicle was completely on Smallwood drive Professor Simmons saw Shannon coming out of the wooded area. Her eyes made contact with Shannon. Shannon was raising something at her.

Professor Simmons hollered, "Its Shannon! She's got a gun!"

She grabbed Tony's head and pushed it down as fast as she could.

Agent Wakefield spun the vehicle around and shouted, "Get down!"

Professor Simmons watched as he pulled out his gun.

Before he fired a shot Professor Simmons yelled, "Don't kill her!"

She didn't know what Agent Wakefield was up to as he got down on the seat of the vehicle and pressed the button to roll his window down. She continued to hear shots that she thought were coming from Shannon. Agent Wakefield got out through the open door on the passenger's side of the vehicle.

He handed Professor Simmons a gun and told her, "Shoot a couple times in response to her shooting. I will try and get in behind her."

The gun looked larger than anything Professor Simmons had every imagined in her life. She knew this was only her mind playing tricks on her but she was afraid of guns.

Professor Simmons said, "I can't, I've never shot a gun before."

Agent Wakefield looked at Tony and asked, "Can I trust you?"

Tony responded, "Yes."

Agent Wakefield removed the handcuffs from Tony. He then took the gun. Professor Simmons stayed close to Tony. Tony was firing one shot in response to Shannon shots. Professor Simmons was holding her ears as the guns were firing around her. She was scared to death.

Suddenly no more bullets were being fired. She peeked up and saw Agent Wakefield approaching with Shannon.

Agent Wakefield shouted, "Hold your fire. I have her in custody."

Agent Wakefield walked Shannon out to the street where the Charles County Sheriff officers had arrived on the scene.

Agent Wakefield said, "My name is Agent Paul Wakefield of the FBI. I'm taking this young lady into custody. She tried to assassinate my witness in a national security case."

The offices looked at Agent Wakefield's badge and said, "Okay, how can we help?"

Professor Simmons stood there shaking with fear. She felt Tony put his arm around her. She was amazed, he made it all better.

Agent Wakefield responded, "I'll need someone to follow me with her down to the FBI building for questioning. I'll take the witness."

The Officer responded, "Alright...I will follow you."

Agent Wakefield said to Tony as the officers walked away, "Well I guess I believe you now. What is this?"

Professor Simmons looked at the small box shaped metal device Agent Wakefield was holding up. She looked at Tony for an explanation.

Tony responded, "This is a private communicator. It's probably to contact General Idit. If she had it she has probably contacted General Idit and they know that I am here and still alive."

Agent Wakefield asked, "Is there any way we can use this to our advantage?"

Tony replied, "I don't think so."

Agent Wakefield said, "Okay. Let's head down to headquarters. Maybe she will be willing to tell us something."

Tony said, "I doubt it."

Professor Simmons couldn't believe Tony held out his hands to be handcuffed again. She thought, *"What an honorable man."*

Agent Wakefield said, "You've earn the right to be trusted. No handcuffs needed."

***

Agent Wakefield, Professor Simmons and Tony all arrived at FBI Headquarters. The sheriff officer was right behind them with Shannon in his vehicle. Agent Wakefield took them all in the building and Shannon was placed in a holding cell. He had Tony taken to one of the interview rooms while he briefed his supervisor, Agent Margaret Reed.

As he approached he asked himself , *"How do I pitch this story to an agent who has been with the FBI for over 20 years and was a dedicated agent. Not to mention she had the ear of the FBI Director. God be with me. At least I know she can make this happen. All I have to do is convience her."*

Agent Wakefield knocked on the door of Agent Reed's office and walked in, "Margaret...I need to brief you on a case I caught."

Agent Reed responded, "Case you caught. What case?"

Agent Wakefield paused, ensured the door was closed and then started, "Yes, I was contacted by a friend of mine...Professor Cassy Simmons. She informed me that we are being deceived by the visitors. She believes that they are not from Shalom but they are from a planet called Gomorrah.

To make a long story short...they are descendants of the people that were here before the city was destroyed. They made a plea for their life and God moved them to another planet in the universe. For 5,000 years they have searched for a way to return and claim what they believe to be their birthright...to rule over this planet. We have to get word to the Director and then to the President."

He knew he would get that look over her glasses. That look that suggested he was out of his mind.

She responded, "You're joking...right?"

Agent Wakefield replied, "There is a man in interview room one waiting to tell you the story. He is from Gomorrah and he has lived here for over a year now. He escaped a year ago and can you imagine his shock at seeing the king of the world he escaped plastered on our TV."

Agent Reed said, "If this is a joke Paul I'm going to have your head for it."

Agent Wakefield responded, "This isn't a joke. I also have a prisoner downstairs in the holding cell. She is the wife of King Abimelech's general. She tried to assassinate Tony...the man in interview room one...because he was telling us the real deal with this visit. We can't wait to long because the UN is going to grant permission soon."

Agent Reed replied, "Okay...I'm going to get the Director on the line and brief him. If this is a joke please stop me before I make a fool of myself."

Agent Wakefield said, "I'll get Tony and Professor Simmons ready. I'm sure you both will want to talk to them."

Agent Wakefield left Agent Reed's office and went into his office where Professor Simmons was waiting. He talked to her about his conversation with Agent Reed. As he was finishing up the conversation Agent Reed walked in the room.

Agent Reed said, "Okay...Paul let's roll up to the bosses office. He wants to talk to you. Bring Simmons with you. Can we trust this Tony guy?"

Agent Wakefield responded, "Yes...he helped me capture the Gomorrite girl."

Agent Reed replied, "Gomorrite girl? I can't believe I'm living this drama."

They went up to the Directors office and briefed him on the case. After discussing the case with the Director they went down to the holding cells to see an interview of Shannon. After watching the interview Agent Wakefield had convinced the Director that he had to get word to the President.

***

The King was attending a dinner in his honor at the White House that evening. He wasn't impressed with the environment. It was nothing like the dinners he through in his palace. He was appalled at the conservative nature of Adaminians.

King Abimelech asked, "Mr. President, your world is slow to grant my peace envoy leave to land on your planet. Why is this?"

The President answered, "These things take a little time King. Permission will be given. I'm sure of it. Tonight let's have dinner and enjoy the entertainment."

King Abimelech stated, "When my peace envoy arrives, I will show you entertainment our way."

King Abimelech was harboring thoughts of slitting the Presidents throat.

"Mr. President," one of the Presidents security team was calling for him. "We have a high priority call for you, sir."

"Thanks Jim, I'll take it in my study. Excuse me a minute King Abimelech but I must take this call," said President Davis.

King Abimelech responded, "But of course Mr. President."

***

President Davis left the dining area and answered the phone in his study, "President Davis."

On the phone was FBI Director and long time friend of the President, Albert Jackson. As soon as he heard Al's voice he thought of how two of them met as interns at a New York law firm right after college.

"Mr. President, I have to speak with you in person...it's very urgent," Al said in a rushed voice.

President Davis answered, "Al...is it so urgent that I must end my dinner with our visitor from another planet?"

"Sir, it concerns your visitor from another planet. We must talk as soon as possible," Al retorted.

President Davis replied, "We are almost done with dinner. Come see me in about an hour."

Al answered, "Yes, sir and I am already here sir."

***

The Vice President of the United States was in attendance at the special UN General Assembly in New York City when the vote was taken. It was almost unanimous that the visitor's peace envoy be allowed to land on Earth.

China was the lone dissenter. They stated their case in the open assembly which is why it ran so long. The Chinese did not believe the story being told by the King and requested the envoy not enter into their airspace. The Vice President called the President to relay the news.

The President had returned to the table with the King.

Vice President Woods asked, "Mr. President...how is your dinner with the King?"

President Davis responded, "George, it's good to hear from you... dinner is outstanding. By the way, the chef you recommended was great. What's the news?"

"Well, Mr. President, it was almost unanimous that the peace envoy from Shalom be allowed to land. Each country wants to provide land for the visitors in the hopes of establishing trade with them. China was the lone dissenter and they denied access to their airspace," Vice President Woods answered.

***

After the conversation with his Vice President, President Davis turned to the King and gave him the thumbs up.

King Abimelech nodded then he responded, "Mr. President, our two worlds will be greatly changed by these events. Each will be the better for it. We will both be new men and you will see that my people have much to offer the people of Earth. History will remember us both."

President Davis added, "King Abimelech, you too will find that the people of Earth have much to offer. May we toast to this great occasion?"

The two men each made a toast and the King excused himself to pass on the great news to his waiting envoy.

***

King Abimelech and his party went out to their shuttle to contact the awaiting ships. King Abimelech was excited at the possibility of destroying this world. He especially wanted to crush China because they didn't believe his lie. He thought to himself they would pay unmercifully for that.

"Royal shuttle to Royal Warship One, over," said the communications officer.

"This is Royal Warship One, go ahead," responded the communications officer onboard the warship.

King Abimelech took the microphone and said, "This is King Abimelech...get me General Idit!"

The communications officer on the warship responded, "Yes sire."

A few moments passed and General Idit came on the line, "This is General Idit."

King Abimelech said, "General...the fools have granted us leave to bring our ships to their planet. Only this place called China asked us not to visit. I want your plan to include the total annihilation of this... China. No one is to be left standing. Is that clear?"

General Idit responded, "Yes sire. I will see to it."

King Abimelech replied, "We will begin our assent to you. You may begin your approach to this world."

General Idit said, "Yes sire. We will approach at impulse speed. They will not suspect anything until the electromagnetic pulse blinds them."

King Abimelech said, "Good."

***

After the King departed the President met with FBI Director Albert Jackson.

President Davis walked in his office and said, "Okay, Al, have a seat."

Al responded, "Thank you, sir."

President Davis asked, "What do you have for me that was so urgent?"

Al stated, "Mr. President you are not going to believe this but we have intel that leads us to believe King Abimelech and his people are not who they say they are and their intentions are not peaceful."

President Davis was puzzled as he responded, "What are you talking about Al? How can you have that kind of intelligence? For God's sake they are from another planet."

Al continued, "Mr. President, we have two individuals who claimed to be from the same planet as King Abimelech and one of them tell us a different story about the King and his so called peace envoy.

The other is the example of total evil bent on killing us all if she could. The good one...if I may...tells us that these people are not coming in peace but in fact they intend to invade and take over Earth. The other one's actions confirm it."

President Davis nervously replied, "Al...I can't believe what I am hearing. I have gone in front of the United Nations and helped champion this peace relation and now you're telling me that we are being deceived.

Al, they've just signed the agreement to let the peace envoy land. The entire world is excited about the possibility of these trade negotiations. Businesses are revving up for the opportunity to sell their products to these people. What would you have me do now?"

Al responded, "Whatever you do, sir, we have to do it fast. I recommend we put our forces on alert and advise other countries to do the same. If we are prepared for an attack and nothing becomes of it, it would be okay. However, if we are not prepared we may be slaves forever."

President Davis hit the intercom button on his phone hard and deliberately.

He shouted, "Sarah, get me the Secretary of Defense and the NSA Director."

The voice on the other end responded, "Yes sir."

President Davis said, "If King Abimelech detects our forces on alert, it will be a sign of war and we don't know for sure that this information is accurate. He will think that we have gone back on our word and war could be imminent because of our provocation."

Al said, "Sir, unfortunately I believe that is what we should do... go back on our word. In essence, we have given them permission to attack."

***

Tony was brought to the White House in a separate car from Professor Simmons and under the highest security. He understood all the security. He just hoped that Earth would be prepared and can defend against the attack.

The lead secret service agent stated, "Bring them both in. Place Professor Mitchell in this room. Professor Simmons will come with me.

Tony looked at Cassy one last time because he thought he wouldn't see her again. He found himself in love with her.

***

Ma'am, the President wants to hear the story directly from you. Please come this way."

Professor Simmons looked at the lead agent and said "Frankly, the President should hear it directly from Tony…not me."

The agent responded, "That's a security risk ma'am and we can't allow that. Until their story is verified, he won't come near the President. For all we know he could be an assassin."

Professor Simmons sneered and said, "That's ridiculous. I know this man."

The agent replied, "With all due respect Ma'am, he didn't tell you he was from another planet either."

Professor Simmons was familiar with the layout of the White House because she had been there on several occasions. However, this was probably her most important visit.

The agent escorting her led her into to the White House Situation Room where the President was waiting with the Chairman of the Joint Chiefs, the National Security Advisor, the Secretary of Defense, and the Secretary of State. The Vice President had not returned back from New York City.

Even though she was an important person she had never been in a room with this many important people. She felt a little overwhelmed.

President Davis was finishing up his conversation with Vice President Woods.

She waited patiently.

President Davis said, "I think you need to hang around the UN just a little longer. It seems we may have to request an assembly meeting fast.

I know this will not make a lot of people happy at the UN but China may not have been far off. "

She could hear the Vice President over the speaker.

Vice President Woods responded, "Really. What should I do in the meantime?"

President Davis answered, "Don't do anything yet. Don't let it out that we might be in possession of information that could change everything. We want to make sure we are right before we do anything."

The Secretary of Defense interrupted, "Sir, taking the time to make sure might give them enough time to attack."

President Davis replied, "We have to take that chance. Professor Simmons is here now. I'll give you a call back soon."

The President hung up the phone with the Vice President and, turned toward Professor Simmons.

He stated "Come on in Professor and have a seat."

She walked in the room knowing that this meeting was going to be difficult. She had to convince these people that Tony was a good man who wanted to save his world. At the same time she had to convince them to defend themselves against an attempt most of them believed would not happen.

She knew that some would question Tony's motivates. She had to be prepared for this eventuality. She had to be convincing and strong. She could not allow her feelings for Tony to come through. She found herself doing as she knew Tony would do…pray."

President Davis said, "Okay, Professor in the interest of time, tell us the short version of this story."

Professor Simmons looked at him stated unequivocally, "Sir… Earth…is being deceived and if you allow that envoy to land they will destroy this planet. That's the shortest story there is to tell."

Professor Davis asked, "Well…can we have a little bit longer story than that"?

Professor Simmons took a deep breath and said, "Sir…about a year ago a small craft landed here on Earth. It was small enough that our radar probably thought it was a meteor or something.

However, aboard that craft were two people from a planet called Gomorrah…named after the city in the Bible. One was Tony Mitchell; whose real name…I just found out is Hai…Professor Hai. His daughter was also onboard the craft. Tony came to work for me in a low level unclassified scientific position."

"Tony or Professor Hai…has informed me that King Abimelech is the ruler of his planet…a ruthless and senseless killer. The planet like the city in Biblical days is pure evil. They have no intention on being friends with us. They are intent on invading and ruling over us."

"We also have one of their spies in custody and as you can see by this video she is pure evil. She tried to assassinate Professor Hai because he was telling us the real plan."

Everyone in the room was watching the video of Shannon being interviewed. They could not believe the evilness that she displayed. She was yelling at the agents and threatening to kill them all. She promised that General Idit would have all their heads on a platter.

The President looked at the Professor. She noticed he was deep in thought, apparently taking it all in.

He said to the room, "Any ideas on how we should proceed? We might have led the way to granting permission for Earth to be attacked."

The Secretary of State spoke, "Mr. President…we cannot go back to the UN with this information. Your presidency will never recover."

The Chairman of Joint Chiefs stated, "Sir, if we don't do something to protect Earth, your presidency will be last thing any of us will be concerned with."

Everyone in the room began blurting out ideas or suggestions before the President had enough.

One general said, "We can send up a missile with six nukes inside the head and blow the suckers out of the sky!"

Someone else asked, "How long would that take to prepare?"

The general responded, "A couple days."

The person responded, "Sir, we don't have that long."

Another person said, "Let's invite the King back down. When they accept we will take them into custody. They won't attack with their leader in our custody."

Someone else said, "That could promote them to attack. What if they really are here in peace and these people are lying to us?"

President Davis shouted, "Enough! Enough…where is this Professor Hai now?"

Al Jackson spoke up, "Sir, he's in one of the briefing rooms under guard.

The President replied, "Bring him to me."

The Chairman spoke abruptly, "Sir we can't do that!"

The President replied, "If I am to go back to the UN with this new information, I am going to do so only after speaking directly to the man who has it…not through a third party. Now, again I say…BRING HIM TO ME!"

Professor Simmons said to herself, *"That's what I said."*
***

The Vice President was standing in the large dining area with all the delegates. Everyone was talking about the possibility of meeting visitors from another world and the economic impact it would have to Earth.

The Vice President on the other hand was wondering what was going on back at the White House that has made the President have concerns over the visitors. He knew President Davis could not divulge any secrets over an unsecure line but he couldn't help but wonder.

The Chinese representative approached Vice President Woods with a smile on her face. She looked as though he had just eaten the Cheshire cat. Vice President had never trusted her. On several occasions they crossed paths and she was always secretive and up to something.

She asked, "So…Mr. Vice President…I hear your country is having second thoughts. Is that true?"

Vice President Woods was shocked. How could she know already?

He responded, "I don't know what you are talking about."

This statement wasn't so far off since President Davis couldn't brief him specifically on what was going on.

He continued, "And how would you know what our thought process is at this point?"

The Chinese representative replied, "We have our ways. We are calling for another assembly in the morning. We believe there's more to these visitors than meets the eye. We will present information that will cast serious doubt of the validity of their "we come in peace" statement. I believe your country already knows what I'm talking about."

She then walked off into the crowd. Vice President Woods started to follow and ask more questions but he didn't want to arouse any suspicions or acknowledge anything for the Chinese. He just continued to wait for his call from the President.

Vice President Woods said to himself, *"I hope we have that much time."*

***

A few awkward moments passed as small talk was being made in the oval office. Everyone was awaiting the arrival of Tony Mitchell, aka Professor Hai. Professor Simmons had done what she could in trying to convince them and the President seemed to be leaning toward going back to the UN. However, he wanted to talk to Tony first.

The President sat and pondered the events of the last 24 hours. He couldn't believe how fast he had gone from hero to possible goat. He didn't care as long as he could save his planet from being enslaved.

The door to the oval office swung open and a secret service agent entered followed by Tony and a second agent behind him. The President noticed Tony's hands were cuffed and the agent led him to a chair specifically set up for him.

Professor Simmons said, "Take the cuffs off him!"

President Davis motioned for the cuffs to be removed from Tony.

He studied Tony for a minute then said, "What should I call you?"

Tony responded, "I go by my Earth name...Tony...Mr. President."

"Tony..." President Davis paused. Then he asked, "What do we have here? I mean...King Abimelech says he is from Shalom. You say he is from Gomorrah. You both have this blood enriched with titanium oxide and a second eyelid. Something is different about you. Then we have the maniac who is threatening to kill everyone."

"However, I must tell you what I'm faced with here. I'm faced with a decision whether to believe you...a man who came to this planet and hid away for a year...or King Abimelech...a man who came to our front door and asked permission to come in. Tell me why I should believe you?"

Tony responded, "Sir...you have no reason to trust me. I came here and hid amongst your people for the last year. However...I did so because I did not know who to turn to with my story. I had no idea if this planet was the same as the one I escaped from with my life. I had to see if I could trust anyone here and then find a way to help my people back on Gomorrah.

Tony continued, "Sir...if I may...I can tell you a story of the ruthlessness of King Abimelech."

President Davis replied, "Go ahead."

The Secretary of State said, "Sir we don't have time..."

President Davis sternly said, "I said...go ahead Tony!"

Tony continued, "I was sitting in my laboratory working out the details of our backup plan to leave Gomorrah in case the overthrow attempt failed when the King's guard came to retrieve me."

"They brought me to the throne room and anyone on Gomorrah knows that when you get summoned to the throne room you will more than likely be killed."

"When I got there King Abimelech questioned me about the coordinates to your world. I told him I didn't have them. I suspected that I would be killed on this day."

"However, what was waiting for me was the worst thing I could have imagined. He brought out my wife and with utter ruthlessness he killed her right before my eyes. To him this was entertainment...the Gomorrah way."

"If you trust King Abimelech you will pay for it with you lives and the lives of all of those you love. That...I am sure of. I will never forget the face of this ruthless butcher and you won't either after you allow him here."

The President's secretary rang the intercom in the situation room.

President Davis responded, "What is it?"

His secretary said, "Sir, there's an urgent call for the Chairman of the Joint Chiefs."

The Chairman got up from his seat and went to the phone.

He spoke into it, "Put it through."

He spoke for a minute and then turned to the President and addressed the room, "The armada is now in orbit. I'm afraid our friend King Abimelech underestimated the time it would take to travel here. We had better move at light speed to put our troops on alert and get our fighters in the air."

***

King Abimelech was standing at the forward section of his royal warship. This room was his private office and gave him the best view of where the ship was headed. He marveled at the spectacle called Earth out of the window. He could not wait to begin the attack and take back the world from which his fore fathers had been exiled.

He knew all of his life that he would be the one to do this. When he was a child he became special to his father, King Manasseh. King Manasseh took him out to all the public events. Of King Manasseh's 21 sons, King Abimelech rose to be his father's prize son. King Manasseh's other sons hated King Abimelech because their father loved him so much.

When King Abimelech officially took the throne of Gomorrah after his father died, he had his 20 brothers brought before him. He knew they all hated him so he gave them an opportunity to leave New Gomorrah and reside in the hills away from all the lands of Gomorrah or be killed. The brothers moved to the hills about 2500 km away from all of the lands of Gomorrah. There they began their own society.

When King Abimelech heard that they were becoming a productive society he sent his army to their land to wipe them all out. He told his army that his brothers were mounting an army to destroy them. He told them that his brothers planned to wipe them out. If they didn't kill them all, the brothers would kill them. This was all a lie.

The truth was that he was jealous of their success and he believed that his people would go and join his brothers in their new society. He could not allow their society to continue.

Remembering the devastation he bestowed on his brothers as payback for all their deeds against him was interrupted by his most trusted aid.

His aide said, "Sire, we are ready to launch the electromagnetic pulse and send the battle cruisers to Earth."

King Abimelech responded, "Adamina…her name is Adamina. Just because the idiots on this planet have changed her name does not dictate to us what we will call her. We will call her Adamina. Now send General Idit to me."

The aide left the room to find General Idit.

Queen Metuka gracefully walked in the room before General Idit arrived.

Queen Metuka spoke first, "My King. Let me be the first to congratulate you on arriving at the footstep of Adamina. Now you will conquer her and take her for your own. This day will be a day that will live in Gomorrah history forever and you will be remembered for centuries to come."

King Abimelech embraced his Queen and hugged her tightly.

He whispered in her ear, "My Queen…you have always been by my side. You will rule over Adamina with me. Once we squashed these miserable Adamians then we will sit in that Oval Office and rule the world!"

General Idit walked in and stood waiting for the King to finish whispering in the ear of Queen Metuka.

King Abimelech concluded, "Now go and ready the women to prepare the celebration. After we crush this world, we will celebrate greater than we have ever done in our history. Now go."

Then King Abimelech looked over at General Idit and said, "General… come in. Are the troops ready? When can I give the order?"

General Idit responded, "Sire…we are ready. I will prepare the men for you to give the order?"

"Gather them together in the launch bay. Tonight we will begin the attack," said King Abimelech?

***

Lieutenant Yaniv was in his quarters with his wife, Renana and their friend Varda. The three of them were discussing a plan to get information to Professor Hai. This information would allow the Adaminians to destroy the war ships. It was crucial for Lieutenant Yaniv to fly one of the shuttles near the city where he thought Professor Hai would have landed.

"My love…I must ask the General for permission to fly with Alpha Brigade. They are the brigade that will be attacking the Northeast part of a place called the United States. I believe if Professor Hai would have gone anywhere he would have gone there" said Lieutenant Yaniv.

"Go my love and may God be with you," said Renana.

Varda interrupted them, "What of my love, Lieutenant Oded?"

Lieutenant Yaniv replied, "There will be two shuttles left on board. Once we have word that these cruisers will be destroyed, one of my men will come for both of you and Lieutenant Oded. We have the codes so that you can escape in a ship and come down to the planet. We will be reunited and Adamina will defeat King Abimelech."

Both ladies nodded their heads in approval but all of them were nervous. This was not the first time they attempted to go against King Abimelech and they remembered the high price of failure.

***

Lieutenant Yaniv was told by his friend who was close to General Idit that Mazal had sent word to him. He told him that Professor Hai was alive and Tamir, who was a spy, was dead. He knew now that with Tamir dead his friend Lieutenant Oded would be killed because he had no more value to the King.

Lieutenant Yaniv had to change the plan. He would have to leave now. Lieutenant Oded, his wife and Varda would have to escape prior to the electromagnetic pulse being fired. It would have to be timed out perfectly but they had no other choice.

***

The men had gathered in the launch bay has the King had ordered. The sound aboard the royal war ship was loud as the men were yelling with all their might in preparation for their attack on Adamina.

The live feed from the second war ship was being pumped into the royal war ship. King Abimelech and General Idit strolled out to the balcony of the launch bay to address the men.

General Idit stepped out…raised his hands to silence the men and said, "Gomorrite soldiers…I present to you your victorious and heroic King…King Abimelech!"

The men went wild with excitement and enthusiasm. They were jumping up and down and yelling, "Hail the King…Hail the King!"

King Abimelech looked at General Idit to have him silence the men again then he spoke, "My brethren…today we make history. Today we attack an enemy light years from our home. We strike back at those who removed us from our land in the early morning light thousands of years ago."

"As it was foretold in the Basar we will make a triumph return to Adamina and take back what is rightfully ours. Today will be that

190

day. Today we will descend upon the slough that inhabits our planet…we shall erase them…and then take our place on the throne. Hail Gomorrah!"

Again the men yelled, "Hail the King…Hail the King!"

King Abimelech ordered, "General Idit…fire the pulse and commence the attack!"

***

Lieutenant Yaniv ran to his quarters to get his wife and Varda. The news that Lieutenant Oded was going to be killed soon had been passed around to the all the men. He had to get them off the ship. Their only choice was to take one of the shuttles before the electromagnetic pulse was released.

The pulse would probably knock out all of the electronics onboard the shuttle but they prayed that they would make it the ground first.

He arrived at the quarters and went in. He found Renana and Varda crying together.

"Come we must go in a hurry," said Lieutenant Yaniv.

Varda stood up and said, "They are going to kill my Oded!"

Lieutenant Yaniv said, "They won't get the chance we are getting him out of the cell now. We must meet them at the shuttle. Come quickly."

They didn't waste time gathering anything. They ran out the door and attempted to make their way to the shuttle bay without being noticed.

***

Down in the cellblock, Corporal Sason arrived to take Lieutenant Oded to be executed.

"I am here to take the prisoner. He is to be executed," said Corporal Sason.

The guard replied, "I got no order concerning moving the prisoner."

"I am here at the order of General Idit. Do you wish to bother him now while the men are preparing for the attack," asked Corporal Sason?

He saw the guard as he was thinking about it.

Corporal Sason said, "I don't think you want to disturb General Idit right now. You could be demoted or worst…killed."

"Okay take him," said the guard.

Corporal Sason went into the cellblock and retrieved Lieutenant Oded. When he got to the cell he found Lieutenant Oded sitting on his cot.

"Come we must move quickly but we must not give our cover away. They think I am taking you to be executed," said Corporal Sason.

"Who sent you," asked Lieutenant Oded?

Corporal Sason said, "Lieutenant Yaniv. He is getting his wife and Varda."

"Lead the way," responded Lieutenant Oded.

The two of them walked out of the cellblock area. Corporal Sason held a laser rifle on Lieutenant Oded to make it look like he was moving a prisoner. Corporal Sason knew it was going to be difficult for them to get to the launch bay because it was at the other end of the ship and two decks up. They would have to go pass many Gomorrite soldiers to get there.

***

Lieutenant Yaniv, his wife and Varda arrived at the shuttle first. They got in and started launch procedures. Lieutenant Yaniv was trained to fly shuttles. During the trip to Adamina he volunteered to be trained. He knew he might need to fly a shuttle to escape capture by the General.

Varda said, "Where are they?"

Lieutenant Yaniv responded, "Give them some time. They have a long way to go."

***

Since there were no more prisoners to guard, the guard went to see his Captain to find out what roll he could play in the attack. When he arrived at his Captain's post on the bridge he found his Captain reviewing plans with General Idit.

The Captain said to him, "What are you doing here? Who's guarding the prisoner?"

The guard replied, "Corporal Sason retrieved him for execution. He said he was acting on General Idit's orders."

General Idit shouted, "Fool! I gave no such order!"

General Idit reached for his weapon.

The guard cried out, "No…Sir…please…"

In one quick motion he pointed it at the guard and shot him down. He was dead.

General Idit stepped over his body yelling, "Get this idiot out of here and find Sason…Now!"

***

Corporal Sason and Lieutenant Oded were passing a group of soldiers on their way to the shuttle. The soldiers were yelling disparaging words to Lieutenant Oded as he passed. Some even spat on him.

Others yelled, "Traitor!"

One soldier yelled, "Let me kill him now!"

Corporal Sason replied, "Then General Idit would kill you where you stood."

The voice on the warships intercom system rang out and silenced the soldiers, "The prisoner has escaped! Corporal Sason and Lieutenant Oded are to be captured and detained. All available soldiers are to search for them now!"

Before the message was completed Corporal Sason began shooting down the soldiers with his weapon.

Lieutenant Oded swung a powerful right hook to the face of one of the soldiers knocking him to the ground. He took the soldiers laser and assisted Corporal Sason.

The two fired their way out of the hallway and ran up the ladder to the next deck. They had to throw their weapons down in order to go up the ladder faster.

After reaching the next deck, Corporal Sason and Lieutenant Oded were about 100 meters from the launch bay when two more soldiers spotted them. Varda had the shuttle door opened but she saw the soldiers between her and Corporal Sason and Lieutenant Oded.

Corporal Sason and Lieutenant Oded attacked the men and began fighting them. It was a tough fight with the soldiers and no one was getting the advantage. Lieutenant Oded got his man's weapon free but the soldier knocked it out of his hands.

Lieutenant Yaniv yelled, "Hurry we have to leave now!"

Varda shouted back, "I'm not leaving without Oded!"

Corporal Sason kicked a laser over to where Varda was standing. He saw her pick it up and point it at the soldiers. Corporal Sason jumped out of the way and Varda shot at one of the soldiers in the back. Corporal Sason jumped over him to help Lieutenant Oded.

He grabbed Lieutenant Oded's man from behind. Lieutenant Oded struck the man across the chin knocking him out cold. The two of them ran to the shuttle. More lasers began firing at them as they ran. Corporal Sason was behind Lieutenant Oded and he felt the painful blast of the laser hit him in the arm. He fell over. He saw Lieutenant Oded turn to come back and retrieve him.

Varda yelled, "No...my love."

Corporal Sason yelled, "Go...save yourself."

Lieutenant Oded ignored them all and came back for Corporal Sason. He grabbed Corporal Sason and dragged him to the shuttle. Varda provided cover by firing back at the soldiers.

Lieutenant Oded said to Lieutenant Yaniv, "Thanks for waiting buddy."

Lieutenant Yaniv responded, "You almost ran out of time my friend."

Corporal Sason said, "Lieutenant Oded you saved my life. Thank you."

Lieutenant Oded replied, "You made a greater risk by coming to the cell to retrieve me."

Lieutenant Yaniv said, "Don't celebrate yet guys. We're taking a pounding by those lasers and we still have to get the launch bay doors open. Let's pray the code still works. Buckle up."

Lieutenant Yaniv punched in the code and the launch bay door began to open.

Corporal Sason said, "Opening the launch bay doors will make the alert button on the bridge blink and alert the tactical officer."

***

On the bridge the alert button began to blink.

The tactical officer shouted, "General Idit…the launch bay doors are opening!"

General Idit responded, "Who is it?"

The tactical officer replied, "I don't know sir…no one has clearance."

General Idit ordered, "Close the doors…now!"

The tactical officer responded, "I'm trying sir but they won't respond. I've been locked out."

"Can we shoot them down," asked King Abimelech?

General Idit replied, "No. That will alert the Adamians. The electromagnetic pulse will knock out all the power on their shuttle and they will crash. Let them leave."

***

The Secretary of Defense was briefing the President while the Vice President was on the speaker phone.

He said, " Sirs, we just receive information that several small satellites just came out of the two ships and they have taken a position around the planet."

President Davis asked Vice President Woods, "What are our chances of convincing the UN to rescind the permission?"

Vice President Woods replied, "Mr. President with all due respect, that will probably do no good. Have you seen their ships? We should put our forces on alert and I recommend…"

The oval went dark and the phone line was dead. The President looked at his Secretary of Defense. Neither of them had any answers.

***

In Cheyenne Mountain, Colorado military members from all the services were scrambling to find out what was going on. Never before had an electromagnetic pulse hit the entire planet at once.

Questions pounded back and forth off the walls of the Operations room. Each question was an attempt to explain what happened. No one had a good, sound reason for it.

Colonel Jack McClelland served in the Air Force for over 20 years. He had just gone through a messy divorce of his marriage of 10 years. He was hurting inside but he couldn't allow his men to see it. When the pulse hit, he was staring at a picture of his two boys. Jason was 8 and John was 3. He missed them so much.

The loss of all the power startled Jack for a second but his mind quickly shifted from missing his boys to his first love…the military.

Colonel McClelland shouted commands everywhere seemingly at once, "Airman Williams…what's wrong with my systems? Son…we're currently blind! Get my system back on line…now! Lieutenant, get my comm working! Let's move people."

Airman Williams replied, "Sir…I think we were hit with an EMP."

Colonel McClelland responded, "That's impossible."

Airman Williams said, "I think it came from space."

Colonel McClelland ordered, "Get me a SAT phone…now!"

***

The shuttle was trying to get to the surface of Earth as fast as it possibly could. Lieutenant Yaniv was racing the engines as fast as they could go. The occupants of the craft were praying hard for a safe delivery. He could not concentrate on what they were doing. His sole mission was to get this shuttle down safely. He knew at any moment the General would launch the electromagnetic pulse and they would be helpless in the air.

Lieutenant Oded yelled, "You're pushing the engines to hard!"

Lieutenant Yaniv said, "I have too if we want to have a chance of getting to the surface before that pulse powers up!"

Renana asked, "Why have they not come after us?"

Lieutenant Yaniv responded, "General Idit knows we will crash if we get hit by the pulse."

Renana said, "God help us…please!"

The craft came through the clouds and Lieutenant Yaniv could see the ground. Then everything in the shuttle went out. There was no power at all on the shuttle. It began to twirl out of control…spiraling down to the ground. They could do nothing but pray. Their lives were truly in the hands of the Lord.

Lieutenant Yaniv said, "That's it…he must have launched the pulse. I cannot control the ship any longer."

Lieutenant Oded was looking out the window and said, "I can see the ground. Maybe we will crash but...oh my God!"

Varda asked, "What is it? What do you see?"

Lieutenant Oded responded, "A ship is headed directly for us! We're going to crash into it!"

Lieutenant Yaniv saw the airliner was free falling out of the sky. All aircraft that had the unfortunate luck to be in the air at the time the EMP was launch was falling fast to the ground. He could see destruction was occurring everywhere.

Lieutenant Yaniv turned the wheel has hard as he could...trying to avoid the airliner, but he could not control the small shuttle. Their lives were in God's hands.

Renana yelled, "Oh God!"

Lieutenant Yaniv closed his eyes knowing that the airliner was going to crash into them. But seconds passed and nothing. When he opened his eyes he saw that the airliner just missed them. God had blessed them today.

Renana said, "Water! Can we steer it into the water?"

Lieutenant Yaniv said, "I see it. The other craft was headed into the water also. Maybe we can try it. Everyone pray for our success."

Lieutenant Yaniv turned the wheel again but just as before he could not control the vessel. It seemed as though the hand of God was guiding them. The small craft began heading toward the Woodrow Wilson Bridge. He was trying with all his might to turn the wheel and avoid striking the bridge. The closer they got the faster they would fall. He thought they would not avoid the bridge.

The shuttle struck the top edge of the bridge and turned 180 degrees. It fell straight down to the water. Lieutenant Yaniv thought that striking the very top of the bridge actually caused the shuttle to spin and slow down enough that the drop downward only caused minor injuries to the occupants. Again...he felt God heard their prayers and the prayers of the people on the bridge for no one was seriously hurt on the bridge either.

Lieutenant Oded said, "We made it! Praise be to God. We made it!"

Renana responded, "Thank you Lord."

Lieutenant Yaniv said, "We've got to get out of here before we sink. We're not totally out of trouble yet. Let's move."

Renana and Varda were the first to get out of the craft. When Lieutenant Yaniv got out there were some people on the river coming toward them in a small boat. He didn't know what to say to them. This was their first contact with people from another planet. He knew all of them were scared.

The boat got to the shuttle and a man shouted, "Is everybody alright? Can we take you to the shore?"

Lieutenant Yaniv shouted back, "We are all safe."

Renana and Varda climbed onboard the small boat first. Lieutenant Oded, Lieutenant Yaniv and Corporal Sason joined them. They had made it to the world they knew as Adamina. However, now they needed to find Professor Hai.

Lieutenant Yaniv asked Lieutenant Oded, "Is the disk okay?"

Lieutenant Oded reached in his pocket.

He answered, "I do have it but it appears it is no good anymore."

Lieutenant Yaniv said, "Professor Hai might be able to restore."

Lieutenant Oded responded, "Let's pray that he can."

Lieutenant Yaniv looked at his rescuers and realized they had more trouble. The Adaminians were holding guns on them.

***

The President was sitting in the situation room waiting to find out what happened. His top advisors were with him when his SAT phone rang.

"This is President Davis...who am I speaking with," asked President Davis?

"Sir...this is Colonel McClelland from NORAD," replied Colonel McClelland.

"What you got Jack," replied President Davis?

"Sir...I believe we were hit with a massive EMP from space. We're speculating that the small satellites were used to send the EMP to the entire planet. We don't have eyes or ears to see anything. We have to believe an attack is imminent but we can't get the word to anyone," replied Colonel McClelland."

"Jack, do you know of any technology that can create an EMP to knock the entire planet," asked President Davis?

Colonel McClelland said, "No sir...never."

President Davis replied, "Do you have a way to cont...."

The lights began to flicker and return to their proper illumination. After a couple of seconds phones began to ring off the hook.

President Davis continued speaking into the SAT phone, "Jack... we have power."

Colonel McClelland answered, "We do too sir but you'd better look out the nearest window and up in the sky."

President Davis moved to the window and his eyes almost popped out of his head. A large battle cruiser was descending toward the Washington, DC area.

Colonel McClelland continued, "Sir, there are seven more headed for different points on the planet. Shall I get our planes in the air?"

President Davis asked, "How do we know this is an attack and not the peace envoy they promised?"

The Chairman of the Joint Chiefs interrupted, "Sir, on the heels of a massive EMP which I can now confirm, took out everything on the planet...I'd say it's an attack."

President Davis ordered, "Get our planes in the air."

CHAPTER 9

AT WAR: DAY ONE

Once the power returned broadcasts were going out all over the world. Different reasons were being given for the lost of all power but one broadcast had it right. WXLV local reporter, Joyce Byrd was broadcasting the story and it was immediately picked up around the world.

Ms. Byrd reported, "This just in from a reliable source in the Pentagon. There is a belief that the visitors from Shalom are not who they say they are but instead they are an invasion force from a planet called Gomorrah. These people are believed to be the ancestors of the people of the Biblical city of Gomorrah."

"They were swept away the morning of the destruction to another planet. Sources also say that we had visitors from Gomorrah on our planet living amongst us and these people provided the intelligence about King Abimelech and his envoy."

She continued, "There are a reported eight ships hovering over major cities across the planet. One of those ships is over Washington D.C. Wait…oh my God…there are smaller ships leaving the bigger ships. It looks like hundreds of them! They are spreading out headed in all directions. Oh my God…they're attacking us! One just…"

Before she could finish the sentence laser blasts struck her building in Washington D.C. The nation's capitol was clearly under attack.

***

The Secretary of Defense shouted, "Get the President out of here!"

President Davis found himself being hurried out of his office toward the underground bunker. He was being briefed by the Chairman of the Joint Chiefs as he was walking.

The Chairman said, "Washington D.C. is taking a pounding by the attack fighters. We have reports that New York City, Chicago, Detroit, Dallas, Miami and Los Angeles are also under heavy attack."

"Four of the eight battle cruisers have positioned themselves to reach all the major cities of the United States. The other four are positioned over Europe, Asia and the Middle East."

"China must have really pissed them off. They're taking the most severe beating of any country.

President Davis went down as one of the blasts struck the White House. The secret service agents grabbed him and hurried him to the bunker.

***

When the blast hit the White House, Tony grabbed Professor Simmons and tried to protect her. Agent Wakefield came running toward them.

Professor Simmons screamed, "Paul…watch out!"

It was too late. The roof above him gave way and he was crushed by the debris.

Tony grabbed Professor Simmons and stopped her from running toward Agent Wakefield.

Professor Simmons shouted, "No!"

She began crying and her body went limp for a second. Tony felt sorry for her. He never wanted her to feel the pain the he had felt in his life.

Tony said, "Cassy you have to get it together. We have to get out of here. They're attack is centered on this city…and this building. Cassy… let's go…now!"

Cassy straighten up and began following Tony through the debris. The two of them tried to get out of there as fast as they could. White House employees were frantically scrambling to get out of the building. Some people were lying on the ground hurt and calling for help. No one was stopping. Everyone was trying to get to safety.

***

Captain Mark Andrews, an F-15 fighter pilot out of Langley Air Force Base, Virginia, instructed his squadron to ready themselves for an all out attack. Twenty F-15 Eagle from Langley prepared for a battle that many of them believe they would not survive but none of them would chose to walk away from. As the Gomorrite fighters began approaching the F-15s their sheer numbers told the F-15 pilots that they would not win this battle.

In command headquarters at Langley, the commander could hear the pilots communicating as the battle began.

One of the fighter pilots came over the radio and said, "Captain I have two bandits on my…"

His radio went dead.

Captain Andrews came over the radio "Langley, we've taken out some of them but there's just too many of them. We have to pull back!"

Langley said, "Captain Andrews pull your fighters back to base. Captain! Captain!"

No voice responded to the commander and the radio was dead. The radar screen now showed only Gomorrite fighters. The pounding of the laser blast rang out all over the world and it was apparent that Earth was being invaded by its estranged brothers.

***

After the power outage ended members of each country had members of their security team running to take them to shelter. The battle cruisers had been seen headed toward New York City. However, it was too late. Vice President Woods was standing in the center of the room when the first blast hit the building next door and rapidly blasts began hitting everything within two city blocks of the U.N. building.

The secret service agents assigned to the Vice President grabbed him and tried to guide him out of the room and to safety. A laser blast struck the building and sent debris flying across the room.

A beam collapsed hitting one of the secret service agents almost killing him. He cried out for help but none was forthcoming. Their mission was clear…get the Vice President to safety at all cost.

The other agent and the Vice President suffered minor injuries. Vice President Woods was brushing himself off when the secret service agent cried out. He attempted to stand and go help him when he was stopped.

The second Secret Service agent asked, "Sir…are you okay?"

Vice President Woods replied, "Yeah…I'm okay. We have to get that beam off of Larry. Give me a hand."

The Secret Service agent responded, "With all due respect sir, my mission is to get you to safety. This way Mr. Vice President…the shelter is in the basement."

Vice President Woods shouted, "No…we need to help him."

Vice President Woods was looking in the direction of the fallen secret service agent.

The agent that escorted him said, "Sir…you can help him best by getting to safety. We'll send someone back for him."

They were on the fifth floor. Fortunately for this agent the Vice President was an athletic man. He ran track in college and continued to run and play basketball regularly. Five flights of stairs were not going to be a problem for him.

Against his better judgment Vice President Woods ran off towards the stairwell with the secret service agent.

He shouted to Larry as he was running, "Larry…we'll send help. Just hang on."

Larry responded, "Yes sir. Get to safety sir."

Vice President Woods knew that help would not be sent. He could hear the attack raining down on New York City like nothing he had ever heard before. He knew that he would never make it out of this building alive.

The Secret Service Agent got the Vice President to the stairwell at the same time as the Chinese representative and her entourage. All of them ran as fast as they could down the winding stairwell. As they got to the second floor a laser blast hit the side of the building, knocking the stairwell from under their feet. All of them fell helplessly down to the bottom of the stairwell.

The stairwell and concrete came falling down behind them. The Vice President looked up and saw his impending death coming. He held his hands up in front of his face as if it would protect him. They all were killed instantly.

***

While the power was out, Solomon was in the Department of Education building on First Street. Everyone in the building was wondering what was happening but no one could give a good explanation.

He was on the 9th floor of the building. They decided to walk downstairs and go outside to see if anything was going on down on the street.

When they got there they found a crowd of people outside. There was a Metro train in the distance sitting on the tracks unable to move. Everyone was talking amongst themselves trying to learn any information they could. Solomon found two of his co-workers, Janet and Lori talking.

Solomon asked, "Hey…you guys heard anything?"

Lori responded, "No…some ex-military guys think it was an EMP but it's lasting to long…so nobody has any ideas."

Janet said, "My friend said she thinks a plane crashed in the Potomac."

Gabriel joined the conversation and said, "I don't know…I have a bad feeling about this."

"I'm with him. I think something is up. Why are the cars not working," asked Solomon?

"Look," Janet said excitedly!"

Everyone looked to where she was pointing and saw one of the large battle cruisers descending in the direction of the White House. As the ship was passing the power began to come back on in the buildings and the fighters began leaving the cruisers.

Now everyone suspected an attack. Some began running to shelter in an adjacent building.

A woman shouted as she ran out of the CNN building, "They're going to attack us!"

Solomon ran over to the woman along with everyone else. Solomon grabbed her and tried to calm her down.

He said, "Calm down. What are you talking about?"

The woman took a deep breath and said, "The news just said they aren't here in peace. The visitors are here to attack us. We need to get out..."

Before she could finish the sound of a laser blast filled the air and stunned everyone in the area. Some were knocked off their feet.

None of them had ever been in a war zone before but now the war zone was under their feet. The Metro train was still sitting on tracks having not moved since the power returned. Solomon had been knocked to the ground. As he looked up he saw a fighter headed in the direction of the train.

A blast fired from the fighter struck the train...blowing a hole in it. The six car train helplessly fell to the ground crushing some automobiles that were sitting on First Street. Screams could be heard everywhere.

Solomon rushed toward the train as each of the six cars fell helplessly off the tracks one by one with a thunderous sound. There were some survivors...screaming for help...begging for mercy.

Solomon's first reaction was to help those who were injured. He had no regard for his own life. Seeing Solomon take off, Gabriel instantly followed. Janet and Lori ran back into the building for shelter.

Solomon yelled to anyone who would listen, "We have to get these people out of here. Give me a hand."

Gabriel responded, "I'm with you."

Solomon continued to shout, "Hey...give us a hand. Some of these people are still alive."

The blasts were still coming and most people didn't care about anyone else but themselves. They ran to take cover. The next blast struck FECA's building; then the CNN building was hit causing debris to fall over into the Department of Education's side of the Union Center Plaza building. Solomon heard the buildings collapsing and the cries for help. Silently he hoped his friends had survived but he feared the worst.

Solomon was able to get a few people to help him but most ran out of self preservation. He looked down First Street and he could see one of the ships coming toward him. The fighter was firing blast at the ground ripping First Street up and throwing concrete in every direction. People were trying their best to avoid certain death. Solomon looked at Gabriel. Both got ready to run but the fighter pulled up and turned around heading to another part of the city. They went back to helping the injured.

It seemed futile to help considering it was so many people. As they were tirelessly working the sounds of the laser blast drifted away from them. Solomon thought the visitors figured they had done enough damage in their area and moved on to another area.

After his mind drifted a bit to his family he regained his focus and started concentrating on helping people. Solomon knew this was only the beginning and he was planning in his mind how he was going to organize a group to fight back. He was not going to allow the enemy to just walk in and take over his city…Washington D.C.

Solomon looked at Gabriel and said, "You know the ground forces are probably coming next, right?"

Gabriel responded, "I know but we can't worry about that now. These people need our help."

***

Ashlee was sitting in her office during the power outage. Marion came in to see her.

"What up girl? Why we don't have any power," asked Marion?

Ashlee replied, "I don't know. It's the strangest thing I've ever seen. I'm going outside…its dark in here."

Marion said, "I'm down…let's roll."

The two of them headed to the stairs. They were on the fifth floor so it was going to be a walk in the dark. They laughed and joked as they went down the stairs but neither of them fully realized what they were in for over the next few days. As they got to the lobby the first face they saw was Simon.

Marion half giggling said, "Hey…Simon. Here's Ashlee."

Ashlee responded, "Shut up girl. Hi Simon…what's up with the power?"

Simon answered, "Hi Ashlee…I don't know what's going on with the power. It seems to be out everywhere."

Ashlee replied, "We're going to wait outside. It's too dark in here."

Simon said, "Okay. Be careful. Something's not right today."

Marion said, "Wow…he really cares about you."

Ashlee replied, "Hush girl…he's just looking out for us because we work in the building he's protecting. That's all to it."

Marion responded, "Dream on sister. He likes you…a lot."

The two of them were outside talking. Others gathered outside underneath the overhang as well. Each group was talking and speculating on what was happening.

Suddenly the power came back on and the news report hit the airwaves. People with radios began shouting to anyone who would listen. Ashlee saw groups of employees start running but it was too late.

She heard laser blasts raining down on the area. With tremendous devastation they began striking the Department of Agriculture, the Smithsonian, and the Department of Energy.

Someone shouted, "Get underground."

Ashlee and Marion began running…trying to get to the underground garage. As they were running the ground underneath them gave way. They both grabbed onto anything they could to hang on to for their lives. Ashlee grabbed onto the end of a bike rack which caught an edge of the building just right to hold her. Marion wasn't so fortunate.

She reached and reached for something, anything that she could hold onto to save herself but nothing was there. Ashlee looked back at her friend and reached out one of her hands to help her but it was just out of Marion's reached. Ashlee saw her go down the hole. To Ashlee it looked like it took hours for Marion to fall crying and screaming but in reality it was seconds before she plunged to her apparent death.

Ashlee was losing her grip on the bike rack. The bike rack itself was beginning to give way under the stress of the building wall collapsing. Ashlee thought for sure this was her last moments on Earth. She began to cry out to the Heavens for mercy…not for herself but for her family and friends. She prayed for her mom and dad. Her sister was at Southeastern River University. She prayed that God would spare her sisters life.

She couldn't sustain her grip any longer. Her hand slowly slipped and slipped until she started to drop but something caught her and stopped her from falling. She looked up and there was Simon. He had grabbed her hand just in time to stop her from falling. Simon pulled her up from the hole and into his arms.

Simon asked, "Are you okay?"

Ashlee replied, "Marion…she's…she's…"

Simon responded, "Come on let's get to the garage. It's safer there."

***

Pastor Bell was in his office when the power went out. The only people in the church were Pastor Bell and his secretary. Pastor Bell was deep in thought about the events. He wondered if he had made a mistake by not turning Tony in a year ago.

He thought, *"If I had turned them in when I met them, none of this would be happening."*

But then again if he had who knows what the government would have done with Tony. His knowledge could have been taken and used against other countries. It's easy to question what he did but in the end he just needs to live with it.

Sharon went into Pastor Bell's office and said, "Pastor…I'm going to run up to the store since all the power is out. I haven't eaten today."

Pastor Bell responded, "Something seems different about this power outage Sharon. I'm going to run home and check on my family. You should do the same."

Sharon asked, "What's going on Pastor? You seem like you know more than you're letting on."

Pastor Bell stood up and looked Sharon directly in her eyes.

He said, "Sharon…please go to your family and make sure everyone is safe."

Sharon began to get worried and simply replied, "Okay."

Pastor Bell grabbed his keys and Sharon did the same. They both went out to the parking lot and got in their vehicles. Each attempted to start their vehicle without success. They tried over and over but neither car started.

Pastor Bell got out of his vehicle first and met Sharon.

He said, "What are odds of both vehicles not starting?"

It was a short walk to the street. Once there they saw several cars had also stalled. The drivers had gotten out of them by now and Pastor Bell knew that the attack was on the way. What could he do to stop it? Then his worst nightmare occurred. He looked up in the sky and in the distance he could see something coming down fast…it was a jet liner and it was headed in their direction.

The roar of the engine got closer. The people on the ground including Pastor Bell and Sharon began to run to safety. The explosion was so loud it felt as if neither of them could hear a sound for a few moments. The flames burst into the air as high as 100 feet. Pastor Bell and the group of people could feel the heat of the burning plane even thought they were a mile away.

There was no cry for help. The jet liner had crashed in a housing area near the church. Pastor Bell and Sharon looked back at the crash and both fell to their knees and prayed.

A few minutes later the ground shook underneath them.

Over and over…it felt like someone was beating the ground like drums.

A man standing near Pastor Bell cried out, "Now what?"

The pounding continued. Over and over it continued like multiple earthquakes were occurring in the distance. All of the people standing… looking at the crashed jet liner turned and looked in the direction of Washington D.C. Pastor Bell knew the city had come under attack. He prayed that his friends would be able to do something to save the Earth from destruction.

One man climbed on top of the church building. He could see in the distance the fighters attacking Washington D.C. He could also see a large battle cruiser hovering over the city. He told Pastor Bell what he saw. There was no joy this day.

Some of the drivers had gotten their vehicles started. Pastor Bell and Sharon ran to their vehicles, started them up and headed to their families. Pastor Bell asked Sharon to start calling members to get them to come to the church. They need to be together during this time.

***

The pounding of the Earth took its toll on the major cities that were attacked. Millions lay dead and others were having trouble finding any hope. Solomon didn't have any trouble believing that the Gomorrites could be stopped. In a matter of hours he had been anointed leader. Mostly because he had a plan and he could convince others to follow him. His military prowess was serving him well.

He was readily trying to organize a small group of men into a resistance.

Solomon and Gabriel were in an underground parking garage conferring with several men who had survived the air assault.

Solomon was speaking, "Men…we need to get some guns, food and establish a base of operations. Any ideas on where we can get the guns from?"

One of the men spoke up, "There was a gun shop on Maryland Avenue. Me, Jeff and Roland can hike over there and pick up some weapons."

Solomon responded, "Head out and be careful. I got a feeling they are going to be putting troops on the ground next.

He turned to two other men and said, "Can you two round up a couple of people and get some food and supplies?"

Sam replied, "Yes sir."

Gabriel said, "What do you want me to do?"

"We need to organize the rest of these people. We need to find medical people. We need to appoint some security people. Then we need to set this place up as a temporary base of operations. We will need to get some people together after we get the weapons to do some recognizance. I know it's a lot of people and they seem hopeless right now. We have to give them some hope. Can you go around and find out what their skills are," asked Solomon?

Gabriel responded, "I'll get right on it. You're a natural at this man."

***

Ashlee and Simon made it to the underground parking garage with some others. The shock was etched on all the faces. No one had any idea what was about to happen. They were all scared. Their lives have been changed. They just sat there in disbelief. Not knowing what to do.

These people unlike the people of Union Center Plaza had no natural leader. No one was standing up and taking charge. Instead they all sat there and wondered how long they had to live.

Simon didn't want to just sit there. He could think of nothing else except to get Ashlee to safety. He secretly loved her. Now he wished he had asked her out a long time ago. He looked at her and admired her beauty.

He thought to himself, *"I guess if this is to happen at least I'm with the one I love."*

He smiled at her and she smiled back at him.

"Simon…if we don't make it out of here…," Ashlee started to say.

"We'll make it. Just keep the faith of a mustard seed," replied Simon.

Ashlee sat up and looked into Simon's eyes and said, "At least I'm with you. Thanks for saving my life."

Simon found the ability to smile after hearing those words. It wasn't just that she had just spoken aloud the words that he just thought about. He couldn't understand why he was so nervous about telling her how he truly felt? He had dreamed about the two of them being together but it was only after he had ceased to become a security guard. He still believed that she didn't really like him because he was only a security guard.

Ashlee broke the silence, "It's not true you know."

Simon asked, "What? What's not true?"

Ashlee answered, "That I wouldn't go out with you because you're a security guard. It doesn't matter to me that you are a security guard."

Simon wondered if Ashlee had the power to read minds.

He said, "Really. Ashlee…I'll get you home safe."

Ashlee said, "Thanks."

In her mind she knew he was only being nice. He could not know if they were going to make it home safe but it was nice to know that he was going to try.

Then she thought, *"What if home wasn't there anymore?"*

***

President Davis was sitting at his desk in the shelter pondering the events of the past 24 hours. He wished he had handled it differently but he soon realized that he could not change that now. Instead he had to get his people out of this war. He had to come up with a plan to defeat this seemingly powerful enemy. But what…what could he do?

His thoughts were interrupted by the Secretary of Defense.

"Sir I have some bad news," said the Secretary.

President Davis responded, "You've got to be kidding…right?"

"I guess I should say I have some more bad news, Sir. Vice President Woods is believed to be dead," said the Secretary.

President Davis looked down. He was very close to the Vice President. The words of his possible death truly sadden his heart. He wanted vindication. He wanted to see King Abimelech dead.

"We have to find a way to take this war to them. How can we do it? Give me some ideas. Where's Professor Simmons and Tony," asked President Davis.

The Secretary said, "We are looking for them. When the attack occurred we rushed in the shelter and loss track of them. When we sent search teams out for them we didn't find them. We will keep looking. They are our best source of intel."

President Davis ordered, "That's your highest priority. Find them."

The National Security Advisor walked in the office.

"Sir…we have intel that the Gomorrites are placing troops on the ground in Northeast DC. They seem to be forming a base camp and the air assault has slowed," said the National Security Advisor.

"General…prepare our troops at Andrews to fight. We have to be able to fight them on the ground or we'll be slaves soon," said President Davis.

The Secretary responded, "Yes sir…my officers have already been preparing. We plan on sealing off D.C. We need to hold them here and keep them from advancing into Virginia and Maryland."

***

Pastor Bell was in the church getting people settled. More and more people were coming in searching for answers and hope. Some of them had successfully made it out of DC before the Gomorrite ground troops began landing. Some were injured and needed medical attention. Pastor Bell had found one doctor and four nurses to help.

Pastor Bell asked, "Sharon do we have anymore towels?"

Sharon responded, "No but we're sending some people out to get some supplies."

Pastor Bell replied, "Thanks Sharon. I'm going to open the warehouse in the back so we can house more people."

The small church building was a temporary structure until the larger building was built. The building work had not been started so the warehouse in back had plenty of open space. Pastor Bell wanted to put as many beds as he could in the open space so that the injured could be helped. Between the two buildings Pastor Bell felt he could house a large body of people.

One of his deacons approached him while he was opening the warehouse.

Deacon Dwight Thompson asked, "Pastor...we need weapons. We gotta protect these people. If we have a large body of people here and that would make a good target for the enemy."

Pastor Bell turned to Deacon Thompson and looked at him with all the seriousness he could muster.

Pastor Bell replied, "Our weapon is the Lord. We will rely on him and not guns to protect us. We will not forsake Him now and He will not forsake us."

Deacon Thompson argued, "Sir...it's not about forsaking Him. The Israelites in the Bible had weapons to defend themselves. We just need to be ready to protect ourselves."

Pastor Bell said, "Dec...I am the leader of these people. They are my responsibility. When God tells me to take up arms and defend ourselves...I will. But that time hasn't come yet. You have trusted me for years...trust me now."

Deacon Thompson replied, "Yes sir."

***

Miguel Sanchez came running into the underground garage where Solomon and Gabriel were setting up camp. He was shouting and everyone turned to hear what he was saying.

Miguel shouted, "We have to leave! We need to get out of here now!"

Solomon ran to Miguel, placed his hands on him in an attempt to calm him down.

Solomon said, "What's going on? Calm down and tell us what you know."

Miguel took a couple of breaths and gathered himself together.

He said, "There are troops coming. A big ship landed off of New York Ave. Massive troops marched out of the ship and they are coming this way!"

Solomon shouted, "Okay…everyone…listen up. There are troops coming this way. They don't know we are here. We must remain as quiet as possible. Everyone get as far away from the door as possible. Take cover behind the cars. Where's those weapons!"

Solomon looked at Miguel and asked, "How many troops are headed this way?"

Miguel answered, "About 40 or 50… maybe less, maybe more."

Solomon said, "Okay we can't move all these people. We have to keep them quiet. I need you to help me keep them quiet. Can you do that?"

Miguel responded, "Yes."

Just then several men who had went to retrieve some weapons and supplies returned to the garage. Solomon went over to them.

Solomon asked, "How many did you get? We have troops headed this way."

One of the men responded, "We have enough to arm at least 20 men."

Solomon said, "Good. We'll need more but this will do for now. We need to position the men in several places around this garage in case those troops come down here. We have to protect these people. Since the elevators aren't working there's only one way in or out of this garage. Let's post men at the entrance in case they come down here."

One of the men responded, "Yes sir."

Solomon continued, "Stay out of sight. We are not ready to take them on. We need to survive this day to organize and fight back tomorrow."

***

General Idit's shuttle landed near the White House. He exited the shuttle, gazed at the death and destruction his plan had achieved. Smoke was rising…filling the evening air. Flames could be seen as buildings burned in the distance. Even smoldering flames could be felt in the White House where he stood. He marveled in his work. Proud of what his men had accomplished in such short time.

Now it was time to finish off the Adamians. He approached the half destroyed building where King Abimelech was waiting. General Idit knew victory was in hand as his troops began to take up positions around the major cities of Adamina.

***

As King Abimelech looked around the half destroyed Oval Office, he noticed a shadowy figure standing in the corner of the room. No one else could see him. King Abimelech recognized him from their previous meetings.

King Abimelech commanded, "Clear the room and do not disturb me."

All at once his servants responded, "Yes Sire."

Once they were out of the room the shadowy figure emerged and walked to the center of the room. He stood in front of King Abimelech with a sinister half smile etched on his face. It was a face that reflected pure evil. His eyes were cold and malevolent. The room began to get cold with evil. His voice was more chilling than his presence.

Baal spoke, "I have given you what you asked. You are the King that has successfully returned to Adamina. Now you must make slaves of the inhabitants and turn their hearts over to me. But more importantly… you soul is now mine."

King Abimelech fell to his knees and said, "I devote my entire existence to you, my lord."

King Abimelech let out an egregious sound. His head and his arms went back and the pain continued to be etched into his face. A cloud like being was being moved from the King's body. His soul was ripping itself from his body.

After a few minutes the soul of King Abimelech was removed from his body and entered the body of Baal. King Abimelech had given his soul to the figure he recognized as Baal.

Baal smiled for he now added another soul to his count.

Baal replied, "It is done."

King Abimelech was out of breath as he watched Baal turn and began to slowly walk away. With each step smoke appeared to engulf him. The further he moved away from King Abimelech the more smoke covered him until he was completely gone. Once he was gone the temperature in the room returned to normal.

King Abimelech returned to his feet and thanked Baal for giving him Adamina.

***

Shortly after Baal had left the room General Idit came in the room. He noticed the look on King Abimelech's face. He had seen it before.

General Idit asked, "Baal has been here?"

"He appeared to remind me that my soul is now his since we are here...on Adamina," King Abimelech replied.

"The troops are ready," said General Idit.

King Abimelech replied, "Send them out. Take as many slaves as possible. We must break them and make them worshippers of Baal."

General Idit responded, "Consider it done."

General Idit walked out of the room.

King Abimelech sat down and thought about his life. He thought about the first time Baal appeared to him. King Abimelech was a young man lost among his father's many sons. He longed for the opportunity to be the favorite son. At night he would pray that Baal would help him become that favorite son.

One night while in his room, young King Abimelech was crying. He was sad because his father choose five of his brothers to go out on a hunt. The room began to get cold. Young King Abimelech grabbed a blanket to put around him. This cold he had never felt before. Out of the corner of his eye he saw a figure forming.

Dark smoke formed at first. Then out of the smoke came a man. His eyes brought fear into young King Abimelech. He fell to his knees in worship.

The dark figure said, "Why do you bow before me?"

Young King Abimelech replied, "Are you not our god, Baal?"

The dark figure smiled and responded, "I am known by many names. Baal will do fine. You want to be the chosen son of your father. You want to be the one to lead Gomorrah back to Adamina. I can give that all to you...if you truly desire it?"

Young King Abimelech said, "Yes my lord. I will do anything for it."

Baal laughed. It sounded cold, evil, nefarious, and heinous. Young King Abimelech had never heard such a noise in his young life. The laugh sent a chill up and down his spine. Fear raced throughout his body. He was scared but yet he was excited because he believed he was in the presence of a god.

Baal finished laughing and said, "I will give it all to you. In return you will give me your soul. Your people are straying away from me. You must lead them back to me. You will make them trust in me again. Finally you must destroy the resistance and one day when given the chance you must kill a man you will know as Gideon. Do all of this and I will grant you your desire."

Young King Abimelech replied, "I will do as you say."

Baal pulled out a contract and asked young King Abimelech, "Extend your hand."

Young Abimelech extended his hand and Baal cut his arm lightly so that the blood fell on the contract.

Baal said, "It is done. You are now the favored son and you will lead Gomorrah back to Adamina. Once you have completed your journey to Adamina you soul will be mine."

Young King Abimelech said, "Yes my lord."

Baal smiled with utter evilness and turned to walk away. The smoke engulfed him as he walk and slowly disappeared. The room temperature returned to normal.

Young King Abimelech walked out of his room and was met in the hallway by one of his servants.

The servant said to him, "Sire...your father is calling for you. Come quickly."

Young King Abimelech responded, "My father? He has never summoned for me."

On this evening young King Abimelech was placed at the head of the table and given the best foods. He was now the favored son and on his way to becoming king.

***

General Idit sent out troops to Northeast, Northwest, Southeast, and Southwest DC. He instructed them to take as many slaves as possible and bring them back to their base camp. If any of them resist they were to be killed.

He sent Colonel Aba, who was a vicious man, to the area where he believed Solomon and the resistance was hiding. The troops were closing in on the parking garage where Solomon and Gabriel were hiding. The lookout saw the troops approaching and signaled to the others that they were coming.

The troops were looking in buildings, searching for people. They were armed with some kind of weapon which looked like a gun. Some of the troops went into the CNN/Department of Education building.

Colonel Aba said, "You men go on that side. You others follow me to this side. Take slaves but if they fight you…make an example of one or two them. Then the others will follow you."

The men responded, "Yes sir!"

The Gomorrite soldiers moved up the stairwell of the CNN and Department of Education sides of the buildings. They were looking for survivors to make them slaves. They arrived at the fifth floor and found survivors. The people saw them and ran for their lives. The soldiers had the stairwells blocked so the running was in vain. Some tried to fight back.

One man held up a chair and attempted to throw it at a Gomorrite soldier. The soldier aimed his weapon at the man and fired a laser blast at him. The blast tore a hole in the man's chest. After witnessing the power from the Gomorrite weapons the others begin to give up in hopes of surviving the massacre.

The soldiers walked their prisoners down the stairwell and outside to the holding area. They were holding all of their slaves there until they could walk them back to the White House. The people that had been captured were of all nationalities, ages and gender. Once the United States was a place where racism ran rapid across the county. Now… they were all united. They were all in fear of their lives. They would all be made into slaves.

Solomon was watching and listening as the Gomorrite soldiers gathered up employees to be made into slaves. They were treating the women brutally and if a man tried to fight back he was killed. It soon sent the message that killing them was easy. The will of the people was broken.

Solomon knew his band of twenty men couldn't attack at this time. They were gravely outnumbered. He planned to rescue them. But for now he had to keep the people in the garage quiet. The soldiers didn't know that there were people down in the garage. They never bothered to search it.

***

The people in the Department of Energy garage were receiving reports that troops were beginning to land on the ground and search building. Simon grabbed Ashlee and the both of them got out of the garage. Night was beginning to cover the city.

Simon said, "Ashlee…troops are beginning to land on the ground. We need to get out of here. You live in Waldorf right?"

Ashlee nodded her head yes.

Simon continued, "Okay…let's go this way. We will cut our way across the city and try to make it to 295. Once we get to 295 we can stay on it until we get to Fort Washington. Once we get there we can stay on 210 to Waldorf. Can you handle that?"

Ashlee asked, "We're going to walk? That's got to be 30 miles."

Simon responded, "It's either that or take our chances here. With all the soldiers coming we might get captured and who knows what will happen to us. I need you to be with me."

Ashlee replied, "I'll try. I'm glad I got that gym membership."

***

The Ronald Reagan building is located close to the White House. The building had taken so much damage that most of the people who work in the building died in the air attack. Those who were still alive were hiding in the basement area near the food court. Among them were Tony and Professor Simmons.

They were sitting near a sandwich shop. Tony was pondering any options that they could pursue. He knew he would be the only one that could figure how to beat the Gomorrites.

Professor Simmons broke the ice, "Tony…what are we going to do? We'll never get to your communicator now and we don't know who to call anyway."

Tony responded, "There has to be a way. God said He would never leave us or forsake us."

219

Professor Simmons said, "We could use His help and more."

Tony replied, "He will come."

Professor Simmons continued, "Look at all these people. Yesterday they were going about their lives doing what they do. Now everything they ever knew has changed. They don't know what tomorrow will bring."

"No longer is driving that BMW or Lexus important. No longer is finding that perfect job the most important thing in their life. Now it's about making it through the next few minutes. Many of them don't know how they are going to do it. All of them have probably never imagined themselves in this position."

"The closest thing to a war zone that any of us here in the United States have ever been in was the 911 attacks. That was isolated to New York and DC mostly but now this attack is everywhere."

"During 911 we ran to our homes and took shelter and felt safe. Now we have nowhere to run. We have nowhere to hide. The Gomorrites will be coming for us and they won't be merciful at all. If there is a God, please let Him intervene on our behalf."

Tony responded, "I have lived my life hiding from King Abimelech and his men. I have concealed my true nature from them for years. This is not new for me. I can tell you that it does not get any easier. God will place before us a way to win this war. We have to have faith that He will. He has brought me and my resistance this far. He will not fail us. He cannot fail."

The sound of laser blast saturated the air as Gomorrite soldiers began taking hostages and killing those who resisted. The attack was coming from the Department of Commerce part of the Ronald Reagan building. Tony and Professor Simmons began running toward the exit near 12th Street. If anyone had to get away from the soldiers it had to be them.

They got out of the building and made it over to 12th Street. People were running in every direction. Tony chose to run down 12th Street toward the mall. Professor Simmons had knowledge of the city but Tony didn't know where to run.

Darkness had begun to cover the city. Tony and Professor Simmons hoped that it would help them evade the Gomorrites.

Behind them they heard a shout, "Its Professor Hai! Get him!"

Another voice shouted, "Hey over here!"

Professor Simmons and Tony began to run over toward the second voice. It was a woman and a small child. The woman was holding a gun. She was visibly scared.

The woman said, "I don't know how to use this thing. Please help us."

Tony took the gun and checked to ensure it was loaded. The soldiers were coming fast. It was three them. They were all armed with their lasers. Tony pointed the weapon at them. He fired several shots in the direction of the soldiers, hitting two of them. The third fired his weapon back at them.

Tony turned and yelled at the women, "Run. Get out of here."

Professor Simmons replied, "I'm not leaving you."

Tony returned fire and the soldier took cover. This gave them time to slip away down Independence Avenue. The soldier radioed General Idit that he was in pursuit of Professor Hai.

General Idit said, "Do not return without him. That's an order."

The soldier replied, "Yes sir."

CHAPTER 10

THE NEXT MORNING

The sun began to rise over Washington DC. The morning light reminded everyone that the attacks were in fact real. Those who were left alive saw smoke rising all over the city. Troops were marching thru their streets... looking to enslave any survivors they could find. Fear covered the city like a blanket.

Simon and Ashlee made it to the I-295/I-395 merge point.

Ashlee cried out, "I can't walk another step. I have to rest."

Simon replied, "We have to keep moving. The sun is rising. We don't know where the soldiers might be."

Through her deep breaths, Ashlee replied, "I don't care if they catch me...I'm just too tired."

Simon replied, "Okay. We can take shelter over there in those apartments. But we can't stay long we have to keep moving."

Ashlee responded, "Okay."

Once they made it inside the building, she followed Simon to an open apartment. They went in to sit and rest. Ashlee was clearly out of breath. She fell on the couch to rest.

She heard Simon doing something around the apartment. Slowly her eyelids were closing as she couldn't fight off sleep any longer. Her last thoughts were of seeing her friend, Marion fall down that hole. Tears came out of her eyes and rolled down her face.

***

Lieutenant Oded found himself in a cell again. Only this time it was on Adamina. This was not how he imagined returning home. This time he was locked with other resistence members. Lieutenant Yaniv, Corporal Sason, Renena, and Varda were being held captive with him.

Their capturers were the same people who pulled them out of the Potomac River. Lieutenant Oded was attempting to explain that they were not the same people who were attacking them. But the people were upset with them.

Lieutenant Oded suspected they were being held under guard at a warehouse. He heard his captures say the place was called the Navy Yard. He wondered if Professor Hai was nearby.

Lieutenant Oded watched as the people appeared confused and scared. One man looked to be the leader of the group. Lieutenant Oded had to get a meeting with him.

***

Ben was an FBI agent, who had been at the White House earlier. He arrived at the Navy Yard looking…hoping to find his wife who worked there. He saw the Gomorrites being held under guard.

Ben asked, "What did these people do?"

Jim McKinney was acting as a leader of this group and responded, "We saw them fall out of the sky in one of those ships. They are part of the enemy forces. We started to execute them but we couldn't bring ourselves to do it. So we're holding them under guard until we can decide what to do with them."

Ben asked, "Why would they come down before the EMP? That doesn't make sense."

Jim replied, "They say they here to help. They say they have information to help stop the attack."

Ben said, "I need to speak with them."

Jim replied, "Go ahead… they're right over there."

Ben walked over to the area where the Gomorrites were being held. He motioned to the guard that he wanted to speak with the Gomorrites.

Ben asked the group, "Which one of you is in charge?"

Lieutenant Oded answered, "I am in charge."

Ben asked, "I was told your story and earlier today I was part of a team holding a person in custody…that was said to be from your world. Who are you looking for?"

Lieutenant Oded again answered, "We are in search of our leader. His name is Professor Hai. If anyone can help us defeat this armada, it's the Professor. Can you help us? Will you help us?"

Ben responded, "We had him in custody earlier however when the attack came we lost him. I do not know where he is now but if your information can help us, I will help you find him."

Lieutenant Oded replied, "What about these people? They believe we are here to do them harm."

Ben responded, "Leave them to me."

Ben knew his sole mission was to find Professor Hai and Professor Simmons. These five Gomorrites had risked their life to get information to Professor Hai in the hope that it would be saved. He went back over to Jim to ask about his wife.

Ben asked, "My wife, Thelma Catchings works here on the Yard. Do you know if she survived?"

Jim responded, "We took everybody's name down in case questions were asked later. Let me take you to Denise. She has a list of all the people that are here. Let's see if your wife's name is on it."

The two of them walked over to where Denise had set up her office. There were several people standing around, worried about friends and loved ones.

Jim asked, "Denise…do you have a Thelma Catchings on your list?

Denise answered, "Let me see."

Denise looked down at her list. After she passed all the names on the list, she glanced up for a second and started to look again. She wanted to make sure that she had not missed the name. She did not want to have to tell another person that their love one was not on the list.

Ben saw her searching the list for second time. He knew that his wife's name was not on the list but he did not want to be a burden.

He knew that he had to find Professor Hai and Professor Simmons. He could not worry about the whereabouts of his wife at this time. He told himself that her name not being on the list just meant she wasn't in the warehouse. It didn't mean she was dead. He had to play his role in saving the world.

Denise finished scanning the list a second time. She slowly looked up until her eyes met Ben's eyes.

Denise said, "I'm sorry... but I don't see her name."

Ben responded, "Thank you for taking the time to look."

He then turned to Jim and said, "Jim... I have to take these people to find the two scientists that can stop this attack. Do you have any men that you can spare to help us? These people and the two professors are the key."

Jim responded, "I can't spare any men. We need to protect ourselves."

Ben replied, "Look...if we don't find these professors we won't have a chance of winning this war."

Jim said, "I don't know about that. All I can do is protect the people here. I can't spare anyone."

Ben looked him squarely in his eyes and said, "Look...Jim...I know this looks impossible but this professor is from their world. Those people over there are from their world. They know more about how to beat them than we do. We need to find that professor to have any chance to win this thing. Do you want to be remembered as the guy that could have helped us but didn't?"

He believed he was getting through to Jim.

Jim responded, "I can probably give you two men. We know their ground troops have taken up positions in DC. It's only a matter of time before they find us here and we have to defend ourselves."

Ben replied, "I understand. We can't have too many people anyway. The fewer people we have the easier it will be for us to move around."

***

Lieutenant Oded overheard what Ben said to Jim.

He turned to Lieutenant Yaniv and said, "You stay here and help them defend this place. Since Corporal Sason is injured they will need your help."

Lieutenant Yaniv responded, "Be safe old friend."

Varda looked at Lieutenant Oded and asked, "I want to go with you. Can I my love?"

Lieutenant Oded responded, "You should stay and help these people. They will need your help and we need to keep our numbers small so we can move around quickly."

Varda replied, "But I can help."

Lieutenant Oded took her by the shoulders and consoled her, "My dear Varda. I love you more than you will ever know. This mission is not suited for you. I must go with them and find the Professor. You are not trained for this. Please understand."

Varda responded through her tears, "I always watch you leave…I always worry. I pray that someday I will not have to endure these things. Tell me my prayers will be answered."

Lieutenant Oded told her, "Your prayers will be answered. Just trust in the Lord."

She cried in his arms as Lieutenant Oded broke away to leave her… again. He felt her arms drop down and she just stood there in tears… he heard her whispering a prayer to God for him.

Ben, the two men, and Lieutenant Oded all left the Navy Yard. They hoped that they would be able to find the two professors.

***

Solomon's resistance fighters had grown overnight to over 50 men. They maintained their headquarters in the garage at the Union Center Plaza. Solomon had organized some of them into smaller groups to hit the Gomorrites. They spent all night organizing and planning their attacks.

Solomon announced to the group, "Tonight we will begin to strike back at our enemy. Mitchell and Troy have provided us with some munitions that we can use to set charges on the enemy's strongholds."

"We need to work in small groups. Working in smaller groups will allow us to move around more covertly and help ensure our success. You know your assigned groups and your responsibilities…anyone have any questions?"

None of the men asked any questions. All of them were ready for their part in the plan. They all wanted to strike a blow against the Gomorrite army. It didn't matter if it was only a small blow. They wanted to do something against them.

Solomon continued, "Okay...if there are no questions then everyone should get as much sleep as possible. You will need it for tonight. It's going to be a long night."

Gabriel walked over to Solomon. Solomon noticed the look etched on his face. It was intense.

Gabriel said, "Hey man do you think we can do this with a rag tag bunch?"

Solomon responded, "I realize this isn't paint ball but we have to fight back somehow. I don't want to be a slave...do you?"

Gabriel nodded his head in an affirming manner.

Solomon was glad he had some training to fall back on. Most of all he was glad his friend Gabriel was with him. He knew Gabriel was an intelligent man who loved strategy. Their paint ball experience could be valuable to them.

His mind moved to his wife. He missed her so much. He prayed that she was safe. She was home on the day of the attack. She didn't have to come to DC because their carpet was being cleaned. What a lucky break he thought. He knew if she was alive that she was at the church with all the other survivors. He knew there was no better place for her to be.

Solomon walked to a private corner in the garage. He wanted to think. He needed to process all of this information. He thought about what he had organized since the war started. He was proud of what everyone had chipped in and accomplished, but he knew it was long from being over. He knew if they were successful the next evening, the Gomorrites would turn their attention to them. That would be the big test for his resistance fighters.

***

Professor Hai and Professor Simmons were sitting inside a building hiding from Gomorrite soldiers when the sun came up. Professor Hai knew that the soldiers would not give up until they captured or killed him. Professor Hai had to do something he knew he would not like. He had to kill soldiers. Not for his own life but for Professor Simmons' life as well.

She was asleep on his shoulder. For a moment he had taken pleasure in her beautiful face lying on his shoulder. He watched her sleep and thought he was so blessed to have met her. A loud boom broke through the silence and woke Professor Simmons from her sleep.

Professor Hai jumped up to see what was happening. He looked out the window and saw Gomorrite soldiers had pulled up to the building.

He heard the sergeant shouting instructions.

The sergeant in charge shouted to the men, "Search the buildings. If you find Professor Hai bring him to me."

The men responded, "Yes sir."

They fanned out into the two buildings searching for Professor Hai. Professor Hai readied his weapon but he knew it would not be enough to defend themselves against a patrol of Gomorrite soldiers.

***

Lieutenant Oded, Ben and the two men rushed away from the Navy Yard. Ben knew that Professors Hai and Simmons were in the White House when the attack started. He surmised that they would still be somewhere in that area.

Ben led them in the direction of the White House. From their vantage point they had a good line of sight to the Gomorrite home base. Two Gomorrite soldiers were walking toward the base when their radio went off.

The voice over the radio announced, "Sir, we have tracked Professor Hai to Independence Avenue. We believe he is inside one of the buildings marked Agriculture."

The voice Lieutenant Oded recognized as General Idit responded, "Capture him and bring him to me."

The voice replied, "Yes sir."

Ben whispered as the soldiers moved away, "We just went past there. Let's head back that way."

The four men headed down the street headed toward Independence Avenue and the Department of Agriculture. The Agriculture buildings were too long buildings on either side of Independence Avenue.

Ben hoped that Professor Hai could stay hidden until they were able to get there. If only Professor Hai knew help was near. They were not that far away but with the Gomorrite ships flying overhead they had to be very careful about their movements.

***

The sun was creeping behind the buildings in the West skyline. Ashlee finally woke up. She was tired, hungry and needed to go to the bathroom. When she came out of the bathroom she saw Simon had woke up.

They ate some chicken and got cleaned up. She helped Simon gather some supplies that they might need for their journey. Simon led her out of the apartment. He looked around and then motioned for her to come.

It was all clear and they began to go down the stairwell. The building they were in had taken some damage from the air assault of the previous day. The stairwell had been loosened so they could not just run down the steps quickly.

Carefully they descended down the three flights of the stairs until they hit the bottom. Simon looked out the glass door.

"Ahhhhh," screamed Ashlee.

Simon turned and saw a man had grabbed Ashlee. He was holding her at knife point.

Simon asked, "What are you doing...brother?"

The man responded, "Give me your money."

Simon replied, "Dude... Do you know what's going on out there? We're under attack by aliens and you want my money?"

The man again responded as he kissed Ashlee on the side of her head, "I gonna take this nice peach and your money."

Simon replied, "Okay, okay man, don't hurt her. Here's all the money I have on me. Upstairs there's some more. You can have that to. Just don't hurt her."

Simon tossed the money on the ground. He had $100 on him.

The man looked at the money and then at Simon. He repeated this twice more.

Simon asked, "Are you going to take it?"

The man pushed Ashlee out of the way and went to get the money. Simon kicked at him.

Ashlee yelled, "Simon... no!"

Simon's kick hit the deranged man and knocked him on his back. Simon pounced on him and pinned him down.

He sternly said to him through his teeth, "There are alien soldiers out there trying to kill us. Why you try to take money that may not be useful anymore? This is stupid. Get it together man or they will kill you!"

The man responded through his tears and whimpering, "Okay man, don't hurt me. I didn't mean it. I wasn't gonna hurt her."

Simon picked up the money and took Ashlee by the arm. The two of them left the building heading for I-295. If they could make it they would be home free.

Just as they got to the end of the street and the ramp to the interstate that would lead them to I-295 was in view, they heard a scream from the man they just left. Ashlee turned and saw two men at the apartment and the deranged man was lying on the ground.

They saw one of the soldiers shoot the man at point blank range and while he was on the ground. The other soldier pointed his weapon at Ashlee and Simon. He shot at them. The laser blast hit Simon in the leg, knocking him to the ground.

Ashlee screamed, "Ahhhhh!"

Simon, in pain, turned to Ashlee and said, "Ashlee... take this gun and shoot at them."

Ashlee responded, "I can't do that!"

Simon replied, "If you don't we'll die for sure. Here... take it... point and shoot."

Ashlee whimpered, "I'm scared..."

Simon sternly shouted, "Ashlee... shoot!"

She turned the weapon at the two Gomorrite soldiers as they were running toward them. The shots sounded like thunder in Ashlee's ears as she squeezed the trigger... once... twice... then again... and again. The recoil from firing the weapon knocked the inexperienced shooter to the ground. Her last two shots went helplessly into the air.

She didn't know how many shots she had fired but she saw the soldiers on the ground. She could not believe that she had taken out not one but two lives even if they were trying to kill her and her new friend. She held her head down and the tears of taking a life rolled down her face.

Simon reached for her...he put his arms around her.

Simon looked at her as she was crying and said softly, "Ashlee... you did it. I know it was hard and painful to you but you saved our lives. It's gonna be okay."

Ashlee dropped the gun to the ground and Simon held her tighter in his arms.

***

American forces formed blockades on I-295 and Branch Avenue to prevent the Gomorrite ground forces from pushing their way into Maryland. Troops from Andrews AFB, Bolling AFB and Fort Meade combined to hold the lines.

Colonel Zack Naylor was in command of the troops at Branch Avenue. The Gomorrite forces were building their camp at Pennsylvania Avenue and Branch Avenue. It appeared that their plan was to march down Branch Avenue into Maryland. They did not expect any trouble. The Gomorrites had orders to take slaves.

Colonel Naylor's men set up mines along Branch Avenue to take out as many enemy soldiers as possible. He positioned snipers along the route as well. At Branch and Suitland his men were entrenched to hold the enemy there and not let them any further. They had to hold Andrews because they expected President Davis to arrive there and set up a base of operations.

Since Bolling was located on I-295 and off the Potomac River, Colonel Matt Jefferson believed that they could hold the line against the enemy and use the Potomac to their advantage. The Navy brought in a battleship to support the line.

The DC Metro police training facility was also located on I-295. They provided extra manpower to support the line. Both lines were ready to defend against their estranged brothers who intended to start their ground assault into Maryland.

***

Night had covered the battleground hiding survivors moving around as they searched for food and water. The darkness gave them an advantage over the Gomorrite patrols. Solomon's resistance fighters were ready to use the darkness to their advantage as well.

Solomon began speaking to his men, "Okay men…it's time. You know your assignments and you know the risk. I don't need to go into detail about the importance of these missions. Each one of you know your responsibility and you know the importance that it will play in helping to defend this planet. Success will help our fighting soldiers in Maryland and Virginia to defeat this enemy. Good luck to you all."

Solomon had put together five units and they each have separate missions in the city. Two of the units were tactical and used explosives to derail the plans of the Gomorrites. Two were designed for recognizance. These units went out and gathered information for the resistance. The last unit was a rescue unit. If they could rescue anyone that was captured by the Gomorrites, this unit would be the one to do it.

Their success will cause the Gomorrites' focus to change from attacking the American forces to defending itself from the resistance. He hoped this would allow the American forces to better defend the country and attack the enemy. He also hoped that the Gomorrite forces would become spread too thin to defend the city. Solomon was very smart and he believed the Gomorrites didn't plan for his style of warfare.

Secretly Solomon prayed that all his soldiers would return safe and the mission would be successful. This was their first time out and he was nervous for them.

***

Gabriel took his men in the direction of the White House. Their assignment was to strike the troop barracks near the White House. Solomon had intel that the Gomorrite soldiers were housed outside the White House. Gomorrite soldiers patrolled the city in shifts. Gabriel hoped to hit them just after a shift had returned from patrol and would be tired.

Gabriel had three men with him including himself. They needed to be small and mobile. They had to stay off the main roads. Being small and mobile allowed them to easily go in and out of buildings and make it all the way to the barracks undetected.

They were counting on this tactic to be successful. Large groups would attract soldiers and they would have to fight their way in and out to achieve their mission. The numbers game would favor the Gomorrites but small tactical units with a specific mission had a better chance of succeeding.

Gabriel and his team came out of the parking garage on First Street and headed behind Union Center Plaza towards 2nd Street. They waited behind some buildings until it was clear. After a couple minutes they ran across North Capitol Street and onto the next street. Then they went down past Georgetown University Law School.

They kept running and hiding between and behind buildings until they reached 12th and Pennsylvania. They stopped to rest there. In the distance they could hear troops moving, vessels coming and going and screams of prisoners being raped and tortured.

There were three barracks and each resistance member had C-4 explosives for each barracks. They had obtained these explosives from DC National Guard members who had joined the resistance. They set the timers for the explosives to go off at 8:00 PM.

***

Donald was one of three men with Gabriel. He was headed to the barracks which was the barracks closest to the White House. He got to the barracks and placed his charges. After the last charge was set he came away from the building and started to return to the rally point.

Halfway back to the rally point he saw a Gomorrite soldier attempting to rape a woman. She was vigorously fighting back. He ran over…crept up behind the soldier and stabbed him from behind. The soldier yelled out in pain and fell on top of the woman. The woman kicked from under him and Donald grabbed her arm.

The woman took the knife from Donald and repeatedly stabbed the corpse of the soldier.

Donald grabbed her and told her, "We have to get out of here… now!"

They both ran toward the rally point with Donald leading the way.

***

Will was a resistance member and the third member of Gabriel's group. He placed his charges and was on his way back to the rally point. As he was running he saw Gabriel waving his hands emphatically. He didn't know why Gabriel was waving at him until he saw Gomorrite soldiers coming toward him.

It was too late. Gabriel hid behind some trees as the soldiers captured his new friend. Two Gomorrite soldiers held him down while one beat him across his face.

Gabriel could hear the soldiers saying, "Stupid...Adamian... did you think you could escape!"

It was clear that they thought Will was trying to escape from the holding area. As he was taking each hit he was glad that they didn't realize that he had just set C-4 charges on their barracks.

As a thunderous blow struck him again in the face, he looked over in the area where Gabriel was last seen. The blood ran down his face and over his eyes. He couldn't see Gabriel now but he hoped that the mission would succeed.

He never told them anything. It was three minutes to eight. Gabriel ran as fast as he could to the rally point. He could see Donald and a woman in the distance when the explosives went off.

Boom! Boom! Boom!

The sound echoed loudly through the night air. After the explosion, Will smiled and passed out.

***

President Davis was sitting in his underground bunker under the White House. King Abimelech had no idea that the leader of the United States was right below him. The Secretary of Defense came into the office where President Davis was sitting.

The Secretary of Defense said, "Sir... we have assurances that your family is safe in Cheyenne Mountain."

President Davis responded, "Thank you. Any word on how things are going up there?"

The Secretary of Defense replied, "I haven't heard anything new yet."

The Chairman of the Joint Chiefs of Staff walked in the room.

He said, "Excuse me Sirs,"

President Davis replied, "It's okay Bob. What you got?"

Bob answered, "The troops are in place at Branch and 295. There's no Gomorrite activity as of yet."

President Davis replied, "Okay... let me..."

The ground above them shook.

President Davis asked, "What was that? Are we striking back?"

Bob answered, "Not to my knowledge Sir."

The three of them walked out the office and into the operations room.

Bob asked, "What was that?"

One of the analyst replied, "We don't know but it appears that the barracks the Gomorrite soldiers were living in just exploded. By our estimates there were probably 100 men in those barracks at the time."

President Davis said, "Whoever did... thank them."

He returned back to his office and waited for the war to rage on.

***

Ashlee took Simon's hand and he slowly pulled her up. They began heading toward I-295. She had to help him walk so Simon's injuries slowed them down.

Ashlee was visibly shaken by her actions. It didn't matter to her that they were trying to kill her. All that mattered was that she took a life. As they walked they saw an enemy fighter fly overhead.

Simon shouted as he pulled Ashlee down, "Get down!"

They both ducked down hoping they weren't seen. When the fighter was gone Ashlee looked up and there were three people standing over her and Simon. She feared that some crazy Americans were going to attack them. She thought, *"Wasn't it enough that aliens were trying to kill them!"*

One of the men spoke first, "Hi... I'm Wayne. This is Millie and Tre. I hope you guys aren't headed toward 295.

Simon answered as he tried to stand to his feet, "We were. We're trying to get to Waldorf."

Wayne responded, "Bad move. The enemy has set up a camp. They are planning to move into Maryland by going down 295. They also have 395 blocked into Virginia. We're basically trapped."

Ashlee felt guilty about her thoughts. These were just nice people trying to get home. She thought, *"I guess everyone hasn't gone crazy."*

Ashlee asked Tre, "What happened to your arm?"

Tre answered, "One of the soldiers cut it in a fight. I took his butt out thought!"

Ashlee said, "Let me take a look at it."

Tre asked, "You a doctor?"

Ashlee answered, "No...I'm a nurse."

Simon asked Wayne, "So where are you headed?"

Wayne responded, "I don't know. We were trying to..."

They all turned as they heard the sound of the explosives by the White House. All of them fell to the ground.

Millie shouted, "What was that?"

Wayne answered, "It sounded like it came from that direction."

He was pointing in the direction of the White House.

Simon replied, "You're right. That can only mean we've started fighting back."

Then Simon said to Wayne, "I have to get her to Waldorf where it's safe. We have to find a way."

Wayne asked, "You know how to drive a boat?"

Simon answered, "No...but if it will get my girl home safe... I'll learn."

Ashlee said to Tre, "There... that's better. I put some cream on it to help prevent infection so you should be fine in a couple days."

Tre responded, "Thanks... it feels better."

Then Tre looked at Simon and remarked, "You got a good catch dude."

Simon smiled and looked back at Wayne.

He asked, "So what's the plan?"

Wayne responded, "Boating down the Potomac."

***

Slam! General Idit's tablet hit the table and everyone jumped at the sound.

He shouted, "You imbeciles! How could you let them get that close to us! I have lost over 100 men tonight because of your stupidity, report to my office at once!"

The soldiers on the other end of the radio knew what that meant. They turned and began to run from the camp.

General Idit turned to his aide and said, "Go and get them. The cowards will most likely run!"

***

The second resistance attack was led by a man named, Malcolm. He called himself Malcolm X after the Muslim leader. Malcolm's father was a member of a black liberation group in the 1970s.

Even though the times had changed Malcolm's father still believed that African Americans were being mistreated in the United States. He raised Malcolm with those same beliefs.

Malcolm's home was in a poverty stricken area of Washington DC. What friends and family didn't understand was why Malcolm lived there. He was a very educated man. Malcolm held a Master's degree in Business Administration and his position in the federal government paid him six figures.

However, Malcolm felt his place was with his people. He was a leader in his neighborhood. He fought to keep crime out of the neighborhood. He fought for equal rights for African Americans. He was a natural leader.

Solomon immediately recognized that Malcolm's leadership skills were going to be greatly needed. He was selected to lead one of the teams and Solomon knew he could be counted on to run the organization if something happened to him.

Before Malcolm went out on the mission, Solomon informed him that if something were to happen to him, he wanted Malcolm to take over as leader.

Malcolm had three people with him named Jamaal, Wilson, and Gina. Their mission was to sabotage the forces at Branch Avenue.

Solomon received information that the Gomorrite forces were forming at Branch and Pennsylvania. They were going to begin their assault on Maryland by coming down Branch. They also had information that the United States military was forming a line at Branch and Suitland to stop the Gomorrites. Malcolm and his team wanted to set up some explosives to slow the Gomorrites and help the US military.

Malcolm and his team came in range of the Gomorrite camp. They were approximately a block away.

Malcolm was instructing his team, "Wilson, I need you to put some C-4 on those ships over there. Jamaal you and Gina go over to that building and plant some C-4 on it."

"It looks like they are using that building as a headquarters. I'm going to do some recognizance to see if we can take something for our use. Let's meet back here in 30 minutes...we straight?"

They all nodded in agreement and went out to their respective assignments. Each member was outraged about the attacks on their city. Malcolm thought about the day before Gina and Wilson were in rival gangs in DC and today none of that mattered. What mattered is they all have a common enemy.

***

Jamaal and Gina approached the back side of the building. Jamaal motioned for Gina to place her C-4 on the back wall near the air conditioning unit. Jamaal went around the front and placed his C-4 on the front of the building.

He was almost caught by two soldiers but managed to stay in the shadows. When he finally returned Gina was waiting.

She said, "What took you so long?"

Jamaal responded, "Had a little trouble."

He then motioned for them to return the way they came. The charges were set to go off at 10 PM. When Jamaal and Gina returned to the meeting point Wilson was already there.

Wilson asked, "You guys good?"

Gina responded, "Of course... don't you know who I represent?"

Wilson laughed and said, "That doesn't matter anymore...we all in the same gang."

Jamaal said, "Cool it guys. Have you seen X?"

Wilson replied, "Naw...not yet."

***

Malcolm was hiding behind six Gomorrite soldiers. He was trying to overhear what they were saying but they didn't have a translator device. He could not understand what they were saying.

Malcolm returned to the rally point.

Malcolm said, "Everything set?"

Wilson replied, "Yeah we're good."

Malcolm responded, "Let's get out of here. We need to put some distance between us and them before the charges go off."

They had gotten about four blocks away when the C-4 went off. The explosives lit up the night sky.

***

Gabriel, Donald and the girl Donald rescued had returned to resistance headquarters. They were discussing the results of their mission with Solomon.

Solomon asked, "Where's Will?"

Gabriel answered, "He was captured. I couldn't save him"

Solomon said, "I heard the charges go off. I guess that means your mission was successful. Who is she?"

Donald answered, "Her name is..."

She cut him off, "I can speak for myself. My name is Kim and I want in. I want to take out as many of these people as I can."

Gabriel responded, "Good we need the help. Do you have any weapons experienced?"

Kim answered, "I spent four years in the Marine Corps infantry."

Gabriel replied, "We could use her in Will's spot."

Solomon responded, "Okay. You set her up."

They heard another explosion in the direction of Branch and Pennsylvania. Solomon smiled.

Solomon happily said, "Sounds like we were successful again."

Gabriel asked, "Was that X's team?"

Solomon responded, "I hope so."

***

Gomorrite soldiers were searching the two Agriculture buildings looking for Professor Hai. Professor Hai wanted Professor Simmons to hide in one of the rooms.

Professor Hai explained, "Cassie... the soldiers are here in the building. You must hide. They don't know about you. They are looking for me.

Cassie sternly replied, "No! I'm not going to let them just capture you."

239

Professor Hai responded, "We don't have a choice there's too many of them."

Cassie began to cry.

She said through her tears, "I can't."

Professor Hai replied, "You must… Cassie… you can help stop this invasion. It makes no sense for both of us to be captured."

Silence fell between the two of them for what seemed like an eternity.

Then Professor Hai continued, "Now… hide in the room. I will go down the hall so they don't find you."

It pained Professor Hai to see tears flowing from her eyes. Professor Hai wiped the tears from her face.

Professor Hai said, "God will protect me."

Professor Simmons said, "You don't understand I have never sought God for anything. I am a scientist and I believe that science was the beginning and end to everything. If there is a God I pray that He does protect you."

Professor Hai guided her into the office room and she hid behind the big mahogany desk inside. Professor Hai thought, *"This desk must belong to someone very important."*

After he walked out the office he glanced back Professor Hai glanced back through the glass window. He was worried about her. He didn't want to see another woman he loved die at the hands of a Gomorrite.

He had to get far enough away from Cassie so that they would not find her. He made his way down the hall to a separate section of the building.

He could hear the soldiers approaching his position. He knew they wouldn't kill him because General Idit would have given an instruction not to. His plan was to take some of them down before his capture.

As they approached he waited until they were close enough. Once they were close he would jump out and pull the trigger. The soldiers came from around the corner. Professor Hai was breathing heavily. He was not a military man so this was all new to him. He heard them get closer and closer. When he believed they had gotten close enough he leaped out and pulled the trigger.

"Click" was all he heard. The gun was empty. He knew nothing about guns and didn't realize that he used all the bullets the evening before. The soldiers laugh as they began walking toward the Professor. The laughter was drowned out by the sound of bullets firing and impacting the soldiers.

A voice yelled, "Professor...get down!"

Professor Hai felled to the floor and stayed there as the soldiers were being cut to pieces by someone. He did not know who it was but he was thankful that God had sent someone to come to his aid. He knew that if General Idit had gotten his hands on him that his life would be over.

When the firing ceased Professor Hai turned to see who was shooting at the soldiers. He happily saw his friend, Lieutenant Oded, a man he believed was named Ben, and two other men. He excitedly got off the floor and ran to hug his friend.

He shouted, "Oded...Oded...I cannot believe it!"

Lieutenant Oded responded, "Professor...It is wonderful to see you again!"

Lieutenant Oded asked, "Professor Hai...are you alright?"

Professor Hai responded, "Yes...we have to get Cassie."

Lieutenant Oded asked, "Who is Cassie?"

Ben answered, "She is the other professor I told you about. Professor Simmons."

Lieutenant Oded asked, "Where is she?"

Professor Hai answered, "She is in a room down there."

Professor Hai ran into the big office room that appeared to be a director's office of some kind.

He shouted, "Cassie! Where are you?"

Cassie hit her head as she jumped up from behind the desk and answered, "Ouch! I'm here!"

She ran to him and jumped in his arms. They embraced each other and she kissed him. He was shocked. No woman had ever kissed him first before. This was not the behavior of women on Gomorrah.

Lieutenant Oded said, "Uh...Professor...we need to get out of here."

Professor Hai looked at Lieutenant Oded and said, "Cassie this is my good friend and fellow resistance member Lieutenant Oded. Lieutenant Oded this is Cassie. She has been very helpful in my stay here on Adamina."

Lieutenant Oded responded, "I see."

Ben interjected, "We better get out of here. I'm sure they will be coming."

Professor Hai said, "Ben is right. Let's get out of here."

They all turned and ran out the way Lieutenant Oded and the others came in.

***

The bodies of the Gomorrite soldiers were found by their comrades. They ran back to their sergeant and reported what they found.

The sergeant didn't want to report this result to the General. He knew the General would be angry and want blood. He thought about the situation then pulled out his weapon and shot one of the soldiers who reported the information to him.

He said to the others, "This man was a resistance member. I am going to report to the General that he aided Professor Hai's escape. I will also report that we are right on Professor Hai's heels. Does anyone of you have a problem with this report?"

All of the men responded, "No sir!"

***

General Idit was visibly enraged when he found out about the second attack which killed his officer in charge of the Branch Avenue attack. Now he had just received word that his men failed to capture Professor Hai.

General Idit shouted, "Now this stinking resistance has followed me here! I will kill them all!"

He whirled his arms around knocking everything down that was in his way.

His aide reluctantly said, "Sir..."

General Idit turned vigorously in anger at the sound of his voice.

His aide continued, "The soldiers who attempted to run are here."

The soldiers were brought in and thrown to their knees in front of the General. He looked at them with utter disdain. He wanted to slit all their throats.

General Idit angrily said, "I should kill you all for your cowardice. But my men are dying at the hands of these idiots. It is your job to go

242

out and find this resistance. When you find them report back to me. I will take a company of men to them and personally kill them all."

One of the men said, "Yes sir. General we will not fail you."

The General turned away from them and the men stood up and ran out of the room. They were grateful for the second chance. They did not want to confront the General again.

***

The time had come to get the President out of the underground shelter. The Gomorrites had not discovered it was there but the Secret Service did not want to wait any longer. The attacks from the unknown assailants gave them the advantage of less coverage at the Gomorrite home base.

They were going to use the secret tunnels to get the President out to a waiting vehicle and rush him to Andrews. The Secret Service agents were instructed that nothing was to stop the President from getting to Andrews and most of all he could not be captured by the Gomorrites.

They began to move out. The plan was working fine as they made it to the street above without incident. The President was placed in a car that was pushed three blocks away from the White House so the soldiers wouldn't hear it start.

Once in the vehicle a Gomorrite patrol spotted them.

One soldier yelled, "Halt!"

The limousine sped off in an attempt to escape. The soldiers started firing at the vehicle. A blast hit the vehicle and caused it to roll over. It came to a stop upside down. The soldiers approached the vehicle but bullets began flying at them. The patrol retreated and called for backup.

Two men approached the vehicle and swung open the door. A Secret Service agent jumped out of the front of the vehicle pointed his gun at the man.

Solomon said, "I'm not your enemy friend."

The agent replied, "Who are you?"

Solomon replied, "I am a man that can get you and whoever you got in here to safety or we can continue to stand and wait for those guys to return. Which one is it?"

President Davis stepped out of the vehicle and said, "You know who I am. Can you get us to Andrews?"

Solomon responded surprised to see the President, "Mr. President. We attacked their forces at Branch Avenue earlier. It's going to be difficult to get you to Andrews but sir my men can handle anything."

President Davis turned to his Secret Service agent, "Let's go with them."

Solomon led them back to resistance headquarters. This was the break that Solomon needed. His attacks were successful and now he was providing protection for the President of the United States.

***

The morning hour was early when Simon, Ashlee and their new friends reached the water. Wayne found three jet skis abandoned probably when the attack started.

Wayne asked, "Can anybody besides me drive one of these babies?"

Simon answered, "Yeah…I drove one once. I thought you said boat?"

Tre answered, "I can get down on one these bad boys. When I was in college down in Florida we road these things all the time."

Wayne said, "Good we can hop on these and ride them up the coast line until we hit Bolling. Our troops should be there. We should be safe from there."

Simon responded, "Let's do it."

Ashlee got on one Jet Ski with Simon. Wayne and Millie hopped on another one and Tre got on the last one by himself. They all started them up and began driving them up the coast to Bolling with Wayne leading the way. They were driving without the lights in the hope that the Gomorrites would not see them.

Before they got a hundred yards a light came on and was shinning down on them. They panicked.

Wayne shouted, "Push it! Let's get out of here!"

All the Jet Ski engines screamed as they attempted to hit the high speeds and race towards Bolling. However, they could not outrun the fighter that was bearing down on them.

CHAPTER 11

THE ADAMIAN RESISTANCE

Laser blasts began raining down from the sky targeted at the Jet Skis as they were racing toward Bolling. One blast was a direct hit on the Jet Ski driven by Tre. Ashlee dropped her head as she knew he was dead. She had never been this scared before. She hung on to Simon as hard as she could and prayed they would be safe.

Ashlee couldn't see Wayne and Millie any longer. A laser blast hit the water near Simon and Ashlee's Jet Ski. It caused a wave to rise up toward them…knocking them off the Jet Ski and into the water.

Now with both of them in the water Ashlee could see Simon helplessly falling deeper and deeper in the water. He wasn't moving. He wasn't trying to swim. She hoped he was only unconscious. She submerged herself under the water and went after him.

She was glad that she took those diving lessons her dad pressed her about last year. She thought, *"Maybe God told him something."*

Once she got to him she wrapped her arms around his chest from behind and brought him back to the surface.

Ashlee used all the strength she had to swim to shore, holding Simon but she couldn't make it. Fatigue was setting in. Her arms got tired.

She began yelling, "Simon wake up! Wake up! I can't make it…I need you to wake up!"

He still wasn't moving but she couldn't give up.

She screamed, "God…help me!"

That seemed to be all she needed. Suddenly she felt Simon beginning to wake up. She felt him begin to swim on his own. The load was off of Ashlee now and she could swim easier. They both made it to shore and collapsed from fatigue.

Simon looked at Ashlee and through his deep breaths he said, "Thanks. I owe you two now."

Ashlee was crying. When she reached the shore she was on her hands and knees. She then fell onto her back with her legs bent at the knees. She was in tears after another brush with death.

Simon crawled over to her and asked, "What's wrong?"

Ashlee leaned over to him and kissed him and he kissed her back.

She said, "I thought you were gone. You can't die on me. I've already loss my best friend. I can't lose you too."

Simon responded, "I'm not going anywhere."

Just then a light shined in their faces.

A voice yelled, "Put your hands up…now!"

Simon and Ashlee both raised their hands at the same time. They were looking deeply into each other's eyes.

Ashlee said in a soft tone, "I give up. I can't do this anymore."

Simon replied, "Don't give up. God seems to love you. He won't let us down now."

Ashlee smiled. God did love her and she needed Simon to remind her of that fact.

The voice said, "You're Americans?"

Simon took his eyes off the woman he now knew he loved and said to the man, "Yes…we are!"

The voice said, "I'm Sergeant Davis from the Bolling Security Forces unit. We thought you were Gomorrite soldiers."

Ashlee screamed, "Oh…thank you Lord…AGAIN!"

Simon replied, "Told you he loves you. We had some other friends with us. Have you seen them?"

Sergeant Davis answered, "We got two people up the coast a little ways. How many of you was it all together?"

Simon responded, "There were five of us."

Sergeant Davis replied, "I will put the word out for the fifth person. In the meantime we have a staging location on Bolling. We're keeping civilians there until we can transport them safely to Waldorf. We will take you guys there. You can rest and get something to eat…if you want it."

Simon and Ashlee began walking with Sergeant Davis and his men. They were headed back to their patrol vehicles when a blast hit one of the vehicles sending pieces of it flying in the air. All of them fell to the ground and the Security Forces team started firing in the direction of the laser blast.

Ashlee was screaming…agonizing in pain. An object was in her left shoulder. Simon saw her and he grabbed her and dragged her behind a rock while the battle raged on against the Gomorrites.

Ashlee yelled, "Pull it out! Pull it out!"

Simon responded, "I don't know if I should Ashlee."

Ashlee grabbed him by the collar and looked sternly into his eyes, "Who's the nurse here. Pull it out!"

She continued to agonize in pain. Simon braced himself to pull it out.

Ashlee quickly stopped him and asked, "No wait…where is the first aid kit?"

Simon looked around and grabbed his bag.

He replied, "It's right here."

Ashlee continued, "Take out some bandages and get them ready. As soon as you pull it out apply the bandages using pressure to stop the bleeding. It's important to keep pressure on the wound. Don't let me pass out either."

Simon responded, "Okay but you know it's going to hurt like heck."

Ashlee replied, "It's hurting now…just pull it!"

Simon got the bandages ready. He got ready to pull the object from Ashlee's shoulder.

He said, "Here goes…"

He pulled it and Ashlee screamed with pain. The Security Forces troops had defeated the Gomorrites and ran over to see what was happening. They saw Simon placing the bandages on Ashlee and applying pressure to the wound. Ashlee continued to cry out in pain.

Sergeant Davis instructed one of the airmen, "Get these two to the staging area."

Then he turned to the other airmen and said, "Let's continue to patrol this coast. Swartz…you and Milsap go down there and patrol for about 100 meters. Jones you're with me."

Sergeant Davis knelt down and told Ashlee and Simon, "This airman will take you back to the staging area. We have some medical supplies there and they will give you something for the pain."

Ashlee replied, "Thanks."

Sergeant Davis looked at Simon and said, "Keep pressure on it and don't let her pass out."

Simon nodded his head to say he understood.

Simon, Ashlee and the airman headed toward a vehicle that would take them to the staging area. Ashlee was leaning on Simon as she walked. She reminisced about her last couple of days. She thought about how she almost died by falling in that hole. She remembered how she couldn't save her best friend. She thought about how she was held at knife point. Then she thought about how she had to take the life of two men that she didn't even know.

Then she was knocked off of a Jet Ski and had to try and save her new boyfriend from drowning. Was he her boyfriend she thought? He had to be. Better be.

Now she had a piece of metal from a vehicle stuck in her shoulder and her new boyfriend had to remove it. The pain was coursing through her body so much she felt herself slipping away a couple of times. She knew she had to stay awake. She just kept focusing on getting home safely…after all her parents had to meet her new man.

***

The President and a Secret Service agent arrived at resistance headquarters with Solomon and some of Solomon's men.

President Davis asked, "You have done all this since the attack?"

Solomon responded, "Yes sir."

President Davis asked again, "How?"

Solomon answered, "I rounded up every able bodied person who wanted to fight back. We sought out every specialty these people had. A little luck brought us a couple National Guard soldiers with access to artillery and ordnance. I just went about inspiring and organizing the resistance to make it happen. I don't plan to give up my city or my world."

President Davis said, "You have done a great job. Your missions last night gave me a chance to escape the White House. Thank you."

Solomon motioned for Malcolm to come over. Malcolm came over and Solomon introduced him to the President.

Solomon asked Malcolm, "Do you think we can get the President to Andrews safely?"

Malcolm answered, "We would have to take several back routes out of the city but it can be done."

Solomon said, "I'm going to lead an assault against the Gomorrites to draw their attention from you. Your mission at dusk tonight is to get the President to Andrews safely."

President Davis said, "I can't ask you to risk your men in an assault. That would be suicide."

Solomon replied, "We won't go all out. We're just going to do enough to keep them occupied and off of you."

President Davis said, "Okay. Can we get someone in the tunnels under the White House? I need to get word to the Chairman of the Joint Chiefs of Staff and the Secretary of Defense."

Solomon called, "Shep! Come over here for a second."

Delonte Sheppard was the best man they had for recognizance. Everyone called him Shep as a nickname. In college he won two gold medals, one in the 100 meter dash and the other in the 200 meter dash. He was able to elude the Gomorrite patrols with his speed.

Shep asked, "What you got, Solomon?"

Solomon replied, "President Davis needs you to go on a mission for him."

Shep said, "Mr. President...I would be honored. What's the mission?"

President Davis explained to Shep, "I need you to get word to the Secretary of Defense and the Chairman of the Joint Chiefs of Staff that I am safe and will be on my way to Andrews this evening. Tell them to give you any information we have that can help your group. Do you know how to get to the tunnels?"

Shep answered, "Yes sir."

President Davis responded, "Okay. Thank you."

Shep said, "No thanks necessary sir."

***

Professor Hai and the others successfully made it out of the Agriculture building and down to L'Enfant Plaza.

Lieutenant Oded said, "Okay Professor…We need a plan. We had this disk drive from Jacob but it got fried when we escaped. It contained a virus designed to disable the warships. What do we do now?"

Professor Hai asked, "Did he tell you anything that could help?"

Lieutenant Oded responded, "Not to me. I was in prison at the time. Lieutenant Yaniv spoke to him directly."

Professor Hai asked, "Where is he?"

Ben responded, "He's at the Navy Yard."

Professor Hai replied, "Then we need to go there. I must talk with him."

Professor Simmons said, "I hope we're going to rest for a minute. My feet are killing me."

***

It was daylight now. The sun had lit up the District again. The war scorn city which was once a tourist attraction is now filled with dust and debris in every direction. Troops continue to scour the city looking for slaves to imprison. There was one Adamian that was hard for the Gomorrite troops to catch.

Shep was making his way to the White House tunnels to deliver the message President Davis asked him to deliver to the Secretary of Defense and the Chairman of the Joints Chiefs of Staff. He had successfully gotten close to the entrance to the tunnels when he stopped in his tracks at what he saw.

Shep saw Gomorrite soldiers coming out of the tunnel and they had hostages with them. Four Americans came out of the tunnel with the Gomorrite soldiers. Shep recognized one of them as the Chairman of the Joint Chiefs of Staff. Shep had seen him on television a couple of times.

There were only two soldiers marching them out. Shep thought he could sneak up on them and rescue the men. He began to make his move until he noticed one of the agents looking at him. The agent was nodding his head as a signal to stop Shep from approaching.

Shep didn't know what to do.

He thought to himself, *"Should I try and rescue them or not? Why is he motioning to me to stop? Do they have a plan already? Let me wait a minute and see what happens."*

Shep saw more soldiers making their way out of the tunnels. There were six of them all together and one of them was highly decorated. The man began yelling at the Chairman of the Joint Chiefs of Staff. Shep moved to a safer location.

Shep could hear General Idit asking the Chairman of the Joint Chiefs of Staff, "Where is your President? Tell me and I will go easy on your men."

The Chairman responded, "I will never tell you anything."

General Idit moved to one of the Secret Service agents and pointed his weapon at him. He looked one more time at the Chairman who would not give in to the General. The General then pulled the trigger and the agent was instantly killed.

General Idit then turned back to the Chairman and asked him again, "Now...I ask you again...where is your President Davis?"

The Chairman replied again, "These men are prepared to give their lives for the President. We won't tell you no matter what you do to us."

General Idit was visibly upset and shouted, "I will find him myself!"

In one motion he struck the Chairman across the head with his weapon, knocking him to the ground.

He then pointed his weapon at the chairman and killed him. He killed each remaining agent asking them to tell where the president was but none of them would give in to the General. He hated them all for not being weak.

Shep fell to the ground in tears. He just watched one of the country's leaders executed in front of him. Now he had to go and report this information back to the President. When he rose he lost his balance and stepped on a branch making a noise.

General Idit looked in his direction and saw him.

He ordered his men, "Catch him and bring him to me!"

***

Ben had quickly and quietly guided the group near the Navy Yard entrance. From his vantage point he thought he would be able to see the warehouse but all he saw was smoke rising in the sky where once there was a building. Lieutenant Oded saw Ben's reaction and pushed his way to the front of the group.

Lieutenant Oded asked Ben, "What's going on…are we here?"

Ben looked at him with pity in his eyes, "I'm afraid…the warehouse has been destroyed. There was nothing left but the burnt remains of the building. It looks like the building took a direct hit.

Ben tried to comfort Lieutenant Oded as he fell to his knees. In the little time that Ben knew Lieutenant Oded he knew he loved his people. He could empathize with him.

Lieutenant Oded cried out, "Varda! My Varda! I will have my revenge!"

Professor Hai dropped to his knees and consoled his friend, "My friend…I am here for you."

***

Professor Simmons didn't know Varda and she had never been to the warehouse but she was moved by the love she witnessed. She cried for Lieutenant Oded. She didn't want Professor Hai to become distracted from consoling his friend so she turned away so he couldn't see her crying. As soon as she turned she saw a young boy standing behind her with a look on his face like he was happy to see others like him.

He was dirty and his clothes were torn but Professor Simmons knew that this child was special because he had survived for three days by himself.

Professor Simmons asked, "What's your name?"

The boy answered, "They took them away."

Professor Simmons asked again, "Took who away? Who took them away?"

The boy answered, "The soldiers…they came and took all of them away. They tried to fight but they couldn't beat them."

Professor Simmons asked, "What happen to the building?"

The boy answered, "They blew it up. They said they wanted to tell everyone that it wasn't good to hide. My name is Carl."

Professor Simmons turned to the rest of the group and said, "Hey... they're still alive! This boy...Carl...just told me they took them away."

Lieutenant Oded stood up and walked over to the boy. Everyone followed. Carl stepped back as Lieutenant Oded approached him. He acted like he was scared of Lieutenant Oded.

Professor Simmons said, "Don't be afraid. He is a friend."

Carl looked at her and trusted her. He took her hand seemingly for protection.

Lieutenant Oded asked Carl, "Son...are you sure they were taken away."

Carl responded, "Yes. They took all of them away. I hid over here. They didn't see me."

Lieutenant Oded turned to the group and said, "We must rescue them. It is the only way."

Ben asked, "How are we going to do that?"

Professor Hai answered, "We will find a way."

***

Shep was running as fast as he could. He had to dodge the laser blast that was being fired at him by the soldiers. He managed to make his way to New York Avenue. He was running down New York Avenue leaving the soldiers in the dust but one soldier was right behind him. He couldn't believe this Gomorrite soldier was able to stick with him but he continued running as fast as he could.

The Gomorrite soldier gained on him. He got closer and closer until he dived at Shep and caught him. The soldier got on top of Shep and started to swing on him. Shep blocked some of the punches and knocked the soldier to the ground.

They both got up. Shep could see the other soldiers coming. He thought about running again but that was fast becoming less of an option. He had no other option but to fight his way out or let himself be capture.

He started hearing gunfire. The soldiers who were running after him began firing back. Now he just had the one soldier to deal with. Shep wasn't a fighter so he hoped he could take this one soldier. He poised himself ready to fight but the strangest thing was the soldier just stood there. Then he raised his hands…giving up. Shep thought, *"Why is he scared of me?"*

Malcolm walked up behind Shep and said, "Well, well, well…I didn't know I was going to have to bail your hide out today."

Shep turned and saw Malcolm holding a gun on the soldier. Jamaal, Gina and Wilson came down the street.

Jamaal said, "We took them out X."

Shep said, "Thanks guys but what do we do with this guy? He was really fast."

Malcolm replied, "Let me handle this. You go back to headquarters and report to Solomon. We have to complete the rest of our mission."

Shep said, "Thanks."

Malcolm and his team nodded and watched Shep walk away down New York Avenue.

Shep made it about two blocks before the sound of a gunshot raced through his ears. He turned and saw the Gomorrite soldier on the ground and Malcolm standing over him. Malcolm fired two more shots into the corpse of the soldier.

Shep was upset. He did not sign on to a mercenary organization. That man may have been an enemy but he didn't deserve to be executed. He was going to report the incident to Solomon and if he sanctioned the execution he would quit the resistance.

Shep ran back to resistance headquarters and looked for Solomon. He was visibly angry. He found Solomon with the President.

Shep walked over to them and began telling them what happened, "Sir…I'm sorry but the Gomorrites found the tunnels. When I got there they were marching some men out of the tunnels. One of them was the Chairman of the Joint Chiefs. I was going to try and rescue them but one of the agents warned me with his eyes, not to try. There were more soldiers in the tunnel. One of them was highly decorated."

"He kept asking the Chairman a question. He was asking him where you were. When the Chairman wouldn't answer him he executed one of the agents. Then he executed the Chairman and all the other men."

"I made a sound and they heard me. They started chasing after me. One of their soldiers was very fast and he caught up to me. Malcolm and his team showed up and saved me."

President Davis was very upset, "We have lost too many good people. We have to put an end to this."

Solomon replied, "We will, Mr. President. We will."

Shep looked at Solomon and said, "I need to talk to you alone."

Solomon responded, "Okay."

President Davis said, "I'll go over here and talk to the people."

Solomon asked, "What is it?"

Shep explained, "When Malcolm saved me there was one soldier still alive. He was the one that chased me down. I asked Malcolm what were we going to do with him and he said he would take care of it. I said okay and left. I was about two blocks away when I heard a gunshot."

Shep continued, "I turned and saw Malcolm standing over the body of the soldier. Look man…I didn't sign up to be in a mercenary group. If that's your plan to operate this thing…I'm out."

Solomon smashed his fist into his hand. He knew this was possible with Malcolm. He liked Malcolm's leadership and wanted him to lead the group if something happened to him but the only thing he feared was Malcolm's liberation history.

Solomon said, "I don't believe in this type of behavior. I specifically instructed Malcolm to bring any prisoners here so we can question them. I didn't want him to kill anyone unless it was in the heat of battle."

Shep asked, "What are you going to do about it?"

Solomon replied, "I will handle it when he returns. You will be with me."

***

It was early afternoon when Simon arrived at the in processing center on Bolling AFB. He along with Ashlee was taken to the triage station for their wounds. Since Ashlee's was more severe she was seen by a doctor quickly. Simon was waiting in the waiting area when he saw Wayne and Millie.

Simon shouted, "Wayne! Hey man, over here!"

Wayne responded, "Hey! Millie look, its Simon!"

Millie waved at Simon and they both walked over to him. Neither of them was injured and they were glad to see him.

Wayne happily said, "Hey man. How are you doing? We thought we were the only ones to make it."

Simon responded as he stuck out his hand to shake Wayne's hand, "Naw man…we made it too. Ashlee is being seen by the doctor. She had a piece of metal in her shoulder. Have you seen Tre?"

Wayne replied, "I don't think he made it. We saw him take a direct hit."

Millie added, "We said a prayer for him. He was a good dude. He helped us get through that first night."

Simon replied, "Wow…I'm sorry he's gone. I liked him too."

Wayne asked, "What are you here for?"

Simon answered, "They want to look at my leg and make sure it's okay."

Wayne said, "Good man. I still can't believe…"

Ashlee came over and hugged Millie and said, "Hey! You guys made it!"

Wayne said, "Hey Ash how's your shoulder?"

Ashlee responded, "The doctor said it will be fine. I'm going out on the floor and help with some of the patients. Simon can you get us set up? They're taking some people to Waldorf in the morning. I might have to stay a while and help with the triage."

Simon responded, "If you're staying then I'm staying."

Ashlee replied, "That's so sweet."

Millie said, "I'm out first thing. I want to get far away from here."

Simon replied, "You know Waldorf may not be safe. The Gomorrites are trying to push their way into Maryland. If we can't hold them then you will be running further south."

Millie responded, "I'll take my chances."

Wayne said, "I'm signing up to fight. I want to do my best to beat them. They need men and I'm down. I can handle a gun as good as the next guy."

Millie said, "Are you sure you want to do that?"

Wayne replied, "Yeah…I'm sure. But hey let's have some fun tonight and tomorrow we can do whatever."

Ashlee responded, "I can't they need medical people. I'm going to take a look at some patients for the doctor."

Ashlee kissed Simon and said, "Bye sweetie. I'll find you later."

Simon smiled and responded, "Okay."

***

Ashlee went off to make some rounds for the doctor. Her patients were toward the back of staging building. They were some of the most severely injured people. She picked up the chart of the first person and looked it over. The sound she heard next sent a shrill up and down her spine. She turned and to her amazement she got the best news she could have gotten.

Marion screamed, "Ashlee! Oh my God you're alive!"

Ashlee shouted, "Marion, my God!"

God had answered another of Ashlee's prayers and she didn't know till this minute.

Ashlee ran over to the bed that Marion was lying in and gave her a hug. She was so happy to see Marion. She thought for sure that she had lost her friend when the attack started.

Ashlee asked, "What happened? I thought you were dead."

Marion responded, "Well so did I. I fell down that hole and landed in the sewer. I was wreathing in pain when a couple of guys who also fell down the hole came and helped me. Girl…it was stank down there! But we stayed down there until we found an opening. Once we did we ran into a bus that was taking survivors here."

Ashlee said, "Wow…you were blessed."

Marion continued, "You don't know the half of it. Those guys had to carry me the whole way. They could have left me down there but they didn't. I thank God for them."

Ashlee replied, "I thank God for saving you."

***

Malcolm and his team came back to resistance headquarters. They were celebrating the success of their mission. They charted the flight path of the supply ships coming to resupply the Gomorrite army. They also were successful in stealing some of those supplies for use by the resistance.

Malcolm and his team were toasting their success when they saw Solomon. He met them just inside the door and he was not happy.

Solomon instructed the members of Malcolm's team to go on in headquarters while he talked to Malcolm.

Solomon asked Malcolm, "Did you kill that soldier in cold blood?"

Malcolm paused. He looked directly in Solomon's eyes… calculating…carefully choosing his next words.

Malcolm answered, "Yes. We don't have room to imprison the enemy. I did us a favor."

Solomon angrily replied, "You did us… We don't kill in cold blood. We only kill in self defense. If we can take a prisoner…we take a prisoner. Killing in cold blood makes us no better than the Gomorrites! You get it?"

Malcolm responded, "Yeah…I get it. We can go around and set charges and kill the enemy and that's okay. But if we gun down one of them…well that's somehow wrong."

Solomon said, "You just don't get it. Maybe I was wrong about you."

Solomon walked off and left Malcolm standing there. Malcolm was angry. He believed that he should not spare the life of any of the Gomorrites. They were the enemy. They came to his planet and attacked them. For that they should pay. Pay with their lives. He was considering leaving Solomon's resistance and forming his own.

***

Solomon went to Gabriel.

He asked, "Gabriel…do you think your team can get the President to Andrews safely?"

Gabriel responded, "I thought Malcolm's team was going to do that?"

Solomon responded, "He was but I don't trust him anymore. I'm giving your mission to him and I want you to take the President."

Gabriel replied, "Okay. When do we move out?"

Solomon responded, "As soon as it's dark."

***

Ben led the group to the IRS building on Constitution Avenue. They found the cafeteria on the seventh floor and ate some food. They discussed how they were going to rescue Lieutenant Yaniv and the others.

Lieutenant Oded spoke first, "We have no information on where they are holding the prisoners. What are we going to do?"

Professor Hai responded, "One of us will have to get as close to the camp as possible and get the lay of the land. Then that person will come back and we can make a plan."

Ben replied, "I'll do it."

Lieutenant Oded responded, "No…I'll do it. I am a Gomorrite and I know how they think."

Professor Hai added, "You're also a wanted man my friend."

Lieutenant Oded said, "If I'm cornered I will just tell them that I am recommitted myself back to the King."

Professor Simmons said, "There's got to be a better way than sending someone into a dangerous and hostile environment."

Ben replied, "Right now there isn't."

A voice said, "Freeze. Don't anyone move?"

All of them froze. Ben and Lieutenant Oded looked at each other in an attempt to come up with an idea to escape.

The voice said, "I'm Trumaine Davis…Metro PD. Who are you?"

Ben answered, "I'm from the FBI. My name is Ben Catchings."

Trumaine replied, "Whew…we thought you might be Gomorrites or something. We've also had problems with gangs thinking only of themselves and we have seen them attacking innocent people. You not only have to worry about the Gomorrites but some of our own are acting stupid."

Professor Hai asked, "Do you have some information on the Gomorrite camp layout?"

Trumaine responded, "I don't personally but we have formed a resistance. I can take you to Solomon. He has information on the layout, their troop movements, resupply lines…everything."

Ben said, "Good. These two scientists can help stop this attack but they have to get their friends out of the camp. They were captured last night."

Trumaine replied, "Well Solomon is the man to talk too. Let's get out of here. Stay behind me…I know the safest route back."

Ben responded, "Lead the way."

***

Ashlee finished her rounds and came back to talk to Marion. She told her all about her journey with Simon. She told her how much she loved him. Marion was very happy for her and she told her that one of the guys that rescued her likes her. Simon found Ashlee and Marion. The three of them laughed and talked for a couple of hours until the sounds of bombs and lasers could be heard.

All of their faces lost their smiles. The sound of people talking that once filled the room had gone. Sadness and fear engulfed the room.

Ashlee said, "It's started again."

***

Trumaine led them back to resistance headquarters. The number of people in the resistance had grown a great deal since the attack.

Trumaine heard Malcolm and Shep arguing as they went by.

Malcolm was angry. He was confronting Shep.

Malcolm asked, "Why did you tell Solomon about the soldier on the street?"

Shep responded, "Because it was wrong, that's why."

Malcolm replied, "What's wrong is trying to imprison the enemy when we don't have a prison anywhere. That's just more supplies that we don't need to use up. You…stay out of my way."

Shep responded, "Not a problem."

Malcolm added, "Next time don't count on us to save your butt."

Shep just walked away.

Trumaine arrived at the room where Solomon usually worked. He knocked on the door. Solomon opened the door and let Trumaine in the room.

Trumaine said, "I have some people who say they can probably stop the attack. One is a FBI agent. Then there are two scientists and a Gomorrite."

President Davis asked, "What are their names?"

Trumaine responded, "The FBI agent's name is Ben. One of the scientists is named Hai…"

The President pushed passed Trumaine and out the door. He saw Professor Hai and Professor Simmons near the entrance to the garage.

He jogged over to them. For the first time since the attacks he felt that they had a chance to turn the tide. If anyone could do it, it would be Professor Hai.

President Davis shouted, "Professor Hai...Professor Simmons! It's great to see you both! Now we have a fighting chance. Tell me we have a fighting chance!"

Professor Hai responded, "Sir...we must find one of our comrades if we are going to have that chance. He is a prisoner of the King."

Ben said, "Sir...who is Solomon and can he get us into the camp to rescue them?

Solomon was walking toward the group when the President turned and pointed at him.

President Davis said, "Here he comes now. You won't believe what this man has accomplished in a couple of days. Solomon..."

Solomon responded, "Yes, Mr. President."

President Davis replied, "This is Professors Hai and Simmons. They need your help."

Professor Hai added, "This is Lieutenant Oded, FBI Agent Ben Catchings and our little friend here is Carl. We need to rescue some friends of ours who are prisoners in the Gomorrite camp. Can you help us?"

Solomon responded, "It is good to meet you all. I have a current layout of the camp. If we do this, it will expose most of my men. I hope you have a plan to win this war."

Professor Hai said, "That answer lies with one of the people captured."

Ben added, "Please...Solomon...we know the danger and we will not ask anyone to join us. Me and Lieutenant Oded will go in alone and make the rescue."

Solomon replied, "We will come with you. It's dangerous and it's more than a two person job. Let's go and look over the map of the layout."

***

Four Gomorrite fighters began their assault on the brigade that was entrenched on I-295. The fighters began firing laser blast at the blockade and American forces began fighting back. An Army soldier was poised on the back of a vehicle. His teammate loaded the rocket launcher while the soldier aimed at one of the fighters. Once the launcher was loaded the soldier fired the rocket at the fighter. It was a direct hit. The fighter burst into flames and came falling down into the Potomac.

As the fighters were mounting their air assault, ground troops started making their way down I-295. American soldiers were returning their fire. The battle of I-295 had begun.

Wayne grabbed a weapon and volunteered to go out and help defend his country. Millie watched him as he suited up for battle.

Millie said, "I have to tell you something."

Wayne responded, "It's gonna have to wait sweetheart. They've started the war and I have to do my…"

Millie interrupted, "I'm pregnant!"

Millie dropped her head and walked around in a circle. She was hoping Wayne wouldn't go and fight but she knew it was in his blood. Maybe the thought of his child being born would stop. At least she hoped.

Millie continued, "I didn't want to tell you before but I'm about two months pregnant. Please don't go."

Wayne replied, "I…you're pregnant? I can't believe it. How did you keep that from me?"

Millie answered, "I found out just before the attack. That's what my doctor's appointment was about."

Wayne responded, "I have to go even more so now. I have to save my country from this takeover. I don't want my child to come into this world a slave. I'm sorry Millie…I have to do this."

Millie dropped her head. She didn't know what to say.

Wayne continued, "I love you Millie."

Millie said, "I love you too."

Wayne hugged and kissed her as he walked off to fight a war against an enemy from another planet.

Ashlee walked over after Wayne left and said, "Did you tell him?"

Millie responded, "Yes."

Ashlee replied, "Come on. Me and Simon are going to Waldorf. You can come with us."

Millie looked at Ashlee with tears in her eyes and whispered, "Thanks Ash."

***

President Davis was briefing the resistance on the information he knew, "Our forces will attack in harmony. The Gomorrite forces began their assault on Maryland down Branch Avenue. The Gomorrite forces sent in fighters first in an attempt to soften the American fighting forces."

"Our troops will remain entrenched to protect themselves from the bombing. As Gomorrite soldiers begin to make their way down Branch Avenue, American soldiers will greet them with bullets and artillery of our own."

"It seems we started a world wide revolution. After the battles started in the Washington DC/Maryland, we started receiving reports of other battles taking place on Earth."

"The Gomorrite ground forces started attacking major centers of the world. New York City was the hardest American city hit by the Gomorrites. We couldn't entrench ourselves and defend all of the major centers across the nation."

"We certainly have learned that the Gomorrites are battle ready and they were determined not to give up. They were determined to win this war but we are just as determined to defend our planet."

"Our Navy fighters tried to defend Southern California from attack but they suffered major losses to the enemy. The Gomorrite fighters have more mobility than our fighters. They can evade attacks better. If we are to win this war it will have to happen on the ground."

***

Lieutenant Yaniv, Renana, and Varda were being held separate from the other prisoners. The Department of Treasury building was being used to house the prisons. There were guards surrounding the building and guards on the floor with them.

The rest of the prisoners were being held outside the building in tents surrounded by guards. Lieutenant Yaniv overheard the guards saying General Idit had to cut back on the number of guards that were guarding the prisoners.

He also overheard that General Idit had to send troops to support the attacks on Philadelphia. Word of the resistance in DC had spawned like uprising around the world. This angered General Idit but this information made Lieutenant Yaniv happy. A resistance movement was beating the General.

***

In the resistance meeting room President Davis, Solomon, Gabriel, Professor Hai, Professor Simmons, Ben, and Lieutenant Oded were discussing the plan to rescue the prisoners.

Solomon was speaking, "The prisoners are being held at the Department of Treasury. Most of them are being held in tents outside. We have good information that the Gomorrites are being held inside the building. It seems the Gomorrites have special plans for them."

Professor Hai spoke up, "He would. They are traitors to the way of Gomorrah. He will save them until the war is over and then make an example of them. But Renana will be forced to be his wife. He has cherished her for years."

Solomon continued, "The best way in is right through the front door. They have cut back on the number of guards…so that will help us. Many of their guards have been sent to support the I-295 and Branch Avenue battles. I have also received word that the war in Philadelphia hasn't gone well either. It seems word of our resistance is spreading."

There was a knock at the door. Solomon paused…walked over to the door and opened it. Trumaine was standing there with another man.

Trumaine said, "Sorry to disturb you but we found this man and his team. I think you need to hear him out."

The man that Trumaine was introducing was Ed Reynolds. Ed was a Navy Seal with experience in covert missions. He had three members of his seal team with him. They were captured in Hampton, Virginia but managed to escape. They came to DC because they heard of the resistance and wanted to help take down the enemy.

What Ed didn't tell them was that his 16 year old son had been captured by the Gomorrites and that was why he wanted to go on this mission. He wanted to save his son.

Ed looked at Solomon and asked, "Can you use our help?"

Solomon sized Ed Reynolds up and responded, "We can use all the help we can. Come on in."

Solomon brought Ed Reynolds into the room and introduced him. Ed acknowledged the President and saluted him. Solomon showed him the layout of the building.

Solomon asked, "What do you think? Can we get them out?"

Ed studied the plans deeper and deeper.

Then he asked, "What about the people down below? Are we just going to leave them?"

Solomon responded, "They can't be our top priority. We have to get the information from the Gomorrite resistance members. With that information we can save everyone by stopping this war."

Ed replied, "Then it's a good plan. I suggest my team lead the assault. We are better trained for this kind of mission. Once we clear the way then your men can enter through the rear of the building while we have their attention."

Solomon said, "I agree. We'll move out at 1730 hours. Mr. President...I suggest you get ready to move out. We will try to get you to Andrews during the rescue mission. This will be the distraction we need to keep them off of you and give you time to get to Andrews."

President Davis responded, "I have decided to stay here."

Solomon blurted out, "Sir...we can't ask you to do that."

Ben responded, "Sir Solomon is right. You are the leader of this country. We have to ensure you are safe and Andrews is the best place for that."

President Davis continued, "We risk too many more lives trying to get me to Andrews. I think the best place for me is here. I believe the radio communications will be ready in a couple of hours. That will have to suffice."

Ben asked, "Are you sure sir?"

President Davis responded, "Yes Ben...I am sure. We need all the men we can to make this assault and rescue. Risking more lives to save me is foolish. Enough have already died for that cause."

Solomon replied, "Alright...we will move out at 1730."

***

At 1730 hours the teams moved out taking different routes to the building. The seal team moved into position and waited for the other teams to get into place. The plan was for the seal team to begin their attack at 1800 hours. While the seal team occupied the soldiers a second team would enter the rear of the building and search for the Gomorrites. Two other teams would remain in the vicinity in case back up soldiers came to assist.

The rescue team was being led by Trumaine. Gabriel's and Malcolm's teams stood at opposite ends of the building and played look out as well as backup in case something went wrong. It was approaching 1800 hours.

Ed looked at his watch and it was two minutes until 1800 hours. He was ready to begin the assault. He had informed his men that they would start the assault just as planned by the resistance.

However, he told them their main objective wasn't to a provide distraction. Their main mission was to find Ed's son. All of his men were in on the plan. He considered everyone on his team family and when someone threatens their family they got revenge. Ed and his team had performed missions in Iraq, Southwest Asia, Iran, Turkey and Latin America. They were highly trained.

It was now 1800 hours and Ed gave the order to begin the assault. The seal team fanned out and approached the building. There were two Gomorrite soldiers standing guard at the front of the building. Ed gave the signal to two seal members to begin firing their weapons at the guards. While the guards were occupied with the seal members shooting at them, the other two seal members began to sneak inside the prison.

Ed and one of the team members made their way to the holding area. They met little resistance since most of the guards had been sent to other locations by General Idit.

Ed and the other seal member were searching feverishly for Ed's son. The prisoners were begging to be freed.

One prisoner shouted, "Please free us! Help us!"

Another one yelled, "Help us! Why are you not helping us?"

Ed was upset that they were making so much noise.

He told them, "Be quiet or the soldiers will know we are here."

Another prisoner shouted, "I can pay you. I have money. Please free us!"

***

Trumaine waited for the signal to enter the building. When he heard the shots he would enter the building. They found a window on the first floor and cut the glass out of it. They all climbed through the window and carefully made their way to the stairs. Their information told them that the Gomorrites were being held on the fourth floor of the building.

Trumaine and his men met no resistance in getting to the fourth floor. Now they had to find where the Gomorrites were being held. They were coming down a hallway when they heard a scream. Trumaine motioned for his men to move into one of the rooms.

A Gomorrite soldier came out of the room dragging a woman by the arm, "Come with me…its time you paid a price for your traitorous acts. Hey Hepher…I'm going to have some fun with this one! She's a wild one!"

The man was dragging the woman down the hall toward Trumaine and his men's position. Once he went pass Trumaine, Trumaine came out of the room and pointed his weapon at his head. The rest of his men came out of the room and took up positions in case someone else came out. Trumaine hit the soldier on the back of the head knocking him out cold.

He whispered to the woman, "What is your name?"

She answered, "Varda. Who are you?"

Trumaine answered, "We have come to rescue you. How many soldiers are still in the room?"

Varda answered, "Only one. Lieutenant Yaniv and Renana are in there also."

Trumaine asked, "Where is the soldier in relation to the door?"

Varda answered, "His back is to the door."

Trumaine motioned to his men to take up positions around the door. On the count of three they would rush the room, take out the guard and rescue Lieutenant Yaniv. One of the men escorted Varda out of the building. As Trumaine reached the count of three, three more soldiers came from around the corners. They were sent by General Idit to retrieve the prisoners. They walked in on the rescue attempt.

They began firing at Trumaine's men. Trumaine rushed into the room. The guard turned to see what was happening and Lieutenant Yaniv jumped up and struck him across the head.

Trumaine asked, "Are you guys okay?"

Lieutenant Yaniv responded, "We will be when we get out of here."

Trumaine asked, "Are you Lieutenant Yaniv?"

Lieutenant Yaniv replied, "Yes. We have to get out of here."

Trumaine responded, "Professor Hai sends his regards. Follow me."

Lieutenant Yaniv asked, "Do you have an extra weapon?"

Trumaine gave him a backup weapon that he had on him. The bullets and lasers were still filling the hallway. More Gomorrite soldiers were coming up. Trumaine's men couldn't hold them all off.

From behind more resistance members showed up and began firing on the Gomorrites. It was Gabriel and his men. They now had the soldiers in a cross fire and it didn't take long for them to defeat the soldiers.

Gabriel said, "I heard you guys might need some help."

Trumaine said, "Thanks."

They heard a loud noise just outside the building.

Trumaine, Gabriel and Lieutenant Yaniv looked out the window and saw numerous prisoners running in every direction for their lives.

Trumaine shout, "What in the world…"

The seal team freed all the prisoners but Gomorrite fighters converged on the area and began firing at them.

Trumaine shouted, "Let's get out of here!"

Gabriel asked, "What happened? That wasn't part of the plan."

Trumaine exclaimed, "I don't know but we need to get out of here fast."

***

The Gomorrite fighters were shooting at anything that was moving. The few ground forces that were in place recaptured most of the prisoners who feared to run because of the fighters. Trumaine and Gabriel's groups split up in hopes that one of them would make it back to headquarters.

In the distance Solomon could hear the fighters attacking. He wondered what went wrong with the plan. Unlike the first night when bombs were the sound of success, these sounds triggered visions of failure…a plan gone wrong.

Solomon saw Malcolm running back to the camp with Ed and a young teenage boy right behind him. The three of them stopped where Solomon stood.

Malcolm turned and swung at Ed striking him in the jaw… knocking him to the ground.

He shouted, "You fool! Do you know what you have done?"

The young boy yelled at Malcolm, "Leave my dad alone. He saved my life."

Malcolm said, "You risked all of our lives and got many people killed. Your own men are dead. You're supposed to be a Navy Seal!"

Solomon stepped in and asked, "What happened?"

Malcolm responded, "This fool didn't bother telling us that he had a son in the prison. He didn't care about our mission. He went there to free his son. In doing so he freed all the prisoners causing the Gomorrites to use their fighters to shoot them down like dogs. I don't know where any of my team is or if they're even still alive. I don't even know if we successfully completed the mission!"

Solomon looked at Ed and said, "You have condemned us all. Son your father may have saved you today but your future may not be bright at all."

Ed sat on the ground looking pitiful. His son sat right by his side.

***

Wilson and Gina had gotten separated from Malcolm. Laser fire was all around them. They were running to safety. Two Gomorrite soldiers were after them. They fled around the corner of 11th and E Street. Bullets flew from across the street at the two soldiers and killed both of them.

Jamaal yelled, "Hey over here!"

Wilson and Gina turned and saw Jamaal motioning for them to come over to him. Wilson and Gina ran across the street and met Jamaal.

Jamaal said, "We have to get to the alternate location and wait until it's clear."

Gina responded, "Just point us in the right direction. Oh…and thanks."

Jamaal replied, "No problem. Our closet safe house is Metro Center."

Wilson added, "We had better move quickly."

They all ran down to the Metro Center Metro station. They hoped they could hide out until it was safe to return to headquarters.

***

The fighters stopped firing their lasers at the escapees. Most of them were recaptured and placed back in their confinement areas. General Idit was furious that the Gomorrites escaped. He had the two guards that were charged with guarding them brought in chains before him.

General Idit sharply spoke, "You idiots…you both will pay for your stupidity."

Hepher shouted, "General…it was Udi. He left his post to have sex with the prisoner Varda! I warned him not to do it."

General Idit grunted and slapped Hepher across his face with such rage that the man flipped over several times.

He shouted, "Don't give me excuses!"

He took out his laser and gunned them both down in cold blood. He then flung the weapon down on the ground.

As he was walking away he shouted to his aid, "Send my EWUs to me at once!"

The Elite Warrior Unit was the best warriors on Gomorrah. They were highly trained and General Idit picked them personally. To be a member of the Elite Warrior Unit you had to demonstrate to General Idit a level of evilness and skill that was equal to his own ability.

He created this unit to do the things an ordinary soldier could not do. He called them in on special occasions to handle special circumstances. This was a special circumstance because the resistance had to be eradicated.

***

The royal shuttle was descending on the White House grounds. King Abimelech was not happy about the latest results. When the news of the escape was told to him, he could not take it anymore. King

Abimelech burst into the room where General Idit was making his plans.

King Abimelech shouted, "General! What is going on! You let the prisoners escape!"

General Idit responded, "I have things under control. I am putting together a plan to get rid of this nuisance for good. I know they are in the Northwest section of the city somewhere between New York Avenue and G Street near Union Station. My EWUs are on their way to search for them. When they find them they will kill them all."

King Abimelech paused and studied his general. He trusted General Idit but for the first time things were not going well in a battle. He also knew if anyone could turn the tide of the battle it was General Idit and his EWUs. He also knew that if he were to go against the General he had better be prepared because the General would not go down easy.

King Abimelech said, "You had better succeed."

General Idit responded, "I will."

***

Shep came back into resistance headquarters running. He ran right up to Solomon.

Shep shouted, "Solomon…they're headed this way!"

Solomon responded, "What?"

Shep gathered himself together and said, "I think they know where we are."

Solomon began yelling instructions, "Okay…everybody evacuation plan Alpha 1 is in effect. Let's move it people."

Everyone in the underground garage began scrambling and moving. They all practice this plan three times a day hoping they would never have to use it. Now they were hurrying down to Union Station.

Once they got underground half of them were to go toward Silver Springs while the other half were to go toward Shady Grove. Solomon's special units would take up positions in the nearby buildings and continue to fight. The plan called for everyone to be evacuated within 30 minutes. He hoped he had that long.

They had to get the President to safety. Solomon went to the President.

Solomon said, "Sir…we have to get you out of here."

Professor Hai asked, "Have we heard from Lieutenant Yaniv?"

Solomon responded, "We have received word that the Gomorrites know where we are and they are coming. We can't wait any…"

Lieutenant Yaniv called out, "Professor!"

He ran over to where the men were standing and embraced Professor Hai.

Professor Hai asked, "What did Jacob say to you?"

Lieutenant Yaniv responded, "He said…something to the effect that the ships are linked. The virus orders all the ships to go to sleep."

Professor Hai replied, "Go to sleep?"

Lieutenant Yaniv reiterated, "Yes…go to sleep. That's what he said."

Solomon jumped in the conversation, "We have to move gentlemen. Let's go. We have a backup tactical center. We must go now."

All of them began to leave headed to the backup tactical center. All of the people had been evacuated to what Solomon hoped would be safe places. At the tactical center they could discuss how to solve the problem with the Gomorrite fighters and battle cruisers. If they could disable those ships the Gomorrite advantage would be gone. But now Solomon's main priority was to get the President and the rest of the people in the party to safety.

CHAPTER 12

DAY FIVE

The Elite Warrior unit found the resistance headquarters but no one was there. Everyone evacuated the underground garage just before they got there. The unit was led by Colonel Chaim. He was General Idit's first cousin. General Idit was a year older than Colonel Chaim but they were close. They were more like brothers than cousins. Colonel Chaim was just as determine to rid the Gomorrites of the resistance as General Idit. General Idit knew he could count on Colonel Chaim.

Once when they were kids around the age of 8 years old they were playing on a hillside. They were pretending to be warriors and fighting off the enemy when General Idit lost his footing and fell down the hill into the water. He was unconscious. Colonel Chaim ran after him and dove into the water. He vigorously swam after him.

Colonel Chaim caught up to General Idit and pulled him out of the water. He tried to revive him and after a few precious moments it worked. General Idit woke and saw his cousin and friend over him. General Idit made a pack with Colonel Chaim that day, that if he ever became the general of the King's army he would bring Colonel Chaim with.

When General Idit reached the rank of general his first move was to keep his pack with his cousin. He promoted the then Lieutenant Chaim to colonel and created the Elite Warriors Unit for Colonel Chaim to operate. General Idit gave Colonel Chaim the best home in Gomorrah and he has his pick of women. The debt was paid but they continued to be the best of friends.

Colonel Chaim looked over the remnants of what use to be the resistance headquarters. He spat on the ground to show his level of respect for them. He then walked out of the garage and surveyed the area.

He looked at his top aide and said, "They are in one of these adjacent buildings…they would not go far. Tal…which direction did they go?"

Tal was a lieutenant in the EWU and Colonel Chaim counted on him for his talent in finding people. He had been known to possess the skills of a tracker capable of tracking individuals no matter where they went.

Colonel Chaim watched Tal survey the area. He walked around looking…searching. Colonel Chaim knew Tal would find what he thought was the best area they would have retreated too.

Tal looked at Colonel Chaim and said, "Sir…if I were the leader of this stinking resistance, I would move all non tactical personnel as far away for the hot zone as possible. I believe that they divided up… some went down this rail track while others went down the track in the other direction. There is evidence on both rails that a large number of people moved along them very recently. The tactical forces are still in the area. If I were him I would have a backup headquarters probably in that building."

Tal was pointing at the Department of Labor building across from Union Station.

Colonel Chaim responded, "Good work Tal. Let's survey the building and determine the best point of egress. We want to take them by surprise."

Tal replied, "Yes sir. I will get right on it."

Colonel Chaim turned to his radio man and said, "Contact Colonel Paul and instruct him to send fighters along this rail. Somewhere in each direction there is a large body of resistance members. Tell him to make sure they die quickly!"

The radio man responded, "Yes sir!"

The EWU members were small in number but deadly in their fighting skills. They were the only unit General Idit had that was highly trained in the art of warfare. The membership consisted of only 10 men but they had been known to take out 200 men with ease.

***

Lieutenant Yaniv and Lieutenant Oded were conferring with one another in the hallway while the professors attempted to find a solution to disabling the Gomorrite ships. Solomon joined them in the hallway.

Lieutenant Yaniv was speaking, "Do you think General Idit will send out the EWUs?"

Lieutenant Oded responded, "Yes. He has been embarrassed. We saw the royal shuttle descending a while ago. You know King Abimelech wasn't happy that you escaped. If General Idit is still alive he has sent the EWUs after us. We must continue to move around or they will surely catch us. With Tal's ability to track they will easily pick up our scent."

Solomon asked, "What's an EWUs?"

Lieutenant Yaniv said, "It stands for Elite Warrior Unit and they are the most skilled warriors on Gomorrah. If they are after you…you are surely dead."

Solomon responded, "I don't know…I have a few tricks up my sleeve."

Lieutenant Yaniv stepped up to Solomon and said with all seriousness, "You have never seen anything like them. Do not underestimate them… if you do you won't have long to live."

Solomon stood there seriously thinking about what Lieutenant Yaniv just said. If it were true then they needed to move quickly. He hoped his people were able to get away. His thoughts were interrupted by Malcolm.

Malcolm ran down the hall.

Out of breath he said, "Someone's coming."

They moved to the closest window with Malcolm leading the way. When they got to the window they could see soldiers moving in on the position. Lieutenant Yaniv moved to another window on the opposite side.

He said, "I got two over here."

Lieutenant Oded moved to another window and said, "There's three over here."

Solomon said, "They're blocking all the entrances."

Lieutenant Oded said, "We've got to move."

Solomon said, "Wait…I have a trick or two myself."

Solomon was holding his arm out and intently waiting for the group of EWUs to get a little closer. Then finally they were in place. Solomon clicked a trigger and…

Boom! Three EWUs were instantly killed.

Solomon said, "Now…we can go."

They ran into the room to get the professors and the President. The explosion gave them the distraction they needed to get out of the building. They headed out of the building toward the university. The university provided computers for them to use. These computers were high powered super computers that can make millions of calculations per minute.

Colonel Chaim went to the position where the explosion occurred. He surveyed the situation. He was angered. Three of his men were dead and someone would pay for it. He was going to kill these resistance members.

He screamed, "How did this happen!"

A warrior replied, "We do not know sir. They had some kind of explosive device. It looked to be remotely triggered."

A second warrior added, "Sir…Tal is one of the dead."

Colonel Chaim responded, "They will pay…so help me Baal."

***

King Abimelech sat in the Oval office. He was extremely upset that his army had not captured Adamina as quickly as he expected. It was the fifth day of the war and the Adamians were attempting to mount a resistance in several places.

The room began filling with that familiar cold that King Abimelech knew all too well. Then the smoke slowly rose up and walking out of it was the all too familiar dark figure King Abimelech had come to know as Baal. He looked cold, calculating…overflowing with evil.

Baal said, "Why have you summoned me?"

King Abimelech replied, "The Adamians are resisting. You promised that this world would be mine!"

Baal responded, "I made no such promise. I promised your successful return to Adamina. I promised that you would be the first king to return here. I did not break the contract. I never promised you a victory over the Adamians.

He pulled out the contract that they signed in blood and showed it to King Abimelech.

Baal read from the contract, "…*in return for receipt of the payment of one soul from King Abimelech, Baal shall ensure King Abimelech is the first Gomorrite king to return to Adamina.*"

King Abimelech shouted, "No! I need the victory!"

Baal smoothly and quietly replied, "You have nothing else to offer me. I already own your soul."

He laughed and the sound was chilling to the bone.

King Abimelech demanded, "But you are our god."

Baal said, "Your god?" I never claimed to be such a thing. You called me Baal…the name of the one you believed in and I chose never to deny it."

King Abimelech asked, "What are you saying? You are not Baal?"

Baal answered, "I said that I am known by many names…you chose to call me Baal. I am most notably known as…Satan."

King Abimelech dropped to the floor. He realized he had now sold his soul to the devil.

King Abimelech said, "You tricked me! I demand my soul back!"

Satan responded, "I have a contract in which I have fulfilled my part. I now own your soul. I also thank you for all the souls that you have led to me."

He then turned and began to walk away. The smoke filled around him and the room temperature began to return to normal.

King Abimelech shouted, "No…don't leave…no…I demand my soul be returned!"

He fell to his knees weeping. His soul belonged to Satan and there was nothing he could do about it.

***

Colonel Chaim vowed revenge for his fallen comrades. One of his warriors saw the resistance member fleeing in the distance.

He shouted, "Colonel…there…they are escaping!"

Colonel Chaim responded, "After them!"

The EWU warriors ran after the resistance members. The warriors were clearly faster but as they closed the gap on the group, shots began coming toward them.

It was Jamaal and Gina. They spotted their fellow resistance members running from the EWU warriors. They fired their weapons at the warriors to slow them down and give their friends some much needed time and distance.

While the EWU was engaged in fighting Malcolm's unit, the resistance members stopped.

Solomon said, "We have to split up. Mr. President you go with the professors to the university. Me and the lieutenants will stay back and buy you some time."

President Davis replied, "No…I can be of help to you. I can fight with the best of them."

Solomon responded, "Someone needs to go with them to protect them."

President Davis said, "I agree but it needs to be someone with military experience."

Lieutenant Yaniv replied, "I'll escort them."

Solomon responded, "Okay go. Professor we need that virus. Taking out those fighters will give us a great advantage."

Professor Hai replied, "We will succeed in the name of the Lord."

***

The battles of I-295 and Branch Avenue were raging on in full scale. Just as Solomon said the air support provided by the Gomorrite fighters were giving them a distinct advantage.

On I-295 Ashlee, Simon and Millie were on the bus and getting ready to head out to Waldorf. Ashlee saw a captain and an airman first class running to the bus. The airman was the driver.

Laser blasts were hitting near the buses position and she saw the airman go down. The Captain turned to help him but soon realized he was dead. More laser blasts struck near the Captain. He got up and continued to run to the bus.

After he reached the bus he shouted, "We're under attack. We need to get out of here fast. Can anyone drive this thing?" Ashlee was shocked when Millie raised her hand and said, "I can."

Simon and Ashlee both looked at her with surprise etched on their faces. Being a petite woman Ashlee would have never imagined she would be capable of driving a large vehicle.

Millie got up and ran to the driver's seat. The Captain looked at her and motioned for her to take the driver's seat. Millie sat down and started the bus. Laser blasts were getting closer and closer to the bus.

The Captain shouted, "Get us out of here...quick!"

Millie punched the gas and everyone jerked forward. A laser blast just missed the bus. Millie punched the gas even harder as the bus left Bolling Air Force Base and got on I-295. She was giving the old bus all it had as she headed toward Highway 210 and eventually Waldorf.

***

It was late in the day when Lieutenant Yaniv and the professors arrived at the university. Professor Hai was going to try and save any information that was on the disk. They found a room with a super computer in it. Professor Hai sat down in the hope that he could work on it. He soon realized that there was no power.

He looked at Professor Simmons but before he could speak she said, "I'm on it."

Professor Hai asked, "How long?"

Professor Simmons responded, "Hang on. This room has a backup system that's isolated from the rest of the university. I just need to find it."

She looked around for a couple of minutes.

She said, "Here it is. Now all I need to do is flip this switch and... walla...we have power."

Once the power was on, Professor Hai started working diligently to see if he could salvage the disk. Lieutenant Yaniv stood at the door ensuring that no one surprised them.

***

Malcolm and his unit had successfully held off the EWUs for the time being. The President, Solomon and Lieutenant Oded joined them in a small office building.

Solomon asked, "What happen to Wilson?"

Jamaal replied, "We were ambushed last night. He didn't make it."

Gina added, "Don't lie. It was my fault. I fell asleep on post and now he's dead. He died saving my sorry behind. I should be the one…"

Solomon interrupted, "No. We can't talk like that. We're all tired. Wilson was a good man and we will miss him. He gave his life for what we all believed in."

He walked over to Gina and put his hands on her shoulders.

He continued, "Gina…Wilson knew the sacrifices he was making. Stop blaming yourself."

After a few moments of quiet, Lieutenant Oded stated, "We should be good here for the night. We'll need to each stand guard. The EWUs won't give up that easy."

Solomon replied, "I'll take the first shift."

Lieutenant Oded responded, "I'll relieve you."

Solomon replied, "Okay. Malcolm your unit will relieve Lieutenant Oded. Let's get some rest. Tomorrow's going to be a tough one."

Jamaal said, "Solomon…one more thing."

Solomon responded, "What is it?"

Jamaal struggled to tell it but started, "It's about Gabriel."

Solomon turned completely toward Jamaal. He noticed Gina's head was down.

He said, "What about him?"

Jamaal continued, "We were fighting in a fire fight. It was tough. They seemed to be all around us. Gabriel kept them pinned down and gave us a chance to escape. He sacrificed his life for the rest of us."

Solomon put his face in his hands.

Jamaal added, "I tried to convince him…"

Solomon said, "You couldn't have."

Jamaal questioned, "What?"

Solomon continued, "He would never have asked anyone else to sacrifice their life for the cause. He felt a leader should make that choice. By making him a leader…I am responsible for his death."

Malcolm interrupted, "It's not…"

Solomon put his hand to stop Malcolm from speaking. He then walked away. He wanted to be alone for a few minutes to grieve his friend's death.

Matti, Tal's replacement asked, "Sir why did we retreat?"

Colonel Chaim answered, "It is getting closer to night. They will find a place to rest. We will track them and set a trap for them. Tomorrow...I will have my revenge."

He looked to the sky and pointed.

He then said, "Baal grant me vengeance on behalf of Tal...my friend."

One of the other warriors who had a radio made his way over to Colonel Chaim.

He said, "Sir...it's General Idit."

Colonel Chaim took the radio and answered, "This is Colonel Chaim."

General Idit asked, "Where are they?"

Colonel Chaim answered, "We know they are close. Very close. By tomorrow morning they will be dead. You have my word."

General Idit replied, "Good. Keep me informed."

***

The battle continued to rage at Branch Avenue. The Gomorrite army had made their way down Branch Avenue as far as Suitland Parkway. Snipers were shooting at the army with all they had to spare.

The Gomorrites were just too powerful. The fighters were destroying the sniper positions and the Gomorrite army went in and won the ground hand to hand battles. They were highly trained for this task and with the support of their fighters they were winning easily.

On I-295 Wayne was seeing his first action. It was tough on him to put the knowledge that he was going to be a father out of his head. He was positioned with a unit of four men trying to shoot down the fighters. They were using surface to air missiles to shoot down the Gomorrite fighters.

Wayne shouted to Tiki, "Shoot it down!"

Tiki was an army soldier trained to use the surface to air missile launcher. He took aim at the oncoming fighters. He steadied himself and just when the fighter was close enough he pulled the trigger.

The fighter tried to dodge the missile but was unsuccessful. It burst into flames at the impact of the missile. They celebrated but quickly loaded another missile for the next fighter. Just after the launcher was reloaded a Gomorrite soldier sprung into their position catching them all off guard. Wayne was quick to draw his weapon and shoot the soldier. But the soldier got Tiki first.

Now no one was trained to shout the launcher Wayne jumped over to Tiki's position and picked up the launcher. With assistance from Bill he steadied the launcher and fired at an oncoming fighter.

The unexpected recoil caused Wayne to fall backwards as the rocket was fired but it struck another fighter and it burst into flames. Wayne jumped up and celebrated.

Wayne shouted, "Yes! That's another one down!"

Bill pointed to the East and said, "Wayne…we got several bogies coming this way. We better get out of here!"

Wayne responded, "You're right…let's move cowboy!"

***

Millie was swinging the bus left and right dodging abandon vehicles and trying her best to get the bus full of injured and medical personnel to Waldorf where they thought they would be safe. Millie couldn't help but think about Wayne. She hoped and prayed that he was safe.

***

Night had covered Washington DC again. Many people prayed for night because the battle would slow to almost nothing. They felt somewhat safe at night but that was an illusion. Some even forgot about the war. The morning light would come just to remind them that this was not a dream.

Renana and Varda escaped with the other resistance members. They both longed for their men. They both prayed for their safety.

Renana asked, "Do you think they are safe?"

Varda replied, "I do not think otherwise. God is with them. They will stop this invasion."

Renana said, "These people…they know nothing of the pain and torture we have experienced on Gomorrah. I feel sorry for them."

Varda replied, "Just a few days ago they had little to worry about. Now we have come to their doorstep and cause them so much pain."

Renana responded, "It is not our fault. We cannot accept the blame for the pain that King Abimelech caused these people. We can only help defeat them."

Varda replied, "I cannot agree. We must accept the blame our people caused...whether we agree with our leaders or not. We should have stopped this on Gomorrah. These people don't deserve to suffer like this."

A lady who was sitting near them walked over and sat down next to Renana and Varda.

She said, "These people...they are your people."

Varda answered, "Yes...I am afraid..."

She interrupted, "Why...why are you attacking us? What did we do to you?"

Varda and Renana both lowered their heads in shame. They were ashamed to be associated with such evil people. Now they were witnessing firsthand the evil that Gomorrites can cause and these people didn't deserve it.

Varda said, "Ma'am...the reason they are attacking is not of God... nor is it my belief. I am sorry you are made to suffer at the hands of such evil. If only you knew how many lives were lost trying to prevent this from happening. I am truly sorry."

The lady just looked at Varda and then back at Renana.

She finally responded, "You don't look evil."

Renana replied, "But we are Gomorrites the same."

As Renana finished her statement laser blasts found their position. Resistance members fled in every direction trying to elude capture or worst...death. The fighters were giving their best effort to kill them all.

Renana grabbed the lady. The three of them ran dodging laser blast as they went. They all prayed that death would not find them this day.

***

Professor Hai and Professor Simmons were hard at work trying to get the data restored from the fried disk given to them by Lieutenant Oded. Professor Hai had the university's finest computer at his hand.

He felt at home again, but his joy was short lived. His task was more difficult than he could imagine.

They had about nine hours of power to get the disk to work or write an entirely new program.

Professor Hai was frustrated as he slapped his open hand on the desk. He shocked Professor Simmons. She comforted him and guided him back to the task at hand.

Professor Hai said, "There is only a small fragment of the disk that can be restored."

Professor Simmons asked, "Does it contain the code that we need?"

Professor Hai answered, "I don't know. Give me a minute."

Professor Hai was desperately trying to restore the data.

Professor Simmons just sat there and watched.

Professor Hai finally said, "There are bits and pieces of the code. We will have to piece the rest of it together with our own code."

Professor Simmons responded, "Okay...how can I help?"

Professor Hai replied, "It is written in the old language...probably a security measure. I will have to write it myself. I am one of only a handful of people who know the old language. Just keep the power on."

Professor Simmons responded, "Will do."

***

General Idit was in the Oval office with King Abimelech. The King was distraught over learning that the figure he thought was Baal was not their god but the devil. He pondered telling General Idit.

King Abimelech sadly looked at General Idit and said, "We have been deceived. Baal is not a god. He is the serpent of the underworld. He is the evil of evil. He is Lucifer. He is Satan.

General Idit's eyebrow rose then he calmly asked, "How does this change our mission? We deserve to live here and we will continue to take what is rightfully ours. I see no difference."

King Abimelech responded, "You are right. Where do we stand?"

General Idit replied, "Tonight and tomorrow we are will be mounting our forces for an all out attack here...Chicago...Los Angeles...Miami...Japan...and lastly the Middle East...where our great city once stood.

These are the places that have given us the most resistance. We will launch our all out attack around mid day two days from now. Our fighters will lay waste to everything in sight. Once this is done the rest of this world will fall."

King Abimelech responded, "Excellent. We will still win this war."

King Abimelech then asked as he drank some brandy from President Davis' private stock, "Are the Elite Warriors tracking Davis and the others?"

General Idit answered, "They should be captured by midday tomorrow."

King Abimelech responded, "This is truly excellent. I want him to see me in his office drinking his brandy before I slit his stinking throat."

***

It was a long night for Professor Hai. He worked tirelessly trying to piece together the code to disable the warship and bring down the fighters. He knew if this advantage could be taken away, Earth's army would have a chance but what about the warships orbiting the planets?

He quickly turned to Professor Simmons and asked, "The warships... orbiting the planet. We will have to do something about them."

Professor Simmons replied, "The President said we launched a missile. It hit some sort of protective shield before it detonated. We didn't damage the ship at all."

Professor Hai responded, "Aaron must have perfected the shield technology. My code must disable that as well."

Professor Simmons replied, "But I don't know if we can coordinate a missile strike now. Our communications network has been severely damaged."

Professor Hai responded, "We will have to try something. Maybe Solomon or President Davis will be able to help in that area."

***

Lieutenant Yaniv was outside surveying the area around the university. He saw in the distance three women running for their lives.

He recognized his wife, Renana, and their friend Varda along with another woman who he didn't know. He ran over to help. As he got closer he saw two Gomorrite soldiers chasing the women.

Lieutenant Yaniv shouted, "Get down!"

They fell to the ground and Lieutenant Yaniv fired his weapon at the two soldiers. He hit the first soldier cleanly killing him. The second solider began returning fire.

Lieutenant Yaniv dived to the ground and covered the women. He continued to shoot at the soldier but soon realized that the soldier had stopped firing at them. He carefully looked up to see if the soldier had moved. He saw nothing.

He looked around more and more but saw nothing. He could only surmise that the soldier returned to his unit to get more men.

Lieutenant Yaniv calmly whispered to the women, "Get up slowly. We have to get out of here."

Varda asked, "Where did he go? Did you kill him?"

Lieutenant Yaniv responded, "I don't think so. He might have ran back to report our position."

Lieutenant Yaniv ran over to the dead soldier and retrieved a communication device. The four of them ran back to the building where Professor Hai and Professor Simmons were working. Lieutenant Yaniv listened for any radio chatter.

The soldier who escaped was reporting their position. Lieutenant Yaniv had to get them all to safety before the reinforcements arrived.

***

Lieutenant Yaniv burst into the lab and shouted, "We have to get out of here now!"

Professor Hai turned and said, "What? We can't..."

Lieutenant Yaniv interrupted, "You don't understand. They made our position. We need to go...now!"

Professor Simmons shouted, "We can download the data and take it to a friend of mines place. He has a computer system that can rival this one."

Lieutenant Yaniv said, "Let's go professors!"

Professor Hai began downloading the code to a flash drive.

Lieutenant Yaniv saw a squad of soldiers converging on their position.

He said sternly, "Come on…they're here!"

Professor Hai replied, "We have to download this code. It's almost done!"

The soldiers were now closing in on their lab.

Varda said to Lieutenant Yaniv, "Give me a weapon. I will help fight them off."

Renana added, "So will I."

Varda took Lieutenant Yaniv's spare gun. Lieutenant Yaniv didn't have a gun for Renana.

Lieutenant Yaniv said to Renana, "Me and Varda will confront them. You get the professors out of here. We will be right behind you."

Professor Simmons overheard them.

She said to Renana, "Here take my gun. It's not much but it's something."

She reached in her purse pulled out a .22 caliber hand gun.

Renana asked, "How many projectiles does it fire?"

Professor Simmons answered, "Only six…sorry."

Renana said, "No need to apologize."

Professor Hai shouted, "It's done!"

Lieutenant Yaniv said, "Renana…get them out of here. We'll hold them off."

Lieutenant Yaniv and Varda began shooting at the soldiers while Renana and the professors exited the room from the opposite side. Lieutenant Yaniv knew their weapons were no match for the soldiers. He was able to take out two of them.

He ordered Varda, "Go…catch up with them."

Varda replied, "No…I can help."

Lieutenant Yaniv sternly shouted, "You are almost out of projectiles… go!"

Varda began to run to catch up with the rest of them. Lieutenant Yaniv was able to kill another soldier before he ran out of ammunition. Now it was two against one. He liked those odds.

The two soldiers were coming down the hall toward the lab. No shots were being fired so he believed they thought the resistance members were running for their lives or out of ammunition.

Lieutenant Yaniv found a knife on the floor of the lab. He took the knife into his hands and waited until they were close to the doorway. He had to make his one shot count. If he was successful in taking out one of the soldiers with the knife he would have to pounce on the other one quickly to have a chance. He waited. He waited and waited. Then he acted.

With one swift motion, Lieutenant Yaniv jumped up and threw the knife at the soldier. It struck him in the throat. He grabbed at the knife but quickly fell to the floor.

Lieutenant Yaniv jumped the other soldier before he could get off a shot. The two of them wrestled on the floor…each one trying to gain the advantage. The soldier's gun was on the floor just out of reach of both of them.

Lieutenant Yaniv and the soldier continued to struggle. The battle raged on as both of them tried to get to the weapon. The soldier grabbed a lab vile and struck Lieutenant Yaniv with it. He used the advantage of those few seconds to grab the weapon.

Both men stood up. The soldier aimed the weapon at Lieutenant Yaniv and smiled.

He happily said to Lieutenant Yaniv, "Now I will be honored by General Idit himself. He will shower me with virgins and untold wealth. Goodbye my friend."

Lieutenant Yaniv responded, "Shoot."

The soldier laughed as he thought Lieutenant Yaniv was talking to him. Then the sound of the .22 caliber hand gun echoed off the walls of the lab and was followed quickly by the chilling impact of the bullet to the soldiers head. He was dead on his feet.

Renana had returned for her husband armed with Professor Simmons' gun. Lieutenant looked at his wife. He knew she loved him and she couldn't leave him.

Lieutenant Yaniv ran to his wife and said, "Thank you my love."

Lieutenant Yaniv took her in his arms and held her tight. He knew she had never taken a life before and he suspected the act shocked her.

Lieutenant Yaniv said softly into her ear, "My love...we must leave. There may be other soldiers coming."

Slowly Renana moved...following her husband to meet with the rest of the resistance members.

***

Varda met them and led them to where the professors were waiting.

Lieutenant Yaniv said, "What do we do now? We can't stay here."

Professor Simmons responded, "I know where we can get a computer. It's a friend of mine and he's the geek of geeks. Follow me."

They all ran out of the building and off into the night. They had to dodge patrols in making their way across the city. Lieutenant Yaniv was keeping a sharp eye out as they went. He could hear the sound of the battles raging on I-295 and Branch Avenue in the distance. He thought, *"It didn't look good for us."*

***

Wayne and his team were holding on at I-295 with all they had to offer but it just wasn't enough. The air support the Gomorrites enjoyed was overwhelming the Americans. Word was being passed around to retreat to Highway 210. Wayne didn't want to retreat.

They had run out of rockets and were shooting with the guns. The Gomorrites were slowly overtaking their positions. It was either retreat or be forced back.

One soldier was yelling, "Retreat...retreat...retreat!"

Wayne continued to fight. Then he saw another soldier pinned down by a Gomorrite solder. Wayne ran to help. He dived at the soldier just in time to stop him from stabbing the American.

Wayne wrestled the knife away from the solider and stabbed him with it.

Behind him the American yelled, "Look out!"

Wayne turned to see another Gomorrite soldier diving at him. He knocked Wayne to the ground and the two battled with all their might. The Gomorrite was on top of Wayne throwing punches at him vigorously. Wayne blocked some of the punches but most of them got through to his face.

289

Wayne was saved by a laser blast that cut the Gomorrite soldier down. The Gomorrite soldier screamed out in agony as Wayne pushed his lifeless body to the side. He saw the American soldier he just saved standing there with a Gomorrite laser in his hand.

The American soldier said, "If they can use them on us then we return the favor."

Wayne replied, "Thanks buddy. I guess that makes us even."

The soldier replied, "Who's counting? Now let's get the heck out of here."

***

As the sun began to rise over Washington DC some of its citizens continued to try and evade capture or worst by Gomorrite soldiers. It was the sixth day of the war and the Americans seemingly were unable to stop the imposing army.

For that matter, no country on Earth seemed to be able to defend themselves against the Gomorrites. With their superiority in the air it seemed the world was going to be ruled by King Abimelech and his Gomorrite army.

The will of most of the people was broken. Many of them were just giving up. They were tired of running…tired of hiding. Food was low if any at all was found. Health was an issue. The hope had been slowly taken away from them. They believed that death or capture would be better.

General Idit was with King Abimelech as the morning sun rolled across the District of Columbia.

General Idit spoke, "It seems we have now taken control of this world and victory is inevitable. Many of the people of this area are in a place called Waldorf hiding from us. We know their location and our fighters and ground troops will be near their position by nightfall. We should have many more slaves to add to our collection. Those who still have a will to fight will die."

King Abimelech replied, "That is good. It seems Satan has delivered Adamina to us after all."

General Idit responded, "What is in a name? Baal…Satan…should it matter to us? You will be the ruler of this world and that…is all that matters."

King Abimelech replied, "You are right my friend. I will return to the Royal Battleship and take my place overlooking this world. Will I be seeing the rest of the world fall like these puny Americans?"

General Idit responded, "We have captured New York, Chicago, Dallas, and Atlanta in this country. We also have captured the countries of England, Germany, Russia and China. The remaining resistance will fall soon. The will of the people has been broken. Many of them are giving up."

King Abimelech asked, "And the president of this worthless country? Where is he?"

General Idit answered, "Colonel Chaim knows where he is hiding. He should be captured today."

King Abimelech replied, "Don't let me down."

General Idit responded, "I will not."

General Idit watched as King Abimelech walked away. He was headed back to his shuttle to return to his Royal Battleship. Secretly General Idit hated him. General Idit knew he could rule better than King Abimelech. He was just waiting for the right time and he felt it was near.

As General Idit watched a cold...evil air overtook the room. It made the General shiver. He looked to his left and saw a shadowy figure emerging from a dark cloud of smoke. He had heard many stories from King Abimelech about this figure and now he was going to meet him face to face. Fear was something that General Idit never felt. Now it was traversing through his body like the blood moving through his veins.

Satan stood and looked at General Idit. He took a deep breath and exhaled.

Then he said, "Ahhhhh...the smell of hate is so good for the soul."

He then turned to General Idit.

Satan asked, "Do you not hate your King?"

General Idit looked in reverence, dropped to his knees and answered, "My lord...he is weak...I despise him greatly but he is my king."

Satan continued, "I can make you King. Is that something you desire?"

General Idit answered, "Yes my lord...I desire to rule!"

Satan continued, "Than you shall be King and you shall become king by killing King Abimelech."

General Idit replied, "Yes my lord. I will do as you ask."

Satan responded, "However, I cannot do anything without your blood on this contract. After I have made you King, your soul will be mine."

General Idit held out his hand and Satan cut his finger and allowed a drop of the blood to fall on the contract sealing the deal.

Satan said, "It is done. Tomorrow morning you shall board the Royal Battleship. Get King Abimelech alone and take his life. You shall be king."

He then submerged himself in the dark colored smoke and the room returned to the normal temperature. General Idit smiled at the thought of his lifelong dream coming to life.

***

The forces at Branch Avenue had suffered defeat at the hands of the Gomorrite Army. The Army was celebrating and making its way toward Waldorf. They stopped at Andrews Air Force Base and were attempting to destroy any threat the base might bring.

Major Lance Freeman had taken control of the base following the commander's death. He had ordered an all out assault against the Gomorrites.

Major Freeman was a 17 year veteran of the United States Air Force. He loved the Air Force. His father was a veteran of the Vietnam War and served in the United States Army for 27 years. Major Freeman was married to Carmella and they had three daughters ages 8, 6, and 4 years.

He thought of his lovely wife and three daughters. He prayed they would survive this massacre unscathed.

Major Freeman and three of his men were defending the Operations building from a battalion of Gomorrite soldiers. They had in their possession the briefcase that contained the codes to the nuclear arsenal of the United States. If the briefcase fell into the hands of the Gomorrite army it would be destruction for Earth. Major Freeman knew he could not allow this information to fall into their hands.

He told his men, "Men...this briefcase cannot fall into Gomorrite hands. There is an access door to the rear of this building. You can evade detection and slip out that door. I will engage the enemy long enough for you to escape. When they are upon me I'll detonate these explosives and everything within a city block will be destroyed. Good luck to you all."

One of the airman responded, "Sir...with all due respect...we're not leaving."

Major Freeman replied, "That's an order airman...go...get to your families."

Another airman responded, "I don't have any family...and I'm staying."

All three soldiers took out their weapons and entrenched themselves for the final battle. Major Freeman knew it was a waste of time and energy to continue to order them to leave. They were American fighting airman...they expected to give their lives for their country and now it was evident that it was going to happen. They all readied themselves for certain death.

The door to the operation building burst open and the Americans let loose with all their firepower. The Gomorrites retaliated. They continued to push through the door. For every Gomorrite soldier killed three more advanced into the building. It was a numbers game and the Gomorrites were winning. The Americans just kept firing away hoping that they could hold them off and keep the briefcase safe.

One of the American soldiers fired his weapon over and over and shouted as he stood. He continued firing at the Gomorrites. When his weapon was empty he went hand to hand with a soldier.

He took the butt of his rifle and slammed it to the stomach of the Gomorrite soldier. As the Gomorrite solider was bent over the airman belted him across the back of his head knocking him out cold.

His victory was short-lived. Another Gomorrite solder fired a laser blast at him. The blast struck him in the middle of his chest. The airman flung his knife at the Gomorrite soldier with his last breath. The knife struck the Gomorrite soldier in the chest...killing him.

The other American soldiers went hand to hand with Gomorrite soldiers as well. They all fell one by one to the Gomorrites until all that was left was Major Freeman. Major Freeman had the briefcase in one hand and the remote detonator in the other. A blast from a Gomorrite laser struck Major Freeman in the shoulder. As he was falling to the ground he took one last look at the picture of his wife and his three little girls and pressed the remote detonator.

His final words were, "God…Bless our country…our world."

The explosion was enormous. A cloud of smoke rose high in the sky and could be seen for miles. The explosion caused collateral explosions and the damage amounted to a radius of four city blocks.

It was more than the major could have expected. The building was located by the flight line and the explosion caused several other smaller explosions to many of the aircraft sitting on the flight line. A C-5 and C-130 were sitting on the flight line filled with fuel. They both ignited and lit up the morning sky.

There were three Gomorrite fighters flying over the building at the time of the explosion. The explosion took out the fighters. The captured American soldiers who witnessed the explosion celebrated because they knew an American had sacrificed their life to take out a good number of the enemy force. They also knew that the building contained all the top secret data the Americans had including the briefcase to their nuclear arsenal.

The Gomorrite soldiers were angered by their joy. They executed several of the American soldiers on the spot as retaliation.

***

The bus with the refugees from Bolling Air Force Base arrived at Redeemer Live Ministries Church in Waldorf, Maryland. Millie guided the bus into the parking lot and everyone began getting off the bus.

Simon and Ashlee were one of the last ones to get off the bus. Ashlee was helping Simon because his leg was still hurting. When they got to the door Pastor Bell saw them and ran over to them.

Pastor Bell reached out and grabbed Simon and said, "Simon…I was worried about you. Are you okay?"

Simon responded, "Yes…thanks to her. Daddy this is Ashlee. Ashlee this is my dad."

Pastor Bell hugged Ashlee and said, "Thank you for helping my son."

Ashlee responded, "Sir…it was your son that helped me. I would not be here now if it wasn't for him."

"Ashlee," a voice screamed out from the other side of the church.

Ashlee looked over in the direction of the voice and responded, "Momma!"

She ran over to her mother and they embraced each other.

Ashlee's mother, Lorraine, said, "I prayed that you would make it home safely!"

Ashlee replied, "I did…we did…me and that man over there. His name is Simon and he saved my life on several occasions. Where's dad?"

Lorraine responded, "I haven't heard from him. You just came from Bolling…you didn't see him?"

Ashlee replied, "No. We got there after a number of people had already been evacuated. He could be at another shelter. Have you heard from my sister?"

Lorraine responded, "I haven't heard from her either."

Ashlee replied, "Then we have to continue to pray…"

The sound of the explosion on Andrews Air Force Base startled everyone in the church. They feared the worst…they feared the Gomorrites were headed their way. They ran outside to see what happened.

When they got there Ashlee saw a cloud of smoke rise up in the air…then several secondary explosions went off afterwards. She saw the three Gomorrite fighters fall to the ground. It was a cause for a celebration…even if it was a small victory for their side.

***

Carmella Freeman looked painfully towards Andrews. She knew the fighting had begun there and that her husband was on Andrews. She also knew that if it came to it her husband would destroy the building he was in and everything he could to protect the briefcase with the codes in it. The explosion brought sadness to her heart as she could only believe he was dead. She held her three daughters tightly and cried.

The youngest daughter asked, "Mommy…was that daddy?"

***

The sunlight pierced the room in which Solomon and his crew were resting. The President was the first one to rise. He was pondering what the day would bring when the ground beneath him shook. He wondered what the enemy had blown up this time.

Solomon broke the President's concentration, "Mr. President…are you okay?"

President Davis responded, "I'm fine Solomon. Did you feel that?"

Solomon replied, "Another explosion. I'm becoming accustomed to them."

President Davis responded, "That's a shame."

They were joined by Malcolm, Jamaal, Gina and Lieutenant Oded.

Lieutenant Oded said, "Are we ready to head out?"

President Davis replied, "As ever."

Solomon peeped through the curtains to see if the coast was clear. He didn't see anything so he motioned for everyone to follow him.

After the last person walked out of the door, five figures emerged from the shadows.

It was the surviving members of the EWU. The resistance members were surrounded and trapped. They could not run anywhere. They had to confront the enemy who had weapons trained on them.

Colonel Chaim broke the silence, "Put down your weapons. We have you at a disadvantage."

Lieutenant Oded said to the resistance members, "We had better do as he says."

They put their weapons down and prepared mentally for their death.

Colonel Chaim said, "Well…this is not how it should be."

He walked around the captured members…looking at each one.

He continued, "My men and I are warriors. We live for combat. The hunt is important to us but hand to hand combat is where real men are born. This was too easy. You walk out the door…we have you at a disadvantage…we capture you. Too easy."

Lieutenant Oded responded, "What would you have us do? Run so you can gun us down? Would that satisfy your thirst?"

Colonel Chaim explained, "I have better idea. There are five of us and five of you. We will pair up and fight to the death. What say you?"

Lieutenant Oded responded, "There are six of us."

Colonel Chaim replied, "Ah yes…the female. To die at the hands of a woman is a disgrace. You disgraced two of my warriors yesterday."

Gina shouted, "Good…they…"

As Gina was speaking, Colonel Chaim aimed his weapon and shot Gina to death.

President Davis shouted, "You coward! I'll kill you."

Colonel Chaim replied, "You can try…Mr. President…you can try. Now we have five on five."

Lieutenant Oded added, "I have untrained warriors against your trained elite warriors."

Colonel Chaim cut him off and whispered, "You have no other choice…except to die on the streets without a fight. Who knows you might win."

He burst into laughter as he motioned to his warriors to lay down their weapons and prepare to fight hand to hand with the resistance fighters. He then turned to the resistance members.

He said, "Let us began the battle to the death. You…Oded…you are mine!"

CHAPTER 13

the Final Battle

The time had come...five warriors...five resistance members...five mono a mono battles. The battle lines had been drawn. Lieutenant Oded's past rolled through his mind. He first met Colonel Chaim on the training grounds of Zoar. They were friends. They trained together daily.

Lieutenant Oded's brother, Ran, was also a part of this friendship. Ran was older so he didn't train with Lieutenant Oded and Colonel Chaim. The relationship between lieutenant Oded and Colonel Chaim ended because Colonel Chaim accused lieutenant Oded's brother of raping his sister.

It was not until later that Lieutenant Oded found out that General Idit orchestrated all of the events. This fueled Lieutenant Oded's desires to join the resistance. Now Lieutenant Oded would have his revenge. Now he could kill the man who wrongfully killed his big brother.

***

Professor Simmons led the group that made it to the home in Northeast DC where Marlin Michaels had lived for several years. Marlin was a computer analyst with the Federal Government and had vast experience in computers. His basement contained a network of computers that he used to track information all over the world. He was the best hacker Professor Simmons knew.

Professor Simmons and Marlin were high school classmates. They kept in touch over the years and now Professor Simmons needed him and his network of computers. They approached the house using care. Nothing looked out of the ordinary. It had the same appearance as all of the other buildings in Washington DC. No one was on the streets for fear of capture or death.

Lieutenant Yaniv entered the house first to make sure it was safe. He carefully searched through the house looking for any evidence that someone was there. As he was turning the corner to a room Marlin popped out with a .9 mm Glock cocked and ready to shoot.

Marlin said, "Tell me who you are or you die."

Lieutenant Yaniv responded, "My name is Lieutenant Yaniv and I am a friend of Professor Simmons."

Marlin replied, "You're a Gomorrite. Today you die."

He began to pull the trigger.

"Don't you pull that trigger," Professor Simmons shouted as she was standing behind Marlin.

Marlin asked, "Cassie? Is that you?"

Professor Simmons answered, "Yes it is and you have a gun pointed at my friend."

Marlin said, "I'm sorry my friend. I'm truly sorry."

Lieutenant Yaniv responded, "No problem. I am glad you did not shoot."

Professor Simmons said, "Marlin…this is Professor Hai. This is Renana and Varda."

Marlin spoke to all of them and offered them something to drink.

Professor Simmons continued, "We need to use your computers. We have some code that can help win this war. Please tell me your computers are working."

Marlin replied, "You serious? You know my stuff is always working. I have backups for my backups."

He headed toward the basement motioning for them to follow.

Marlin continued, "I have been tracking transmissions all over the world. Did you know there are pockets of resistance fighters all over the world? Man if only we can give them some support."

Professor Simmons responded, "We can give them that support. Can you communicate with our military?"

Marlin responded, "Yes I can. They don't know where the President is and Andrews was overtaken this morning."

Lieutenant Yaniv said, "The President is with my friend and some other resistance members. We can only pray that they are well."

Professor Simmons replied, "We may need to communicate with the military to coordinate a strike against the warships in orbit."

Marlin responded, "Are you serious? Cool."

Marlin reached the bottom of the stairs where he introduced them to his system of computers. Marlin's system impressed Professor Hai.

Professor Hai said, "This is an impressive computer system. Where can I get started?"

Marlin responded, "I intercepted some chatter from the FBI about you before the attack. The Gomorrites have been looking for you since they got here. Take my seat. It's an honor."

***

General Idit stood at his command center and received reports from his colonels that the troops were ready for the final assault on all the known resistance targets.

General Idit came over the communication system and addressed his colonels, "Gentlemen...the time has come for us to begin the preparations for the final assault. This assault will secure victory for us and we will rule over Adamina forever. Gather your troops and ensure they are ready. In four hours we will launch our final assault. Hail Gomorrah!"

All the colonels responded, "Hail Gomorrah!"

***

Jamaal stood poise to take out the Gomorrite warrior he was matched against. Jamaal was a fighter. He had a black belt in Aikido. Aikido is the Japanese martial art form developed by Morihei Usbida. This art form involves gaining control of your opponent or throwing them away from you. He like many Adamians had no experience in a death match.

His opponent was a powerful looking man. Jamaal planned to use speed to take down this man.

He said to Jamaal, "You are no match for me. I will break you down and then kill you easily."

Jamaal responded, "Bring it on."

The two of them circled each other. The EWU warrior inched closer to Jamaal and performed a sidewinder kick to Jamaal's face. Jamaal blocked the kick but stumbled backwards. Jamaal saw him coming toward him but it was too late. Jamaal was hit in the face with several powerful blows, knocking Jamaal to the ground.

Jamaal shook his head as he was amazed at the combination of power and speed of his opponent. He couldn't just admire him though he had to beat him...or die.

Jamaal jumped up off the ground and sidestepped the punch. He grabbed his opponent by the wrist and used his momentum against him. Jamaal pulled the warrior by him and then caught him in the face with his elbow, drawing blood from his mouth.

The EWU warrior was surprised by the move and he was actually impressed by Jamaal. He wiped the blood from his lip and then spit.

He said to Jamaal, "Impressive...but you will not defeat me."

Jamaal responded, "We'll see about that."

Jamaal caught his opponent in his side with his arm while he was lunging at him. Jamaal shifted his hip and flipped his opponent to the ground. Jamaal's feet were swept from under him.

Both men were on the ground. Jamaal felt his opponent jump on top of him and grab his throat. Jamaal tried to remove his powerful hands from his throat.

Jamaal brought his legs up and wrapped them around his opponent's throat. He was able to pull him backwards forcing the release of his hands from his throat.

Jamaal was drained from the choking. He made it to his hands and knees but he was grabbed from behind. His opponent grabbed the top of Jamaal's head and the bottom of his face at the chin. He twisted Jamaal's head and snapped his neck like a twig.

Jamaal eyes rolled to the back of his head. His body just dropped to the ground. The remaining members of the resistance viewed Jamaal as a brother. Malcolm viewed him as a son.

Jamaal was now dead and the Gomorrite's Elite Warriors had won the first battle.

***

Professor Hai proudly announced, "I did it! I have completed the code that will disable the warships and the fighters."

Professor Simmons replied and asked, "That's great. How does it work?"

Professor Hai answered, "It turned out to be simple. The royal warship is in control of the entire network of computers that are in use by the Gomorrites. One command from the royal warship can be sent to every computer in the network. We can essentially hack into the network and command the system to do what we want it to do."

Professor Simmons asked, "How do we hack the network?"

Professor Hai answered, "That's a little more difficult. We need to get to one of the computers in the network. Jacob provided us with a backdoor administrative account and password. However, we need to be on one of the computers in the network. The Gomorrite security system would take days to hack from the outside."

Professor Simmons said, "So…the bad news is getting to a computer in the network. That's going to be nearly impossible."

Marlin said, "Not really. I know where one is that we can use."

Professor Simmons asked, "What? How?"

Marlin answered, "I have been tracking their ships and their movements since the attack started. One of their ships was shot down about two blocks west of here. I went over there a couple of times to see if I could hack their network. Needless to say Professor H is right…it's almost impossible to hack their system. But if we have an account and password…it will be easy."

Lieutenant Yaniv said, "Lead us to it."

Professor Hai added, "We have one more problem."

Professor Simmons asked, "What is that?"

Professor Hai answered, "The Gomorrite upload program requires a password to get started. The only person who knows this password is Aaron. It could take a while to hack the program and start the upload."

Lieutenant Yaniv said, "Hopefully we won't have any problems but if we do everyone should be armed. Marlin do you have any weapons?"

Marlin answered, "I have a couple of guns over here."

Marlin led them to a chest where he kept a .9 mm handgun and an automatic assault rifle.

Lieutenant Yaniv asked, "Why do you have these weapons?"

Marlin responded, "This isn't a safe neighborhood…it's better to be prepared than to not."

***

Malcolm was a strong and streetwise man from Southeast DC. He learned to fight in the streets. He was a man who was bent on doing whatever it took for his people. His father fought in the streets of DC as well. He taught Malcolm how to fight in case he got into a situation where he needed to fight his way out.

Ten years ago Malcolm and two of his friends were visiting friends in South Carolina. On the way back they stopped along the road to get some gas. Three white males were at the stop staring at them. One of the men made a comment about Malcolm and his friends poisoning their neighborhood with their ghetto ways.

Malcolm's friend, Wes jumped up and wanted to fight right away but Malcolm held him back as he attempted to defuse the situation. Malcolm tried to be diplomatic but two of the white men were not allowing him. The third man was helping Malcolm defuse the situation by trying to keep his friends calm.

However, one of Malcolm's friends made a negative comment about their mothers. The fight then broke out. Malcolm took on the man who started the situation. Malcolm's boxing skills were very good. He pelted the man across his face, knocking him out after several well placed punches.

Malcolm felt bad about the fight and the outcome. He chose to never use his skills again. However, now he had no choice. He was motivated because the Elite Warriors had just killed his friend Jamaal. Malcolm had become like father and son in the days since the first attack. Malcolm took care of Jamaal and he felt the pain of losing him worst than any of the others.

Malcolm asked, "Solomon can I speak with you a minute?"

Solomon answered, "Okay."

The two walked out of earshot of the rest of the resistance members.

Malcolm continued, "Solomon…I have to confess something."

Solomon responded, "What is it."

Malcolm struggled to find the right words then he continued, "I killed him."

Solomon looked at him with shock.

Malcolm continued, "It was an accident I swear by it. We were arguing. We shoved each other. I must have shoved him hard. He went over the bridge railing and into the water. I tried to grab him but…"

Solomon shouted, "I can't believe you!"

Solomon grabbed Malcolm by the collar. The other resistance members ran over and broke the two up.

President Davis said, "We don't need this now!"

Malcolm said, "I just needed to clear my conscience."

He then walked over to begin his battle with his opponent.

Solomon didn't know if he should be angry or not. Malcolm said it was an accident. Now he needed Malcolm to win this battle for the world's sake.

Col Chaim announced, "This is my quickest warrior Cain."

He then looked toward Cain and said, "Make short work of him."

Malcolm bounced around on his toes mimicking professional boxers as he moved around Cain. He was stalking Cain and looking for a weakness. He studied Cain and Cain studied him. Malcolm cut off the distance between him and Cain and threw a right hook to the body of Cain. He followed that hook with an upper cut to the jaw.

Cain had a look of surprise on his face. Cain performed a spinning kick to Malcolm's chest. Malcolm caught his leg in mid air and attempted to fling the smaller man to the ground. However, Cain spun around and his other foot caught Malcolm in the face. Cain landed on his feet and Malcolm was on one knee.

Cain performed a double kick to the face of Malcolm, knocking him backwards to the ground. Malcolm jumped up and rushed Cain. Cain tried a back flip with a kick to the face of Malcolm but Malcolm just moved out of the way.

When Cain's feet hit the ground he was met with two ferocious left jabs to the face by Malcolm. The punches knocked Cain to the ground but he quickly got back to his feet. Neither of these fighters could kill with their bare hands and Colonel Chaim was getting impatience.

Colonel Chaim threw a knife in the middle of the two fighters and shouted, "End this…now!"

Each man looked at the knife. Malcolm went for the knife first. Cain did a two hand front flip. As his feet hit the ground he spun and kicked Malcolm in the face. He followed that move with a kick to the stomach then a scissors kick to the face of Malcolm as he was bent over.

Malcolm staggered a few feet backwards. Cain did another two hand front flip with one hand grabbing the knife. His feet hit the ground in front of Malcolm. In one quick motion he rose the knife up and thrust it in the neck of Malcolm, severing his Jugular vein.

Malcolm fell to the ground holding his throat. President Davis took a step toward Malcolm in an attempt to help him.

He was held back by Lieutenant Oded who said, "Don't. If we don't abide by the rules we all die."

President Davis shouted, "We can help him!"

Colonel Chaim responded, "It is to the death. If you break the rules then you forfeit and you all die now."

Malcolm continued to struggle for his life but it was slowly slipping away from him. His mind flashed on his children. He knew he would never see their smiling faces again. His beautiful wife would never nag him for not doing things around the house. He hated her nagging but now he wished he could hear it one more time.

After about two minutes Malcolm drew his last breath and his body fell limp on the ground. He was dead. The Elite Warriors now had killed two resistance members. One more death by a resistance member would end the tournament and they all would die.

***

Marlin was leading the resistance members to the downed fighter. He had been to the site several times trying to hack the Gomorrite system. He knew the way without thinking.

Marlin came around the corner a block away from the site and ran directly into a Gomorrite patrol of four soldiers. Lieutenant Yaniv knocked him to the ground and fired off several rounds before they could respond.

He took out two of the soldiers before the others began firing back. Varda moved to a position to help Lieutenant Yaniv while Renana got the professors inside a building to safety.

Renana shouted, "This way...move...we have to make sure you live!"

Professor Simmons responded, "Tony...keep your head down!"

One of the soldiers got off a clear shot at Professor Hai. Professor Simmons saw the soldier shoot at Professor Hai and she pushed him out of the way...taking the brunt of the blast herself.

The laser struck Professor Simmons in the left shoulder with a force that knocked her body forward. Professor Hai turned in time to catch her before she hit the ground.

Professor Simmons reached up and caressed his hair.

She said, "You have to save this world. It is within you to do. I love you."

Through his tears Professor Hai said, "Cassie...no...no...please...I love you too."

Renana saw what happened and ran over to Professor Hai. She grabbed him and pulled him inside the building. Varda shot the soldier that killed Professor Simmons and Lieutenant Yaniv killed the last soldier.

They all ran over to Professor Hai. They watched as he continued to sob at the lost of another woman he loved.

He continued to say, "No...please."

Renana and Varda both were shedding tears. They both knew of the lost that Professor Hai suffered on Gomorrah when his wife was killed by King Abimelech. Now he has traveled to Adamina only to find love and have it taken away again.

***

King Abimelech was standing on the bridge of the royal warship waiting to hear from General Idit. The call came over the communication system.

General Idit said, "This is General Idit. Put me through to King Abimelech."

King Abimelech answered the hail, "General. I am here. How is it going?"

General Idit responded, "The final preparations are being completed. We will start the assault in a few hours."

King Abimelech replied, "Good. Contact me once it starts."

General Idit responded, "I am docking with the royal warship now."

King Abimelech asked, "What are you doing here? You should be overseeing the final attack."

General Idit answered, "My colonels have it all under control. I can better serve you by your side on the bridge."

King Abimelech replied, "So be it. King Abimelech out."

General Idit responded, "I will join you in a minute. General Idit out."

Queen Metuka softly spoke, "I do not trust him."

Under his breath King Abimelech said, "Neither do I."

***

The morning sun was beating down on the pavement as the third battle was getting ready to take place. The resistance members were down two members and the Elite Warriors were about to end this tournament.

The three resistance members were talking.

President Davis said, "I will go next."

Solomon responded, "Sir…I can't let you do that."

President Davis replied, "It is not your choice son. We all have to fight or we all die. Our only chance is to fight this thing out and hope we can win it."

Lieutenant Oded said, "The President is right. We have no other choice. I have to go last because Colonel Chaim is mine."

Solomon replied, "Sir…let me go next."

President Davis said, "Son…I am a good fighter. I am in great shape and I have a chance to win this fight. Lastly, the next lost seals our fate. I can't have you carrying that burden for me. If the President of the United States is to die then let it be on his terms."

Lieutenant Oded said, "Solomon…let him go next."

President Davis added, "There…you're outvoted two to one. If I don't return…continue the fight."

President Davis stepped out as the next fighter for the resistance.

The Elite Warriors announced Tzur would be the next fighter. When Tzur emerged from the group President Davis saw that he was a giant. He was ripped with muscles. President Davis' fighting skills consisted of some martial arts training as a teenager along with some boxing training in his 20s.

Lieutenant Oded walked up to the President from behind.

He whispered in his ear, "Do you know the story of David and Goliath?"

President Davis responded, "Yes."

Lieutenant Oded continued, "Call on the name of the Lord and victory will be yours."

President Davis remembered the Bible stories he learned in school.

He thought to himself, *"Could all those stories be true? Is the Christian God the answer to beating these evil Gomorrites? Was Jesus really the Son of God?"*

He decided now was as good a time as any to give his life over to the Lord. He knew he could not win this battle on his own.

He spoke aloud, "with all of you as my witness, I profess to that I believe Jesus is the Son of God. I believe He died for my sins. I accept Him as my Lord and Savior. Jehovah...I call on your name. Use me as a tool to deliver us a victory."

Tzur and the other Elite Warriors broke out in laughter.

Tzur shouted, "Look...he is praying already! Trust me Mr. President...I will kill you so that you die quickly. Then you will meet your God face to face."

They all continued to laugh.

Lieutenant Oded and Solomon dropped to their knees and began praying...not just for themselves but for all of Earth.

Tzur pulled out a knife and flung it to the ground between them.

Tzur shouted, "Mr. President...if you can get to the knife first, I will let you kill me. If I get there first then I will slit your throat and send you to your God."

President Davis responded, "I do not need the knife."

Tzur and the other Elite Warriors laugh even more at that statement.

President Davis bent over and picked up a stone the size of his hand. He held it there and stood ready to throw it at Tzur. He imagined what

David was thinking when he was ready to face Goliath. He silently prayed that the Lord would be with him.

Tzur said, "Go ahead Mr. President…throw your little rock."

President Davis wound up and threw the rock as hard and has fast as he could at Tzur. It seemed as though the rock grew in density as it moved through the air.

The rock stuck Tzur between the eyes and blood gushed out in all directions.

Tzur slowly fell forward on his face. He was dead.

***

Colonel Chaim could not believe his eyes. His best warrior was defeated by an inferior opponent with the use of a simple rock. He wanted to kill both Solomon and Lieutenant Oded were they stood but he had to honor the terms of the tournament.

It was now two to one still in favor of the Elite Warriors but now the resistance believed they could win.

***

General Idit arrived in the hanger bay of the royal warship. He exited the shuttle craft and saw King Abimelech waiting on him.

King Abimelech said, "This is not what we planned. You were to wait on the surface and oversee the victory from there."

General Idit replied, "As I said, Sire…I would be in a better position to serve you by being at your side during this triumph battle. It will be a glorious victory and we will be able to watch it together."

King Abimelech sighed and turned his back to walk off. He never fully trusted General Idit but he knew the General was the best man to run his army. Now at a critical juncture of the battle he chose to arrive on board the warship instead of personally overseeing the battle. Something was not right about this and the King would have to tread carefully.

***

The next resistance fighter would be Solomon. Solomon believed in God and he was a member of Pastor Bell's church in Waldorf, Maryland. He walked away from President Davis and Lieutenant Oded to gather his thoughts for this battle. They were still celebrating the President's victory over Tzur.

Solomon never imagined himself fighting for the world he loved so much and his life. He quietly prayed to ask God to be with him in this battle.

Solomon spoke softly, *"Lord, be with me now as I go into battle. Cover me with your Spirit so that I may have victory over our enemy."*

Solomon reached back into his memory. He thought about the days when his grandmother made him memorize the 23rd Psalm. He thought there was no better time than the present to recite it.

He began, *"The LORD is my shepherd; I shall not want. He maketh me to lie down in green pastures: he leadeth me beside the still waters. He restoreth my soul. He leadeth me in the paths of righteousness for his name's sake. Yea, though I walk through the valley of the shadow of death, I will fear no evil. For thou art with me; thy rod and thy staff they comfort me. Thou preparest a table before me in the presence of mine enemies. Thou anointest my head with oil; my cup runneth over. Surely goodness and mercy shall follow me all the days of my life. And I will dwell in the house of the LORD forever."*

As Solomon was speaking, a beautiful white pillar of smoke formed near him.

A voice from within the smoke said to Solomon, "Solomon…I am with you. My Spirit will cover you and protect you. Go now and defeat your enemy in my name."

Solomon fell to his knees at the sound of the voice.

Solomon held his head down in reverence to the Lord and spoke, "Thank you Lord but what of my friend…Lieutenant Oded?"

The voice responded, "I am proud of you. You ask not of yourself but of others. Was I not with David when he fought Goliath? Was I not with Samson?"

Solomon replied, "Yes my Lord you were there but I still have fear."

The voice said, "My prophet Elisha asked me to open the eyes of his servant and show him what he could see. Your journey is just beginning so I will do for you what I did for Elisha's servant."

Solomon looked all around him and he saw the street was full of beautiful white horses and chariots of fire round them. Solomon could not believe what he saw. He knew now that he could not be beaten with the power of the Lord at his side.

The smoke disappeared as quickly as it had appeared. Solomon looked around and no one was paying attention. He walked back over to President Davis and Lieutenant Oded.

A voice shouted, "Know that my name is Hanan and I am the one who will kill you."

He stepped out from the group of Elite Warriors.

"I will have my revenge for my fallen brother, Tzur," shouted Hanan.

Solomon proudly stepped forward and proclaimed, "In the name of the Lord my God Jehovah...I will defeat you!"

Hanan laughed and said, "I will send you to Hell and spit on your corpse. This I will do in the mighty name of Baal!"

Colonel Chaim announced, "There will be no weapons in this battle. These two appear to be evenly matched. To proclaim victory you must kill your opponent by hand."

Hanan said, "I will snap your neck Adamian."

Solomon replied, "You can't because the Spirit of the Lord covers me."

Hanan said, "Baal is my lord and he will grant me victory over you and your God."

For a second Solomon was caught off guard as Hanan moved toward him with a swiftness that exemplified Elite Warrior training. He threw an uppercut to Solomon's chin that only grazed him. Solomon felt quicker than he had ever felt in his life. It was as though he was not in control of his movements.

After Hanan's uppercut only grazed Solomon he tried to come back with a round house kick. Solomon with relative ease ducked the kick. Hanan was frustrated. The anger was etched on his face. He threw an overhand right at Solomon. Solomon grabbed his wrist, turned his body underneath Hanan and flipped him to the ground.

Hanan brought his legs up and with both feet kicked Solomon in the face. Solomon staggered backwards but regained his balance.

Hanan got to his feet and said, "Enough of this...I am going to kill you!"

Solomon said, "Let's do this."

Hanan ran at Solomon…braced himself and threw a punch with all his might. Solomon stepped to the side and wrapped his arm around the throat of Hanan and squeezed it as hard as he could.

Hanan tried mightily to break the hold of Solomon but Solomon's strength was greater than he had ever felt it before. He knew it was not him alone who was able to hold his arm on the throat of his powerful enemy.

Hanan fought and fought until he had no breath left in his body. He fell to his knees and then to the ground…dead at the hands of Solomon. The resistance had now tied the battle and the once confident Elite Warriors now feared defeat.

***

Professor Hai had reached the grounded shuttle and with Marlin's help he gained entrance inside. He and Marlin were attempting to gain access to the Gomorrite network while the others guarded them.

***

About a block away from the fallen fighter were Gomorrite forces lurking in the shadows.

The sergeant in charge of the patrol said to his lieutenant, "Sir…the man has returned to the fighter and he brought with him some others. Among them were Professor Hai and Lieutenant Yaniv."

Lieutenant Uzzi was in charge of this patrol. He had ten soldiers with him. They had been watching the site of the downed fighter because General Idit had received reports that their network was attempting to be hacked and it was coming from this location.

Lieutenant Uzzi was sent to capture the man and bring him back to Gomorrite Headquarters. He never imagined that he would get the bonus of capturing Professor Hai and Lieutenant Yaniv as well. Now these two men along with Lieutenant Oded were the most hated resistance members alive.

Lieutenant Uzzi ordered his sergeant, "Surround them. Do not allow them to escape. If they do…you had better be dead."

The sergeant responded, "Yes sir."

***

Onboard the royal warship stood King Abimelech and General Idit, as they prepared to launch the final attack.

General Idit came over the communication system to speak to all the Gomorrite forces, "Men...today is the day that we take back Adamina for our own. Today we will launch the final assault on the few remaining resistance strongholds. Today King Abimelech will claim Adamina as his kingdom!"

The men yelled and raised their weapons high in the sky while stomping one of their feet on the ground. It was the day that general Idit had trained them for.

General Idit announced, "Men...I present to you...your great king...King Abimelech!"

King Abimelech began speaking, "As General Idit said...today is the greatest day in our history. Today will mark the triumph return of the Gomorrite people to Adamina. Over 5,000 years have passed since we were exiled from our home. We were swept away in the morning light for no reason. This God...Jehovah...left us for dead on a baron planet. But Baal...the mighty god Baal saved us!"

The men started yelling as loud as they could, believing that Baal had saved them and returned them home as King Abimelech proclaimed.

King Abimelech continued, "Now we will enslave those who are lucky enough to survive and kill the rest. Then we will mark this day with a great New Adamina celebration!"

The men yelled even more.

King Abimelech shouted, "Hail Gomorrah!"

The men yelled in response, "Hail King Abimelech...hail Gomorrah!"

General Idit ordered, "Commence the assault."

The colonels in charge of each regiment began their part in the final assault all over Earth. Near Waldorf the people who had been relocated to Redeemer Life Ministries Church could see the fighters rising in the sky as they were preparing for their final assault. This was a sight they had not seen since the first day of the war. It was a mighty symbol as the fighters lined the morning sky. All the people at the church could do was drop their heads and pray.

***

Now it was time for Lieutenant Oded to face his nemesis Colonel Chaim. The winner of this battle would decide the fate of the others. Two Elite Warriors watched as well as Solomon and President Davis to see how the final battle would unveil.

President Davis whispered to Solomon, "When Lieutenant Oded wins this fight we have to be ready. I don't think they will just lie down and die or let us capture them."

Solomon looked at President Davis and agreed.

Colonel Chaim said, "Just like the last battle. No weapons...just you against me."

Lieutenant Oded responded, "For the record...my brother never raped your sister."

Colonel Chaim replied, "So you say, now that you are faced with dying at my hand. A coward like you would say anything to avoid death."

Lieutenant Oded responded, "I am a man of the one true God and I only speak the truth. You have been lead down the wrong road by your so called friend General Idit. It is a shame you have not seen it."

Colonel Chaim replied, "Enough of this talk. It is time for you to die."

Colonel Chaim ran at Lieutenant Oded hitting him in the stomach with his shoulder. He lifted Lieutenant Oded up into the air and slammed him to the ground. The two of them rolled over and over on the ground with neither of them gaining an advantage over the other one.

Lieutenant Oded made it back to his feet at the same time as Colonel Chaim. They slowly began circling each other. Lieutenant Oded was poised to attack but he knew to be cautious. He knew Colonel Chaim was a very good warrior one mistake could mean death.

Colonel Chaim swung at Lieutenant Oded striking him in the face. Lieutenant Oded counter punched him with a punch to the stomach and then to the face. Colonel Chaim responded with a punch but it was blocked by Lieutenant Oded.

Lieutenant Oded then threw a round house kick to the face of Colonel Chaim hitting him in the mouth. The kick drew his blood and his anger.

Colonel Chaim wiped the blood away from his mouth and spit the rest on the ground. The two men squared off again. Colonel Chaim jumped at Lieutenant Oded and knocked him to the ground. Colonel Chaim punched him several times in the face.

***

While the battle was raging on, President Davis whispered to Solomon, "When Oded wins go for the gun next to that BMW over there. I'll go for the one over by that 300. Shoot to kill quickly."

Solomon replied, "Got it."

President Davis said, "If we die…It has been an honor fighting with you."

Solomon responded, "I think we will live to see another day."

President Davis looked at him puzzled by the remark. He had just given his life to God and could not understand what Solomon had been shown by God.

***

Lieutenant Uzzi's men surrounded the position where Professor Hai was located. They opened fire on them.

Lieutenant Yaniv shouted, "Take cover. Shoot anything that moves!"

Varda shouted, "Professor…hurry…we are under attack!"

Marlin said, "They're after us. We got to hurry."

Professor Hai replied, "I'm moving as fast as I can. I'm in!"

***

Lieutenant Oded grabbed Colonel Chaim by the shoulders and flung him to the ground. Again both men made it to their feet and squared off against each other.

Lieutenant Oded threw another round house kick at Colonel Chaim striking him in the chest. He then moved in and struck Colonel Chaim in the face with a right and left hook. The blows knocked Colonel Chaim to the ground.

Colonel Chaim fell near a rock. He picked up the rock as he was attempting to stand. In one motion he threw the rock at Lieutenant Oded and followed it by tackling him to the ground. He picked up another rock and readied himself to strike Lieutenant Oded in the face in the hope of killing him.

Lieutenant Oded blocked the punch and flipped him over. He then turned and wrapped his arm around the throat of Colonel Chaim. He squeezed and squeezed as Colonel Chaim fought for his life.

Colonel Chaim continued to fight for his life. Cain reached in his belt and threw a knife to Colonel Chaim. Colonel Chaim caught the knife and attempted to stab Lieutenant Oded with it.

Seeing this President Davis and Solomon darted for the guns and shot at Cain and Saul. Saul was killed immediately but Cain made it behind a car. Solomon went to get behind him while President Davis continued to fire at him.

Lieutenant Oded tried to dodge the stabbing attempt by Colonel Chaim but the knife caught him in the arm. He was able to knock the knife out of Colonel Chaim hands and struck him in the face with his other fist. He then grabbed the knife and stabbed Colonel Chaim in the heart with it.

Lieutenant Oded said, "I did not want it to end like this. Again… my brother did not rape your sister."

Colonel Chaim grabbed the hand that Lieutenant Oded was using to hold the knife in him and said, "Why would he lie?"

Lieutenant Oded replied, "Jealous."

Colonel Chaim looked at Lieutenant Oded as the life drained out of him. He still would not bring himself to believe Lieutenant Oded. Colonel Chaim's last breath was used to curse Lieutenant Oded and his dead brother.

Solomon was behind Cain and shouted, "Drop the weapon!"

Cain turned and aimed at Solomon. Solomon shot first and killed Cain.

The three men met in the middle of the street where they had fought to live another day.

Solomon said, "With God's help we are victorious."

Lieutenant Oded added, "Now we have to find ours friends and stop the attacks on Earth."

Solomon heard gunfire near their position. They decided they would go in that direction and hopefully they could find their friends and if they needed help…they could provide it.

***

Simon was standing outside the church next to his father, Pastor Bell. They were joined by Ashlee and her mother.

Simon asked his father, "Is this it? Did we survive that long journey just to die here?"

Pastor Bell replied, "Don't give up on God. He will never leave us or forsake us."

Ashlee took Simon's hand and they looked at each other.

Simon looked at Ashlee and said, "If I am to die, I can't do it like this."

Ashlee responded, "What do you mean?"

Simon turned to face Ashlee.

He continued, "Will you marry me?"

Ashlee was shocked. She looked at her mother and then Pastor Bell. They both had shock looks on their faces. Then she saw Pastor Bell smile.

Ashlee looked at Simon, smiled and said, "Yes."

The two of them embraced each other deeply while everyone else continued to watch the fighters approach their position.

Everyone was frozen in their positions and the fighters continued advancing toward them.

***

General Idit asked, "Sire, can I speak with you in your private office?"

King Abimelech looked at him and suspected the General was trying to get him alone.

King Abimelech answered, "Whatever you wish to tell me, you can tell me here."

General Idit asked, "It is about our friend and the smoke. Are you sure you want me to tell you here?"

King Abimelech was surprised and agreed to go to his private office.

The two of them was alone in the office.

General Idit began speaking, "Satan came to visit me after you left yesterday."

King Abimelech suddenly turned and asked, "What? Why did he visit you?"

General Idit continued, "He was attempting to turn me against you."

Surprised that General Idit would share this information, King Abimelech asked, "And what did you say to him?"

General Idit answered as he walked over to the King, "I told him exactly how I felt about you. He tempted me by offering me the throne."

King Abimelech responded, "What? I am glad that you sided with me my friend."

General Idit placed his hand on the King's shoulder and said, "No Sire...I did not."

As he was speaking he grabbed his laser and placed it at the heart of the King.

As the King struggled to fight, General Idit pulled the trigger and said, "You are a failure as King. Now it is my turn to lead."

The blast did not sound because the weapon was pressed against the King. His lifeless body fell to the feet of General Idit.

General Idit stepped over the body and walked over to the communications system.

He pressed the button to make a ship wide announcement, "King Abimelech is dead. I am the new King. Bring Queen Metuka to me at once."

After a few moments two of General Idit's men brought in the body of Queen Metuka.

King Idit asked his servants, "What happened?"

One of the servants answered, "She poisoned herself."

King Idit replied, "It is well...she would have died at my hand anyway."

The communication officer came over the system and said, "King Idit...we need you on the bridge."

King Idit responded, "What is it?"

The officer replied, "Sire...there is a ship approaching the planet."

King Idit stepped out on the bridge and asked, "Where is this coming from?"

Colonel Bar was the first officer on the bridge and replied, "We do not know Sire. It is not coming from the planet. We now can confirm that there are two ships approaching and they will arrive in 20 minutes."

***

The Gomorrite patrol lead by Lieutenant Uzzi continued to attack Professor Hai's group at the fallen fighter. President Davis, Solomon and Lieutenant Oded arrived just as they were running out of bullets to defend themselves.

President Davis took up a position behind some of the Gomorrite soldiers while Solomon and Lieutenant Oded took up positions flanking the President on his left and right.

Varda shouted, "Lieutenant Yaniv we are running out of projectiles!"

Lieutenant Yaniv responded, "I know. Just try and make everyone count. We have to hold this position."

President Davis, Solomon and Lieutenant Oded began opening fire on the Gomorrites from behind.

Renana shouted, "It is Lieutenant Oded!"

Lieutenant Yaniv replied, "Just in time old friend...just in time!"

Varda shouted inside the fighter, "Professor...hurry! We can't hold them much longer."

Professor Hai was talking under his breath, "It is not working. I can't understand why it is not working."

Marlin said, "I don't have any idea what you are doing. I don't understand any of this language. I'll go help them fight these creeps off."

Professor Hai shouted, "Go...go!"

As Marlin got up to grab a gun and go fight Professor Hai grabbed him by the arm and said, "Be safe young man...we have lost too many lives already."

Marlin responded, "Thanks Professor."

***

The two ships that the Gomorrites were tracking dropped out of warp around Earth. They opened a communications channel to the Gomorrite warships.

The captain of the lead ship said, "This is Captain Amos of the Shehar vessel, Eden. Stop your attack on this planet or we will be forced to intervene."

King Idit said, "Shehar? They don't have ships like those ships. They are a primitive people. How could this be?"

The first officer asked, "Sir…what should we do?"

King Idit ordered, "Open fire on them."

Both warships began firing on the two Shehar ships.

Captain Amos shouted, "Give all the power to the shields. We must keep those shields up."

He looked at the man standing next to him and said, "If your friend has anything ready, now is the time to do it."

The man took the communication device he had on his person and began speaking into it.

***

The battle continued to rage between the Gomorrite patrol and the resistance fighters.

Inside the fighter Professor Hai could not make his code work. He didn't know what else to do. He thought failure was imminent.

His communication device began sounding. He didn't expect to hear this device go off. No one that he knew of had one of them any longer.

The voice over the device said, "Israel to Professor Hai or any resistance members…please respond."

Professor Hai asked, "Israel? Is that you my friend?"

Israel answered, "Professor! Yes it is me…Israel!"

Professor Hai asked, "It is good to hear your voice. Where are you?"

Israel answered, "I am onboard the Shehar vessel Eden. We are fighting for our lives against the Gomorrite warships. Professor…"

Captain Amos interrupted, "I hate to interrupt this reunion gentleman but we could use some help about now. Our shields strength is down to 35 percent."

Israel asked, "Professor...can you get the code to work?"

Professor Hai answered, "I am trying my friend but Aaron put a password on the upload program. I have written a program to determine what the password is but I have not got it yet."

Israel replied, "Professor, I hate to rush you but we can't take much more. The Gomorrite warships are more powerful than ours."

There was no response.

Israel shouted, "Professor...Professor!"

As Professor Hai was deep in thought, watching his cipher program try and find the password, he saw an illumination of lights before him like he had never witnessed in his life. In the center of the illumination was a group of children playing. They were dancing around in a circle singing a song. Professor Hai smiled as he remembered how simple life was in those days.

Then he remembered the game they played in the prime numbers. They had to dance until the leader yelled "stop". The last person to stop had to say the next prime number. He remembered that he and Aaron were the best at this game.

Then one of the girls in the vision stopped and walked toward him. He recognized her as his wife as a little girl. She just smiled at him.

He realized then that Aaron probably used the first 32 digits in the list of prime numbers as his password. He frantically entered the numbers in the program. The upload immediately began.

Professor Hai shouted, "Yes! Thank you Lord!"

He got back on his communicator and announced to Israel, "Israel the code has been uploaded. Is anything happening?

Israel answered, "Professor...nothing is happening. We are about to be..."

Professor Hai prayed that he had not entered the code too late. He could hear what was going on aboard the ship.

The Eden's first officer said, "Captain...the shields are down to 10 percent!"

Captain Amos looked at Israel and said, "We cannot hold out much longer. We need to..."

The operations officer onboard the Eden shouted, "Their shields are dropping!"

Colonel Amos ordered his weapons officers, "Fire all weapons… now!"

Professor Hai thanked the Lord for sending him the vision. He got to see his wife one more time and saved two worlds from destruction.

***

King Idit felt the jolt of his royal warship being struck by weapons fire presumably from the SheHar vessel. The hit was harder than any of the previous hits thus prompting him to look sternly at his First Officer, Colonel Bar.

Then Colonel Bar shouted, "Sir…our shields are dropping!"

King Idit shouted, "What are you talking about? Get them back up…now!"

Aaron added, "We have a virus. It's shutting down all our systems!"

Colonel Bar yelled, "Fix it! Or we will be destroyed!"

Aaron responded, "Sir…I am trying. I just need about five minutes more."

The Colonel Bar shouted, "Our engines are overloading. We are going to explode. We need to get out of here."

Colonel Bar shouted, "Hold your position Lieutenant."

The operations officer got up to run to the escape pods but was shot down by Colonel Bar.

King Idit said, "Coward. Aaron…what is the status?"

Aaron responded, "There is not enough time…Baal you have forsaken us!"

King Idit saw the figure he had come to know as Satan standing at the forward section of the ship. He realized that no one else could see him. Satan was grinning as he stared at the newly crowned king.

King Idit shouted, "You lied! You said I would be king!"

Satan responded, "But I didn't, you are king! Now it is time to collect. Give me your soul."

King Idit dropped to his knees in agony as his soul began ripping from his body. He tried in vein to hold on to his soul but he couldn't. He could hear Satan laughing with each pull on his soul.

Finally it was ripped from his body and he laid down on all fours, weak and vulnerable to death. He slowly got to his feet and saw Satan smirking at him.

King Idit said in a weak voice, "You tricked me."

He looked at Satan expecting a response but none came. Instead Satan only pointed his finger. King Idit looked in the direction he was pointing.

Colonel Bar said coldly, "Fool, you have led us to death."

The last thing King Idit saw was the laser shot coming toward him fired by Colonel Bar. The shot pierced his chest on through his cold and evil heart. Another Gomorrite king was dead.

Right after King Idit died, both Gomorrite warships exploded in the cold loneliness of space.

***

Lieutenant Oded took out the last Gomorrite soldier attacking the downed shuttle. They all went in to see what Professor Hai was doing.

Professor Hai said, "Israel is aboard a Shehar ship. I am waiting to see if we were successful."

They all heard a loud noise in the sky. Everyone ran outside to see what happened. Professor Hai looked up in the early afternoon sky and behold, he saw two large fireballs in the sky. He didn't know if it was the Shehar ships or the enemy.

Israel called on the communicator, "Professor we have destroyed the ships!"

Professor Hai responded, "Praise the Lord!"

He told the others that the two royal warships had been destroyed.

Renana looked at her husband and asked, "Is it finally over?"

Lieutenant Yaniv answered, "Yes my love. It is over."

Professor Hai watched the two of them embrace as they finally could celebrate their freedom.

He then turned and noticed Varda running over to Lieutenant Oded. They both embraced.

***

Varda said to Lieutenant Oded, "My love…it is over!"

Lieutenant Oded replied, "Praise the Lord! He has granted us victory over our enemy!"

***

President Davis looked at Solomon and said, "You know…when this is all cleared up I might have a job for you in my administration. You interested?"

Solomon answered, "I think I would like that Sir."

The two shook hands as President Davis turned to Professor Hai.

President Davis asked, "Where's Professor Simmons?"

Professor Hai looked down and answered, "She died… saving my life. Too many have died trying to save my life."

President Davis replied, "Without you Professor we all would be dead or slaves. I think Professor Simmons knew that and that's why she made the sacrifice."

Professor Hai responded, "Yes sir she did. I only hope I can help this world continue to know peace."

President Davis said, "Oh my friend…I think this world will want nothing else but peace from now on."

President Davis embraced Solomon and Professor Hai. They were joined by Renana, Varda and Lieutenants Oded and Yaniv.

President Davis said, "Lieutenants…there is a place for both of you in my administration. Are you interested?"

Lieutenant Oded responded, "Sir…I am no longer a lieutenant. That rank was attained in the army of a ruthless and evil king. I no longer serve him. I can openly serve the Lord my God…Jehovah!"

Lieutenant Yaniv added, "I as well…It is good to know freedom."

President Davis replied, "It is good to have you all in America. My home is your home."

***

The people in front of Redeemer Life Ministries Church could not believe their eyes as the fighters fell from the sky one by one. Pastor Bell rejoiced in the Lord as the fighters were crashing down on the Gomorrite ground forces.

As Pastor Bell watched the two fireballs in the sky he said, "You did it my friend. You did it."

Simon asked, "Who did it?"

Pastor Bell answered, "A friend who I met a year ago. He came here to save us and he did it."

Liz came running up to Pastor Bell and hugged him.

She asked, "Do you think my father did this?"

Pastor Bell answered her, "I can think of no one else who would have done this great work in the name of the Lord."

***

All of them standing there smiled as joy now filled their hearts and minds. Before they were worried about their very existence but now where fear took up resident joy was now living. Many who didn't believe in the power of Jehovah now believed.

Just seven days ago there was talk everywhere of removing God from every public place and even the money in which Americans spend every day. Now...everyone was praising the name of the Lord.

A few days after the end of the war a billboard in New York City was lit up. It said, "Romans 14:11, "For it is written, "AS I LIVE, SAYS THE LORD, EVERY KNEE SHALL BOW TO ME, AND EVERY TONGUE SHALL GIVE PRAISE TO GOD."